"I THOUGHT I WOULD NEVER SEE YOU AGAIN."

Her whisper came back: "We are forever."

She clung tightly. They said nothing. He walked slowly, carrying her into the dark, and there among the carriages he lifted her weightlessly onto the driver's seat. It seemed unimportant that he could not see her features. She was there, close again and real again. Their hands clung together the way they had done that night in the veld. The two occasions became one.

"Colorful."   —*Publishers Weekly*

"Burke writes with authority . . . recommended."
                   —*Library Journal*

Kimberley

COLIN BURKE

St. Martin's
Press

KIMBERLEY

Copyright © 1985 by Colin Burke

Printed in the United States of America

First mass market edition/September 1986

ISBN: 0-312-90501-7
Can. ISBN: 0-312-90526-2

10 9 8 7 6 5 4 3 2 1

CONTENTS

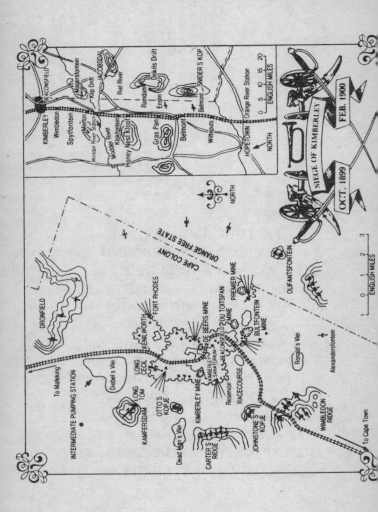

SIEGE OF KIMBERLEY
OCT. 1899   FEB. 1900

Left panel (detail map):

To Mafeking

DRONFIELD

INTERMEDIATE PUMPING STATION

Diebel's Vlei

KAMFERSDAM

LONG TOM
OTTO'S KOPJE

KIMBERLEY MINE

Dead Man's Vlei

CARTER'S RIDGE

JOHNSTONE'S KOPJE

WIMBLEDON RIDGE

LONG CECIL

FORT RHODES

KENILWORTH

DE BEERS MINE

BEACONSFIELD DU TOITSPAN MINE

KIMBERLEY SANATORIUM

Reservoir

RACECOURSE

PREMIER MINE

BULTFONTEIN MINE

Ronald's Vlei

Alexandersfontein

OLIFANTSFONTEIN

CAPE COLONY
ORANGE FREE STATE

To Cape Town

NORTH

0   1   2   3
ENGLISH MILES

Right panel (regional map):

KIMBERLEY

BEACONSFIELD

Wimbledon

Spytfontein

Modder River

Honey Nest Kloof

Klokfontein

Merton
Station

Riverton

Kraaipan

Riet River

Ramdam
Enslin

Gras Pan

Belmont

Witteputs

Wittkop

Klip Drift
Magersfontein

JACOBSDAL

Dekils Drift

SNIDER'S KOP

Belmont
Orange River Station

HOPETOWN

NORTH

0   5   10   15   20
ENGLISH MILES

· 1 · | PRELUDE AND ARRIVAL

If he is still waiting there, I shall walk toward him and get past without even seeing him.

Emma watched herself in the mirror of the small toilet compartment, resenting the rising color of her cheeks. She prepared herself to confront the corridor, getting hold of the door handle to steady herself against the rocking motion of the train. But her hand, like her mind, refused to move. The hesitation grew into inactivity and she stood absently holding on, listening to the metallic clicking of the wheels on the rails.

I am being stupid, stupid. The thought became a silent shout. To be intimidated by a man waiting in a corridor is such juvenile nonsense. He may not even be there anymore. How is it that I am even unable to deal with the idea of someone else knowing that I have just emerged from a lavatory? Will he be thinking about that when he sees me? Well, what of it? What if he stares? It is a fact that men stare at women. It is a thing they do, covertly or openly. Since the beginning of time they have done it. If you ignore them, they think you are disturbed and affected by them. If you become angry or upset, they still seem to believe they have made the beginnings of a conquest. It is only my fault that

1

I have this naive inability to either face up or ignore. Where did I not learn? Have I been so protected? Shall I blame my husband for sentencing me to a quiet life at Birchleigh? Shall I blame him for leaving me in the suffocating care of my mother? Shall I blame my mother?

I shall go back along that corridor and ignore the man. Open the door and go; you are making altogether too much of this.

But she remained where she was, holding onto the handle. Here is one of those moments where you could make a fool of yourself by being too aggressive—or too nice, for that matter.

He stared at me on the platform in Cape Town. He deliberately eyed me in the corridor as we boarded. He is waiting in that corridor now, I know he is.

Emma began to turn the handle, then let it close again. Sarah could manage this. She is the one who gaped when he brought his horses off the train to water them at Beaufort West and again at De Aar. She was not looking at the horses but at him, returning his arrogant stare. For Sarah, there is no exploitation by men. She meets the advances halfway and takes them or leaves them as she sees fit. If that is a technique, then I shall make a point of never learning it. I shall not be subject, like my sister, to the demands of mere eyes. She is no example to me and I none to her. I fight the demands. She hardly resists. I select once, as if there will never be another opportunity.

Emma turned the door handle again. I am being stupid about something I have to live with. So let me go and deal with it. It will be good practice.

She got the door open and stepped out into the small vestibule, pausing before turning into the corridor, wishing someone would come through from the next coach, someone she could fall in behind and follow. But no one came, and when she turned the corner, he was there, leaning beside an open door with one leg creating a barrier across the passageway, one highly polished riding boot propped against the bottom of the window frame.

Emma began to walk toward him. The walk became a determined march.

He is pretending not to see me. It is impossible to be unaware of someone marching noisily along a narrow passage toward you and bumping a valise along the panels to make quite sure their presence is felt. This is the insufferable type who is accustomed to being noticed, who arranges this sort of thing, who traps you with eyes and innuendo.

She marched right up to the tall, shiny-booted obstruction and stopped helplessly, feeling her cheeks going redder than ever, hating them for exposing her. Must I really ask permission to pass him? I feel like lashing out with this valise. He is pretending to be dozing, but there is the silly hint of a smile. Please, oh please, don't let my voice go high.

"May I pass, please?" Her voice came out lowish and gratifyingly stern.

The eyes opened; the smile became a grin. The practiced eyes searched for hers, but the expression on her pretty face was directed sternly at the obstructing knee.

"Oh, I do beg your pardon." The voice was deep and pleasant, out of character with the behavior.

The leg came down and she squeezed past, keeping the valise between them. A few more steps and she had reached her compartment door. She struggled with the door, horrified that he might decide to help her. As the door opened, she heard a roar of laughter from the open compartment she had come past on the way and a heavy Irish accent: "You're wasting your time, Bart," and any doubt about the man's intentions was dispelled. She got inside, closed the door quickly, and settled herself into her corner.

I've come through this awful ordeal, struggled with the door, banged it closed, and here they are, my own family, all blissfully unaware, without even the flicker of an eyelash. She smiled at her sleeping family and her own foolishness.

Emma wriggled herself into a more comfortable position beside her mother's unbending arm. She watched the others sleeping, their heads bobbing and swaying with the movement of the train. She looked out at the red world, the stone-scattered earth, the sparse dusty bushes, all in tones of red, the same color as the dust spurting past the window.

Is this what the equator divides, the green, green north and the dust-red south? Green for soft, red for hard. This then is hard country. What are those expressions—"empty desolation," "cruel wastes"; the ones one reads without really identifying? This is where Geoffrey has fought, on hard, dry ground, on tired, dusty horses.

But Emma's dreams had given it a green background, grassy plains, with wooded hills and high sentinels of gray rock. Even the chargers of her imagination shone like the hunters at home.

Home. We are a long way from the comforts of Birchleigh. A long way from the security, the peaceful seclusion, the quiet, the waiting. Oh yes, the boredom. At least this is better than boredom, and whatever comes up now, I shall not be alone in facing it. I shall meet my husband again this evening for the first time in two years, for the first time in a foreign place.

Emma shivered and dabbed at the perspiration on her forehead.

She watched her sister sitting opposite, her head nodding down with sleep and then jerking up without waking, then nodding down again, her usual perfection of every hair in place slightly ruffled by conditions that were proving a slowly losing battle, even for Sarah's determined combing and dabbing.

She watched Mark slumped in the corner beside Sarah. Dear brother, our so-called man in the family, so neat and so precise, suddenly caught in a position that would never suit his elegant image. Had he ever been seen like this? Fine dust coloring the brown hair, creases in the material at his shoulder from almost two days of being cooped up on the train. What is that poor Savile Row suit going to look like after six hundred and fifty miles in this rumbling, dust-seeping carriage?

Then on Emma's right, her mother, riding out the bumping and swaying with all the dignity of a granite Boadicea. Lady Freestone-Grant, protector of the family fortunes, controller of the brood, keeper of the family myths. "A Freestone-Grant would never do anything like that, and about your Grant great-grandfather, did I ever tell you that his brother who had been a colonel in the Inniskillings, went out to the Americas, and I often wonder whether that general who had done so well was an off-spring."

Shall I always be in awe of my mother? Shall I never understand the rigid order that produces her unquestioned decisions? Her combination of wisdom and strength on the one hand and social affectation on the other seems to have held her firmly together for as long as I can remember? But are her decisions unquestioned? For instance, why is she here? After all those years of holding court at Birchleigh without ever going away, why has she undertaken such a journey? Does the answer lie with her beloved son, Mark, and his new insurance enterprise with Geoffrey? Or with Sarah, who has insisted on joining the escapade, and whatever hopeful match she may make along the way?

Not with me. Oh, Lord no. Good old Emma, she made a good match. Geoffrey is a good fellow. Did his stuff at Sandhurst, proved himself with the Hussars and in action with the Colonial Forces.

It could just be a combination of all of us—clinging to her offspring, who all at once are flying off like a small flock of migrating birds.

Nevertheless, it's rather like the Queen walking away from her throne, giving up all that comfort that was built around her. Were it not for Geoffrey, I would be there, not here.

Now you could say, Mother was leading her own Hussars into a new battle for the African interior. She would see her role as essential because the Empire did not expand by force of arms and money alone, but by the social graces. While Mark and Geoffrey made their contribution to imperial glory, Mother would spearhead the action on the social front, sweeping through the parties and gatherings, storming the right dinners, and not returning home until she was satisfied that her brood were getting all the proper advantages.

So here we are together, thought Emma, a far cry from everything we know and heading for who knows what. If Mark is to be believed, we are heading straight into the beginnings of a war. But Mother's opinion seems better informed: "Those Boers would like a war, but they are really just farmers. Confronted with a few crack regiments, they will surely be thrown into confusion and go sensibly back to their pastoral pursuits." From all reports it seems most unlikely. In fact, would Mr. Rhodes be on this very train on his way to Kimberley if the threat were real? In any event, the Freestone-Grants, with their thoroughly military background, will not be out of place in a possible uprising. But this time the women will be there. It is time the women get involved. When I think of all the waiting for Geoffrey. Geoffrey in India. Geoffrey at Sandhurst when he might as well have been in India. Then, after we were married, Geoffrey in Africa. Waiting. That is mostly what my married life has consisted of. It seems to have turned me into a cynic at twenty-five. No, not a cynic. *Cynic* has a clear meaning. It hardly applies to anyone as confused as myself. That is why I'm supposed to be soft. Sarah's hard. Does that imply weak and strong? Do I resent Sarah as a result? Do I resent Sarah because she despises my apparent softness? Am I just a lower form of life called female who thinks like that?

But I am not a Freestone-Grant, thought Emma, I am an equally military Stevenson now. "You know Emma Stevenson? The pale little wife of Captain Geoffrey Stevenson of the slashing saber. Yes, the same one you've read about, hero of the Matabele wars."

What is it like being married to a hero? I must find out, thought Emma. And at last here is the opportunity.

It was impossible to believe she would be seeing Geoffrey in just a few hours in Kimberley.

The train sped across the hot Karoo, the smoke from the chimney belching up and over, the dust sucking up from under, those two acrid elements combining into a choking gas that found its way into the carriages and set every man and animal coughing and sneezing.

It got into Bartholomew Bannock's nose and he bent forward to sneeze, causing Paddy O'Flaherty, sitting opposite, to lean away with a pained expression before swallowing the last of his halfjack of whiskey.

He held up the bottle upside down.

"Will you look at that, Bart? Wasn't I tellin' you it would last all the way to Kimberley?"

Bannock shrugged. "We're not there yet."

The big Irishman leaned across and pulled down the carriage window to throw out the empty bottle and immediately struggled to close it against the dust blowing in. The fat Italian lying on the bunk above also began to sneeze noisily.

"Shut the window, you damn fool," yelled Bannock.

O'Flaherty managed to close it and slumped back in his seat, unimpressed with the disturbance he had caused.

Bannock suppressed his growing irritation not only with the heat of the sealed-up compartment, which offered the impossible choice of closed windows or a constant stream of dust, and not only, for that matter, with O'Flaherty and his drinking and singing and incessant loud conversations with the Italian, but with his own anxiety over the horses.

His real concern lay five coaches back with a truck full of thoroughbreds and the young jockey Van Breda, who was in with them, at best trying to keep them calm and on their feet and at worst being trampled to death.

They had each taken a turn with the horses—himself on the first leg from Cape Town to Beauford West, then O'Flaherty as far as De Aar, then little Van, who had looked worried as a lamb going into the slaughter as he went in among that forest of stamping hooves. He may have been small, he may have been mute, but he could talk to those horses by better means than words. The voiceless jockey gave sharp whistles and gestures of the hands that they seemed to understand perfectly. But the animals had been excited and ill at ease from the start.

For Bannock it had been a return of the nightmare of the voyage out, when Marcus had kicked down his stall and tried to gallop around the wet, heaving deck, sliding headlong into the scuppers and by some miracle not going overboard. After that he had dreamed each night of the great stallion jumping the rail and crashing down into the turbulence.

It had all come back as the truck pulled out of Cape Town station, with Marcus racing fit this time and taking it out on the two mares, kicking and savaging them as if they were responsible for the misery. He had gone for Bannock himself, who at first tried a swing of the leathers, then tried reasoning with those blazing angry eyes. It was a repeat of that night on the deck when he was dragged with both hands desperately gripping the halter, staring through the spray into those same hysterical eyes, trying to contain his own feelings of hysteria as the quarters went lower, hooves stamping, slipping back toward the thin cable of the rail with the burgeoning swell heaving up from below.

But like all good characters, and with the good example of the rest of the string who settled down in the truck almost immediately, Marcus calmed himself into his usual dignified stance, balancing on spread forelegs, even nudging his great love, Lady Potter, in seeming apology.

Bannock was brought back to reality by O'Flaherty launching into one of his noisy conversations with the Italian above.

"Now about that information you got about how a man can pick up a diamond claim around Kimberley?"

The huge, swarthy face appeared over the edge of the bunk, the mustache bunching to expose the coming words.

"I told'a you, they make'a rush. You take'a the peg and peg'a your own place. The diamonds they are everywhere. Sometimes'a many, sometimes'a not so many. You got'a be lucky, Mr. Flaritti."

"O'Flaherty," roared O'Flaherty. "Did yer not know that every good Irish name starts with an O? Oh-flah-her-ty, not Flerrititti."

The Italian tried again. "O Flerritti?"

"O'Flaherty, for God's sake."

"O Flehitti."

"Right," said O'Flaherty with a cunning look. "Right oh, Mr. Paddykelly."

The reaction from above was immediate, the Italian raising his great bulk on one elbow. "My name is Mario Pacelli. Pah-chell-li." The big lips enunciated like an opera singer's, pulling his mustache into a bushy oval.

O'Flaherty was delighted with the consternation he was causing above. "In that case, Mr. Paddykelly, I'll just be goin' on callin' you Paddykelly and you can go on callin' me Flerittiti and then we'll both be after understandin' one another." And before the Italian could respond: "I shall now sing you both one of my favorite songs."

"No you won't," snapped Bannock, who had become conscious that the train was braking as it negotiated a bend. With the screech of brakes came an almighty jerk and he imagined the horses stumbling forward while Van scaled the walls of the truck to avoid being crushed. But the train continued on slowly and they could see a station through the dust across the bend.

"Now listen to me." Bannock demanded O'Flaherty's attention. "You are a little drunk. Shut up, Paddy." He anticipated the protest and went on. "If I am right, this is the last stop before we reach Kimberley, so this time look sharp with the watering. At De Aar, Parader was lucky to get any at all."

"We should have brought a groom," complained O'Flaherty.

"I told you we couldn't afford it," Bannock sighed wearily. "We had to catch this train." He realized that O'Flaherty was looking away. "We had to, not so?" he insisted.

"Sure." O'Flaherty was sulking.

"Well, the first-class tickets were all we could get, and that took almost everything we've got."

But O'Flaherty was not going to allow the subject to be changed. "Three of us can never be handlin' six great boundin' beasts, and I'll be remindin' you that my days of groomin' and horse-holdin' are supposed to be over. The promise it was, from your own lips."

"We can find help in Kimberley, but in the meantime, you're a groom, Van's a groom, even I'm a groom, so get used to the idea."

"Sure, that's understood," said O'Flaherty magnanimously. "I'm just remindin' you of me rights for the future."

A few more jerks and squeakings of brakes and the train slowed to a crawl. They saw a sign pass by in the window announcing HOPETOWN, with a tin shack village beyond that appeared to offer little of what its name promised. But if the village looked desolate, the low-level siding was alive with people, mostly military personnel, officers in red jackets, troopers in khaki.

As the train made its final fitful jerk to a standstill, Bannock and O'Flaherty swung down onto the platform and quickly made their way back through the waiting soldiers to the truck with its precious cargo of thoroughbreds.

Van Breda was up, clinging to the side timbers with a reassuring grin and wave of the hand that might just as well have expressed his delight at being relieved from his duty in the truck for the last leg of the trip. His sign language got through better to O'Flaherty than to Bannock. But Bannock was beginning to understand the gestures of the head—the nod for yes, the nod for no, the smile for right, the frown for wrong. It was the finger signs and complicated waves of the hand that still confused him.

Bannock climbed up beside Van Breda and counted six shining backs all standing up and seemingly in good order.

"You wait here," he ordered, "and get the feedbags off while I find out how long the stop will be. They stay in the truck. This time the water comes to the horses; less trouble that way."

The jockey gave his agreement sign and scrambled back down into the truck.

Up ahead, the engine was taking on water as men swung the bowser into position, which meant a stop of at least twenty minutes.

While Bannock and O'Flaherty went in search of water for the horses, most of the passengers climbed down to stretch their legs, among them Lady Freestone-Grant, leaning on her son's arm and accompanied by Sarah. Emma, in no mood for running the gauntlet of grinning soldiers, pulled down the window and settled herself comfortably to watch the proceedings from the coach.

In no time the dull siding took on the atmosphere of a garden party, with a slow intermingling of parasols, the smartly suited gentlemen of Mr. Rhodes' entourage, and the shining brass and accoutrements of the officers' uniforms.

Emma watched her mother bear down on two of her acquaintances from the Colonial Club in Cape Town, giving the gracious smile reserved only for those in senior and influential positions.

There was that man again, Mr. Boggle-eyes, the passage-blocker, not looking quite as cocksure of himself as earlier. He was making aggressive gestures to someone who looked like the stationmaster. She could see Sarah, who had wandered off on her own, taking an interest in what was happening there. In fact, a small crowd was gathering around to watch what was becoming a heated altercation.

The stationmaster was joined by a red-jacketed captain, and Boggle-eyes let loose at both of them.

I wonder what he is going on about, Emma thought; he seems pretty angry.

Bannock, in fact, was fuming.

"I'll be damned if you think you can take my horses off this train for a couple of cannons, no matter how many pieces of official paper you show me. I also have a piece of paper that says that truck is paid for all the way to Kimberley."

The stationmaster took the opportunity to escape and go about his duties.

The adamant captain spoke quietly. "You are wasting your time, sir. If you will keep your voice down, you will save us all a lot of bother and I can explain that we are on the verge of a state of emergency."

"What emergency?" demanded O'Flaherty over Bannock's shoulder.

"I am not at liberty to discuss that." The captain stared at them coldly, uncomfortably conscious of the crowd of spectators drawing around. "All I can tell you is that this is a military priority. These guns have been drawn up this far by road and they are now required urgently up the line. Your animals can be accommodated here pending a later train, or," he held up his hand in anticipation of the protest, "since it is unlikely that you will find an unoccupied truck, I would advise you to walk your horses to Kimberley. It's less than fifty miles from here."

"Walk?" Bannock stared in disbelief.

"You could make a claim on the quartermaster in Kimberley. Chances are you'll be compensated."

"You're mad," shouted O'Flaherty. "Do you realize these are valuable thoroughbreds who have never set foot on hard ground the likes of this?"

The captain smiled patiently, and only O'Flaherty knew that look of Bannock's, who was coming close to losing his temper.

"Listen, you—"

"My name is Captain Graham."

"I don't care what your name is. There are three of us to handle six horses. Are you going to offer me any assistance in that way? And what about our baggage and feed stocks? Are you going to supply me with mules?"

Two other officers and a sergeant had appeared, standing around in support of the captain, who now looked more sure of himself.

"I shall arrange for your goods to be held in safe custody in Kimberley. If you set off straightaway, there are seven stations between here and there, plenty of water and feed available all the way." He smiled again. "If you get in a bit of trotting, you should arrive before the heat tomorrow."

"Thank you for the advice," Bannock spat out.

"Not at all," said the captain cheerfully. "I am quite sure your racers could do with a bit of exercise after being cooped up on the train. You might say, off the train and into training, what?" His fellow officers laughed.

"What would be the punishment for punching an officer?" O'Flaherty's temper also began to show, and the military men stopped laughing and closed ranks in an answering show of scorn.

From where Emma sat she could vaguely hear the raised voices amongst the general hubbub, but the scene looked orderly enough, the crowd having divided into two clear groups. There was a gathering of people toward the engine, who would be paying their respects to Cecil Rhodes, which had happened at each of the stops; and another, more agitated one of curious spectators who had gathered to watch that fellow have his argument and were now following down towards the truck where the horses were kept.

She leaned out to see what was happening there. The truck was being opened. Her own curiosity was becoming too much for her and she decided to go and investigate what it was all about for herself. It was an opportunity to see the big chestnut again, the one that pranced and posed like the horses in the paintings in the study at Birchleigh.

Emma ignored the looks from the men, who made room for her as she walked toward where she had last seen Sarah. The ramp was down, and by standing on tiptoe she could just see, between the heads of the crowd, the flying manes and tossing heads of the horses bursting into the sunlight.

There was a moment of anxiety as she found herself caught in the crush, but then she saw Sarah's golden plait and pushed through toward her.

Sarah was at the front of the crowd, standing beside that man, the owner of the horses, who was holding two sets of reins. Above him two thoroughbred heads bobbed, mouths chomping nervously at the bits.

Before Emma could get her sister's attention, Sarah had stepped forward impulsively and asked, "Do they intend giving you any help with the horses?"

Bannock jerked around with an irritated expression that changed when he saw Sarah. There was an awkward pause, during which he studied her from head to toe and up again.

Sarah reddened.

"I don't think so, Miss . . . ?"

"Sarah Freestone-Grant," she blurted out, immediately frowning at her own clumsiness. "I think it is awfully unfair."

Emma found herself sharing Sarah's embarrassment in

the face of the very self-assured man who was now looking at her inquiringly. She clutched at Sarah's elbow, and for a moment, the two normally poised young women were at the mercy of a disarming smile.

"Bannock is the name, Bartholomew Bannock, and I appreciate your concern—" He was cut short by the horses pulling away. He managed to get out, "Thank you, Miss Freestone-Grant, and thank you, Miss . . . ah . . . ?" He pulled the horses back, staring at Emma, the brown eyes holding her, demanding her.

"Mrs. Stevenson," said Sarah firmly. "My sister. Her husband is in Kimberley. We are going to meet him there."

That was quite unnecessary, thought Emma, about my husband in Kimberley to a total stranger. She was amazed at Sarah, who was now smiling headlong at the man, but relieved that the brown eyes had transferred their attention there, and even more relieved when Mark pushed through the crowd and took them both by the arm. He spoke without taking any notice of Bannock.

"Mother was looking for you," he puffed. "It's back to the carriage and ready for the off."

Bannock struggled with his charges but made sure he got the last swinging-away look from Sarah.

The crowd drew back quickly as two mule teams clattered onto the platform from the far end drawing the contentious field guns, both well sewn up in hessian that clearly proclaimed in profile what was underneath.

The oncoming mules upset the thoroughbreds, who in turn sent the spectators scampering for safety. Bannock and O'Flaherty were being pulled across the platform while Van Breda, who had dropped the saddles he was carrying, and a few of the troopers tried to give assistance. It was all confusion, Bannock, Van Breda, and O'Flaherty skidding along in a losing tug of war with six rearing, kicking opponents.

"Get them off the platform," shouted Bannock. But the choice was taken out of his hands when the closest mule team stumbled sideways on taut reins in a threatening wall that forced them down a stone ramp and off the platform. The thoroughbreds tugged backward, dancing up the dust, until they were on open ground, well clear of the station. Once there, in typical fashion, they calmed down as if nothing had happened, only to rear and dance again as the train whistle blew to recall the passengers.

Emma had settled into her place at the window, longing to look out at the proceedings but trapped by her mother's choice of her as audience for a full bulletin of her adventures on the platform. While Lady Freestone-Grant's voice droned on, Emma remained irritatingly conscious of Sarah, who was leaning out of the window, no doubt hoping to be noticed from outside.

"I have now had the opinion of various influential people, and I can tell you quite categorically that there is to be no war.

"I particularly have the assurance of that lieutenant-colonel, whatever his name is, from the boat. You may also remember meeting him at Government House in Cape Town."

Mark nodded and Sarah smiled in turn as they were singled out for reactions that required no comment.

"There was also one of the leading lights of De Beers, who happens to be a close friend of Cecil Rhodes—who, by the way, greeted me very charmingly before returning to his private carriage. And that carriage! The way it was described to me made it sound a rather vulgar affair—all done over in deep crimson and gold, buttoned velvet, even cut-glass chandeliers. Quite Czarist or at best majestic. Hardly diamond magnate, I would have thought. What was it I was saying? Oh, yes: the opinion was unanimous that the idea of war at this time is quite ludicrous."

"Quite right," said Mark from opposite, and Lady Freestone-Grant shifted her attention to him, no doubt as a more appropriate respondent in a military discussion.

The train whistle sounded again, a longer, more final warning.

"There is a perfect analogy for all this: Gilbert and Sullivan. Very apt, don't you think? Troop movements, ultimatums, oom pah pah, general diplomatic hysteria. My dear, it is plain that both the politicians and the very modern major generals have become so bored that they need this type of diversion. I mean to say, there is no enemy, is there? Imagine a line of lancers charging at a bunch of farmers! Frighten them to death."

Mark waited patiently for his mother to run out of breath to get his few words in, while Emma's attention became fixed on the scene outside.

She had to hide her amusement when the train jerked forward, forcing Sarah to sit down with her back to the scene and frustrating her view of whatever object it was that held her interest. Emma, who was facing backward, could see the object clearly. Bannock had mounted the big chestnut stallion. It was moving around prettily, glistening with golden reflections of sweat and good grooming.

The train moved off slowly. The soldiers saluted and waved.

She watched the man with his horse. He was out of the saddle again to check the girths. He slid off in a catlike movement, tall and thin, with unruly black hair. At this distance he looked elegant, in spite of the red dust on his boots and tight white breeches. It was the way he moved. He moved like the kind of man Emma had once dreamed of. The perfect man in control of the perfect horse. It was that very image that had first attracted her to Geoffrey. Beautiful hands that never seemed to have to grip the reins, a mobile and fluid figure in the saddle as if an extension of the horse's every movement.

But this was indeed a horse of another color. It seemed the most perfect animal Emma had ever seen. Maybe, as it had done for Geoffrey, it created an illusion about its rider.

Certainly this man was nothing like Geoffrey. This is an adventurer, of fairly plausible manners but insensitive intentions. There is at least one of them in every company of men, every team, every battalion. He practices a process of seduction with every woman he meets. He only has to see her and his eyes begin their work. It was an effective process, Emma had to admit, no matter how distasteful. It was not even that there was any emotional effect, simply that it was uncomfortable to be visually caressed, to feel as if one's clothing had become transparent for those intense brown eyes. Yet she had hardly been singled out. Sarah had gotten the same treatment, and so would any other pretty female who came along.

The train picked up speed, the horses shrank to the size of ants in the distance. Lady Freestone-Grant rattled on, eyes on her son to make sure he was listening.

"There is nothing unusual about the local population becoming restless in any colonial context. In India it was always thus. Your late father was forever on some or other alert. You wouldn't remember that, of course."

Mark reacted obediently with a small shake of the head.

"I assure you, the sight of a few guns being rushed from one place to another was a perfectly ordinary, everyday affair. It really is no different here. Did you hear anyone comment on those guns? *I* certainly didn't."

Mark nodded as expected and smiled and let the matter rest. He turned and considered his sisters, both of them far away in their own thoughts.

"Who was that man you were talking to?" He aimed the verbal arrow at Sarah.

"What man?" Lady Freestone-Grant immediately surveyed the target while Mark smiled mischievously.

Sarah faced them coolly. "His name is Mr. Bannock, the owner of those horses. I suspect he is related to the Bannock who won a few of the classics when I was at school."

"Indeed, yes," said Lady Freestone-Grant, always glad of some evidence of family background. "How did you manage to meet him?"

Sarah must have eliminated every nice and proper reason she could have given in a moment, for she replied, "I introduced myself to him."

Mark began to laugh, Emma looked studiously out of the window, and Lady Freestone-Grant waited for an explanation in icy silence.

It was in that pause that Emma found she had lost sight of the horses in the heat haze that shimmered the outline of the tin roofs of Hopetown.

For the first ten miles Bannock had said nothing. He slumped in the saddle, setting a slow walking pace for the other two, who, knowing his mood, kept well back.

Each of them rode one horse and led one on a bridle —he on the brown gelding Parader, with the stallion Marcus prancing alongside; O'Flaherty on the big gray gelding Hussein, leading Lady Potter; Van Breda on MacHattie, leading Pot Pourri.

The gentle-natured Pot Pourri had been selected as the packhorse, carrying an ungainly load that happily did not weigh very much: six full feedbags, six halters and hobbles tied together, and canvas for improvising a drinking trough when necessary. There was very little food for the riders. The bread, cheese, and dried meat purchased in Hopetown they carried in two saddlebags supplied by the gunners.

They were as out of place as a line of camels in arctic wastes: six thoroughbreds a long way from the soft going of the Cape, still nervously sniffing out the waves of hot air, carefully, suspiciously, placing their hooves between the brittle yellow clumps of dry grass and rock outcrops, stumbling from time to time on the stones that scattered the veld.

Bannock was in a state of deep depression. This latest setback had triggered off all his worst misgivings. Was this the right direction to be taking? Should he not have simply sold the string once the trouble started in the Cape? Sold all of them—except Marcus, of course—and shipped back to England, where he knew what to expect from the stewards and the jockeys and the touts, even the bookmakers.

Once the arguments had started in Cape Town, the nobbling of Marcus, the fight in the club, the general ganging-up from all sides, it had become a question of get out or go on losing out.

You can eat them up at Port Elizabeth, someone had said. But Port Elizabeth was too close for comfort. You could take your pickings on the diamond fields or even on the Reef, they said. Most of the time you would be going against badly handled second stringers and three-quarter-breds, donkeys by comparison to some of yours.

That had sounded good. But nobody had said anything about cannons and a possible state of emergency.

He turned to see how the other horses were coming on. They still looked good, heads up, impatient with the slow pace, and with very little sweat, considering the blazing afternoon heat. O'Flaherty and Van Breda were almost asleep in the saddle, and he was beginning to feel the same way.

They had last tasted water at the Orange River bridge two hours earlier. The next prospect now loomed ahead in the form of a brick tank at a small siding.

Their approach forced them onto the rough stony road that converged with the railway line to run alongside a short platform and a small stone dwelling, which turned out to be empty and abandoned. Inevitably, the horses sensed the presence of their long-awaited drink and crowded together as the three men dismounted. There was a trough and hand pump below the tank, and to Bannock's relief, the water gushed out in answer to O'Flaherty's efforts. The horses drank and were led into the late-afternoon shade of the small building.

Bannock went out to the tracks and looked pensively

to the north. That train would soon be arriving in Kimberley, while they would have to see out the entire night and a good part of the following day before arriving. He had decided on a few hours' rest later in the cool of the evening, but not too late, when it would be too cold for rest without blankets.

He walked back toward the horses. O'Flaherty and Van Breda had switched the saddles and unpacked the loose items off Pot Pourri's back, dividing them into two lots before strapping them, one on Hussein and the other on MacHattie. Van Breda brought Marcus, ready-saddled for Bannock to mount. The great horse shifted around on his hooves as if he were preparing for a race and Bannock had to chase him in a half circle before jumping for the saddle.

He watched O'Flaherty, who, in spite of his size, slipped up onto the saddle like the most agile of jockeys. But now he was on Lady Potter, who was one of those light-framed, long runners, unaccustomed to carrying that amount of weight.

"I don't like your bulk on that mare for any distance," said Bannock.

O'Flaherty stiffened in the saddle. "And what about your bulk, all six foot of it?"

"Weight is the problem, Paddy, not height."

O'Flaherty's excitement had transmitted itself to Lady Potter, who pranced and reared while her resentful rider kept his attention on Bannock.

"Listen here, Bartholomew,"—he used the name in full when he was angry—"let me point out that this dear horse will never enjoy better hands on her reins and never has she known a seat, no matter how heavy as you say, that's trained in Ireland to go with the bumps and jumps and never a jerk."

Bannock, in spite of his mood, had to laugh, because give O'Flaherty his due, he was busy demonstrating the very points he was making.

The ice was broken. They all laughed as Van Breda

mounted up and a square dance started in a stamping circle of rising dust as the three turned this way and that, reaching out to catch the reins of their partners for the next long walk.

They settled into the trough of somewhat broken ground running beside the railway tracks, with O'Flaherty his old self, going ahead at a bouncing walk, singing one of his songs of endless verses. Next came Van Breda, with Bannock bringing up in the rear, fighting a mild war of nerves with Marcus, who was taking a long time to settle down.

O'Flaherty suddenly stopped singing and Bannock realized he was reining in and staring toward the horizon on his left. There was dust rising over there on a higher plateau, a long, flat ridge.

They all stopped and watched.

"What do you make of that?" asked O'Flaherty.

"Riders." Bannock's eyesight was better. "Look to the north of the dust. About a dozen of them."

Van Breda was making furious hand signs, which were lost on Bannock but not on O'Flaherty.

"I agree," he said. "It must be cavalry."

"Not cavalry," observed Bannock. "No pennants, no lances. Do you know what I think those are? Those are the Boers."

O'Flaherty was inclined to agree. "The fightin' farmers. Sure, if it's them, there's nothin' to be worryin' about. You know what they're sayin', it's a lot of fuss over nothin'."

"That's not quite what they're saying. What I heard was, they're banding together and looking for trouble."

"And they'll soon be gettin' tired of it. I'm tellin' you, it's a lot of fuss over nothin'."

"I'm not so sure. If there's a lot of fuss, it's not over nothing."

Bannock studied the dust cloud. There was something sinister about the way it blew back into a swirling form that became alive with threat. The group of riders was moving fast. Who would go at a gallop in that heat? And the dust was lying off to the south, which meant they were approaching, or at least heading in the same general direction.

"Let's move on," said O'Flaherty. "If they're lookin' for trouble, it's with the army, not us."

Bannock hoped he was right about that and trusted to the great distance that separated them and the height of the railway tracks, which must to some extent obscure their progress.

As O'Flaherty led on, he began singing again, only this time less enthusiastically, more softly, as if the sound might find its way up there.

But something was happening on the ridge. The dust was gone. There was no sign of the riders. Bannock reined in and strained to see, cursing himself for not having retrieved his binoculars from the train. For a while he could make out nothing. The ridge shimmered in the late-afternoon heat. They could be standing still or coming this way.

Then he saw dust again, lower down the ridge, with the minute figures of the riders descending and eventually disappearing below eye level behind the rise of the railway tracks. They were approaching and there was nothing else in this barren wilderness they could possibly be heading for but themselves.

The string ambled on at the same pace, as if by an unspoken agreement between the three men to make no assumptions and proceed as if nothing was happening.

It took some ten minutes before they heard the hoofbeats and saw the heads bobbing on the other side of the tracks. Then the riders exploded over the top, stepping and jumping over the track, bringing a cloud of dust with them as they drew up in a wide circle, sending the thoroughbreds into a frantic dance of disapproval.

Bannock held his reins wide to at least keep Marcus' head straight, while the rest of the big horse jackknifed about like a boat in a storm. He surveyed the strange and

menacing band who surrounded them. If they were the
Boers, they looked like anything but harmless farmers.
They looked sullen. They looked dangerous. They were
untidy, at first sight appearing to be in uniform, yet no two
of them wore the same clothes. Looking around the circle,
there was corduroy, khaki, and leather, new breeches and
old working trousers, English riding boots, miner's mud-
larkers, and one or two in rough suede shoes.

Their one common denominator was armory. Each of
them wore fully bulleted bandoliers and new-looking rifles
slung across their backs.

The Boer leader singled out Bannock as the one to
speak to and cantered forward aggressively to confront him.

"*Goeie middag,*" he called out, and suddenly he was
smiling broadly. "This is your horses? Who is the owner of
this horses?"

"I am," said Bannock. "And what the bloody hell do
you want?"

The Boer went on smiling. "We are from the Jacobsdal
Commando. We are under orders to look for horses."

"I didn't know there was a war on." Bannock allowed
Marcus to chop forward before checking him. The Boer
reined back, but the smile remained.

"Oh, no, *Mijneer,* there is no war,"—a pause for emphasis—"not yet. We are still short of horses. We are looking for good horses like this. We pay good prices. And this
is a good one, hey?" pointing to Marcus. "What do you say,
Mijneer? Tell me your price."

"These horses are not for sale." Bannock's voice rose
to a shout but he took control, tried to reason. "They are
not riding horses. They are racehorses, so they are no good
to you."

"*Wat sê hy?*" The Boer appealed to his followers.
"*Watte soort perde?*"

One of his men called out, "*Reisiesperde, Komman-
dant.*"

"*Goed.*" The Boer was jubilant. "That means they are running fast. *Nou goed,* all the better."

"You are wasting your time and ours," said Bannock. "We are late and we must move on. Let's go, Paddy," he called to O'Flaherty, who immediately turned and led off straight at the surrounding horsemen.

The horses parted and they were through, but the Boers spread out behind and followed at a walk while the leader rode up alongside Bannock.

"*Nie wat, wag, wag.* Wait, *Mijneer.* We are not finished talking yet."

"Yes we are." Bannock dug his heels into Marcus, jerking on the lead rein to make Parader follow. In three long, cantering strides he had brushed off the Boer, whose small horse had shied away in fright, and come alongside O'Flaherty.

"Listen, Paddy," he said urgently. "We are about to go for a gallop."

"You're mad." O'Flaherty glanced back at the strung-out threat. "They'll be shootin' at us right away."

"I don't think so. He's bluffing, Paddy. Are you listening, Van?" he called over his shoulder. "When I give the word, slip the halters off the other three and chase them."

O'Flaherty was horrified. "They'll be runnin' all over the place, more as likely back in the wrong direction."

"We have no choice. It's a question of maybe losing three horses or the lot."

The Boer had tripled his mount alongside again. He was laughing. "I think you must sell us this horses." The threat became more obvious. "We must have them. You will get a good price."

Bannock looked back, gauging the distance to the line of Boers some way behind, then made his decision. Pulling over the reins, he allowed Marcus to swing his rear quarters toward the Boer leader, forcing him to pull away. At the same time, he pulled Parader toward him and slipped off his halter.

The others followed suit immediately, each of the lead horses receiving a crack with the loose halters.

They were off on the start of a new kind of race, getting into their stride so quickly that the Boer leader found himself galloping into a wall of dust and flying grit.

"Stay close to the tracks," shouted Bannock, leaning back on the tightest rein he could hold on Marcus, who was in danger of overtaking the loose horses.

They were on rising ground, where the railway line climbed to pass between two rock-topped hills. Bannock looked back, to see some of the Boers following at a gallop, spreading out to avoid the trail of dust that hung in the windless heat. But they were getting smaller as the pace of the thoroughbreds quickly increased the gap.

The decision to chase the three loose horses had worked well. They forged straight ahead at a calm gallop, stretching out at no more than the equivalent of a three-quarter-pace workout, but fast enough for the purpose. It had worked well so far.

Suddenly, MacHattie veered up the bank and cleared the rails at the top, sliding down to run a parallel course on the far side.

"You stupid damned dog," shouted Bannock, letting Marcus speed up and riding closer to the embankment to stop the other two from following MacHattie's example. He was not risking Marcus for any other horse, but O'Flaherty was about to risk Lady Potter as he charged her up the embankment. At the top the mare shied away, refusing to jump the rails.

From his elevated position, O'Flaherty looked back and immediately waved to the others and began to rein in.

"It's all right," he shouted. "They're off in the other direction."

Bannock and Van Breda rode up to join him, and

through the thinning dust they watched the group of Boer riding off in the direction from which they had come.

"Van, you fetch MacHattie," ordered Bannock. "Put a bridle on him for the time being; we'll catch up with the other two later."

"Did you see those strange fellows," O'Flaherty puffed incredulously, "with the long leathers and the feet stuck out forward and those stubby little horses with the funny paces?"

"Tripling, they call it, Paddy."

"What are you tellin' me now? Do you think I don't know what a triple is? It's a ridiculous pitter-patter sort of pace where you're as likely to trip as keep on triplin'. I can't believe it, the way they stick their feet out like that, ready for the fall."

They rode on along the embankment beside the line, watching Van Breda over to the left getting the bridle onto MacHattie without dismounting. Up ahead, Parader and Hussein were strolling on together.

"I'm hungry," said O'Flaherty. "Do you know that Italian Paddykelly, fine man that he is, he is a chef, did you know that? He's one of the world's great cooks, and sure, he's a man with a dream. He's worked in all the great hotels, but all he wants is his own little restaurant in Rome, servin' up the greatest food you ever tasted."

"Sounds more like an opera singer."

"Now there's a reason for that." O'Flaherty was off again. "Certain Italians and certain Irishmen have a lot in common, like Paddykelly and meself. We both appreciate the finer things in life."

"Like wine, women, and song." Bannock started laughing and decided it was more from relief than from O'Flaherty's prattle.

"You're close to the point there, Bart, but you've got the order wrong. Like food, as I said. I would place food —no, maybe good whiskey and wine—no; definitely good food, that's first. Then, of course, the finer types of liquor, which both Italians and the Irish really understand." He ignored the pointed laughter from beside him. "And then, as you said, the song. Take the good Catholic hymns that are sung the world over, and the grand old songs of Ireland. Even the sadder ones are very like the opera."

"And what about the women?"

"Oh, I'll be leavin' those to the true experts like yourself. Like the snooty-nosed little blonde you were workin' on in the train. Think I don't notice these things?"

"I don't know what you're talking about," said Bannock, remembering the snooty-nosed little blonde and her equally snooty-nosed sister. A very interesting and untouchable pair of females. But even if you could not touch them, you could think about them. Bannock thought about them, undressed them, even tried making love to them, and came to the conclusion that he preferred the married one to the one who gave him the eye. Pity.

They caught up with Parader and Hussein near the top of the rise between the two hills and waited there for Van Breda to follow up the hill leading MacHattie, who cantered alongside, obediently responding to the magic whistles of the little man. Their dust stream made an insignificant mark on the vast sea of red veld going gray with the failing light, tinted red again by the sun at the horizon.

Bannock could see another smaller stream of dust on the distant ridge where he had first noticed it. The Boers were still on the move, and if the reports were correct, there were others on the move throughout the territory. Something about them did not add up to the description he had been given. They looked rough and ready, yes, but there was a style, an enigmatic force, gray-eyed and intense; even the strange way they rode was fluent and businesslike. Something about that man, the leader. He smiled all the time, but his eyes were not smiling, he was never ruffled. And Bannock knew that if that man had had a fast horse, things would have been different. He thought, I hope I don't have to meet any more like him.

When Van Breda came up, they rode together over the top of the hill and there they saw the possible reason why the Boers had turned back: a Union Jack, minute in the distance, hanging limply above what might have been a police or military post. There were a few horses picketed beside the small building, but no siding or railway platform.

"And what about diamonds?" Bannock asked O'Flaherty.

"What diamonds?"

"I'm talking about you and your Italian friend and the diamonds you plan to pick up in the streets of Kimberley. Where do they come in your list of priorities?"

O'Flaherty put on his pained look. "Sure, you'll never be understandin' these things. You've got a one-track mind and I don't mean horses. The diamonds are there, begorrah. Not in the streets, but on the outskirts. You have to go through all the proper formalities. Makin' the claim, gettin' the necessary license, et cetera. Paddykelly and meself will be gettin' together on the matter. It's all arranged."

"Forget it. You'll be too busy looking after six horses."

O'Flaherty ignored him. "I shall now sing you one of those dear songs that never fail to bring tears to the eyes."

As the sun went down, O'Flaherty's booming voice brought no tears to the eyes of Bannock or Van Breda, but it must have come as a surprise to the buck and the jackals, and eventually to the men down at the post they were approaching.

"We are coming into Kimberley, ladies." The inspector closed the compartment door and set off again on his tour of announcement.

Emma watched her hands trembling as if they did not belong to her. She watched them in detached fascination as they moved, gathering her things together.

"Where is Mark?" her mother complained. "He must take care of everything. Sarah, go and find him instantly. Never mind." She smiled at Emma. "I am quite sure Geoffrey will have done everything necessary for our arrival. Oh, this heat."

The train steamed slowly past a big mining complex, a metal tower with spoked wheels holding cables on the top, a number of low, rusting buildings, a flat-topped hill of dumped waste ground, and a wide dam of muddy water. The smoke from the engine floated out, catching the last rays of the sun. Suddenly, for Emma, Kimberley was a reality. Kimberley, but not Geoffrey. She tried to picture him again, but all she could see was the uniform, clear in every detail: the glinting buttons, the epaulets, the saber.

Then she remembered he was no longer a cavalry officer. Geoffrey not in uniform. Geoffrey an insurance man. How do you imagine that? Maybe now that he was a civilian he would change, become a helmetless, spurless human, the kind who talk to their wives, who even woo their wives, touch them and hold them, often.

Did that mean there was still hope? Geoffrey a conventional man with working hours and hours for coming home. There might even be a home to come home to. Those famous decorations would be put away, to be worn only on formal occasions. The circumstances would dictate the changes, the change in habits. It was easy enough to predict those changes. But could they dictate love? Emma doubted that. There was never enough passion between them for even passion to die.

But any hope is worth embracing. From the time Geoffrey had surprisingly announced his intention of resigning from the cavalry, the promise had grown. Then the offer of a partnership with Mark set off the present chain of events. Instead of returning to England, he had traveled direct from his last commission, with the expeditionary forces in Natal to Kimberley, to establish connections with De Beers while waiting for the family to arrive.

Mark opened the door and looked in. Lady Freestone-Grant was ready for him.

"Where have you been, Mark? I want you to watch everything. Put nothing on the platform until we are all ready. These miners are very rough types, from all reports. We must all stay together once we leave the train. And please keep an eye out for Geoffrey."

There was something about the way she referred to Geoffrey, as if he were her other son. That made sense to Emma. Think of Geoffrey as a brother. She had known him since childhood. Yes, like a brother then. And now? Was there not a sad truth in that the kind of feelings she had toward him these days were not unlike her feelings for Mark? One feels no passion for one's brother, so maybe that long familiarity, overfamiliarity, maybe that accounted for the way her feelings had become so confused. Would it be like going to bed with her brother tonight?

Emma looked up as the roof of the station closed over to reveal a truncated version of Paddington, giving the same impression of vast gray metal overhead, beams arching like rainbows, rococo pillars of iron—an impression that soon shrank by comparison. There were only two platforms. But there was another difference. This little Paddington was covered in bright bunting. Streamers cascaded down from cardboard cut-outs of the Queen's head, countless Union Jacks fluttered up amongst the smoke, a military brass band pumped away in competition with hundreds of cheering voices. A right royal reception for the Empire's king of Africa.

While Mr. Rhodes arrived in triumph, Emma's agitation grew worse. She followed Sarah into the passage, and they shared a window with Mark, watching the welcomers crowding forward in pace with the slowly moving train, toward Rhodes' coach up front.

Emma's knuckles were white where she gripped the window. Why am I so apprehensive? Maybe I know why. Because I am about to be reassured. I am about to be told not to worry, that my fears are groundless, that I am not to bother my head with mere theory or conjecture, that I should leave everything to him. Every urgent question I have ever asked him has been smothered thus.

She remembered again that last magnificent reassurance of Geoffrey's as he set off for Africa two years ago: "You must understand, my dear, we have not been given a chance. Fate has been against us. We have not even been allowed to give each other a chance." Is that what all career officers told their wives? If so, their credibility would have to be in question. She had been offered no options. Oh, to have been an army wife. But even at the time of their marriage seven years ago, when the next and imminent assignment was the Matabele campaign, the conditions did not permit. Even the boat trip was not allowable: "You cannot wait at the coast on your own. I could not take that responsibility. I have to know you are safe."

But I could have taken that responsibility all on my own.

Emma looked out at the crush of military uniforms. It's a man's world, this, she thought. Or a boy's one, if you were an officer like Geoffrey. Men who were boys, boys who never really grew up because there was no need to. When you can strut about and jingle your spurs and flash your metal tokens of status, in the officers' mess, in the clubs and bars, strut to numbers on the parade ground and once in a while on the battleground, where some, for one sober moment, become men by dint of death.

"There he is," Mark shouted above the din. "There's Geoffrey."

Emma had to search, but then she saw him looking around anxiously from where he seemed to be trapped by a group of senior officers. He really stood out like some rising young diplomat in his civilian suit. There was no mistaking that fine head of sand-colored hair casually— no, carefully—untidy. Tall, thin Geoffrey; thin nose, thin face, thin and wiry all the way down. Oh, yes, as a woman assesses a man, Geoffrey was beautiful. The beautiful image covered everything—speech, movement, everything you could see or hear. But she had lived with only a ghost of what was behind that facade, somehow assuming that what was hidden would emerge and make their lives complete.

She thought, I have scratched that surface too long. My beloved myth is wearing thin.

Geoffrey saw them and made his excuses before pushing his way through the crowd.

She thought, Here comes reassurance. She trembled in the corridor as he climbed onto the train and squeezed past the disembarking passengers to get to her.

"My dear girl." He kissed her on the mouth and cheek. "How wonderful to see you at last." He was smiling down at her, holding her by the shoulders, and all she could think was, Holding by the shoulders is not an embrace. There was going to be no embrace.

Sarah took the initiative and did embrace him, by force, Emma thought. Lady Freestone-Grant offered her cheek and Mark his hand, and immediately the two new business partners were discussing prospects. Emma remained joined to the conversation only by holding on to Geoffrey's hand, excluded as if that hand were a groom's holding the reins of an attendant horse. She moved with them automatically as they followed the porters who had come aboard to fetch their luggage.

On the platform the noise was deafening. Emma watched Geoffrey; he was more talkative, more animated than she had ever seen him. But she had seen him animated before. It came back to her that Geoffrey was not without passion; not in his dreams, when he shouted and squirmed and lashed out about the bed. Then he was a fighter, spurred on by what? Fear? At first she had not believed that. But the dreams had their dialogue. Those slurred words and shouts became repeated again and again, until they were understood.

Major Everett, a fellow traveler who had been on the ship and bound for Mafeking, came up, bowing to Lady Freestone-Grant but heading straight for Geoffrey Stevenson.

"Captain Stevenson, I presume." They shook hands and he went on, "The champagne is for Cecil Rhodes, the fanfares are for the heroes of Empire, and you, of course, are one of their living representatives here."

"Thank you," Stevenson answered, a trifle embarrassed. But he was flushed and in his element.

Emma felt more isolated than ever as the round of pleasantries began. Geoffrey looked as if he had never dreamt a bad dream, never called out in the night, "No hope . . . no hope . . . no hope," in a way that took on the rhythm of the gallop; shouting, "I shall not be taken . . . I shall not be touched"; then screaming, "Come on, die, you bastards, die with me"; then waking up sweating, denying that anything had happened.

A gentler Geoffrey broke into her thoughts. "So I gather you already know my wife, Emma?"

"Yes, indeed, I know your beautiful wife, I know the whole family." The major beamed around at them.

Emma retired back into her isolation as her mother took charge of whatever conversation was to follow. She was being invited to bring her family to a later reception in honor of Mr. Rhodes at a place called the Sanatorium, which in spite of its misleading name, it was explained, was in fact the luxurious institution where Rhodes stayed whenever he was in Kimberley.

There were three cheers for Rhodes, and Emma saw him momentarily as he stepped down from the carriage, his square, mustached face set in a grimace, which if one was closer could no doubt be seen as a smile. It was the same and only expression she had seen at each station where he took the air. A strong face, an unchanging face, ideal for a poker player. But Rhodes played with nations and people and diamondiferous holes in the ground as the stakes.

Stevenson led the way out of the station with Emma on his arm, the Freestone-Grant entourage following and the porters behind. He looked down at her seriously.

"There is something we are all going to have to discuss. There is going to be a war. I don't think it will be much of a war, but unless we decide to get away from here quickly, we may well be trapped for the duration."

"Does Mr. Rhodes know that? We all felt nothing could happen if he was here."

Their whispered exchange was not lost on Lady Freestone-Grant when they gathered outside the station.

"Why so serious, young man? Is something the matter?"

Stevenson looked at Mark and then at his questioner. "I was just saying to Emma there seems a strong chance of a declaration of war here. We are going to have to put our heads together and decide what to do under the circumstances."

The porters began loading the baggage onto one of the two carriages drawn up for them.

"Oh, I think you can put your mind at rest about that." Lady Freestone-Grant was smiling again. "I believe my sources of information are of the best, and they say the Boers are being kept thoroughly in their place."

Stevenson frowned. He answered sternly, "My information dates from this morning. The Boers are heavily armed and dispersed throughout the country. There is an ultimatum that must be answered by tomorrow."

Lady Freestone-Grant smiled patronizingly. "We shall find out tonight. All the right answers from all the right people."

Stevenson was showing signs of annoyance. "You don't have to wait until tonight, ma'am. There is about to be a war."

·2· | THE CLOSING OF THE RING

To watch Major Gordon Masefield scribbling on his pad, it would have been difficult to tell whether he was intensely attentive or intensely bored. His expression never changed: eyes down, lips set tight in a permanent sulk, double chin forced into a roll that overlapped the collar of his tunic. It looked more like boredom as the CO's voice lectured on its deadly monopitch.

But with Masefield you could never tell. His antique gold propelling pencil quivered and stopped bolt upright, and quivered at its work again, sending off glints of reflection, enough on their own to distract the attention of his brother officers. Not that it took too much to bring attention to Masefield. He was surprisingly fat for an officer. "He's an officer and a half," someone once joked in the mess, careful not to be heard by him. Certainly he could have taken up a chair and a half of the spindly bentwood type used for meetings in the plans room at army H.Q. in Lennox Street.

The image of a figure of fun stopped abruptly at his figure. Masefield remained every inch an enigma. He was just not a funny man. If anything, he was sinister, too articulate to be put down. In his short time in Kimberley, he had made no friends, and remained too aloof even to make enemies. Most confusing of all was his position on the staff, Communications Officer, that new designation whose areas of responsibility were vague and undefined. Besides the fact that Masefield could be seen from time to time entering or leaving the CO's office, no one could tell you precisely what he did. His answers to questions in meetings were reticent at best and invariably were taken over and evaporated by the CO in his inimitable style of generalization. He was known to ask questions, to gather information, but never to give any. Kimberley Command had gained a large inscrutable inquisitor, and only the Commanding Officer of the garrison, Colonel Kekewich himself, might know what he was about; and even then, he only *might*.

While Colonel Kekewich's voice droned on, to a careful observer it would have appeared that the gold pencil was not simply writing but also drawing, almost certainly doodling.

The colonel's voice was saying, "Until the result of the Boer ultimatum, which expires at five P.M. this evening, our defense plans remain secret. If the result is what I expect, we are likely to come under siege for as long as it takes the main army to get up here."

He twisted the gold pencil until precisely the right amount of lead emerged. The new point drew a neat ring and began to sketch cannons in a wider ring around it.

The colonel's voice was saying, "We are faced with a distinct difference of opinion between the Cape Ministry, whose opinion we take with a pinch of salt, and our own General Staff, whose opinion is law. On the one side, there is mollycoddling of the Boers; on the other, a quiet call to arms."

Masefield drew a small bugle in the middle of the ring.

"The Boers? They are rallying like ants, armed to the teeth with German rifles, German and French artillery. On the other hand, they are an undisciplined rabble who know nothing of military strategy, which implies that whatever happens, if anything happens, it will happen and be over fairly quickly."

Masefield drew a nice explosion.

The lecture went on. "This is our standing force in Kimberley. Bear with me; if you've heard it before you shall hear it again: a battery of artillery, Diamond Fields Artillery that is, with six seven-pounder guns which belong in a museum; then two companies of volunteers, the Diamond Fields Horse, of two hundred, all ranks and no available horses—a company of horse sans horses, can you believe it?—and the Kimberley Regiment—regiment, mind you—of four hundred and twenty ranks in all. Then we have Robinson's Cape Police, five hundred throughout the district, spread out along the railway almost as far as Mafeking. Our potential force when all recruitment is finalized will be about three thousand six hundred men of all ranks."

The pencil traveled up the page to where an equation had been written: "Ultimatum equals War over Peace." Below "War" it wrote, "2 to 1 on." Below "Peace" it wrote, "100 to 1."

The colonel was saying, "Captain MacInnes, as you know, has drawn up the plans for our ring of defenses. I think it is an excellent interim arrangement, and I shall ask him to show you what has been decided on: the earthworks, the redoubts, the entrenched positions, and all the relative details of administration, stores, general deployment—in fact, the whole defense plan."

The pencil made a large affirmative tick on the drawn ring of cannons.

"Gentlemen, we have thirty-four thousand souls in our care, ten thousand of whom are the African mine laborers. We are defending the second largest town in the Cape Colony. Think of our numbers, then think of thirteen and a half miles of perimeter, and you can begin to gauge the task."

The pencil had scribbled the equation: "13½ over 6 × 7 pounders."

The colonel was saying, "It will become necessary to turn Kimberley into one vast fort."

The pencil began to draw battlements.

Bartholomew Bannock walked along one of the higher ramps of the wood-and-iron grandstand and thought of Epsom and Goodwood and Doncaster. He looked out over the run-down racecourse, shorter than anything he knew—hardly a mile all the way around—and of a type of going he had never imagined could exist, a yellowed stubble of dried-out grass on sun-baked red ground.

He walked down to where the little English trainer, an ex-jockey, was sitting, looking at him. He turned around and faced a sign that read MEMBERS & OFFICERS ONLY, and thought that some things were fairly standard wherever you went.

Eventually, he asked, "What if the whole thing doesn't happen, Mr. Watson?"

"It's happening already—Charlie, mate, Charlie is the name. This town has got more soldiers than people. They're carrying sandbags around in the night. They're polishing up their guns, and I told you, everybody's trying to buy my horses. So you can expect the same thing."

Bannock was distracted, and his companion looked to see what had caught his attention. O'Flaherty was coming on in the distance, riding beside a mule cart he had somehow acquired. It was a moment of relief. It was all there: the forage, the baggage, and the saddlery.

"I'm short of money, Charlie, but I'm not selling any of my horses."

"You're not going to have the choice, sport. There's going to be no more racing here. They told us. Bert Michaels left with his string last week. Weatherby's gone up to the Reef. Nobody's left. You'll find the rest at Port Elizabeth one of these days, and that's where you'll find me."

Bannock lit a cheroot, took a seat on the stand, and listened to Watson.

"You've got two ways to go. You can set off with me in the morning on the long walk. No trouble with grooms. The Basutos are good handlers, and once they get into the racing game, they are all for heading for the big centers. You've only got to feed them on the way. It's a long walk to Port Elizabeth; take about three weeks. But it keeps the nags in trim, and when you arrive, the racing's keen, and with your Marcus you won't be short for long. Cor, what a stallion that is. That's the one way. The other way, you're a racing man where there's no racing, so you'll have to sell. And who better than honest Charlie Watson, who's got the ready booty. Maybe not enough for the stallion, but there's a couple of others I could manage and you could manage without."

"Forget it," said Bannock, spitting.

"Then you're coming for the ride?"

"No." Bannock gave it some thought. "I think I shall be going to Johannesburg for that summer handicap."

"On foot?"

"On foot and hoof, my friend."

"You'll be too late, mate. That way you'll just be giving your horses to the Boers; they'll take them."

Bannock climbed up to the back of the grandstand and leaned over the open railing below the roof to watch O'Flaherty arrive.

O'Flaherty called up as he dismounted, pointing first at Bannock, then at Van Breda, who was coming from the stable, to include them both in what he had to say.

"Those stupid buggers have stolen a couple of our bales. I wanted to kill the rotten shit, that fellow at the station, the omidorne. Thank the Lord I got there in time to stop them takin' anythin' else. And I want to tell you somethin' else that you won't believe: those two cannons," he pointed a wild emphasizing finger, "those two rotten perishin' cannons that put us off the train, they are standin' there useless as you like, with the hay bags tied on them and the snotty-nosed little soldier standin' there on guard. And shall I tell you something else again? The military have never heard of compensation. What horses, the officer said, what compensation is it you're talkin' about?"

"I see you have a bottle of whiskey," observed Bannock.

"It's me own money, God be praised, what's left of it," shouted O'Flaherty, patting the beloved bottle in his pocket.

Watson had also climbed up to the back of the stand. He nudged Bannock, pointing to a one-horse trap that was driving into the stable enclosure toward them.

"Here comes trouble. Mr. Graham Pope-Evans himself."

"Who's he?"

"Secretary of the Turf Club, one of the De Beers gents. He's the one who passed the word you were here. I heard it from Maskell the bookmaker, who got it from him, and I came straight over."

"Well, then, let's go down and have a nice chat with him."

As they climbed down the stand, Bannock noticed two riders moving at a walk on the far side of the course. One was an elderly gentleman, the other a girl in full riding habit whom he recognized. It was one of the two pretty blondes on the train, the unmarried one. The reckless one?

Bannock and Watson came around the side of the stand in time to hear O'Flaherty say, "I think you'll have to talk to the owner himself." O'Flaherty and Van Breda had stopped their unloading to watch while the driver of the mule cart ran round to take the reins of the hackney from Pope-Evans.

Watson made the introductions. "This is Mr. Bannock, the trainer from Cape Town. And this is Mr. Pope-Evans, secretary of the Kimberley Turf Club."

Pope-Evans, a short, fat, balding man, alighted and glared up at Bannock.

"Mr. Bannock, I trust you are quite comfortable here in these new quarters you have just taken over?"

Bannock chewed on his cheroot. "I'm a registered trainer, sir, and this is the racecourse. It's the first place we came to on our way in."

"Yes, but you do not own it," complained Pope-Evans. "It is still our racecourse, and you could have had the manners to request permission before installing your own horses in the course stables. But never mind." He stopped the obviously irritated Bannock from speaking. "This is of course a courtesy we extend to visitors and new arrivals, so you may leave them here. But only for a few days, I'm afraid. There's going to be no racing, you know."

"I'm going on to Johannesburg," said Bannock.

Pope-Evans smiled politely. "I think not, Mr. Bannock. If the reports are correct, nobody will be going to Johannesburg or anywhere else." He climbed back onto the trap and looked down at them.

"I believe you have a good stallion?" he asked. "If you're interested in selling him . . ."

"Not a chance," snapped Bannock.

"Let me know if you change your mind." With a nod and a graceful turn of the whip, Pope-Evans maneuvered his prancing hackney around the cart and left.

"I think you should go to Port Elizabeth with me," said Watson.

But Bannock was looking in another direction. The blonde girl on the horse had turned and was trotting briskly toward them, while the elderly gentleman waited at the far rail.

"What did you say earlier, Charlie?"

"I dunno." Watson looked puzzled. "What did I say?"

"Here comes trouble."

"Nice piece of trouble," remarked Watson.

"His kind of trouble," put in O'Flaherty.

Emma scribbled an indecipherable line on the pad in her lap. She tried to gather her own thoughts despite the continual chatter of her mother and Sarah.

They were sitting around a cane table in the shade of an acacia tree that dominated the hotel garden. The pretense at letter writing was her escape from a discussion of everything that had happened and would happen: the fabulous military men, the silliness of the local fashions, and the absurd concept of a war between farmers and the British military machine. They were waiting for Mark and Geoffrey to join them for lunch. Mark had gone off to attend a meeting at De Beers, and for some unexplained reason, Geoffrey, the future partner, had not gone with him.

From where she sat she could see Geoffrey now and then, stopping at a French window opposite, hands solemnly behind back, walking away and appearing again while he talked to the old colonel, who could not be seen. Poor Geoffrey, she thought, and poor Emma. It had not been much of a reunion. They had spent two unhappy nights together, the first no worse than the second.

On the former occasion, she had been very conscious of their first private moment alone. A time for a revision of understanding after so much parting. But Geoffrey had been a little drunk, from the champagne as much as from the praise and acclamation: "You are undressed, sir. Where is your famous sword?" and "How many did they say you wiped out in one charge?" and, again and again, "This is really an honor, sir," from captains and young lieutenants.

He had handled it all with the perfect qualities of aplomb and modesty. She had actually looked forward to their moment of reunion. But oh, Geoffrey, not Geoffrey. For him, reunion had been a peck on the cheek at the station. For him, it was simply a matter of giving to her that night what she must have so missed. She looked for his eyes, while he looked to undress her. So nothing had changed, and Geoffrey merely could not understand. Proving once and for all that he had no understanding of her, no logic in that kind of crisis, no ability to come down off his high horse and deal with the matter.

The sex act had taken place like a brisk exercise canter that rocked the bedsprings and worked up a sweat for the rider. It was the same old wordless ride.

It had been the same last night. She had tried to negotiate something, tried to make him talk. It would have to be talk first, establish love again, then love and make love, in that order. Nothing else would do now.

She watched Geoffrey standing in the window, wondering what he could be talking about so seriously. Her mother's voice broke in. "Here's Mark. And about time. I am becoming famished. Where is Geoffrey? Does anybody know? Do you know, Emma?"

"He's inside, Mamma, talking to Sarah's old admirer."

"Oh, really, Emma." Sarah decided to be flattered, while her mother needed to explain.

"Hardly an admirer, Emma. Colonel Thrumpton is a retired officer who kindly offered to take Sarah riding. He must be all of seventy."

Emma had been watching Mark coming across the lawn. He now waited with folded arms for the conversation to end, while the carriage that had dropped him rumbled on down the street. He waited for his mother's attention, her permission to speak.

"I've just had the most extraordinary experience. The meeting ended early and Ivor Morton, one of the accountants, excellent fellow"—Mark was breathless with excitement—"he has taken me on a sightseeing tour of some of the mines. I have been to De Beers' Mine and the massive Kimberley excavation just north of here, and we have driven a mile to the south to Beaconsfield to see the Du Toitspan Mine. Apart from the buildings in the center of town, it's a town of mines and workshops and endless tin shanties, and all covered in a layer of red dust."

Lady Freestone-Grant showed polite interest. "Did Mr. Rhodes attend your meeting?"

"Oh, heavens no. As far as I can see no one ever comes into contact with Rhodes—not on business matters, that is. I'm quite sure he delegates everything. Do you realize what it means to own De Beers? The whole of Kimberley and much of the surrounding country is a De Beers concern. They own every inch of the ground, all of this. Virtually every man in the place works for them, and Rhodes controls it all. He is the proprietor." Mark found himself talking to Emma, whose enthusiasm always matched his. "It really is an extraordinary town, if you look beyond the dust and the shambles. They actually have electric lighting, although most of it is down the mine shafts. But the most remarkable thing of all is that hole in the ground. It's the most breathtaking sight, and Morton has promised that he will arrange to take you all to see it."

Sarah and Lady Freestone-Grant looked restive, and Emma decided that Mark needed support. "How big is it?" she asked.

"It's the biggest man-made hole in the world, literally gouged out of the earth by thousands of diamond-seeking fanatics. It's three thousand five hundred feet deep, about as deep as Table Mountain is high, and there is water down there, a great lake that appears as a pool from the heights."

"Oh, must you, Mark?" Lady Freestone-Grant was tiring of the subject. "I'm sure it is quite vast, and I am also quite ready for lunch."

But Mark was still carried away. "Mother, would you believe it if I told you that as I looked down there was a glimmer of reflection which came and went, and it was birds? There are flocks of birds that fly across those depths that the eye cannot see. Does that not impress you?"

"That impresses me, but frankly, at this moment in

time I am more impressed with the idea of lunch. Where is Geoffrey?"

Emma felt a little guilty for knowing exactly where he was and saying nothing.

He was at the window again, watching her, and if she only knew it, far from those problems that affected her, he had immediate problems of his own. Behind him, sitting in one of the easy chairs, was Colonel Thrumpton, who, although he was supposed to, he could not remember from India. But he was nevertheless a dear old rambling man who had taken an interest in his mother-in-law and family at the Rhodes reception.

The colonel was wandering on at that moment.

"I may be retired, Geoffrey, but I must say, I am glad to be here at a time when my experience may come in useful."

Stevenson nodded at the nicety and answered the question that had come before. "You are suggesting, then, that I should postpone my plans and hold myself ready to join Scott-Turner's mounted force? I wonder whether I have any choice in the matter. Don't misunderstand that—"

The colonel interrupted him. "What were your plans, Geoffrey?"

"Well, that's a difficult one." Stevenson remained at the window. "My plans are at once a problem and an embarrassment. I mean, they are not quite formulated yet. Mark is the one we should be talking to, and I must discuss this with him later. It is really through his contacts in London that we are able to go into this venture."

The old man smiled. "I am trying to think of you as an insurance man."

Stevenson continued, without looking around. "But whereas Mark was correct at the time in thinking Kimberley should be our headquarters, things have moved fast in the mining world. In my talks with the De Beers people, and considering the growing Rhodes interests in the

Transvaal, Johannesburg has become a better place for us to be, even as a starting point."

"I have told you what I think of that."

"Right." Stevenson turned around to face the colonel, then started pacing the room. "The unrest, the risk, and the full-toss war, if you are to be believed. Right; that is my worst worry. What can you imagine got into Mark's mind to bring everybody out with him, the entire family? What got into Lady Freestone-Grant, for that matter?"

"A long-suppressed desire for adventure, my dear chap. It was never the exclusive prerogative of the young." Colonel Thrumpton chuckled. "I still suffer from it myself." The old man smiled warmly at Stevenson. "You really are at liberty to call me Simon. In private, I mean. I should prefer that."

Stevenson stopped and smiled back. "From Sandhurst to my dying day, you remain sir. You can change habits, but not the kind of indoctrination we embrace."

"Very well, Captain." They both laughed, and the colonel went on. "The point is that I still know more of the situation than you do. You must believe me that by tomorrow Kimberley could begin to come under siege and then your family, and other like families, many thousands of good people, including, quite incredibly, Cecil Rhodes himself, they could all be trapped here for the duration, and in that case we are going to need not only every gun, every soldier, every able-bodied civilian, but most of all, we will need a few star turns like yourself, motivators of morale. We have quite a few already. In fact, with you, we will have at least five of the famous saber swingers of the native wars. Will you make yourself ready?"

Stevenson stopped again at the window, looking out. He answered quietly, "Of course, sir."

The colonel stood up. "We shall have to find you a horse, and that will not be easy. Most of the seniors have charged in to book the better ones from the De Beers stud."

"You are rushing ahead, sir," said Stevenson. "There is no war yet." He turned around, smiling. "But I think I might have found the horse I want, war or no war. There is a racing trainer who has just arrived. Name of Bannock, apparently a relative of the famous racing Bannock."

The colonel nodded. "George Bannock, Paddington Boy, Derby of—what year was that? And second the year after."

"Quite right," said Stevenson. "At any rate, he has some good animals, and all things being equal, he's not going to need them. I am going by Sarah's judgment, and she is a good judge."

"This Bannock—he is a friend of yours?" asked the colonel carefully.

"No, an acquaintance of Sarah's."

The colonel looked relieved. "Oh, I get it now," he said. "When I took your sister-in-law out riding today, she excused herself to speak to someone at the racecourse."

"Right," said Stevenson, "and she arranged for me to see those horses tomorrow."

Bannock had lain awake on his bed of straw for what seemed like hours. The bed was made of hay bales, laid end to end, behind the bar in the small officers' lounge below the grandstand. He lay there staring at the steeply sloped ceiling, watching the reflection from the windows change from darkness to gray to dull yellow to the red of dawn.

What am I doing here? Why am I continually complicating my life? Maybe my father was right. At this moment I could be a very expensive racehorse vet, filing teeth, blistering legs, pumping stomachs, counting my assets.

Bannock's father had always assumed he would be a veterinary surgeon. He had never stopped to think. He was the trainer, his sons were other things. He was aware that Bartholomew was a rider and a horse lover; he even knew that this was the son he could talk to about horses. It was natural he should be a vet.

"That's a solid, respectable thing to be, my boy. If you love horses, that's the most dedicated and meaningful way you can love the brutes."

He had never stopped to look. Because then he would have seen how Bartholomew had acquired that training touch that separates the racing artists from the craftsmen. He would have recognized that there were times when it was not only his own ability that brought some of the winning runners to hand.

But the son also loved his father. He did his bidding, went to Dublin, struggled through two years of university. And all Dublin did for him was take him deeper into the love of the thoroughbred dream, the history, the changing concepts of breeding.

In the end, the instinct that took over was the racing one that was bred into him. He left the university and applied for his own training license, and the clash came.

It was to be years before his father would relent and grudgingly admit that the son could do what he could do. But by the time that all was forgiven and he wanted him back in the fold at Newmarket, the son had become his own trainer. Struggling, maybe, but in the eyes of the old hands, a brilliant prospect.

Even that was forgiven. For Bannock, it felt like the beginning of the greatest relationship in racing history.

Then George Bannock died and Bannock discovered he had a brother who despised the family occupation, and two sisters who were not even vaguely interested.

Bannock stretched where he lay, producing a squeaking of straw from the hard bales.

What was this day going to bring? He had that old sickening feeling. It was going to be bad. Not worse, just predictably bad, the way it had been since that day his father died and he had had to get away from Newmarket and out of England. Was life finding out his weakness? Was it something wrong he was doing, something negative? Was it a continuous fault to strike out at anything and anyone who got in the way and to find that even the seemingly weak had their weapons of retribution?

But those conditions existed. He was not imagining that there was always someone who wanted to take him down, waiting for him and finding a way, starting with his fine, respectable, legal elder brother Matthew. Yes, Matthew had neither liked nor understood the racing world.

"You don't understand," he had said. "Every horse Father owned—including the stud, all the yearlings, all the horses in training—belongs to the estate, and no matter what you say you were promised, you cannot take any of them over. As sole executor, I am not at liberty to do what you are asking. I simply have no knowledge of an arrangement for you to take over certain horses this season."

Bannock had listened in a rage and thought, How could my father have sired this parsimonious horse-hater? He sat up straight on the hay bales, throwing off the horse blanket, shouting, "It's you who don't understand," as he had shouted at the time.

"Listen," he had appealed to Matthew, "there are priceless animals in the Newmarket stable, there are nominations that have to be fulfilled. They have got to be kept in training the way Father would have wished, and not by that deer-stalker, shooting-stick idiot you have appointed, who couldn't train a donkey to stand still."

Matthew had smiled at him, plainly enjoying every minute of his frustration, for once making no attempt to hide his dislike of his younger brother.

"Personally, Bartholomew, I think you are a bloody fool. You had the opportunity to manage Father's racing stable, but you had to go off and prove what a great trainer you were."

"I'm beginning to do just that."

Matthew had remained smiling. "With two winners in

one year? Not much of a record in the shadow of George Bannock."

"I don't have the clients yet. Nor the finance. Whatever happens, Matthew, we are a racing family. You can sell the studs if you must, but you cannot sell the string."

That had seemed Matthew's moment of spiteful triumph. "My dear brother," he preached, "I think I know my duty as executor, and I most certainly understand my position in law. Everything except the family home will be sold. We have sisters and other dependents to be considered. As for you, Father was not very pleased with you, and I trust you will be grateful for whatever you are given."

Bannock was not going to have that. "Father and I understood one another. I loved that man. We had our problems, but I had more in common with him than you or anyone else in the family could ever have had. But I'm prepared to make a deal with you. Just give me the string."

"You are asking for a fortune you would never qualify for. At best, you might be able to afford to buy back one or two of those animals."

"No racing man would resell Marcus Aurelius at any price. He would have to be out of his senses."

"Then you will have to forgo that little obsession."

"Matthew, I have a growing obsession to come round your desk and punch you through the wall."

"Violence is one of the characteristics of instability in people like you, Bartholomew. If you try it, you will be in jail within the hour." He paused, no longer smiling, and added, "If it were left to me, you would get nothing."

That was the last time he had seen or heard of Matthew. Within a week, he and Paddy O'Flaherty had sailed from Tilbury with the only five horses he owned in the world, as well as Marcus Aurelius, whom he had smuggled out of the old family stable the night before.

Taking the great horse was an obsession so strong that it blanked out the effect of his brother's hate and any real regret on his own behalf. Only much later did it dawn on him that Matthew would have seen it as a pathetic mistake on his part that established him as a criminal, giving up everything he could have claimed for one mere horse. It was a bargain that needed no seal. There would be no repercussions from Matthew, or any of the family, for that matter.

He thought, did my father see his family the way I see them? Or don't see them, is more to the point. Incredibly, they were never interested in horses or racing. That's what really separated us. That's why they don't exist for me.

Bannock lay back on the bale again. He smiled when he thought of that night at Newmarket when he and Paddy had gotten the stable manager and the head groom drunk, searched through the files in the manager's house until he found the papers for Marcus Aurelius, then blanketed up the big stallion and led him off into the night.

There had been little choice of destination. America offered the competition, but the family connections ruled that out. With a ship ready to leave, South Africa became the escape route, with the prospect later of Australia or even America, once the dust had died down.

But here I lie, he thought, owner of Marcus, hopefully not to be recognized as Marcus Aurelius, one of the world's great horses, in a country where the next best wouldn't see his heels after a few furlongs. Here I lie, nobbled and chased out of town by a few influential crooks in Cape Town, flat on my back and on a racecourse where there is no racing, with a bunch of expensive horses and not enough money to buy a bag of oats. If I'm going to have to stay here, I am going to need money to stay here. If I'm going to get away, with or without Charlie Watson, I'm going to need money to get away. It's going to be a bad day, Bart Bannock. You're going to have to sell a horse to one of these keen buyers. And that is going to hurt.

He could hear O'Flaherty talking loudly to someone outside, and then the door was banged open, heavy boots crossed the room, and a newspaper was thrown down on his chest.

O'Flaherty leaned over the bar and announced, "Read that. Go on, just read that and see what you think."

Bannock snatched up the paper and examined the front page of the *Diamond Fields Advertiser*. The banner headline read: PROCLAMATION: STATE OF SIEGE.

O'Flaherty watched him impatiently, waiting to speak as soon as he'd read through the details, but Bannock spoke first.

"We've got to get out of here fast. You or Van will have to go and find Charlie Watson right away—"

O'Flaherty interrupted. "Bart, there's a man outside. He brought this newspaper—"

Bannock was not listening. "No, I'll go myself. You and Van can start getting everything together—"

"Bart, will you listen to me," O'Flaherty insisted. "There's an army feller outside, insists on speakin' to you. He's snoopin' around the horses. He's interested in the horses, do you hear?"

Bannock closed his eyes in a moment of blinding frustration. He began to see his little complex of stables and grandstand as the place that was coming under siege.

"What are we goin' to do?" asked O'Flaherty. "Are we goin' to get rid of this feller and make a bolt for it?"

They stared at each other, but Bannock's thoughts were still far away. Whatever impetuous decision he was about to make was likely to lead them into more trouble than ever. Slow down, he thought. Think first, act later. We don't know enough about what is going on. Paddy was looking too excited, and that could be dangerous.

Bannock swung his legs over the bale, climbed into his breeches, and reached for his boots.

"Where's my shaving water?" he demanded as he got to work with the boot hooks.

"Shavin', is it?" O'Flaherty was horrified. "Is shavin' all you can think of at a time like this? That man is waitin', Bart. He's a very important officer."

"You're forgetting your duties." Bannock rummaged

in his leather bag for razor and strop, pulling out a shirt and throwing it over his bare shoulder. "If Van isn't cooking up a bucket of water, he'd better get to it quickly."

O'Flaherty knew that tone of voice. He was out and away to the stables before Bannock reached the door.

The sun was losing its red already above the horizon, promising the usual blistering day. There was no sound or sign of war. It all looked perfectly peaceful, the horses pointing out from the loose boxes waiting for feed time, Van and O'Flaherty at the fire at the far end of the stables decanting hot water from a large paraffin tin they had found into a bucket. All peaceful—except for the large, rotund officer leading his mount from one stable to the next, peering in at the horses.

Ignoring the visitor, Bannock walked across to the drinking trough and set to working up some pressure on the hand pump.

"Mr. Bannock," the officer called out, and began leading his horse over while Bannock thrust his head and shoulders under the intermittent bursts of water, continuing to pump with one hand and contemptuously ignoring the man until he had to deal with him.

"Mr. Bannock?"

Bannock stood up straight, water streaming down his face, to confront the fat officer, who was regarding him with an amused expression.

"I am Major Masefield, on the staff of Kimberley Command, and I'd like to have a word with you about your horses."

The threat had arrived, and Bannock was in no mood for it. "You'd like to buy all my horses?" he asked.

"Not quite." Masefield was smiling. "But almost. This is quite unofficial, but I am looking for good mounts on behalf of a number of officers, some whose mounts are not so good and some who have no mounts at all. It's entirely up to you."

"Thank you," said Bannock.

Masefield overlooked the sarcasm. "They are all prepared to pay, of course, and Staff are busy at the moment working out a scheme whereby horses could be taken over on a daily compensation basis."

"Nobody is going to take over my horses," Bannock said flatly.

"Of course. Nothing of that sort has been decided yet. But if things get hot here and you have to wait long enough, your horses may simply be commandeered." He made his point smilingly. "And then if you want to fight to the death for them, you will have your opportunity."

O'Flaherty, who had come up and heard the last remark, banged down the bucket of steaming water on the corner of the trough and glared malevolently at Masefield.

"How much are you prepared to pay for a good horse?" Bannock fixed the strop to the handle of the water pump and began sharpening his razor.

"What are you thinkin' of?" exploded O'Flaherty. "You're not goin' to sell him any one of our horses?"

"Shut up, Paddy," snapped Bannock, keeping his attention on Masefield. "How much would you pay?"

"Obviously, that depends," said Masefield.

"Have you got the money in your pocket?" Bannock began shaving, looking into the small cantilever mirror borrowed from the veterinary bag.

O'Flaherty was still staring at him in disbelief. "Do you know what we've sacrificed for those horses? Do you know what each one of them animals means to me?"

"Keep out of this, Paddy," warned Bannock and went on shaving, concentrating on the major. "Do you know what a racehorse is worth, Major Masefield?"

"Be realistic, Mr. Bannock, there is no such thing as a racehorse here, only warhorses. And only warhorses are going to be valued and fed. I would not like to make too fine a point of the fact that your horses, if you were to hang on to them, could become worthless or, as I said, commandeered. But in answer to your question, you can be quite

sure that some of my colleagues are good judges of
horseflesh, some of them veritable bloodstock enthusiasts.
They would naturally come down, see for themselves, and
speak for themselves. I am merely trying to ascertain your
attitude."

"Bring them along, Major. I may have to sell one
horse. One, do you hear? And I will decide which one that
will be."

"Ah." Masefield was looking past Bannock. "I see you
are about to have visitors."

"Damn." Bannock began furiously pulling on his shirt
as he saw the open carriage approach with two men facing
and two blonde, hatted heads from behind. He had entirely
forgotten the arrangement with that girl, the pretty prospect from the train who wanted to bring someone to see the
horses.

The carriage drew up in front of the drinking trough
and immediately there was a confusion of greetings, with
Sarah calling out, "Good morning, Mr. Bannock. Sorry to
be so early," then holding back when she realized one of the
men in her party had recognized the major.

"Hello, Masefield. I hope you haven't snaffled up the
one I'm after." The tall man was on the ground offering a
hand to the ladies.

Bannock was stunned at the implication. He had innocently assumed that this friendly arrangement was for a few
horse lovers to look over his horses and, at the same time,
further the possible romantic intentions of the blonde toward himself.

Sarah made the introductions as she alighted.

"My brother-in-law, Mr."—she smiled conspiratorially at Stevenson—"or is it Captain Stevenson. My brother,
Mr. Mark Freestone-Grant. My sister I think you met
briefly, Mrs. Emma Stevenson. This is Mr. Bannock, whose
beautiful horses were banished from the train in favor of
two nasty cannons."

It was obvious they knew Masefield, who greeted them

all and led his horse off to follow Stevenson, who had walked away down the line of stables, inspecting each horse in turn.

O'Flaherty nodded in open-mouthed appreciation at the two beautiful young women until Bannock dismissed him.

"It's feeding time," he snapped. "As soon as they're fed, you and Van get them out to exercise two at a time on the course."

"Have you heard the news that we are under siege?" Sarah flashed her big eyes at Bannock.

"Yes, I have."

"My mother calls it a storm in a teacup, and from all accounts it will last about a week."

Her brother looked pained. "Shall we join the appraisal committee?" he suggested, leading off to where the other two leaned on a stable door looking in at Marcus.

As they came up to them, Masefield turned and drew Bannock to one side.

Masefield said quietly, "By pure coincidence, this is one of the officers I was supposed to be acting for."

"I'll deal with it in my own way."

"Fine," said Masefield. "But in the meantime, if you have any change of heart or you need advice or you run into an argument and need arbitration, you'll find me at army headquarters in Lennox Street."

"This is an amazing horse," Stevenson called to them, and they walked over to join the group ogling Marcus. "I gather you are a relative of George Bannock?"

"I am his son."

"How strange." Stevenson was looking at him quizzically. "You call this horse Marcus. Didn't your father win one of the classics, season before last, I think? Oh yes, Marcus Aurelius. Am I right?"

"Yes."

"You are surely not suggesting that this is the same horse?"

"Yes, it is."

"Then why the shortened name?"

"He is still registered Marcus Aurelius."

"Forgive me for being amazed, but is he lame or gone in the wind?"

"He's perfectly sound."

"Then whatever made you bring such a great prospect to a place like this?"

"That's a long story."

Suddenly it became apparent to the others watching that Bannock was a lot less friendly than any of them might have assumed. But Stevenson was not giving up.

"It really makes one wonder what you are doing here. I would have expected your prospects on the turf in England to be even better than the horse's. But as you say, I'm sure that is a very long story. The point is, are you going to sell him to me?"

"No."

"Then what in heaven's name are we doing here?" Stevenson looked patiently around at the others, but even the normally effusive Sarah was too nervous to comment.

"I'll consider selling you one of my mares," said Bannock.

"You'll consider?" Stevenson stared at Bannock, putting on a show of incredulity for his audience. "Let me spare you a lecture on the disadvantages of mares on the parade ground or in the field."

"Let me give you a short lecture on the thoroughbred racing stallion." Bannock remained calm. "He'll kick your parade ground into a shambles. He'll bite off their ears and have their backsides."

Stevenson went rigid with anger. "Look here, Bannock, there are ladies present. I shall come back later on my own and see if there is anything that can be arranged. Whatever happens, I must find a horse. I am not a bargainer, do you understand?"

"Neither am I," said Bannock.

"But I am a buyer."

"You're in the queue."

Stevenson swung on his heel. "Come, ladies; come, Mark."

Marcus chose that moment to bare his teeth at Emma's straw bonnet. Bannock dashed forward, grabbing her arm and clouting the menacing mouth in the same instant.

"I'm sorry," he said to the surprised girl, "but I'm afraid he is no respecter of beauty."

He watched them return to the carriage, Stevenson flustered, Sarah glancing over her shoulder apologetically, and Emma looking down, embarrassed. Masefield was on his horse waiting to follow them.

The whip cracked, the carriage moved—and Emma looked back at the only man she had ever known to ride roughshod over Geoffrey's superior image.

Bannock lashed the whip down, taking two hands to the reins as the horse pirouetted in a rising dust devil. Out of six rather excitable horses, he had decided to saddle up Parader as the most handleable for riding into town. But Parader seemed to be infected with his owner's dislike and resentment of Kimberley. He eventually settled down, ears back, long neck bent, poised for the next offending freight wagon or mule cart. It was an impotent moment in the search for Charlie Watson.

Ahead lay the town center, behind was the mining area of Beaconsfield, and way off to the right, the village of Kenilworth. There was little option. The town center was, if nothing else, the best place to inquire.

Bannock gathered Parader into a trot, whacking his boot with the whip as a further warning of who was to come out on top in any coming test of will. He rode past a large stone church where hundreds of people, no doubt refugees from the outlying farms, were gathered with their carts and carriages piled high with furniture and belongings. Most of the traffic on the road was military. Wagonloads of sand-bags, stores, and fodder, guns drawn by mules, and mounted parties going both ways. The noonday heat beat down and the dust rose up and Parader liked none of it, least of all the restraining crack he suffered from time to time.

Then they were riding into the town proper, with large buildings leading on down Du Toitspan Road and a few more off to the left and right on the cross streets. He rode across Lennox Street, recognizing the army headquarters and drill hall by the flags and regimental crests. There were hundreds of men queueing there. The farther he went, the more bustle there was, with crowds of people lining the streets, talking excitedly or looking confused. He wondered why many of them were looking at him until he realized it was the horse that was attracting the attention—eighteen hands of prancing thoroughbred of a type not common in these parts.

The Grand Hotel bar came up on the left. If anyone knew Charlie Watson, it would be a barman. He dismounted, tying the reins to a pillar of the iron verandah, tossing a coin to the first of three black boys who came up to mind the horse.

Bannock strode into the crowded bar, elbowed his way through, and asked his question.

"I'm looking for Charlie Watson, the trainer. Do you know where I could find him?"

"Certainly," the barman shouted over the muttering chorus. "I know Charlie Watson."

"Where can I find him?" Bannock shouted back.

"No, sir, I can't help you. I don't know where he lives, but he has his stables out at Taylor's Kopje. I'll tell you what; if you go around behind the hotel, up the small road, and down the first alley in that direction, you'll find Finnegan the farrier. He does all the horses. He'll know."

"I'll buy you a drink later," shouted Bannock as he left.

Outside, the three little black boys were being dragged halfway across the street by Parader after having made the mistake of untethering the reins. Bannock laughed as he caught up with them, and gave them one of the last of his precious coins. He rode around the back of the building and found the lane and the farrier's yard.

Finnegan, who looked too old to be beating out shoes, straightened up from his anvil and stared questioningly at Bannock.

"I'm looking for Charlie Watson," Bannock asked as he dismounted.

"Where in heaven's name did you find a horse like that? Are you taking that to Charlie Watson, did you say?"

"No, I'm looking for the little man. Can you tell me where to find him?"

"You won't find him, sor."

"Why not?"

"He's gone, the lord knows where. I had my boy down there at Taylor's yesterday putting on shoes for him. Then he was down there again at first light this morning, and the good Lord be praised, never a horse, never a saddle or bridle, never a bale of hay, and not a sign of Mr. Watson himself. He's gone, sor, without paying his blacksmith. Charlie's never done anything like that. I can't understand it."

Bannock slumped. It was a bad day, all right, and getting worse. He had depended on Charlie Watson's optimism, even on his promise of buying a horse or, alternatively, of getting out with him. But do you listen to promises from that sort of character? Charlie Watson was a sharp little bastard; a typical fast-talking little crook.

When Bannock mounted up, he had the same three black boys waiting to hold Parader's mouth, and as the big horse lurched backwards they were pulled off the ground together. They followed as Bannock rode off, and he shook the whip at them as a sign that they were no longer needed.

He trotted back through the streets of the town and put

Parader into a gathered canter the moment they reached the open road. The horse was hot, sweating all over, the lather building up where the reins stroked the neck, but he was behaving better, albeit out of nervous exhaustion.

He was heading back for the racecourse and O'Flaherty's long-faced resentment, that or his roaring temper. It occurred to him that the trouble with Paddy was more over being left out of the decision to sell a horse than over the principle of actually selling one. O'Flaherty had always had more to say than his position warranted, even when he had deserted the Newmarket stable as a groom to follow George Bannock's son, right into hell if necessary. There was no logical way to handle Paddy except with the fist, when he was drunk, and even that would have been a risky practice when he was half-sober. So Paddy was a force on his own, a foolish wayward force, and, after all that, a loyal and faithful one.

Bannock had decided. There was no way out of it. He would have to sell a horse. And if he was going to be trapped in Kimberley by the siege, he would eventually have to sell another and another, or what was it Major Masefield had said? Not be able to feed them, or lose them to the army. Damn Charlie Watson, damn this whole lousy dust bowl of a country. If it is still possible to get out, we will get out and take our chances.

He took the turn-off for the racecourse, riding free from the Du Toitspan Road dust, and after a few strides found the road blocked by a trap and one-in-hand that he recognized. He rode past the bobbing hackney and reined in to confront Mr. Graham Pope-Evans of the Turf Club, with an equally rich-looking passenger beside him. This could only be more trouble, Bannock thought, and waited patiently to be ordered off the racecourse.

"Good day, Bannock." Pope-Evans was surprisingly pleasant. "We have been searching for you everywhere." He turned to the man beside him and said, "Over to you, sir."

The large, side-whiskered gentleman surveyed Bannock and the way he controlled the restless Parader with no visible sign or effort.

Bannock, who had summed up the situation in his own way, was not waiting for the man to make his assessment. "You're a little late in the day, gentlemen," he announced. "I've had plenty of offers, but luckily for you, I have declined them all so far."

The large man appeared unimpressed. "I'm not interested in your offers."

"Why not?" Bannock asked. "How do you like this one?" patting Parader's mobile neck. "Parader, brown gelding by Grand Parade. Not the greatest racer, Grand Parade, but a great sire. You must know his progeny. And a dam from another great line, Marchioness."

"Mr. Bannock," the large man cut him short impatiently, "I am not in the market for a horse. Will you kindly listen to me, because I have a proposition for you. From the inquiries I have made about you—"

Bannock interrupted. "Who are you? What's your business? Who the hell are you to make inquiries about me?"

Pope-Evans looked shocked and embarrassed, while the big man laughed himself into a temporary state of coughing, at the same time pointing a finger for attention.

"My name is MacGrath. I represent De Beers—"

"Who the hell is De Beers?"

MacGrath stopped smiling. "You are standing on their ground, Mr. Bannock. De Beers owns the whole of Kimberley, every diamond, every man jack alive in it, and a lot more besides. If you are interested in our proposition, we will do business. If not, we will deny ever having heard of you."

"That sounds very impressive," said Bannock. "What's the proposition?"

"As I was saying, what I discovered from the inquiries

I made was that you are short of money and that you have a stable full of mouths to feed."

"That's my business."

"Don't be so sure of that. We could go into the matter of why you had to leave Cape Town in a hurry. However, that's of no interest to me, so can I make my proposition?"

"Why not?"

MacGrath's expression was serious, speculative. "This is in the strictest of confidence," he said. "The engagement we are offering you entails a fair degree of risk, which will, of course, be paid for accordingly. In short, we need dispatch riders with fast horses to take and bring messages across the enemy lines."

"What enemy lines?"

"The Boers are beginning to appear. They have not surrounded the town yet, but they will."

"And you expect me to ride through the middle of them?"

"I said there was risk."

"That sounds more like a death warrant than a risk, Mr. MacGrath. How much are you going to pay?"

MacGrath pointed at the horizon. "There is far less enemy activity out there than you would imagine. It is doubtful whether they will ever have enough people available to totally surround the town."

"How much are you going to pay?" repeated Bannock.

"Handsomely, Bannock, handsomely."

Bannock's thoughts raced. The risks could be considered later. It might even be a shortcut way out of Kimberley. "I need money now," he said.

"I shall send you down a hundred guineas before this evening. Call it a sign of faith. It will serve as advance payment for your first journey on our behalf. If you are as tough as you appear to be, you are the right man for us. The payment for each trip you undertake will be negotiable according to how we agree on the risk. You will be supplied with feed, food, veterinary service, and anything else you may require. You will work exclusively for us. The first trip will take place in the near future. Do we have an agreement?"

"Yes." Bannock had a question of his own. "What is the story you heard about what happened in Cape Town?"

"Only that you were in a lot of trouble."

"They told you what I did. Did they tell you why?"

"Not precisely."

"They pulled my horse up in the clumsiest demonstration of mouth-sawing I've ever seen on a racecourse. He couldn't lose. I bet on him the way I've never bet. The stewards hummed and hawed, and I chased that jockey clear around the Peninsular. When I caught up with him, he was ready to welsh on his patrons, who turned out to be quite a respectable group of racing gentlemen."

"And you took the law into your own hands."

"There was no law, unless it protected them. So yes, I did what you're saying. I went and broached them in their club."

"And punched them all senseless."

"At a time when four of them were jointly engaged in punching me senseless."

"Not quite the way I heard it, but I like this version."

"Then the police and other shadowy people followed us around and the stables were set alight. Did they tell you about that?"

"No."

"Well, I don't give a damn what they told you. It just looks as if you need me and I need you."

MacGrath nodded. "Bannock, the agreement only stands if no one knows of this, with the exception of your own men, who may be involved on the same terms. No one else, Bannock. Particularly no one to do with the army. Is that understood?"

"Yes," said Bannock, and reined in his excited horse as the whip cracked and the trap sped away without so much as a farewell.

Bannock settled Parader to a standstill and laughed as he realized that his own mouth was agape.

"A hundred guineas," he shouted aloud. A hundred guineas this very day, when a few minutes ago he had been penniless.

Impetuously he shook the reins, then leaned back tight on them as Parader sprang into a fast canter toward the racecourse. The relief was wonderful. He would worry about the risk and whatever else was entailed later.

O'Flaherty was waiting at the off-saddling enclosure behind the grandstand. He stood his ground with arms sternly folded as Parader clattered to a stop right in front of him.

He glared up at Bannock. "I don't know where you'd be comin' from at such a gallop, but that gent from the Turf Club was here lookin' for you."

"I know, I know." Bannock dismounted and grinned at O'Flaherty. "Before this day is out," he announced, "you and Van will have a few pounds in your pockets for steak and whiskey."

O'Flaherty was shocked. "Which one did you sell?" he demanded in an agonized whisper. Bannock wondered why he was whispering, and then he saw why. There was a horse with sidesaddle tied up at the stables and the unmarried Freestone-Grant girl, perfectly turned out, was walking toward them.

"I haven't had to sell a horse, Paddy. I'll tell you about it presently," he said quietly.

O'Flaherty went off shaking his head as Sarah came up, examining Bannock from the boots to the eyes.

"You're looking a little dusty, Mr. Bannock," she mocked.

"I don't know how you've managed to stay so clean and tidy," he returned.

"That is not much of a compliment."

"And beautiful."

"That's better. I am supposed to be out riding with old

Colonel Thrumpton, but he has gone to the Kimberley Club. He said for a meeting; I suspect for a siesta." She smiled, looking at him straight in the eyes without making any attempt to say anything further.

Bannock recognized the conditions, so well known to him, of head-on flirtation. He took the liberty of examining the beautiful girl who faced up to him, hands and whip behind her back, the expensive calf leather boots pointing out below the stylish riding skirt that rose in folds to her narrow waist, the high breasts straining forward in the white blouse, the diamond scarf pin, the mass of blonde hair tied above the head in plaits, the fine, arrogant eyes locked on him.

He broke the silence. "Is this a social visit, or are you one of those serious horse buyers?"

"This," she announced gaily, "is a serious social visit. I wish to apologize for my brother-in-law's behavior this morning."

"Where did he get the impression that I wanted to sell all my horses?"

Sarah smiled guiltily. "Maybe he thought you needed money more than horses now that we're under siege. We are under siege, you know, even though the enemy is staying sensibly out of sight."

"Is your brother-in-law aware that you are apologizing for him?"

Sarah giggled. "Good heavens, no. He would be horrified. Terribly upstanding, our Geoffrey, but a good sort really. A war hero, you know. Slashing around with his saber in the native wars." She burlesqued the action with her whip. "It was all over the newspapers at the time. We were very proud of him, and when he could not get me, he took my sister, Emma, as compensation."

"I trust neither you nor he are regretting the fact?"

Sarah giggled again. "Oh, lord no. I am just not the camp-following type. And Geoffrey—well, he may have a few tiny regrets, but he certainly has nothing to complain of. He did very well for himself when he joined the family."

Bannock laughed dryly. "Is there some special advantage in belonging to your family?"

"Certainly," said Sarah. "A certain amount of influence, mostly through Mother, and an awful lot of money. We all have expectations, you know."

"Well, let me be the first to congratulate you, Miss Freestone-Grant."

Sarah was unabashed, "My friends call me Sarah. Bartholomew, is it not?"

Bannock smiled and nodded distractedly. "There is still something I don't understand about your brother-in-law. Surely the army would have supplied him with a horse?"

"Oh, no," said Sarah, "he is not army. He was retired and bent on business in partnership with my brother, Mark. Well, that was the position until yesterday, and now, with this emergency, I expect he will go slashing right back into action. But army or not, he would have wanted a horse of his own and Geoffrey is frightfully fussy about horses. If we had gone on to Johannesburg as planned, Geoffrey would have ridden magnificently beside the coach, you see. As it is, we are all trapped in a suite in this funny old establishment called the Shields Hotel. I hope you may decide to call on us there, Bartholomew. And by the way, where are you staying?"

The moment of truth had to be dealt with. "It would be wrong to say that I was staying anywhere," said Bannock, "but let me show you where I sleep."

He went ahead and invited Sarah into the door with the sign that read BAR MEMBERS & OFFICERS ONLY. She walked in boldly, followed him across to the bar, and looked down at the straw bales he indicated.

"Do you really sleep there?" she asked in a tone of wonder.

"It's quite comfortable," said Bannock. "It adapts into

a double bed by the simple procedure of adding another bale alongside."

"How interesting," said Sarah, ready to give as good as she got. "Is that in case you wish to take one of your horses to bed with you?"

Bannock looked at this girl who talked too much and bragged too much and decided that he would nevertheless enjoy making love to her.

"My dear girl," he said, "it is not horses one rides in bed."

She stared at him coolly for a while, then said, "I really must be going," and turned and walked calmly out of the room.

Bannock went out and leaned on the door, watching Van Breda and O'Flaherty respectively holding her horse and helping her mount. She cantered across from the stables, pulling up in front of him.

He waited for the verbal backlash, but instead she asked, "May I come again?"

"What a good idea," said Bannock and watched the beautiful slim body ride away, deciding that he'd been right the first time, that she was one of those reckless young ladies whose delicate upbringing had never managed to impress on her the need to be shocked by all the usual things that should have shocked her.

Something had woken Emma up. There was a jerking movement beside her. The whole bed began vibrating, and she almost screamed in horror, knowing what was happening. She lay still, holding her mouth with both hands, as Stevenson's fist crashed down on the bed, only just missing her. He was panting one moment, holding his breath the next, calling out in inarticulate mumbling.

Words came hoarsely: "No . . . no . . . no . . . no," a rhythm like the height of passion of sex. But Emma knew how the words came, the whispers of terror between the war cries, breathlessly forced out at a gallop while the fist that lashed one way and the other and thumped down onto the bed gripped a phantom saber.

"I'm done for . . . Oh God, I'm done for. . . . No . . . no . . . no." The fist came down again and Emma flung off the covers, slid out of the bed, and stepped backward in the dark, her hands across her mouth again to muffle the sound of her own gasping breath.

She could just see him, silhouetted in the pale light of the window, leaning on one rigid arm, flailing about with the other, his legs jerking, his head jerking, his mouth wide open in a silent scream.

Suddenly he sat bolt upright in bed, breathing heavily but evenly. He sat like that for what seemed a long time, and slowly, his breathing returned to normal. Emma wondered if he was awake. She tried to call his name, but her lips moved and nothing came out.

He moved, feeling about the bed, feeling for her.

"Emma?" He spoke quite normally.

Emma found herself involuntarily moving farther backward. Then he struck a light and she saw him reaching over to light the lamp, sweat dripping down his face, blinking around at the room until he saw her, and then staring at her incredulously.

"You were dreaming," she heard herself say.

"I'm quite all right." He leaned over to see past the light. "What is it, Emma?"

"You were in battle." She heard herself saying what she had always imagined getting up the courage to say to him. "You were fighting for your life. It's a dream you always have."

Stevenson shook his head impatiently. "Emma, really," he appealed. "I am quite all right. Come over here, my dear. Why are you standing there as if you had seen a ghost?"

"I did see one." She tried to keep the tremor out of her voice. "Your ghost, Geoffrey."

"I beg your pardon." Stevenson pulled himself across the bed and sat on its edge. "What are you suggesting, Emma? That there is something wrong with me? I may have had a nightmare. There is nothing extraordinary about that."

"But it has happened before, so many times."

"When? At Birchleigh? How many times are you suggesting?"

"Almost every night we've been together. I tried to speak to you about it."

"I cannot remember that."

"You could—no, not could, you *would* never speak to me."

"Come here, Emma. Come to bed. I insist." He touched his forehead and seemed surprised at the sweat.

She stayed where she was. "No," she insisted, "we must talk about it. Whatever this problem is, whatever it means, it affects me, too. It is part of the remoteness that separates us."

"What on earth do you mean?"

She was trembling. "You must talk to me or I will leave this room and not return."

Stevenson sagged forward, arms on knees. He looked down for some time, lost in thought.

Emmas was not going to be talked down and reassured again. He was preparing himself to do so. He was about to reassure, to be terribly kind. It was going to sound logical, but it was not going to be logical. It was impossible that a nightmare of such violence did not carry through to consciousness with at least a hint of the horror of a moment before. You are lying, Geoffrey, she thought. Why are you lying? Must your pride transcend my feelings? Are your own feelings above the faith we should have in each other?

Stevenson looked up. "Emma, I am worried about you.

I watched you at the reception the night before last, our contretemps that night, and in fact every time we have been alone. It is you who are remote."

"You swing your saber with feeling, Geoffrey, even in your sleep. You swing it back at me as if I had struck at you."

"What is this silly fantasy?"

"I tell you what is happening and you make me look like a liar." She heard her own voice rising. "You make me look a fool."

"What is this nonsense about a saber?" He sounded sad.

"You sleep with it in your hand, you swing it in your dreams." She knew what she was going to say but could not stop herself. "What a pity that you cannot point your sword with feeling for me."

"Are you being vulgar? What are you trying to say?"

"You have a dream of passion, Geoffrey. So do I. But mine is a passion of love, where minds make love and genitals follow on down there in their own natural way."

He was stunned. "I cannot believe it is you saying these things. Are you suggesting that I do not love you?"

"Not with the kind of love I dreamt of."

"Then you must stop dreaming."

"Oh, no, Geoffrey, it is you who must stop dreaming."

He spoke quietly. "Now you are certainly being offensive."

She had to go on. "Stop striking at ghosts in the night."

He was barely audible. "I am no tilter at windmills."

That stopped her. "Oh God, I know that," she apologized. "I am not denying your courage. You have earned everything in that way and I have been your greatest admirer."

He sighed deeply. "Somehow, Emma," he said slowly, "somehow we shall have to reach an understanding. I had no idea that events had gotten to this. As much as I am surprised at your outburst, I can understand your point of view."

Emma shivered at the prospect of hope. She waited to hear more.

"It seems our problems are ones of communication. I think your word *remote* applies, but hardly in the way you meant it. It is simply that we have been apart so much, don't you see that, Emma? We have not been given a chance to even practice communication with one another. Admit that, Emma."

She shivered again, but this time with despair. She had heard those words before. She was being reassured again, put in her place again.

"Emma, answer me." He smiled confidently. "Come on, communicate."

"Shall I agree with you because I am too tired to argue?"

"No. Come along, my dear girl." He was entirely himself again. "Argue, by all means. At least that is a form of communication."

"I always bared my soul to you. You have never done that with me."

Stevenson looked amused. "Emma," he said patiently, "was there ever much to tell you? Are you interested in battles and mess bills and billiards?"

"Geoffrey, that is not relevant—"

He interrupted. "Of course it is. Because I mutter in my sleep from time to time, which I am quite sure you and a thousand other people do too, because of that are you imagining some hidden intentions or assignations on my part? Don't you understand I am a pretty plain and straightforward sort of fellow? I have no secrets, Emma. I have been a straightforward "saber swinger," as you say, and, if you don't mind my saying so, a jolly good one at that."

Emma looked for the words. Could it be as simple as this? Could such a pattern of horror be reduced to normality by the usual few reassuring words from Geoffrey?

He smilingly held up his hand to stop her from speaking. "I have just thought of an extraordinary piece of news which I am guilty of not communicating to you." He paused for impact, and Emma thought, We are lost to a man who will admit nothing.

"From tomorrow, I am to volunteer my services to Her Majesty's Forces in Kimberley for as long as it takes for relief to arrive. And I trust that my new uniform, which is taking shape at the tailor's, is ready before that event occurs." He held up his hand again. "There is more. As of tomorrow, the fifteenth, I am promoted major, which I think you will admit is quite a coup, considering the short involvement it promises to be. In fact, I meant to tell you —rather amusing—they are having a bit of trouble locating the enemy, if that is the proper term in this case. The whole approach is rather amusing. For example, I shall not be going out with Scott-Turner's sortie tomorrow because my uniform will not be ready." He roared with laughter. "The truth is, I am quite relieved, since they have not yet been able to provide me with a suitable mount." Only then did he realize that Emma had neither shared his amusement nor reacted in any way.

She thought, We are lost to a mind that can only respond to orders and bugles.

"Come to bed, Emma," he said gently. "We shall talk more tomorrow. We shall communicate, by Jove." He patted the cover. "Come to bed."

Emma moved forward slowly. She would go to bed as humbly as was required this time. But the long-practiced humility was gone; the blind humility, gone.

Hussein stepped carefully along the moonlit path, the newly discovered shortcut into town. Bannock let the reins hang slack as the big gray nosed down suspiciously from time to time, behaving well, considering the darkness and the eerie warm wind blowing up waves of invisible dust.

Over to the left, he could just make out the ghostly tin roofs of the native camp and the long, flat ridge of the reservoir.

He took a firmer hold on the reins, sensing movement up ahead, and in a few more strides he could make out soldiers, two, maybe three, moving toward him from a sandbagged barricade that flanked the path.

"Who goes there?" One of the soldiers seemed excited at what must have been his first opportunity to challenge someone that night.

Bannock held Hussein back as rifle bolts engaged and two soldiers confronted him, weapons pointing.

"The name is Bannock. I am billeted at the racecourse, and I am going into town to find one of my men, who I suspect is drunk and incapable."

"Righto, Mr. Bannock. You can proceed, but you must report to Lennox Street in the morning for a permit. From now on everybody outside the perimeter needs a permit to pass through."

"Can you tell me where a man who is bent on getting drunk and staying drunk could be found at three o'clock in the morning?"

"In a gutter somewhere, more than likely, sir." The two sentries laughed.

"Are there bars that would still be open?" Bannock asked.

"You're not in the backwoods now, sir. Kimberley is a civilized town. We have licensing hours. The only place you'll get a drink at this time of night is the Miner's Comfort Society on Market Square"—the sentries laughed—"or Mrs. Burtin's House of Fun in Victoria Road. Just ride around until you see a bunch of horses tied up somewhere. Maybe your man is not too drunk to hammer the bedsprings." They both laughed again.

Bannock rode on. He was in no mood for humor,

remembering previous searches for Paddy, remembering Cape Town every time the great singing drinker got some money into his pocket and more often than not landed up in a cell. He would never have denied Paddy the money, but this time there was a need for discipline and readiness, as Paddy well knew.

When Van had awakened him with a series of hand signs, nods, and rollings of eyes that he had eventually interpreted as meaning that Paddy had gone off on Parader and not returned, Bannock had been dreaming of escape. The idea of escape was becoming another obsession. To take the money and ride out and keep riding. It was a reasonable theory. If one rider could outrun the Boers, so could three. Hide out during the day and keep moving at night and head toward the Cape, where the Boers were outnumbered. Unlike Paddy, he could easily sacrifice three of the horses in an emergency. Now he was being honest with himself. His real obsession was with Marcus. It was like fighting for the survival of one's own family. Marcus was the symbol of his father, of some vague faith in the future, even of possessing something really valuable. He had to admit that if there was any love in him, it was centered on that bloody horse . . . that beautiful horse.

He rode into the silent town, searching up and down the streets for telltale tethered horses. In Victoria Road he found such a group of horses, but Parader was not one of them. He took to trotting up one block and down the next, cursing Paddy, who was supposed to be back on watch at the stable giving Van his chance to sleep. As it was, he had given the sleepy jockey his revolver, with instructions to stay awake and keep watch on the horses from the grandstand. They would have to be on constant guard from now on, in a desperate town where there were too many riders and not enough horses.

He entered a street and saw Parader, standing hands taller than the horses tied on both sides of him, with an empty Cape cart and carriage drawn up just beyond. As he approached, three small figures ran toward him, the three ragamuffins of his last visit to town. They took hold of Hussein's bridle, exchanging looks that connected this big gray and the big brown Parader of the last time. Bannock saw his horse tethered and went to the door of the house, where he knocked loudly.

The door opened and a heavy pugilistic character dominated the opening, as if he wished to smother the muttering voices and swirling smoke from within.

"What do you want?" asked the hulking figure.

"I want to speak to a friend of mine who is inside there."

A huge hand came forward, pulling Bannock into the entrance hall while the door slammed shut. Immediately, O'Flaherty's voice could be heard in the background.

"What is your friend's name?" demanded the hulk.

"Get your hand off my coat," warned Bannock, and as the man let go, he walked purposefully through toward the sound of O'Flaherty.

He found himself in a big, dimly lit room. There were men sitting at tables drinking and playing cards. No one took any notice of him, and as his eyes became accustomed to the light, he picked out O'Flaherty sitting with his back to him, holding forth to two other men. Before he could get to him, there appeared the inevitable fat madam in flowing black crepe, who had taken up a position in the middle of the room and smilingly dismissed the hovering doorman with a wave of her hand.

Bannock smiled back and pointed meaningfully at O'Flaherty's back, but the madam, whose mind was on business, beckoned to a sleepy-looking girl dozing in a chair at the far end of the room.

O'Flaherty was saying, "I've always had this great interest in the culliny . . . the cullirry . . ."

"Culinary," one of his companions prompted.

"Well, isn't that what I said? The culinary arts. It is truly fascinatin' to learn these things you are tellin' me."

"This is Clara." The madam waved a fat arm at the sleepy girl behind her.

"Not at the moment, thank you," said Bannock. "I just want to have a word with my friend."

O'Flaherty swung round at the sound of his voice and waved a grand welcome at the empty seat beside him. "Bart? Now where would you be comin' from at this late hour?" he inquired, leaning away a little apprehensively.

"You are supposed to be back at the stables."

"Of course, I was just tellin' me friends." O'Flaherty waved a hand at the two men opposite, evidently a little drunker than he had at first seemed to be. "I was on the very point of leavin', but there was a lot of important things we were discussin', the diamonds," he rambled. "You remember how we discussed the diamonds? It's not so easy, we are goin' to have to go carefully with the diamonds. Oh, I nearly forgot," he said, waving again at the other two at the table. "You remember Mr. Paddykelly from the train?"

"Pah-chell-li," Pacelli corrected.

Bannock nodded. "Come on, Paddy," he said, "we have got to get back."

"In a minute, in a minute." O'Flaherty must have known the risk he was taking defying Bannock, but he was carried away in a moment of drunken enthusiasm. "I'm still drinkin', my friends are still drinkin'." He shouted across the room, "Missus what's-your-name—Cecelia, bring my friend a brandy. Now as I was saying', Paddykelly is the head chef lookin' after the fat stomachs at the Sanatorium. You want to hear about this place. That's where the great Mr. Rhodes and his cronies are stayin'. And this is the other head chef, Carloleeni."

"Carlo Cellini," put in Pacelli sadly.

"Tell Bart here about the way they eat at your place. Tell him what Mr. Rhodes says every time. Come on, Bart, just listen to this. Go on, Paddykelly, tell him about the jam bon."

Pacelli, obviously a practiced raconteur, sat up

straight, squared his shoulders, and launched into his story, with O'Flaherty nodding encouragement.

"First we serve the *jambon,*"—this time pronounced correctly—"raw, you say in English, ham. On the menu, ee'sa jambon de Parma. Meester Rhodes he ee'sa talking, waves he'sa hand. Who ee'sa care? Pacelli himself will hav'a de Parma. You rather hav'a pâte de foie, Meester Rhodes? Wav'a the hand. Gigot d'agneau? Oh no, Meester Rhodes ee'sa talking. The caneton à la bigarde? Take it away from me, he say. Then everybody ee'sa eating nice and Meester Rhodes he say, giv'a me plain'a beef, rare, he say. He say, giv'a me good bloody English beef, he say, with'a gravy." Pacelli looked sternly at each of them in turn. "What's kind'a sauce ee'sa gravy? Ee'sa flour paste."

"There ee'sa gravy and'a gravy," Cellini said carefully, "with'a little espagnole in."

Pacelli glared at him. "Gravy and'a gravy is not'a sauce and'a sauce."

Cellini was not to be put down. "Something like'a sauce," he suggested.

Pacelli waved his hands in circles. "What'a kind of chef ee'sa thees?" He looked away in disgust.

O'Flaherty shouted across the room, "Where in hell is my friend's brandy?" He was attracting the amused attention of the men at the other tables.

The madman bore down on them. "Will you stop your shouting this minute," she hissed. "You're upsetting my guests."

"Shhh." O'Flaherty held up a finger and continued in a hoarse whisper, "Quiet, everybody. We'll not be wantin' to upset poor Charlie at his work." The men nearby who heard him roared with laughter.

"Did you say Charlie?" Bannock was suddenly interested.

"Sure, Bart, you know Charlie."

"Charlie Watson?"

"Himself as ever was."

"Where is he? Is he here?"

"Right in that room there."

"That's very interesting," said Bannock, glancing toward the door O'Flaherty was pointing out. "I want a word with him."

Bannock stood up with a determined expression, and the two Italians also stood up, deciding it was a wise moment to leave.

"Good night, O'Flehitti," said Pacelli. "Good night, Meester Bannock."

O'Flaherty also stood up swaying slightly, holding out his arms. "Good night, dear Paddykelly," he said, "and dear Carloleeni."

"O'Flehitti," Pacelli pleaded, "please'a call me Mario and this ee'sa Carlo, not'a kelly and'a leeni."

"So be it," said O'Flaherty magnanimously, "and the blessings of the holy father be upon you both."

"Il Papa," smiled Cellini, understanding.

The two Italians immediately crossed themselves and O'Flaherty, inclining his head, reverently joined them.

"See you at Mass," he called out as they left.

"You bloody hypocrite." Bannock laughed. "When did you last go to Mass?"

O'Flaherty looked hurt. "Did you happen to see a priest anywhere in the Karoo?" he asked. "They've got a fine man here, Father Murphy, and a fine church, Saint Mary's, and a bishop and all. And let me tell you that in the ordinary way, you'll find me regularly at the sacraments. Me old father used to say to me, Paddy, he said, if you miss Mass, your luck will surely go to hell, and I've always remembered that."

Bannock was impatient. "How long has Charlie Watson been in there?"

"Too long, Bart, too long. Maybe he's gone to sleep on the job."

O'Flaherty lurched across the room and banged on the door in question. "Hey, Charlie," he shouted. "I thought you went in there for a sprint and now you're doin' the full fourteen furlongs. Come on, Charlie, Bart wants to speak to you."

For a moment the madam was speechless. She waddled across the room, then she screeched, "Get away from that door. How dare you? Magnus," she shouted, "Magnus, come here."

The big pugilist was into the room and through the tables, but he hesitated when he found O'Flaherty looking at him coolly.

"Throw him out," screamed the madam.

"No, don't throw him out," said Bannock, who was quietly standing next to the pugilist.

"Don't you interfere," said the madam, calming down a fraction. "He's causing trouble and he must leave." She turned to the pugilist. "Just take him outside and put him down gently," she suggested.

"Leave my friend alone," Bannock said calmly.

"You keep out of this," sneered the pugilist, squaring up to O'Flaherty.

"What are you all talkin' about?" asked O'Flaherty innocently.

"Hit him, Paddy," said Bannock.

"Oh, no," said O'Flaherty, quickly pointing to the other side of the room. "Not while that's goin' on over there."

The pugilist looked around and O'Flaherty's fist crashed into the side of his face, sending him headlong onto a table, which broke up under his weight in a splintering explosion.

The madam screamed and backed off against the wall. Bannock looked menacingly around the room, but the men were all standing up looking nervous, some smiling, while the pugilist was on his back turning his head slowly from side to side.

At that moment, the door opened. Charlie Watson looked out. The door promptly closed again.

"Come out, Charlie," called Bannock. "Come out or I'll kick the door in."

There was silence for a moment, then the door opened and Charlie Watson stood there fully clothed, with a saddle over his arm. Behind him, the girl in the bed held the sheets up to cover herself and watched with great interest.

"After you, Charlie." Bannock gestured the way out, but Watson hesitated.

"Where're we going, sport?" he asked nervously.

"We're going outside for a short, friendly discussion."

Watson had no choice. He led the way out, through the room full of silent people and onto the veranda, where he made for his horse with the saddle poised.

"Drop the saddle on the ground, Charlie," ordered Bannock.

Watson looked worried. "Saddles go on horses, Bart, not on the ground."

"Put it down, Charlie, and come and sit here with us," Bannock suggested soothingly.

Charlie sat down on the step of the verandah, still clutching his saddle as if for protection. Bannock and O'Flaherty sat down on either side of him. The three ragamuffins, whose life evidently revolved around watching tethered horses, came and sat in the dust in front of them, for all the world like the three carved monkeys, shifting their attention from one speaker to the next as if they understood the conversation.

"All right, Charlie boy, Paddy and I would like to hear your story."

"Story? What story? There's no story, Bart. I just decided not to go. Too much of a risk."

"And then you disappeared. If you were not such a big lover, we might never have found you. Where did you disappear to, Charlie?"

"I had to move my string, Bart. They told me to get out of Taylor's Kopje. It's right out there in the firing line. I had to move into town, don't you see?"

"But that's strange, Charlie. Nobody knew where you were, even your friends. Do you know what I think?"

"No, what, Bart?"

"I think you're a dispatch rider."

Watson laughed nervously. "Ah, Bart, you are a one. I think I get the drift. I think we are back in the same business, you and me and Paddy. Hey, Paddy, is that right?"

But O'Flaherty was leaving it to Bannock's line of questioning.

"Imagine us riding dispatch for the army," posed Bannock.

Watson's face showed no expression. "It hardly pays, Bart," he said. "Three shillings a day and two shillings for the horse. I'm surprised a superior character like you agreed to it."

There was a long pause, during which the three ragamuffins became confused, not knowing who to look at next.

Then Bannock spoke. "I think you know a man called MacGrath, Charlie."

"Ah," said Watson, eyes darting away in conspiratorial surprise.

Bannock let it sink in. "I think there may be two sides to what you are doing, Charlie."

Watson nodded. "I think I may be doing just what you are doing, for the same reason."

"But Mr. MacGrath doesn't pay so badly."

Watson laughed. "Mr. MacGrath is what I call a good owner. I'd race for him anytime, sport."

"It's a nice clean way out, Charlie."

"Agreed," said Watson.

"To Port Elizabeth."

"Oh, no." Watson was shocked. "You don't understand, mate. Galloping away from a few Boers is possible, but crossing the country with a string of horses is suicide." He went on excitedly, "You don't know those Boers. Their horses might not be so fast, but they can ride and they can shoot, and they never give up. What's the matter with you? We can play Peter against Paul and we can make a lot of money in a short time, because this thing won't last, mate. There's the whole British army coming, and when they get here it's going to be all over, unsaddle and weigh out."

Suddenly, Bannock felt depressed. Obviously, Charlie Watson could see a way to double-deal the army and De Beers, and in the process make a fair amount of money. If he and O'Flaherty were to break out, it would have to be on their own, in the way he had planned. And it would have to be soon, before the Boers surrounded the town.

"Saddle up your horse, Charlie. We're all going home."

Bannock mounted up and threw a shilling each to the three ragamuffins, who danced along with them, unable to believe their luck. They rode around into Du Toitspan Road.

Watson drew alongside Bannock and said, "We must work this thing together, sport. I know more about the country than you do. I can tell you the places, and we can give one another the tips. I can show you how to ride on the top of the kopjes so you can see both ways and scarper off the best way when you see trouble coming. And when the army tells you one way and De Beers tells you another, I'll tell you which is right. If you're going to Barkly West for De Beers or the Orange River for the army, you've got to know every rock and every bush and every place they can hide and wait. I like you, mate," he said, "and if I can help to keep you alive, I will. This is where I get off. The Sanatorium, where the king of De Beers lives. I've got stabling in the back with the army. The army is snaffling all the spare stabling in town. It's all full or I'd get you in there. Good night, mate, or good morning. Look at it, it's morning."

It was five o'clock and the first light was spreading as Watson turned off and Bannock and O'Flaherty rode on down the Du Toitspan Road toward Beaconsfield and the road going south to the racecourse.

Suddenly, there was an indescribable noise. Bannock recognized the piercing scream of sirens, which seemed to come from all sides. The horses jumped as if they had been lashed. Bannock watched Watson's thoroughbred pirouetting on the adjacent road. He could just hear the sound of women screaming in a nearby house and, struggling with Hussein, he looked back to see the three little monkeys trying to hear no evil, heads down and hands to their ears.

The first alarm was sounding.

·3· | ALARMS AND BUGLES

The gold propelling pencil tapped reflectively at each detail of the handwritten memorandum. Major Masefield pressed his eyelids closed, then opened them to assume once again the unblinking stare that disconcerted so many people.

The pencil checked each line from the top. "To the CSO, from Masefield. 19th October, 1899. Re CO's questions on communications. With railway line torn up and telegraph lines cut we are immediately dependent on dispatch riders and native runners. The system discussed is already in action except that effective provision is yet to be made for these people to move about in spite of curfew, etc. It is not going to be easy in the light of the Boers massing on the border and already signs of them around Kimberley.

"We are going to have the newspaper people demanding details of what is happening down south. They will have to be censored in some way since they are likely to create a state of alarm even worse than your confounded sirens."

Masefield's small, thin lips arched slightly in the wide expanse of his face. Hardly a smile, yet for him it could have been the equivalent of laughter.

* * *

Bannock lay on the straw bed staring without focus into the mass of corn-blonde hair spread out directly in front of his face, tickling his nose. Each hair came into sharp definition, then blurred again into a golden screen. Sex had always been a soporific; this was the ideal aftermath, to let the vision blur and the mind wander in peace, or, even better, to sleep. But he was wide awake, very conscious of every sound: a creak in the ceiling beams, O'Flaherty's voice in the distance as he self-consciously shouted orders to Van more loudly than was necessary.

What had essentially been missing had been replaced. And it had required so little prompting, responding to a look or two. No conscious feelings of romance, no particular intentions at all. Sarah had managed it all herself. And he had done his stuff.

A voice came from beyond the screen of hair.

"I'm glad that I don't have to sleep on this. My back feels broken."

He laughed and began to get up. "It's not the bed that broke your back."

Bannock was pulling on his breeches when she spoke again.

"I'm not accustomed to sleeping with vulgar horse trainers in their forage stores."

He looked at her while he buttoned up his breeches, and she was smiling.

"Oh?" he asked. "Where do you normally sleep with vulgar people?"

Sarah sat up, holding the horse blanket over her knees. She became serious. "Bartholomew, please understand, I am not accustomed to sleeping with men."

"Do you mean with the exception of this exception?"

"There was only one other exception," she said quietly, "and I was properly engaged in that case."

She began to tie her long hair into its familiar plait.

Bannock leaned on the bar, his eyes following the long, shapely legs as they emerged from under the blanket and hung over the side of the straw bales, with the black skirt bunched up above.

"You must be feeling terribly reckless," he teased.

"A trifle grubby, and covered in straw. I really can't believe it. Me, rolled in the hay. That always seemed a singularly ridiculous peasant pastime."

"Your first mad sin," suggested Bannock, "and with a grubby old horse trainer you were not even engaged to. Do you always make love with your clothes on, Sarah?"

"I think you will agree that one has little choice when suddenly seduced."

"That's an exaggeration."

"Grabbed and ravished."

"With full consent."

"I feel mown down, smashed apart, and . . . Oh, dear, I'm not sure what I feel."

"Well, you think about that while I go and have a wash," said Bannock, crossing to the door in his bare feet and breeches.

He stepped outside and immediately understood that something was wrong. O'Flaherty was standing at the far end of the stables gesticulating at him, his mouth wide as if he were shouting a warning, but with no sound coming out. Bannock was on the point of asking him why he could not simply say what he wanted to say, when O'Flaherty pointed urgently. Only then did he turn and see the cause of all the alarm.

Standing at the off-saddling enclosure, facing the other way, was a tall, thin officer in service uniform, tunic belted with revolver and saber, breeches and spurred boots, hands folded behind his back flicking a riding crop. He was inspecting Sarah's horse, which was tethered there.

Bannock felt awkward in his one-garment attire, and even more so when the officer turned around. It was Geoffrey Stevenson.

How the blazes did Stevenson get there without me knowing? But then he remembered hearing the horses being taken out one after the other for watering. He would not have noticed another set of hooves coming in. Well, it was too late. The man could think whatever he liked. And by his frowning expression, he had already drawn his own conclusions.

"I have caught you at an awkward moment, no doubt." Stevenson made no attempt to disguise his dislike.

"What do you want, Mr. Stevenson?" Bannock was also going to make no pretense of being polite.

Stevenson stared at him, then looked around pointedly at Sarah's sidesaddled horse, then back again at him. "It's *Major* Stevenson," he said curtly.

Bannock folded his arms on his bare chest and waited for Stevenson to go on.

"I have come as I said I would, to make you an offer for a horse. Before you say anything, I want you to know that I've thought carefully about our last conversation and come to the conclusion that it was unrealistic to think of using a stallion in the class of yours as a cavalry mount. I quite understand your determination to keep him to yourself."

"Oh, good," said Bannock.

Stevenson seemed to miss the irony. "In which case, the choice becomes less critical, from your point of view as well as mine. My one reservation is mares. I will not use a mare in action. Which leaves your bay colt, which I thought a lot of, and, of course, the two geldings. But wait, one other reservation. One of the geldings is gray, a hopeless color in the field. Well then," he finalized, "it's the colt or the big brown gelding."

Bannock seethed and said nothing.

Stevenson waited for him to react. "I am leaving the choice to you."

"There is no choice," said Bannock. "I have also given

the matter further thought, and I have decided not to sell any of my horses."

Stevenson tapped the riding crop on his boot. "I shall try to explain this to you patiently," he said. "At any time now, there will be guns firing on us. The Boers are bringing in artillery, you may be sure. What are you and your horses going to do then, Mr. Bannock?"

"I'll be minding my own business."

"No you won't You will be the only noncombatant in this town. I take it you are not figuring in the defense of Kimberley?"

"That is also none of your business."

"Your business will never be that private, Bannock. Word travels fast. We have had a full report on your behavior in Cape Town. Apparently the Turf Club people there would like to ask you a few questions, and so would the police, if I'm not mistaken. It makes one wonder what a few inquiries in England might reveal. It does seem insane that Marcus Aurelius should be out of the running for the big stakes."

Bannock's folded arms tightened as he fought against his rising temper. "Where do you manage to pick up all your gossip?" he asked.

"You are being insolent, and that is unnecessary."

"And you are guilty of slander, which is foolish. I am not the kind of man who can be threatened into doing anything."

"Really?" Stevenson's face went red with anger and he pointed his riding crop at Bannock. "You listen to me—"

Bannock interrupted. "Take your whip out of my face," he said slowly.

Stevenson suddenly calmed down, took a step away as if to leave, then turned and said, "You have made an awful fool of yourself. When I came here, it was to do you a favor, considering that I already had sanction in principle to have a horse commandeered—"

"Confiscated," said Bannock.

"Call it what you may. The matter will now be out of my hands. I think you will find the quartermaster less accommodating."

Bannock watched him march toward his horse, mount, and ride off.

From behind Bannock came the voice of O'Flaherty, who had been leaning on a stable door listening. "I say we pack up and get out of here tonight."

"Not yet," said Bannock. "I'm riding out for De Beers tonight, and I'll see the lay of the land first."

In the heat of the argument he had forgotten Sarah, who had just emerged from the barn door furiously dusting off the skirt of her riding habit.

"Tomorrow night, Paddy," said Bannock. "We'll go tomorrow."

Lennox Street was crowded with military personnel and animals. In the heat of the midday sun there were carts drawn up, idle teams of mules with their traces hanging loose, soldiers lounging on both sides of the road and others drawn up in full kit, sweating as they marched out from between the main headquarters building and the drill hall.

Bannock had been kept waiting on the army headquarters verandah for over half an hour. He had paced up and down restlessly through the depressing cream and public-works-department-brown colonnade, raging to himself about what he assumed was going on inside. He had recognized Stevenson's horse tied up at the hitching rail when he arrived. It was the same heavy cob ridden, and no doubt owned, by Sarah's old colonel friend.

As he paced back toward the main entrance, Stevenson came out, saw him, ignored him, and strode on down to his tethered horse. Bannock watched him mount and ride away, his mood not improved by the look of cool satisfaction on the other man's face. Stevenson was going to get his horse at any cost. The question was, how could he be stopped from doing that?

The sentry in front of the verandah slammed down his boot on the about turn and marched slowly, machinelike, toward the entrance steps, the gleaming bayonet bobbing like a remonstrating finger. Bannock felt conspicuously out of place among the symbols of war, an impression reinforced each time an officer marched in or out, looking him up and down with expressions of curiosity and disdain.

Should he be there at all? Should he not be back at the racecourse preparing to get away after dark that same night? He had argued the alternatives with himself from the moment he had set out, almost glad of the present hold-up that allowed some time to come to a decision. He understood this type of crisis so well, where, whatever decision he made, impetuous or otherwise, would be likely to be a bad one. But he was past the point of the impetuosity he was famous for. He knew what he had to do, only subject to what might have been hatched up between Stevenson and Major Masefield. The time for escape was tomorrow night, not tonight. Tonight he would fulfill his first and last dispatch ride for De Beers. It was his opportunity to check out the map and directions he had been given to reach his destination, a trading post near the Modder River Station. By tomorrow, he would know the extent of Boer activity in the area. He would be there and back before first light, with a clear idea of the very escape route they would take the following night.

They would go down as they had come up, from Hopetown, but with the three loose horses carrying packs. He and O'Flaherty had planned that side of it carefully. They would travel light, taking only their essential possessions and equipment and just sufficient feed to see them through the seventy miles to the Orange River, where they would cross to virtual safety. After that, it would be a long, slow journey to Port Elizabeth.

A corporal emerged from the main entrance. He

looked around the verandah until he saw Bannock, and came over to him.

"Mr. Bannock?" he inquired. "The major will see you now, sir. If you will follow me?"

Bannock followed him through the loudly echoing corridor with its strong atmosphere of antiseptic and boot polish, around a corner, into an anteroom where three army clerks were busy at desks, and through to a large office filled with files and papers. In one corner Masefield was writing at a rolltop desk, his huge frame depending on the delicate-looking mechanism of a swivel chair.

The corporal snapped to attention and announced, "Mr. Bannock, sir," then turned and left.

Masefield went on writing. Bannock waited until he looked up.

"You know why I am here," Bannock said. "You said if I ran into problems I should come and see you."

"Mr. Bannock, sit down." Masefield put his pen down and swiveled round to face him. "Let me give you a short but edifying instruction. It is obvious that you have never been involved in a military situation before, and this is the worst kind of military situation. We are in a state of war. We are coming under siege. We are operating under emergency regulations—"

"Which enables you to confiscate my property?"

Masefield's mouth tightened in a slight but unmistakable expression of disapproval. "That is the very least of it," he said. "This is what you fail to understand. Insulting, let alone threatening, an officer of Her Majesty's Forces at a time like this is a punishable offense. You are extremely lucky that the officer concerned is also a gentleman. He admits to a certain amount of provocation on his part—"

"If you call demanding to take over what constitutes my livelihood provocation, I would agree."

"Stop worrying about your livelihood; it doesn't exist. If you want something to worry about, worry about staying alive."

"I would just like to establish my rights."

Masefield smiled ironically. "Oh, as to that," he said, "you have none. Except, that is, the right to volunteer. In the meantime, the quartermaster has issued a requisition for three of your horses. In terms of a proclamation issued yesterday, you will receive compensation in the form of one shilling per day per horse. If a horse dies or is killed on active service, you will be paid its full value, the value to be established by agreement between yourself and the quartermaster's office."

"Three horses?" Bannock leaned forward, staring in disbelief. "I thought he needed one horse, not three."

"I have it here on the list. A colt and two geldings." He looked up. "Which leaves you and your men a horse apiece. Don't complain, Bannock," he warned. "You'll be out of order."

Bannock closed his eyes and tried to think against his rage. Suddenly, the well-laid plans were meaningless. Could they get away effectively with just three horses? Would they lose the rest, lose Marcus, if they hung on? Hold on and talk yourself calmly out of this situation. Get out of here and try to think again.

Masefield's voice came though. "Have you thought of volunteering?" he asked calmly.

Bannock opened his eyes. He had to keep his temper and get out of there. "What would I do?" he asked.

"Difficult question," said Masefield thoughtfully. "You are a rider, which should be useful. I doubt you have the discipline for the mounted corps, or even the Town Guard, for that matter. You could ride scout maybe, but it's questionable whether you know the area well enough. You could also ride dispatch, but I think there are enough dispatch riders at present. The trouble is, these people are true professionals at their jobs, which almost rules you out. I think you must volunteer, and then we can decide where you fit in."

"I'll volunteer immediately if you will return at least one of my horses to me."

"You will simply volunteer, damn you." Masefield slammed his fist down on the desk. His double chin vibrated as he blurted out angrily, "You had your chance to sort this matter out amicably and you threw it away. Now shut up, Bannock, and listen. Do you know what the army does to people who go against them in wartime? They shoot them."

Masefield was still speaking when Bannock swung off the chair and strode out through the door. He pushed past an orderly struggling with a bunch of files and papers in the next doorway and maneuvered himself between two groups of officers talking together in the long passage.

He had almost reached the front entrance when the walls appeared to move. There was a thundering crash, and his hands went involuntarily to his ears. In the same instant, he felt himself thrown sideways against the wall, then helplessly onto the floor. The exploding sound reverberated on. Pieces of plaster cascaded down from the ceiling. The sound began to abate, and he could hear men shouting and horses neighing. The orderly who had been carrying the files looked around miserably at the confusion of papers strewn across the passage. The group of officers began getting up and dusting themselves off.

Bannock stood up and made his way outside as another explosion occurred, this one less severe.

The road was alive with movement: men running across in both directions, horses bolting, and a team of mules careering away down the street, loose harness dragging behind. For a moment Bannock imagined they had come under artillery fire, but he soon saw the source of the explosion. To the south, an enormous billowing cloud rose up, curling high into the sky in a great towering column.

"It's the De Beers dynamite stocks," shouted one of the officers. "The whole bang shoot has gone up."

Bannock looked around for his horse. The hitching rail

had been torn away. The horse was nowhere to be seen. He set off up the street to find it, but, only partly aware of what he was doing, marched aimlessly in the path of running men and excited animals.

The world was closing in, throttling his mind like the surrounding siege. Anger blacked out everything but the picture of three horses.

How do I face Paddy and Van? They expect me to fight. I've got to fight back, but against what? The garrison? They've found a way to beat me. They've cut off my life-blood. They've castrated my pride.

"Shall I fetch you a drink, Mother?" Mark Freestone-Grant was halfway out of his seat at the small table near the window where he was playing chess with Emma, when the offer was declined.

"No, no, continue your game," ordered Lady Free-stone-Grant from where she sat in the far corner of the room. "The others will be here in a moment."

The gaunt *mater familias* was seated in a high-backed chair, regal and relaxed, her fingers touching together in a meditative pose as she surveyed her private living room in the Shields Hotel.

"Are you feeling better now?" Emma asked solici-tously, without looking up from the chessboard.

"I am quite recovered," came her mother's voice, "al-though I do abhor loud bangs at any time and cracked windowpanes and, above all, hysterical people. If I had to calm down one member of the staff who came to calm me down, there were at least four, including the manager."

The door opened and Emma and Mark were distracted from their game by a gasp from Lady Freestone-Grant, who clapped her hands in a gesture of appreciation for Steven-son's new parade uniform. He stood in the doorway resplen-dent in braid-edged red tunic, gold-striped black pants, and immaculate top-boots.

"Major, you look most elegant," said Emma.

Lady Freestone-Grant considered him appraisingly. "Kindly pour the drinks, Geoffrey," she said, "and you two may continue with your game while I have a short discussion with my other son."

Stevenson strode over to the silver drinks tray. "Sherry, ma'am?" he asked. "Emma, sherry? Mark?"

"I shall get my own, thank you." Mark remained engrossed in the game.

The old lady followed every movement as Stevenson put down the sherry for Emma, then brought her drink over to her and held up his own in a silent salute.

"What is the matter with your arm?" asked Lady Freestone-Grant. "A war wound already?"

Mark and Emma both turned to see.

Stevenson balanced the glass in his fingers, exposing a bandaged wrist.

"Oh, no, it's nothing, really. I took delivery of a horse this afternoon and we were schooling it to gunfire. Horses which are unaccustomed to loud reports tend to react badly. Really, this is nothing." He dismissed the wrist with an exaggerated frown and sipped his drink.

Lady Freestone-Grant leaned forward conspiratorially. "Is she coming?" she asked quietly.

Stevenson smiled. "She was on the point of dashing off in old Thrumpton's carriage to view the result of the dynamite disaster from the barricades. She seemed displeased that the invitation should have come from me, but I managed to insist."

"What nonsense," said Lady Freestone-Grant. "I really cannot understand what has come over Sarah. She knows perfectly well that we get together for drinks every evening. Even if this matter had not come up, I was on the point of having a serious talk with her. You must understand, Geoffrey, that in the normal way, Sarah has always been very open with us."

Emma had turned round and was listening. "What is

wrong with Sarah?" she asked. "What are you two discussing so privately?"

"I must say, I was thinking the very same thing," said Mark, moving his knight but also obviously conscious of what was being said at the far side of the room. "If there is something amiss, shouldn't we all be quite open with one another?"

"What should we all be open with one another about?" Sarah was in the room before anyone realized. She took hold of her wide skirt and crossed the room, settling herself on the window seat beside the chess players. "No, I shall not have a drink, thank you," she announced, reacting to Stevenson's movement toward the tray.

Lady Freestone-Grant quickly adjusted the line of conversation. "Well, Geoffrey, I am pleased to hear you have found a horse at last. I trust it is a good one?"

"I suspect I shall be putting it to the test tomorrow on my first sortie."

"Oh, dear," said Lady Freestone-Grant. "I'm afraid I do not like to hear of anyone going into action."

Stevenson laughed. "Oh, no, there is little promise of action. All the Boers have done so far is pinch some of our supplies coming in from Riverton, including some guns, unfortunately. That was yesterday. And today they raided a few head of cattle from the perimeter, and some say they are directly responsible for the dynamite explosion. We shall try to find them and punish them—that is, if they are to be found; they are very elusive so far. But never fear, De Beers have enormous resources of food, staples, and cattle. We will not go hungry." He found Emma staring at him, questioning him. "You are not to worry, my dear," he said, putting his own interpretation on it, "it will be an exercise canter." Then he added a secret taunt for her: "You will lose no sleep over this."

"Where did you get the horse?" Emma asked her question.

Stevenson downed his drink and headed for the silver

tray. "Emma," he said while he refilled his glass, "you remember that fellow Bannock? Of course you do, you were there." He crossed back to hold the floor and waited until he was satisfied he had all of their attention, then he went on. "Well, you cannot imagine how much trouble we have had with this character."

"Who is 'we'?" Sarah asked evenly.

"I shall come to that. As I was saying, Emma, you remember how I offered for a particular horse and he haggled about a horse I did not want, and the money, and so on."

"I don't remember him haggling," said Emma firmly. Sarah suppressed a laugh.

Stevenson was put out, visibly annoyed. "I may be expressing myself badly," he said, "but there was an argument, a damned obtuse one on his part. At any rate, I shall cut a long, boring story short by explaining that I exposed myself to a further meeting with him, which resulted in further insults and trickery on his part. And what happened on this occasion you must take my word for. This fellow was setting up impossible bargains with horses he has absolutely no use for, so there was nothing for it but to put him in his place."

"I find that really surprising." Emma was frowning.

"I find it unbelievable." Sarah's temper was starting.

"Now wait a minute, sisters," said Mark in an effort to restore calm. "What is this? A conspiracy?"

"Wait," said Stevenson, "there is more. In the way that bad news travels, the bad news for Bannock traveled up on the last train to reach Kimberley before the lines were cut. A gentleman who knows all about Turf Club matters in the Cape passed it on to us at the Kimberley Club, and as I am already going into more detail than I would like, let it suffice to say that this fellow is a rogue, involved in races that were not run true and incidents involving drunken violence. There is also an interesting piece of conjecture about a stallion in Bannock's possession, which is worth little here but would fetch a fortune as a stud animal in England."

"I think you are aware"—Sarah was at the breaking point—"that Bartholomew Bannock is a friend of mine."

Stevenson smiled sympathetically. "I think that when all is known," he said, "you may decide to choose your friends more carefully."

"How dare you?" Sarah let go. "You have obviously cheated him out of one of his horses."

Suddenly she was on her feet looking toward her mother, who reacted immediately.

"Kindly sit down, Sarah," Lady Freestone-Grant commanded. "I shall have something to say to you presently."

But Sarah was in no mood for orders. "I wish to be excused," she snapped, and marched out of the room, forcing the surprised Stevenson to stand back for her.

They were all left in stunned silence.

Mark looked around at Stevenson and his mother and asked, "What on earth is all this about Sarah?"

A dry laugh came from Lady Freestone-Grant. "Sarah is acute," she said, "Sarah is quick. But oh dear me, your sister is not very clever." She held up her glass to Stevenson. "I shall have another sherry, if you don't mind."

Stevenson took the glass but remained where he was, irresolute and puzzled. "I seem to have botched this. I thought that faced with the evidence—"

Emma interrupted him. "How reliable is your evidence?" she asked.

Stevenson was dumbfounded. "I beg your pardon" was all he could get out.

"May I say something?" asked Emma.

"By all means," he said guardedly.

"I met this unfortunate man with you. I have no special impression of him except that he is obviously trapped in Kimberley against his will. But I have to say this: your version of what happened that day does not tally with mine."

Stevenson shook his head in a search for words, but Lady Freestone-Grant spoke for him.

"You're out of order, Emma. You must ask Geoffrey to explain the whole matter to you later."

Mark looked at Emma in disbelief. Her rebellion was so out of character.

Emma watched a vein pulsing at Geoffrey's temple and a small, nervous twitch at the corner of his mouth. She knew, as instinctively as she could detect the signs, that whatever was wrong with Geoffrey was getting worse. The nightmare were slowly, inexorably coming to life. She only knew that she had to defy him. It was the lesser of two evil ways to behave: to defy and make some kind of contact, or to give in and remain remote, ineffectual, and frustrated as ever.

"Did you really force him to give up that horse?"

"Later, Emma." She heard her mother's voice but she had Geoffrey's attention, the eyes seeming to go through and past her to focus somewhere beyond reality.

He said dully, "The army has taken over three of his horses. By coercion, if you like. But I am not here to explain or justify anything to you at the moment."

"Now come on, you two." She heard Mark's voice but she hung on to Geoffrey's eyes, defying them to look away.

"But you do seem intent on justifying yourself," she said.

Emma was aware that her mother was slowly standing up. She heard her say, "I think I shall be excused."

Geoffrey stared at Emma like an owl. "You don't understand," he said. "If you knew what your sister was doing with this fellow—"

"Sarah is past the age of consent."

Mark got up to help his mother toward the door. Emma watched them go out together. Suddenly, she realized that Geoffrey had taken an aggressive step toward her. He was shaking with rage, and she began to regret inciting him. But there was no responding anger in her and not even a trace of fear.

He blustered, "If you have so little consideration for your sister, who is being seduced by that . . . that rotter—" Perspiration had broken out on his forehead. The twitch at his mouth was more pronounced. "That bastard!" His voice became hoarse. "I'll see him hang! I'll see him lose every horse he owns! Do you hear me?" he was shouting. "I'll see that the authorities and everyone knows the kind of man he is so that he can be dealt with."

Emma closed her eyes and listened to the hoarse breathing, the way he breathed when he woke from the dream. The bad dream was infringing on consciousness, the violence of the dream becoming applied to a different subject, not fighting for his life with the saber, but the same violence. And she was alone with it.

She stood her ground, afraid to move, even to retreat. She waited, keeping her eyes closed, listening to the gasping. Then, as if the real crisis were over, the gasping changed to heavy breathing. And slowly, painfully slowly, the breathing became more even, as it did after each nightmare.

She heard him sigh deeply and say quite normally, "I say, Emma, what is going on here? Where has everyone gone? Shall I pour you another drink?"

She refused to open her eyes. She thought, I share this nightmare. It has become mine as much as his.

The sound that began as an indecipherable mutter in the distance had soon grown to the unmistakable thumping of galloping horses. Bannock held the snaffle ring at Pot Pourri's mouth as lightly as he could so as to keep her calm, and at the same time strained to see through the screen of thorns. It had been fortunate that when he first heard the sound there was one of those rare clumps of dry thorn trees nearby.

The riders came into sight, difficult to make out in the dark, obviously Boers, with cross-slung guns and felt hats, going past toward the west as fast as their tough veld ponies would carry them. Amazingly small horses that hesitated for nothing, riding down bushes and clattering over rock outcrops without flinching.

They were gone, the dying noise lost in the creaking and buzzing of crickets and cicadas. He patted Pot Pourri in gratitude for her good behavior. She had become a true friend in one night, and he realized with amazement that since acquiring her, two years before he had left England, he had never ridden her.

"You're a marvel, my girl," he told her, and led her on foot to the top of the next rise, which he judged should be very close to Kimberley.

Sure enough, there was the wide configuration of skyline in the distance, with the ironwork and pulleys of the Bultfontein minehead over to the right.

Bannock sat down on a rock and took out the rough map MacGrath had drawn for him. He had to hold it up close to make out the details; it was too much of a risk to strike a light. According to the map, he was just east of Ronald's Vlei, with the racecourse due north of him and only about a mile away. The position was perfect, considering he had to avoid the manned posts marked with crosses at Bultfontein on the one side and Beaconsfield Park on the other, and the big redoubt at the reservoir farther west. Fortunately, the searchlight at Premier Mine to the east had little effect at this distance.

He consulted his watch. Just after four; time to move before first light and the last ironical mile where the danger of death threatened not only from the Boers, but from the rifles of his own people. His orders were explicit. If there was any activity in the area of the racecourse preventing him from going straight in, he was to ride west to the Du Toitspan Mine, where it was arranged that the Town Guards on duty would let him pass without question. Most of the volunteers in the Town Guard were De Beers employees, so Bannock drew his own conclusions.

He mounted up, to the unaccustomed feel of well-stuffed saddlebags pressing back against his thighs. It had been a surprisingly easy ride, going straight out into the moonlit veld the previous night. He had heard horses and movements in the distance as he rode south following the precise directions he had been given, but he had seen nothing. Pot Pourri had settled down to a self-chosen pace, a long, striding, comfortable jog that, even taking into account four good rests, had covered the fourteen miles to Merton Station in under three and a half hours. The station had been deserted, and he had soon located his destination, the trading store, a half a mile due east toward Magersfontein. There he had been whistled down by what would become his image of a professional dispatch rider for all time: a tall, rugged man in khaki, campaigning boots, and sheepskin vest, whose humorous eyes belied an untalkative, even unfriendly manner. Their exchange of sealed envelopes and rolls of newspapers took no more than a minute, and Bannock was left packing his saddlebags while the silent man cantered off into the dark toward the Orange River, leading his spare horse by impatient jerks.

The return journey had been even less eventful, but difficult in another way. He had hardly come five miles when storm clouds obscured the moon and left him virtually at the mercy of Pot Pourri's instincts. And that was when he really grew to appreciate this fine-boned mare.

In the normal way he would never have chosen her for such a rugged assignment, yet he would have been wrong. She kept her head every inch of the way, sensibly stepping aside for thorn bushes and other obtrusions, never really shying, never growing nervous. Now he wondered why he had ever neglected this elegant lady with the fine, dished face and the big brown eyes. She had done well as a racer, surprising him again and again with her ability to stay. He remembered her winning over two miles at Manchester. He was astonished at the time, and irritated with himself for having sent her out more for exercise than with any real hope. She was a great compensation in the loss of his other horses, and he felt secure in the knowledge that if anything came at him, he had the right vehicle for escape: a horse that could outrun any Boer mount and hold a fast gallop for four miles or more at a stretch.

Bannock rode toward the town slowly, restraining Pot Pourri in a gathered walk. She was as fresh as when she started out. He could hear nothing except the crickets and see very little of the town ahead, but he had studied this area outside the perimeter carefully and knew that it was as flat as a pan, save for small, loose stones on the surface. Over to the west there was a flash of lightning and, a few seconds later, a long, low rumble of thunder.

Bannock's hands reacted on the reins to a strange moaning sound that soon increased in volume to a ghostly wailing. He recognized it immediately as the warning sirens situated at the main redoubts and throughout Kimberley. The noise became impossible. Pot Pourri reared and spun around hysterically. He hung on tightly as the din emanated from the town in vibrating waves, each siren screaming at a slightly different pitch, making an insane chord that no ears could tolerate. Eventually, the scream died down, and the wailing receded back into infinity.

Bannock brought Pot Pourri under control again, relieved that he had been on her back, not having to watch her break loose and gallop away into the dark. He began to laugh at the idea of that ludicrous warning system frightening the life out of every soul in Kimberley, and warning them against what? The veld around him was as empty as the hills behind. At this moment, the enemy was a ghost and an illusion.

Lightning caught his eye, and thunder rolled. He proceeded at a walk and blessed the clouds that obscured the all-revealing first light.

He thought about the plan for the following night, and

felt very confident. Everything had been taken into account in that decision. It was imperative to escape the sterile siege, where every condition was against him. He had made peace with himself about the loss of the three horses. As long as he had Marcus, he could survive, if only by breeding him. Port Elizabeth had become a symbol of salvation. They could not beat him anymore. With three honest horses, one honest jockey, and his only friend no matter what his faults, old Paddy, the only friend he could ever depend on.

He had put the risk to both of them. Paddy wanted to come in spite of the risk, in spite of his dreams of digging up diamonds in the back streets of Kimberley. Van wanted to come because of his simple dream of riding winner after winner and his virtual reverence in the presence of Marcus. He smiled when he thought how easy it was going to be for them, traveling light, poised for the escape gallop at every moment, and with only seventy miles to the Orange River and safety. They could do most of it through the night and complete the dangerous part of the journey with a fast ride the next morning.

What were the problems going to be? MacGrath? He would hand him the dispatches and say nothing. He had earned the money, done his duty by them. Masefield? He hoped never again to confront that fat, shrewd officer. But there was no reason why he should run into him during the day. Sarah? There was every reason why she might turn up. She could be a problem. She would be told nothing. He knew her type so well, the type you can never get to know. She was selfish enough to be able to come to terms with his departure quite quickly. It would be a mistake to consider her. Charlie Watson? He had an instinctive distrust of that charming little fellow, that cynical little man. He would not seek Charlie out; he would decide how much to say only if he saw him.

The lightning came bright, lighting up the rails of the racecourse ahead. Bannock felt exposed in that instant and lifted Pot Pourri into a steady trot as the thunder sounded loud and long and heavy drops of water began to fall, bringing up the strong smell of wet dust.

When he thought he heard a sound in the distance, he pulled to a stop again. There was a faint rumbling. Not thunder. It was somewhere over in the west. He watched the horizon at the far end of the town carefully. The next flash of lightning showed an antlike line of what must obviously have been cavalry, spreading out into the veld down toward the south.

He heard the sound of a bugle call bleating urgently in that direction, as the rain began to splatter down.

"Sergeant," shouted Stevenson, wiping the rain out of his eyes and re-cocking his helmet.

"Sir." The sergeant pulled up at his side.

"We'll take up formation in line at the bottom of that ridge."

The sergeant moved off shouting, "Columns of three! At a canter!" then, after looking back for Stevenson's nod, "Forward!"

Stevenson collected the tall throughbred into a canter, its coat shining wet with rain. He looked a sight for any cavalryman's sore eyes. Only a true horseman would have known Stevenson was fighting to restrain that powerful mouth, his stirrups canted forward, his hands tight at the reins. No doubt he must have regretted at that moment his compromise from snaffle to the heavy pelham he was pulling at with the curb chain slacked off; he must have wished for a martingale to stop the long, impetuous neck from flailing up at his face. But he looked magnificent and was obviously elated as he got control and skidded the big horse to a standstill in the mud below the ridge.

The sergeant was shouting, "Left wheel!" and the riders pulled up in ragged formation at the next command, with Stevenson on his restless thoroughbred facing them.

"Right turn! Face together! Hold that line steady!" the sergeant shouted from his position alongside.

Along the ridge, Stevenson could see the column of Cape Mounted Police and two of Kimberley Light Horse drawn up in close order at the foot, but a long way farther back. Farther on again through the mist of the rain he could see what might have been cavalry commander Scott-Turner's party actually climbing the ridge, and there was the sound of gunfire from that direction.

"Hold your formation," he shouted to his troop and, swinging the thoroughbred around, galloped up the steep ridge on his own. He reined in at the top, struggling with the impetuous horse as he surveyed the scene. All was confusion. There were hundreds of Boers milling around on foot and on horseback, striking tents and trying to move wagons and carts, evidently startled into action out of their sleep. Groups of riders were already speeding away in the opposite direction, and a rear guard of Boer riflemen was taking up position on the near side.

Bugles sounded from behind, one after the other chanting the order to disengage.

"Retreat?" Stevenson was astonished. "Why retreat? It's the enemy who are retreating, damn it."

Then guns were firing, bullets ricocheted, whining away off the rocks at the top of the ridge. The horse went wild as he turned it. He struggled to hold his seat as they slid frantically down the rain-soaked bank. By the time he reached the bottom, the horse was out of control, and he galloped toward the drawn-up formation, which broke up to make room for him as he sawed at the mouth, shouting, "Damn you, hold up, damn you."

He gained control some thirty yards farther on and roughly turned the horse, letting it prance back toward the troop. He was aware that his men were trying to hide their mirth over his struggle with the thoroughbred.

"You may laugh," he shouted, beginning to laugh himself, his face streaming with rain, "but I'll see your faces in a fight presently."

The thunder cracked. The light was improving, in spite of the rain and heavy clouds. Stevenson waited, watching three officers gallop toward him from the main column. He recognized two captains from the other troops and Major Peakman. As they reined in, Peakman spoke breathlessly.

"Lucky for you, Major, Colonel Scott-Turner was out of position, because so were you. You're too far on the flank and a ruddy sight too far forward."

"With respect, sir, I was simply trying to anticipate—"

"Stay in line, Major Stevenson. We are going to attack, but the colonel's instructions are specific. We expect the Boers to retreat, and we will disengage on signal."

"Why on earth—"

Major Peakman interrupted again. "This is a show of force, sir, and that is all. Those are the orders. They apply to all of us. You may keep your opinion for later."

The three officers turned and galloped away back to their stations.

Stevenson restlessly walked his mount in circles and figure eights as if he were schooling a dressage horse. He seemed amused and elated, but his expression changed sharply as the call to advance came. He heard the sergeant give the order and the chorus of squelching hoofs as the column moved forward, but he was already galloping ahead up the bank, opening the reins wide as the horse slipped and then gathering again as it regained its footing. He reined in at the summit and this time went forward slowly, watching the whole squadron magnificently top the hill. But he was not too pleased with what he saw lying ahead. The Boers on his side were well on the retreat, already out of any danger of capture. There were stragglers, but only far to the right, and they would soon be overrun by Scott-Turner's people.

Stevenson showed his frustration, drawing his saber and swinging it in an exaggerated signal for his troops, who had just then come over the top of the ridge. He let his thoroughbred show its strides, galloping away toward the deserted camp, veering across on a course that would bring him close to the rest of the column. For a while he allowed the gallop, splattering through the mud and swinging his saber petulantly on one side like a polo stick. He soon realized he had left his troop standing, and spent the next fifty yards pulling the powerful runner to a standstill. He drew up beside a covered wagon with half-inspanned oxen, its stores strewn all around in the mud. Sitting still in the pouring rain, he watched the round-up of some prisoners in the distance. Behind him, the sergeant shouted his orders to the troop to pull up and re-form.

Suddenly, Stevenson lashed out with his saber at the canvas of the wagon. The sharp blade sliced three ways, opening a flap to reveal the ammunition boxes inside. He nudged his horse slowly along the side of the wagon, slicing again and again at each section of the canvas, creating a perfect pattern of openings in a demonstration of surgically precise and deadly sword swinging that held the attention of every man present.

"Sergeant," he called back, "you may take these oxen prisoner."

The three of them leaned on the inside wall of the stable looking at the big brown mule. Besides being enormous, it was fat and dozy-looking, with unnaturally long lop ears. O'Flaherty wore a persecuted frown.

"Go on, Bart," he pleaded, "you've got to admit it's a fine, healthy beast."

Van signaled enthusiastic agreement.

But Bannock was still worried.

"How did you get it here? I suppose you paraded it through the middle of town?"

"Not at all," O'Flaherty protested. "I was the master of discretion, even with Finnegan the farrier. I told him we didn't need a mule at all, really. And then I told him how Marcus had a sheep in his box all those years to keep him calm, and how the sheep died and we had to put a chicken in there, and I think he understood, there being such a shortage of small animals in the town."

Bannock struggled to remain serious. "So you told him you were going to push this hulking freight mule into the loose box with Marcus. It sounds like a tight fit to me."

O'Flaherty looked hurt. "It makes a lot of sense puttin' a mule with a stallion. It's not as if you've never heard of such a thing."

"A small mule, Paddy."

"And into the bargain, Finnegan is under the impression that this is one of them ridin' mules."

Bannock was skeptical. "Have you tried to ride it?" he asked.

"When have I had a chance for that?"

Bannock laughed. "It sounds like one of those old mule stories to me. But if it ever has to be ridden, it's going to be your pleasure, friend. You know what mules are like when they're not riding mules."

They all stared dubiously at the massive mule.

"Has it got a name?" asked Bannock.

"I've called it Macushla and look at that, just look at that big ear flickin'. Sure, it knows its name already."

"It's not a girl, Paddy."

"Well, it's not anythin', is it? It's just a big, poor thing with a dear Irish name. But talkin' about the discretion, when I came out of Finnegan's, I climbed on to Lady Potter calm as you like with never even a passin' glance to that mule, and the mule was led all the way back by a small black boy, bless him, who I paid out of me own money."

Bannock glanced at his watch. "It's now just after five. We'll start checking the light at about nine-thirty. Once it's dark enough, we'll be ready to go. Now, there are just one or two things I would like to point out to you two about your brilliant plan. First, you can forget about that load." He pointed to the enormous loaded backpack in the straw at their feet. "You can't expect to take all that clobber."

"What are you goin' to leave behind?" asked O'Flaherty. "The racing saddles? The horse blankets? Your clothes and boots? The fodder?"

"You can throw off most of that feed," said Bannock. "We'll be out of danger by mid-morning tomorrow and we'll find either a feed store or some grazing. With all this rain, we're going to have no trouble with water. Now point two, and this could be the sad, short tale of Macushla."

"I know this one," said O'Flaherty. "We leave her in the lurch."

"At the first sign of trouble, we leave her. If we are chased, it's our only hope. She stays where she is."

O'Flaherty sighed. "Van and I worked that one out earlier."

Bannock wanted to be sure of his sentimental friend and the wordless jockey he could never fathom. "You understand, then?" he asked.

Both men nodded.

O'Flaherty and Van Breda got down on their knees and began to untie the huge backpack, but they were both on their feet again at the sound of approaching horses. Bannock cursed and went out to close the stable doors.

"Get out there, Paddy," he ordered. "If it's Masefield, I don't want him to see the mule."

O'Flaherty stepped outside, holding the door, and they heard him say, "Well glory be to God, if this isn't becomin' the social center of Kimberley." He looked back in, smiling. "Every time you look around, there's another visitor arrivin', and sooner of later all the fine ladies of the town will come to have tea with his dear self, the great lover."

"Oh, no," said Bannock, pushing past O'Flaherty, expecting to see Sarah.

But he stopped in his tracks when he saw who it was: the wife of Stevenson the hero, Sarah's sister. He was not pleased as he watched the light carriage being pulled up and braked by its native driver. He had seen his fill of this family. The ones he was already acquainted with were trouble enough.

"Keep that stable door closed," he ordered, and walked across to help the lady down.

But she was already on the ground, looking embarrassed yet determined. Bannock prepared himself for the onslaught about her poor defenseless sister or her mistreated husband.

"Good evening, Mrs. Stevenson."

She glanced around apprehensively.

"There is a matter I must discuss with you urgently. Is there somewhere we can talk?"

"Please come this way."

Bannock walked ahead of her to the bar, where he pushed the door open and stood aside, waiting for her to enter. He watched the neat bonnet go past, the rings of shining yellow hair showing under, the small body hidden among folds of velvet cloak. She was a beautiful little female, surprisingly young to be Stevenson's wife.

She stood in the middle of the room rummaging in a large handbag. He pointed to a straight-backed chair in front of the bar, but she didn't seem to notice. She placed her handbag on the bar and continued to rummage until she found what she was searching for.

She looked up. "I feel a little foolish, Mr. Bannock, and I hope you will be patient with me."

He waited, very much on his guard, but he knew nevertheless that he was unnerving her.

"Please—do you mind?—I think I should explain right away." She stumbled over her words but kept her eyes directly and, he thought, defiantly on him. "It came to my notice . . . the matter of the horses. . . . I must be careful that you do not misunderstand me."

He decided to reassure her. "Please, sit down, Mrs. Stevenson. Take it slowly."

She sat down and collected her thoughts.

"To put it simply," she said, "I think you have been mishandled. But the circumstances have created a wrong impression. What I mean is, you are under a wrong impression about Geoffrey . . . my husband."

"You don't need to do this, Mrs. Stevenson."

"You don't understand," she said more urgently. "Geoffrey is under a great strain. He would never have behaved like this in the normal way. I wish I could tell you more, but . . ."

Bannock tried to help. "You are under no obligation to tell me anything, and frankly, I think the matter is closed. You really should not humiliate yourself."

"That is not the reason I came here." She got up and held out a canvas banking bag to him. "Here is two hundred guineas. It was all the money I could raise at present, but it is a gesture toward the full amount your horses are worth, which I shall see to it you are paid."

Bannock was utterly disarmed. He kept his hands behind his back and struggled for words.

"I will never accept that," he blurted out.

"You must. Please understand, it is for Geoffrey's sake as much as mine. I know that he has prejudiced himself against his normal nature. He is not like this at all."

She was becoming distressed. Bannock took her gently by the shoulders and made her sit down.

"Will you listen to me, Mrs. Stevenson?" he said firmly but politely. "Your husband faced me with some accusations based on hearsay—"

"I would never take that into account."

"It gave me a reputation I don't entirely deserve."

"I believe that is none of our business."

"Oh, but it is. If horses have a value, so do reputations. They are not the prerogative of the rich, you know." He knew he was making her more uncomfortable. "Will you be patient with me if I tell you something?"

"Yes, of course."

"I come from a long line of horse people. I work in an industry where bad reputations come about without effort. But I am a racing man, and proud of it. I love it, do you understand? The horses, the competition, the heartaches, the obsession with winning."

"Of course, I understand that," she answered quietly.

"But this is what I really want you to understand: contrary to what has been said, I have never nobbled a runner, but I have suffered at the hands of people who have."

"Mr. Bannock, please."

He just went on. "This is beginning to sound ridiculous. I'm no saint, nothing as boring as that. I've never been a great respecter of rules and conventions. For example, it could be said that I stole my best horse from my father's estate, but I traded a considerable inheritance for that. Now you get this, Mrs. Stevenson; my pride, which I have been telling you about, makes it impossible for me to come to terms with your pride. So please keep your money."

Emma looked down, at a loss.

"I thought I would manage this so well," she said. "It was difficult for me." She hesitated. "I mean . . . to go behind everybody's back."

"I think you are magnificent." Bannock thought she was magnificent in more ways than one. He watched the perfect face come up, the candid eyes stare at him straight and true. How could she belong to a pompous ass like Stevenson?

"I promise you this, Mr. Bannock: as soon as conditions allow, I shall talk seriously to Geoffrey, and I am confident that he will want to treat you correctly. Somehow, we will make it up to you."

They stared at each other. There seemed nothing more

to be said, but Bannock tried for words. Against all logic, he wanted to keep her there, to talk to her.

"Look here—"

"There is just—"

They had both started to talk at once, when they heard a horse galloping away. Bannock cursed O'Flaherty for going off at the last moment, no doubt to stock up on whiskey.

Emma had collected up her bag and stood facing him.

"I can understand what Sarah sees in you," she said, smiling. "You are a straight talker, no nonsense, and I suspect no one will ever put you down."

Bannock smiled back at her. "I have been put down in the past," he said. "The only difference now is that it cannot happen without my knowing about it and, I'm afraid, not without a fight."

She went to the door and turned, "Maybe you need a few more people fighting on your side."

He opened the door for her. The reckless Bannock took over. "I'd have you on my side any day."

Emma blushed and walked purposefully to the waiting carriage. She was up and seated before Bannock could get there to assist her.

"I shall keep my promise. Good-bye, Mr. Bannock."

Bannock saw only the smile of a generous child, a child's beautiful smile on a face that made him gape stupidly as the carriage drove away.

When he turned around, he was surprised to see O'Flaherty still there, walking toward him.

"I heard a horse. I thought it was you." Bannock inquired.

"Not me." O'Flaherty looked upward dramatically. "That was someone else."

"Who?"

"And you are in trouble."

"Come on, Paddy. Stop playing games."

"It's as well you are leavin' or all your beautiful ladies will be scratchin' one another's eyes out over you."

"Who the hell was it?" Bannock's irritation grew as he realized his guess must be right. "Was it Sarah?"

"It was herself," said O'Flaherty, being a little more careful. "She rode in here like a storm cloud, gave me a sign to stay back and not call you, then watched through the window at yourself leanin' over nicely pattin' the other one."

"What are you talking about?"

"Well, I don't know what you were doin' with the other one, but this one, she sits there grindin' the teeth and rollin' the eyes, and before you can say good day, she's off and away again, puttin' the whip in unmercifully. But you can't blame her, can you? She was here last night lookin' for you, and again this morning. Every time lookin' ready to kill."

"When did you say?"

"Last night after you rode out, and this morning when you were over at De Beers. Let us pray she doesn't come back again with murder in her heart."

Bannock shrugged. "As you say, Paddy, it's just as well we're leaving."

"Amen," said O'Flaherty with great dignity.

Bannock stretched and yawned. "I'm going to sleep for a while," he said. "Keep an eye out and wake me if anybody comes. Oh, and Paddy, make sure to wake me before nine."

He went off to the bar, suddenly tired and conscious of the fact that he had not slept properly when he had lain down earlier in the day. This time he stretched out on his back on the straw bed, closed his eyes and tried to shut out all thought, but again, without much success.

He was sorry to leave the De Beers involvement unfinished. MacGrath would expect him to report back the following evening. It was just another piece of evidence to add to his unstable reputation. There was nothing for it. Charlie, at least, would understand why he disappeared in the night; he would see it as a piece of sporting behavior. But not Sarah. That was a different pretty kettle of fish. Sarah might rant and rave, or she might remain delightfully cool. There was no way he could judge how she would behave. He really didn't know her at all, but he knew her face and its expressions. He knew her body and its curves. The illusion was perfect, and very welcome. He could hear her urgent breathing, gasping. Feel the body pressing against him, feel her scratching hands on his back.

He turned over restlessly in the bed, face down, and tried to shut out the dream and sleep, but the warmth came back. The heat, the fast breathing. Only now the face had changed. It was her sister, looking up at him with that anxious expression. The face dissolved and disappeared.

Bannock woke up in a sweat and, kneeling on the straw, he tried to recall that face. He wanted the moment back, to bring it back and keep it happening.

That was the last thing he remembered when he was shaken into wakefulness by O'Flaherty's heavy hand. They went out into the dark, and there everything was prepared for their departure: the mule, ears hanging and sleepy, seemingly oblivious of the heavy backpack; the horses all saddled and ready, with Marcus pacing around as if it was time for early-morning gallops.

They mounted up, Van Breda on Pot Pourri, O'Flaherty on Lady Potter, leading the mule, and Bannock on Marcus going straight ahead to show the way past the rails at the southern boundary.

It was almost pitch dark, the moon covered by storm clouds that had gathered earlier than on the previous night. Marcus objected to having to feel his way, constantly backing off and being cajoled forward. All they could see was the faint sweep of the searchlight at the Premier Mine redoubt. But ahead, nothing.

The prospect was gloomy in every sense of the word. Bannock realized that they would make very little progress through the night unless the storm cleared to reveal the moon at some later stage. He could hear O'Flaherty cursing the mule.

He called back, "Keep together. The animals will calm down if they're together."

But Marcus continued to be suspicious, jerking around, plunging and blowing and snorting in a way that was too loud for comfort.

There could be no resting until they were well clear of the town, and there would be even less reason to relax until they were past the Boer fortifications.

Suddenly, a bright light snapped on in front of them, beaming directly into their eyes, sending all three horses into a frenzied dance while the mule waited patiently in the middle of the melee. There came the sound of loading rifles. The bobbing lamp went off, leaving them temporarily blinded.

"Bejases," shouted O'Flaherty. "What do we do now, Bart?"

Out of the darkness came a voice. "Mr. Bannock, will you get down, please. All three of you, off your horses, if you please."

That was Masefield's voice, and Bannock felt murderous. He dismounted and led Marcus forward until he made out Masefield's large form sitting on a shooting stick. In the gloom beyond, a group of soldiers stood in line with their rifles pointed.

"They can lower their rifles, Corporal," Masefield called out, then turned to face Bannock. "Were you off on a hunting trip?" he asked.

Bannock thought fast. "Is there any law against riding out of Kimberley?"

"I told you the other day, the army has its own laws. We tend to shoot anything and anybody who gets in our way." But he laughed and stood up, waving the shooting stick. He pointed with it. "Come over here, Bannock; I want a private word with you." He pointed the stick at

O'Flaherty and Van Breda. "You two wait where you are, if you please."

Bannock followed, mad with frustration, and watched Masefield settle his large bulk in what looked a clever balancing act on the spindly shooting stick.

"Now, Mr. Bannock." Masefield leaned his hand on his thighs as if settling down for a long discussion. "If you think I am going to ask you a lot of questions, you are quite wrong. However, I am going to explain a few things to you in fine detail. If during this explanation you have too much to say, or anything to say, for that matter, I shall arrest you forthwith and interview you in a cell. Is that understood?"

"So you are not arresting us?"

"Just listen to what I have to say. Army intelligence, Mr. Bannock, is not a misnomer. You have been under surveillance from the beginning, and I must say that I have had to retract certain assumptions I made about you. While you were out dispatch riding last night for interests, let us say for the moment, unknown, or at least unspecified— while you were out, one of our dispatch riders was killed, and his body deposited right under the reservoir redoubt. And even taking into account that your instructions were impeccable, I am impressed by your cool performance."

"Why didn't you stop me, then?"

"Just listen, Bannock, this is not for your convenience. When your man bought the mule today, one of my men followed the animal. You need not recriminate with Finnegan. He knows nothing."

Masefield turned his head and shouted, "Corporal, over here, please."

The corporal came running and snapped to attention.

"What's in the pack?"

"Clothing, sir. Personal possessions, soap, razors, saddlery, enough feed for two or three stops. Do you need a full list, sir?"

"No, thank you, that is all."

As the corporal marched away, Masefield remarked

casually, "This hardly looked like a dispatch ride. You were leaving."

"I'd still like to know why that should be an offense," asked Bannock. "There are refugees coming in and people going out all the time."

"In, yes; out, no. And in your case, the options are nil. There is enough evidence to lock you up for the duration. Now this is what I want to say to you: I know from information at my disposal that your new employers are well pleased with you. For my own reasons, I am going to suggest that you continue to give them service, and for reasons which I shall presently explain, I shall expect you to cooperate with me . . . on the quiet so to speak."

Bannock could not resist laughing. "You mean I am to be a double spy?"

Masefield smiled, a look of careful assessment. "Listen and you will learn," he said. "A siege is a strange situation. Separating the army from its General Staff is like chopping an arm off the body and asking the hand to perform. Without telling you too much, you must believe that my motivations are of a higher order than those of the organization you are mixed up with. Your principals are simply in business. Mine, on the other hand, represent the difference between victory and defeat. The messages you carry constitute a situation of meddling and interference which can only cause confusion."

"Why don't you put a stop to it?"

"It is not as simple as that. You are riding for Rhodes, which means we are dealing with a man who may have more influence than the entire General Staff put together. I can only do what I am allowed to do. What is your answer, Bannock? Are you with me?"

"If that's an invitation, it sounds more like a threat." Bannock gave himself a moment to think, and the decision came easily. Agree to anything and everything; the moment for escape would come.

The fat major said nothing, and Bannock began to see

in him his brother—the same staring-eyed, vengeful spirit. He could easily have been his brother, riding his shooting stick like the ugly advocate sitting at his desk in formal consultation, faintly bored, speculative, offering nothing, waiting patiently for an answer.

"If I were to agree," Bannock jockeyed, "would you return my horses to me?"

Masefield laughed scornfully. "I never thought I would hear a man trying to bargain with a gun at his head." He stopped laughing. "You know as well as I do that the Major Stevenson arrangement cannot be retracted. But I hear he has settled firmly on one of the three horses. I shall see what can be done to return the other two to you."

"Then I agree."

Masefield leaned his head back in an attitude of mild disbelief. But he spoke quite affably. "Which brings me to my next point. That fine stallion of yours. I find it quite extraordinary that that stallion is a grandson of the great Saint Simon."

"Who told you that?" Bannock was suspicious and on his guard again. "Oh, yes, of course; I should have known who told you that."

Masefield went on as if Bannock had said nothing. "I have decided that an animal as valuable as that would be less exposed to danger in the army stables at Lennox Street than out on the racecourse."

Bannock saw his brother's eyes in Masefield's head. He was being tormented by another fat, vengeful devil. He was beaten again.

"You're going to impound it," he said bitterly.

"In a word, yes."

"That breaks our agreement."

"On the contrary, my dear chap, it binds it."

"You are a bastard."

"Oh, come now, we value your services too much to let you flit away in the night. Your horse becomes a harmless hostage. You may send your own groom up for a specified time each day. There is a quite adequate exercise paddock there. You may give complete instructions to the army groom. You have my word that your stallion will not be employed or interfered with in any way whatever. You see, Bannock, in your case, the army has had to draw a pretty fine line between being unreasonable and being stupid."

Emma knocked and called, "Sarah?"

She listened at the door, then turned the handle and entered. She was surprised to see Sarah sitting at the dressing table brushing her hair.

"Oh, you are up already. Will you be going riding?"

"No," said Sarah. "I think I have lost interest in riding for the present."

"I am sorry I was unable to speak to you last night," said Emma.

"That is quite all right. I understand." Sarah remained concentrated on the mirror and her hair.

"But you said it was urgent."

"Urgent yes, but private. It was no good with Geoffrey present."

"You are being very mysterious, Sarah."

"I am being mysterious?" She went on brushing. "It is you who are being mysterious."

"I don't understand." Emma was becoming irritated.

Sarah caught Emma's eye in the mirror. "You said I looked tired the other day; now I think it is you who look pale and tired."

"I have not been sleeping very well."

"Ah ha."

"Why are you provoking me, Sarah?"

"Where were you yesterday afternoon?"

"I was with Geoffrey at the exercise paddock."

Sarah continued brushing. "Let me try again," she said. "Where were you yesterday evening?"

"I was here, as you know."

There was silence for a while. Emma realized that somehow Sarah knew about her visit of the previous day. She could not imagine how. It seemed impossible, unless she had gone out in the middle of the night to see Bannock.

Sarah turned around on her chair and looked straight at her with that malicious smile that always spelled trouble.

"You amaze me, Emma. I have always suspected you of tricks and evasion. You have always been such a clever little girl, haven't you? Always getting the prize. Little eyelashes pointed down while the men forged in, and only the best for Emma. Nothing less than the head boy, the *victor ladorum,* the sword of honor, the marriage of the year. So clever, but never caught out. Always the innocent, good little person. But this time you have taken on something you could never handle."

"Oh, Sarah, say what you have to say."

"Thank you for putting it in the right context. You are hardly going to expose yourself, so maybe I should do it for you. I know where you were yesterday because I was also there. I saw that fellow touching you, innocent little Emma."

Emma sighed and prepared to explain. "It was necessary that what happened yesterday be a private matter."

"Oh, I quite understand."

"Your sarcasm is wasted. I had to see that man purely to explain something about his dealings with Geoffrey. I hate being surreptitious, but it was something I saw as a duty."

"I would adore hearing you explaining that to Geoffrey."

"I really don't feel under obligation to explain anything to anyone, but what you would not realize is that Geoffrey is under a lot of strain. He had a ridiculous misunderstanding with Mr. Bannock, as you know, to do with horses and, incidentally, to do with you."

The malicious smile remained. "You went to that . . . that fellow to apologize for your husband's behavior?"

"Not to apologize, Sarah, only to explain. I had to explain something that even you are not aware of."

"Ah, more mystery. Little Emma's ulterior motive still shrouded in mystery."

"I'm forcing myself to be patient with you, Sarah. There was no motive other than to restore understanding."

"Oh, come now, how could you achieve understanding with a man you could never hope to understand? You know nothing of men like Bartholomew Bannock. Even I know precious little of the type. But stable rats only come out in the open by chance. He is after you, now. I saw him. And he'll get you, of course."

"You are raving."

Emma was not being provoked, but Sarah was losing her composure, becoming shrill. "Poor Emma, can't sleep at night thinking of horsey hands touching her."

Emma began moving toward the door. "I will not listen to this," she said. "We can talk again when you're calm."

"I am not interested in talking to you—"

"You are shouting, Sarah. Keep your voice down."

"I am interested in talking to Geoffrey. Geoffrey and I understand one another."

Emma turned round and walked back toward her sister.

Sarah screamed at her, "What do you know about men?"

Emma's hand shot up and struck Sarah across the face with a force that jerked her head back. Emma looked down at her reddened hand in astonishment. She could not believe the force she had used.

Sarah sobbed quietly and babbled, "He will get you, he will get you."

"No, he won't," Emma said softly. "I really have no interest in him."

"Dirty, horse-smelling rat."

Emma stroked Sarah's head. "It's all right, Sarah," she said. "Everything will be all right."

· 4 · | DOUBTS AND ARGUMENTS

"Over here," came the voice from behind the thorn trees, and Bannock laughed at the cloak-and-dagger measures as he carefully steered Pot Pourri away from the track, through the maze of dry gray prongs, hoping all the while that the noise of shelling from the far side of town would not frighten her into a confrontation with the thorns.

"You're quite a practiced old spy, aren't you, Mr. MacGrath?" said Bannock as he came upon the large man, who cut a surprisingly fashionable figure on his big horse, in bowler hat, tweed hacking jacket, and mahogany top boots.

The fat, bewhiskered face was smiling. "Please understand," he said, "I am not accustomed to lurking behind bushes, and until recently I was not accustomed to dealing with riders in the night. But since you were so insistent upon seeing me, I felt the degree of privacy should not be overemphasized. So let's hear what it is you have to say, without further delay."

"The army knows what I'm doing. They want me to go on doing it, but report to them on the side."

"Who in the army?"

"Major Masefield."

126

"Ah, yes; Masefield. I've had dealings with him. He was most put out on hearing that Cecil Rhodes was being regularly quoted in the London newspapers. He wanted to know why we could get through so easily while the army had trouble even getting messages to the Modder River. What we are doing is against military regulations, you know."

"What did you tell him?"

"Denied everything. He tried to trick me; almost succeeded. An extremely clever fellow, Masefield. It seems you handled yourself quite cleverly, too. You impress me, Bannock. I am very pleased with you, although I must admit to a degree of surprise that Masefield was not able to merely convince you to do what he wanted without divulging it to me. Maybe you can explain that."

"You pay better."

"That sounds a very human attitude." MacGrath nevertheless seemed skeptical.

"And they've taken three of my horses. They have my stallion as a hostage. But don't worry, the money isn't everything. My impression of Major Masefield isn't very good. He's an evil sod. They should send him out on patrol and let him sweat off some of his self-confidence and lose a bit of excess weight at the same time."

MacGrath looked reflectively down at his own large stomach. He smiled. "Never underestimate fat, shrewd men, Mr. Bannock. Maybe they mean something quite literal when they talk about food for thought. How are you to pass our messages on to them?"

"That hasn't been worked out yet."

"Well, I'm quite sure we can work out some shortcut of our own. You secrete our sealed dispatches somewhere and hand them a few innocent envelopes and newspapers, something like that."

"You realize, of course, that they will want me to carry messages for them as well now."

"I see no harm in that."

"So you want me to continue?"

"Oh, good gracious me, yes. To stop would mean you have reported to me, and arouse suspicion. In any event, most of our communications are relatively innocent. I think you must understand that our objectives are essentially no different from those of the army. We are all working for the same cause, though of necessity not quite together. There can be no secret that Mr. Rhodes is a little impatient with the progress of the local military staff. He wants action. He wants an end to the siege. He wants the mines back in operation. He wants dynamite and coal coming in. He does not want ten thousand African laborers standing idle. Essentially, he wants the relief column as soon as possible. And believe me, he is in a position to influence it at the highest levels. He has his own vast empire to account for, and there should be no reason why he should have to tolerate unnecessary censorship or interference. If you knew Rhodes, you would understand why he will not be made impotent by the usual confusion of officialdom. The essential difference between the dispatches you will be carrying for them and those you carry for us is that theirs are reports going out and instructions coming in from the General Staff down south. The generals must be seen to be running things. On our side, we are communicating at the highest political and military level in London and in the Cape. So whereas the army dispatches are of scant interest to us, ours must not get into their hands."

"Understood."

"So there you have it, Bannock. You are now a double agent, engaging in double talk with a fat, shrewd major on the one hand and an even fatter and, I trust, shrewder company official on the other. So just go on doing what you are doing until they stop you. You are doing an excellent job. If all goes according to plan, the relief column will be here soon. We are working on it."

They listened to the distant whining and thumping of the shelling. It had become a routine occurrence. Each day the Boers bombed one chosen target; each day saw people and animals, military personnel and their equipment moving out of the target area. The interview was over.

"Good day, Bannock, and good luck with your ride tonight. Now I shall attempt to sneak out this way."

Bannock turned and maneuvered Pot Pourri carefully in the opposite direction, toward the racecourse. He smiled to himself when the other big horse jumped and bucked as it scraped the thorns. The mare carried her head high, fighting to better a stiff canter, and even at that pace she turned her intelligent head outward listening for the gunfire, flicking an ear for each far-off report and each answering bang from the Kimberley batteries.

When the racecourse came into view, there were two strange horses tethered at the stables. More visitors. O'Flaherty was right: the place was becoming a general meeting point. Was it Stevenson back for another threatened duel?

As Bannock rode in, he recognized both animals. One was Sarah's, with the familiar sidesaddle; the other, Masefield's cob. But neither of their riders was anywhere to be seen.

Bannock dismounted and followed O'Flaherty's grooming whistle to where he found him on one of the loose boxes, busily brushing Lady Potter.

"Where are these people?" he asked.

O'Flaherty went on brushing. "The major went off someplace. I couldn't be tellin' you where he went. The lady arrived later, and she's to be found right where you'd expect." He stopped brushing and inclined his head. "Over there in your sleepin' quarters."

O'Flaherty returned to his whistling and brushing while Bannock set off for the grandstand. Sarah appeared as he approached, leaning in the doorway of the bar, looking none too friendly, tapping her riding crop onto the folds of her skirt.

She began speaking before he got up to her.

"I don't know what to make of you, Bartholomew. You seem to be out for all you can get."

Bannock recognized a female crisis when he saw one. "What's your problem, Sarah?"

"My problem"—she arched her head back to avoid his eyes—"is you and what I'm hearing about you. Your sordid reputation has arrived from Cape Town."

"And you would like me to explain it all to you?"

"Not at all." She kept her head up and turned away. "It's all been explained. What does need to be explained is your latest attempt at womanizing. You must learn to know when to keep your hands off."

"What are you talking about?" Bannock knew what she was talking about and didn't like it.

"You know what I'm talking about, Bartholomew. You've known a lot of women, I'm sure—at least a lot of common sluts. That's where your talents lie. That's where your techniques are most effective. You must learn to stay in your own territory. You're a slut man, aren't you?"

Bannock began to laugh in spite of himself. "Come now, Sarah, there's only one technique. You should know there's nothing different about me."

"How modest of you." Sarah maintained her aloof pose, but the crop swung in agitated jerks behind her.

Bannock might have been amused, but he attacked. "You lay them out and hold on tight and give it to them, straight as a lance and hard as a hammer. It works for the elegant ladies as much as for the sluts, with legs open, mouth open, everything open. That's the rule of the bed."

"Shut up, you vulgar pig."

"You're quite right. I've done my bit, on top and underneath, back to front, standing up, bending down, and rolling around."

"You think you're very clever, don't you?" Sarah was not ready to let her anger go.

"No, I think it's always women who believe they are so clever. They imagine that once they've got a man to bed they've got him, but isn't it sad, all they've got is themselves. The truth is, they don't get him, he gets them."

"You know nothing of reasonable women and reasonable men. You are a whorer, that's all."

"What does that make you, Sarah?"

Sarah seethed and said nothing. Bannock was becoming bored with the situation.

"All right, Sarah, why don't you just tell me what you came about."

"I thought you could explain a few things. You've been seeing my sister?"

"I think it would be more correct to say your sister has been to see me."

"What about?"

"That is confidential."

"Indeed. But you did see Emma and you did lay your grubby hands on her."

"Nonsense."

"I happen to know that, but I'm not sure Emma's husband knows that." She paused and emphasized, "Yet."

Bannock shrugged. "I don't give a damn who knows. I don't give a damn about any of you. Your insinuations are a lot of nonsense and you know it. What kind of sister are you, anyway?"

"You don't give a damn about Emma?" she challenged, with a thin smile.

"Yes, if I were to consider anybody, it would be her. She's a nice little lady."

"And you find her quite attractive," she goaded.

"Yes, very attractive," he gave back.

"Isn't it a pity she has a husband?"

"Yes."

Still the threatening smile. "Well, you'd better pray he doesn't find out about this, because you would no longer be dealing with ladies you can exploit but a gentleman of a caliber you could not even begin to understand. He will deal with you and dispose of you as he sees fit."

Bannock was unimpressed. "Go home, Sarah. Go tell him whatever it is you wish to tell him. Just get the hell out of here, will you?"

He was on the point of turning away when Sarah stepped out into the open and struck at him with the crop, catching him across the face. He shook his head and turned back instinctively. She lashed out again and again, but his arm was up to ward off the blows.

"Go home, Sarah. If you don't go now, I'll give you the thrashing you deserve."

Sarah was white-faced and out of breath. "You've caused all the trouble you will be allowed to cause," she got out hoarsely. "You will presently be put in your place."

She rushed off toward her horse, the blond hair shining, the riding habit swinging about her long legs, and Bannock felt a slight pang of remorse at the loss of a beautiful body. He also felt suspicious about the whereabouts of Masefield, seeing the large horse again tethered beside Sarah's. If he had only known, all he had to do was look up.

While Sarah rode away, Masefield was still leaning on the top of the grandstand, watching over the back, from where he had listened to every word of the conversation. He called down to Bannock.

"What an interesting fellow you turned out to be. All you have to do now is arrange a secret assignation with the mother and you'll have the whole family on their backs."

Bannock regarded the fat, smiling major relaxing on the rail above.

"Do you always lurk in the background and listen to private conversations?"

Masefield chuckled. "Have you ever punched a woman? Come on, tell me."

Bannock turned and walked away.

Masefield called after him, "You're a study, do you know that? You're a study."

* * *

The waiter came from the bar of the Kimberley Club balancing the tray of drinks on one hand, striding noiselessly down the passage of plum-colored drapes and polished teak. He was on the point of entering the smoking room when he heard the whine of a shell and paused, holding the tray with both hands in expectation. The explosion took place somewhere in the distance, but with enough force to set the glass chandelier tinkling. The waiter continued on his way toward the two officers in the far corner of the room.

Geoffrey Stevenson waited, saying nothing while the drinks were poured and the man went away. Then he looked up at Colonel Thrumpton, making no attempt to hide his impatience.

"I am not sure that I follow your drift, sir. Am I to be disciplined in some way?"

"Good heavens, no; quite the opposite."

"Then let me try to understand what you are saying. It sounds as if you are criticizing my behavior in action."

"No, no, not criticizing. I have started off here very badly. I do wish that Staff would handle their own subtle suggestions."

They both paused and listened to the whining flight of a shell, which exploded farther away than the first.

Colonel Thrumpton took a reflective sip. "Now listen here, Geoffrey, I have just remembered there is a perfect way to illustrate the point. Would you take the word of Robert Berkeley on anything?"

"Well, yes, of course I would."

"Commanding officers in the field miss very little. He thought a lot of you."

"I am flattered." Stevenson looked appropriately down at his glass.

"But he was concerned for you. At the time when your exploits in Matebeleland were reported in the London papers, he confided in me that he thought you a bit . . . how shall I say . . . ?"

"A bit reckless, no doubt," Stevenson suggested patiently.

"No, it was more than that. He thought you a little obsessive at times."

"Obsessive?" Stevenson plainly disliked the word.

"Do not misunderstand; let me quote him as my memory serves. He said you carried the saber like a symbol, like a flag."

Stevenson laughed in apparent disbelief. "How should I carry a saber?" he asked.

"I think what he meant was that you took that sword as seriously as a gun, that it put you in danger. That, in short, you are too brave for your own good."

"Oh, really, sir." Stevenson smiled, but his patience was wearing thin.

"He intimated that you were extremely lucky to come out of the campaign alive."

Stevenson leaned forward and glared at the old man.

"What kind of suggestion is that to a British officer?" he demanded. "Are you suggesting that a cavalry officer should hold back in some way? Are you suggesting that my first priority in battle is to save my own life? I know a lot of dead British officers who would not take kindly to that idea."

Stevenson sat very straight and very still, the almost imperceptible twitch at work in the corner of his mouth. As he grew more tense, the old man seemed to become calmer, less intimidated.

He said, "The discretion that keeps you alive also keeps you fighting."

Stevenson's voice rose to a sharp pitch. "Oh yes, of course," he said, "live to fight another day and all that."

"Now hold on, Geoffrey, if I have upset you it is only that I've not expressed myself very well. Can I tell you something else that might help, about a bird I go hunting after? It's called a coucal, and if I could describe its beautiful call to you, you would know it right away. Its uniqueness lies in that one keeps hearing it but seldom sees it."

"I take it there's some special significance for me in this bird story."

"Hear me out, my boy. You could say the coucal is an expert coward." Thrumpton sipped his drink and watched his staring companion carefully. "But who can judge the good judgment of a bird that survives? It knows its own strength and challenges nothing bigger than itself. Yet it is a king in the world of birds, and the terror of all rodents and other creatures smaller than it. It hugs its own territory, creates its own siege, always remaining in the defensive ring of its own making. Be a coucal, Geoffrey."

"You are suggesting that I be an expert coward?"

"No, simply that you use enough judgment to survive. You have done enough in the past, and you are needed for the future." The old man leaned forward, gray eyebrows and wrinkles contracting together. "I mean to say, you can do nothing if you are dead."

Stevenson maintained his icy formality. "With respect, sir, you are preaching a very simple sermon."

"Grant me a moment more of your respect, and listen to an old coucal who takes no particular pride in his own survival. I'm sorry to say this, Geoffrey, but I must put it plainly. You not fighting primitive savages now, you are fighting men with guns who can aim. To stand up in their sights is to die. You are not here to sacrifice your life in that way. You are here to lead and inspire those fellows behind you."

Stevenson leaned across to pick up his saber in its scabbard from the chair beside him. He held it out in his hands like an offering.

"If this is a flag or a symbol to the men, it is a pretty bloody one. You should see their faces when this blade comes out. Suddenly, they want to see blood, they want to kill. You should see the faces of the enemy when the sword and lances are out. In half the time it takes to load a gun, a good horse can cover five lengths of its own body, and within an instant of that time, the saber does its work." The long scabbard shook slightly in his hands. "The point you have made, Colonel, is quite wasted, because I am not a suicidal idiot. But I must put it to you that I know of no way of carrying a fight to the point of confrontation without going out in the open and fighting and striking with any weapon that comes to hand." Stevenson was trembling and breathing heavily. "And by the way," he said, "the Matebele had rifles, plenty of them."

"Is this the saber?" Colonel Thrumpton asked quietly.

Stevenson slammed the sword down on the table and answered loudly, "This is a saber like hundreds of others," then, realizing he was shouting, lowered his voice. "You want to know if this is the weapon I did all my cutting down with? The answer is yes, yes, yes, it is."

Thrumpton picked up the sword and examined it. He pulled the blade slightly from the scabbard and slammed it shut again, smiling at the younger man. "Geoffrey," he said.

"Yes, sir." Stevenson was making a conscious effort to control his breathing.

"Do not place your life in the hands of this anachronism."

The only visible sign of life was a large group of Boer horsemen silhouetted on the brow of a low hill to the west. But there were sounds. The darkness was alive with it all around, sinister noises so subtle that he could not identify them, and for the present he was satisfied to keep very still and listen.

Bannock had to study a new attitude in himself on these night rides, a new nervousness. From the moment he had ridden out the previous evening, there was a continuous sense of danger. Always noise, and not always in the distance. Voices close at hand that brought him to a standstill again and again. Foreign, guttural words, in that Boer language he had heard so little of. The movement of horses, often galloping in clattering chorus, that he recognized as the short-paced stocky movers he had seen previously. At one time he had hidden among rocks and watched a movement of artillery in astonishment. There must have been a hundred guns at least, drawn at a furious pace toward the Kimberley positions. The days of the desultory siege were over. The Boers meant business, and it was obvious that the myth of the band of ragged farmers was about to be exploded.

Bannock watched the outline of the Boer commando on the hill. They were standing still in loose formation, most of them having dismounted. They were waiting. What unnerved him was that others must be waiting who could not be seen.

He strained to see in the dark, yet wished that dawn would never come when he could see and be seen. The undetectable noises were still there—not horses, not marching. It was a soft hissing and murmuring, behind and in front and to the east. There had been a long volley of rifle fire from the Kimberley fortifications ahead, accompanied by distant shouts and screams. And then silence. And then, once again, the eerie sounds.

Bannock talked soothingly to his nervous mare, stroking her shivering nose, walking her slowly, his left hand at her mouth, his right hand holding the reins at the withers, ready to mount and ride at the first sign of danger.

His usual night senses deserted him in the face of these inexplicable signs: the murmuring, the strong scent of cattle dung, the characteristic smell of native perspiration. There were sounds of oxen lowing, but farther ahead.

He pulled up short as he heard muttering voices just in front of him and went down on his haunches to look for silhouettes against the graying sky. And then he saw them: heads of men who were squatting or kneeling, endless swarms of them. There were wide eyes staring at him from only a few yards away. Some were greeting him: "*Hau, nkosi.*"

His first instinct was to mount and gallop away in the opposite direction, but the great murmuring hiss he had first heard from behind was coming closer, closing in on him. He was surrounded by a swarm of dark figures.

The squatting natives in front stood up, keeping a respectful distance from the excited horse. They seemed to be clearing a path for him. There was a message being passed forward into the darkness, becoming a sibilant note in the distance. Bannock went carefully forward, leading Pot Pourri down the black, silent passage until there was a stirring again and footsteps approached from in front, and he heard a low, urgent voice giving orders to all those around. The voice came close and Bannock stopped, to be confronted by a great black man in khaki bush shirt and shorts, shining muscles bulging out of the tight sleeves.

"*Nkosi,*" the man greeted him. "I know your face. You are the man of the racecourse. I am Mabala, the chief."

Bannock was impressed, and relieved at the friendly reception. "You are chief of all these people?"

Mabala laughed. "No, these are the Basuto, the Mpondo, the Shangaan; these are all the tribes who are mine boys. I am Mabala, the Zulu Induna who is here when their chiefs are not here. They listen to me. I am their mine chief. Why are you riding here in the night? You are brave. Are you not afraid of the Boers? They will kill you."

"Yes, Mabala, they will kill me if they see me."

"You are clever to come in the dark."

"I must get back to Kimberley before it is light."

Mabala grabbed his shoulder. "Come," he said. "We go together."

The passage opened again and Bannock followed the big African, leading Pot Pourri at a fast walk. The first faint light was coming from the horizon, and he realized they were in the middle of a horde of thousands of natives, all on the move toward the Kimberley perimeter.

The light increased and Bannock became anxious about the telltale height of his horse standing out above the moving crowd, but they were closer to the perimeter than he had judged. As the path continued to open, they could see the lookout post of the reservoir redoubt just ahead.

"Climb on your horse, *nkosi*. I will lead you."

Mabala helped Bannock up and took a firm hold of Pot Pourri's reluctant mouth.

"You know horses," said Bannock.

"I rode in the native corps at Ulundi," said Mabala proudly. "I owned my own horse."

Mounted men had ridden out from the redoubt and were patrolling the front of the advancing horde.

"You there," shouted one of the horsemen, riding into the oncoming throng toward Bannock.

"I am carrying dispatches," Bannock shouted, holding up his new army passbook.

The soldier came up to him. "Report to the duty officer at the redoubt, if you please," he ordered.

"I don't report to anybody," said Bannock. "I have my own orders."

Bannock's remark took the soldier by surprise. He covered his embarrassment by swinging his crop at the crowded natives. "Make way, make way," he shouted.

There was an angry murmur from all around, and Mabala snapped an order that produced immediate silence. Another minute brought Pot Pourri clear of the crowd, and Bannock was pulled up short, shocked at the scene in front of him. Town Guards were busy loading the bodies of dead Africans onto a cart.

The soldier drew up again. "We thought it was a Boer attack," he said. "It was still dark, there was no warning. We didn't know."

"Where do all these people come from?" Bannock directed his question at Mabala.

"The mines wanted these people to go back to their homes," said Mabala. "They say it is war now, not mines.

They say there is no food for natives. We must all go home. I had to go with them to lead them in the dark. The Boers, they stopped us. They said, go back. Then the soldiers shoot."

Bannock shook his head in disgust at the bloody sight.

The soldier gestured with his crop. "Will you move along, please? We have to get this lot into town."

"I am grateful to you, Mabala," said Bannock.

"I will see your face again, *nkosi.*"

Mabala saluted as Bannock turned his horse and cantered toward the racecourse. He was hungry, thirsty and depressed, and in no mood for the open cart with trigger-happy Town Guardsmen on the back that swerved around in front of the oncoming Africans to block his path.

"Let him through," came a shout from the soldier who had first apprehended him. But he was already right in front of them, holding up his military pass.

"What's it like out there?" asked the driver curiously.

"Dark," snapped Bannock. He reined Pot Pourri past them and cantered on.

He rode round the southern rail and up to the courtyard of the racecourse as the first red of dawn touched the roofs of the grandstand and the stables. He was about to shout for Van Breda to get up and start the fire when he noticed that there were two men with their horses waiting under the thorn trees at the off-saddling enclosure. One of them approached him as he dismounted in front of the stables. He heard him say, "Wait there, Mark, if you don't mind. I shall handle this on my own."

Bannock groaned at the sound of Stevenson's voice and waited for him to come up, spurs clinking, hand on the hilt of his sword, the perfect picture of a cavalry officer.

"We found your bed unslept in. One assumes you were up to your mischief in some other bed last night."

"What are you talking about?" Bannock was momentarily taken aback. He began to tie Pot Pourri's reins purposefully to the hitching rail, holding back from the instinct to punch. But he needed to find out what Stevenson was getting at.

"I am talking about your womanizing exploits. About your expert ability for getting on the right side of pretty women. I am talking, in fact, about my wife, sir. No, not sir—bastard. Seducer—damned seducer."

"Your wife?" For a moment Bannock was confused. He thought about the implication of her visit, but Stevenson was not waiting for explanations.

"Yes, my wife," Stevenson blurted out furiously. "It was bad enough having to stand aside while my sister-in-law made a fool of herself with you, but my wife? Oh, no, that is another matter."

"You'd better get out of here before I do you an injury." Bannock spoke quietly, the warning signal for the worst of his temper.

"Do me an injury? What nonsense. What right have you to become violent?"

The end stable door swung open and Bannock saw O'Flaherty stagger out half-asleep and stare in their direction.

"What the devil is going on?" O'Flaherty demanded.

"It's all right, Paddy. Keep off, I don't need you," said Bannock, turning back to Stevenson. "Now you get out of here," he threatened. But there was a flash of metal, and he found himself looking into the point of Stevenson's saber.

Freestone-Grant called out, "Geoffrey, I say, hold on there."

"Stay out of this, Mark," Stevenson answered hoarsely.

Bannock watched the end of the sword. It was shaking, vibrating to the fury of the man who held it.

"Now listen," Stevenson said hoarsely. "This weapon has killed brave and honest men. It would think nothing of disposing of a rogue like you."

"If you don't put your silly sword away, you're going to die with it in your hand."

Stevenson's eyes were fixed on Bannock's Even after he heard the metallic click below, it took some time before it registered and he looked down.

Bannock held his heavy service revolver fully cocked and pointed at Stevenson's stomach. Bannock watched the sword shaking in front of him, and watched Stevenson's face in amazement. It was contorted, twitching; his eyelids were flickering.

"If you want to die, try a stab," said Bannock.

O'Flaherty had come up and was standing to one side, staring in disbelief. Freestone-Grant came running toward them.

"Have you both gone mad?" he asked, boggling at the weapons.

Bannock said, "Will you explain to your friend that if he's having a duel, he's on the losing side. And will you also explain to him that I am not interested in his sister-in-law, or his wife, or any of his bloody family, for that matter."

Stevenson shrugged off Freestone-Grant's hand, but he was staring into space. Slowly, he focused on Bannock again. "I was told only yesterday not to place my life in the hands of this weapon. All that remains is for you to shoot me and prove that rather obvious piece of advice to be true."

"For God's sake, Geoffrey," Freestone-Grant appealed to him. "Calm down, old chap. Put the sword away."

Bannock replaced his revolver in the holster under his leather coat, and the sword slowly went down. He watched the twitch at the corner of Stevenson's mouth, realizing that there was something very wrong with the man. There was something equally wrong with what he was saying. As much as he wanted him to finish this affair, Bannock was curious to know what had caused the outburst and how exactly Stevenson's wife was involved. She had said he was under a great strain, would never have behaved like this in the normal way. He thought back: that beautiful face, the expression in her eyes, it was desperation. The man he was facing was not normal.

"What did you do with my wife?" Stevenson asked weakly, and it dawned on Bannock that he had come here without his wife's knowledge. There was some confusion, some mischief. No one had known about her coming here. Except Sarah.

"You don't seem to be communicating properly with your wife," said Bannock. "She came here with one intention, to uphold your good name. That's the advantage of having a good name in the first place. I, as you know, have a bad name, which you seem intent on making worse."

"What did my wife say to you?"

Bannock was beyond care of discretion. "She came to pay me for the horse you cheated me out of."

Stevenson stared in disbelief. "Why on earth would she do that?" he said, almost to himself.

"She said you were a man of honor who would never normally do a thing like that."

"I can't believe it," said Stevenson.

"Well, believe it or not, go and discuss it with your wife. Leave me out of it."

It was as if Stevenson became conscious of Bannock once again. "You are quite right," he said. "What I say to my wife is my own business. She plainly misunderstands this situation. But let us be sure that you understand it. That horse I have of yours is out doing duty, defending the town and saving your useless neck."

"Before you go any further," said Bannock. "I'm going to show you something."

He went to his horse and snapped open the near saddlebag, pulling out a wad of envelopes and newspapers.

"Take a look at this," he said angrily, coming back to face Stevenson. "Look at that," he said, holding an official envelope in front of Stevenson's face. "Would you like to read the latest news from the outside world?" He held up the folded newspapers and fanned them out. "Well, you can't. They are confidential and not for mere officers to look at." Now Bannock was shouting. "And that"—he pointed to the saddle—"is the bed I've been sleeping in all night. Bringing the messages that are going to save your bloody useless neck. Shall I tell you what I think now? I think your wife is a woman who can be trusted and I think your sister-in-law, Sarah, is incapable of being mishandled. She can handle her seduction scenes perfectly well on her own. And if you don't get away from here right now, I'll ask Paddy O'Flaherty here to save me the trouble of putting you out of action for the duration."

Freestone-Grant put his hand on Stevenson's arm again. "Come, Geoffrey, I think we should leave."

But Stevenson remained staring at Bannock for some time. He put his hand to the corner of his mouth as if he had just become conscious of the twitch, then turned abruptly and marched toward the horses, with his brother-in-law following, looking anxiously at him and then back at Bannock.

As if to send them on their way, the morning shelling started somewhere over to the north. Stevenson had trouble mounting Parader, who reacted to the heavy thump of the cannon fire by scrambling around in a circle, forcing him to jump and swing himself into the saddle. In a demonstration of good horsemanship, Stevenson turned Parader and held the other horse's head while Freestone-Grant mounted, then found his stirrups and cantered away.

O'Flaherty watched in disgust. "I never thought I'd see the day that grand thoroughbred was made to look like an army moke. We could have kept that horse," he complained. "All you had to do was be tellin' them that I was also dispatch ridin' and we could have kept that horse. You can still demand that. Do you hear me?"

Bannock was watching the two retreating riders. "I told you," he said absently, "your duty is here with Van and the horses."

"I'm the very man to be doin' that kind of work,"

O'Flaherty went on complaining. "When it comes to creepin' in the dark with never a sound, there's nobody can match me."

Van Breda appeared with tin mugs of steaming coffee, and Bannock gestured gratefully. They stood sipping and listening to the thump and whine and explosions of the distant shelling. But there was another sound, a deep, resonant murmur of native voices. It was growing louder, and they could be seen approaching the southern rail of the course, a great, red scene colored by the dawn, the figures and everything around matching the deep red color of the ground. The three men turned to watch.

O'Flaherty said, "Where would all these people be comin' from? Do you realize they'll be comin' through here? You won't be able to see for dust."

"Mine natives," explained Bannock. "De Beers sent them out and the Boers sent them back. There's no work for them here. God knows what they're going to do with them."

The approaching mob moved and wavered like a nervous shoal of fish as three batteries fired in quick succession from the south, the whine of the shells echoing back to indicate a target somewhere in the area of the reservoir. The smaller guns at the perimeter had begun to answer, and Van Breda ran to calm Pot Pourri, who almost pulled the hitching rail away.

"I have to deliver the mail." Bannock handed over his empty mug and went to mount up, but waited when he noticed the mule cart that had stopped him earlier careering around the southern rail in front of the natives and heading straight for the stables.

The cart drew up. Mabala was on the back with the Town Guardsmen. He smiled broadly and greeted Bannock as he jumped off. The driver of the cart pointed down at him with his whip and addressed Bannock.

"This is Mabala," he said. "He was with mine security. He has been put in charge of this lot that's coming in. The orders are for most of the natives to be billeted on the racecourse."

"Billeted here? In what?" asked Bannock.

"In tents. The army is sending down hundreds of tents later today. You'll have to move. It's the end of the racecourse, that's certain. Once the blacks move in, they use cow dung for their floors. The smell will drive you out."

O'Flaherty laughed. "We've been after livin' with horse dung and cow dung all our lives. We'll not be worryin' about that."

"Have you ever smelled a thousand bush blacks in one place?" sneered the cart driver, and the group of Town Guardsmen on the back of the cart sniggered.

O'Flaherty was not giving up. "What's goin' to happen to these poor souls now that the minin' has stopped?"

"It's not going to be easy for them," said the cart driver. "The army pays them one pound for every head of cattle they can steal from the Boers, and they can sell their illicit diamonds. It's amazing how they can hide diamonds. You can search them and there's nothing. They hide them under stones and go back for them. But diamonds only buy money. And if the food gets shorter, money won't buy food."

"Are we ordered to leave?" asked Bannock.

"Not that I know of," said the cart driver. "But if you want to stay, talk to Mabala. He's responsible for them settling down here."

Bannock was not satisfied. "Why can't these people go back to the native camp?" he asked.

"They've pulled it all down."

"That's crazy," said Bannock. "Tents are no protection against shrapnel."

"What are you worrying about? The Boer cannons are mostly on Carter's Ridge. You're right out of the way here."

"For your information, they are setting up batteries right round the southern perimeter."

"Then you'd better start hiding in your stables, mister."

Bannock was not amused. "Thanks for all your advice. You can go now."

The man laughed. He cracked his whip, and the mule cart raised a cloud of dust as it rumbled away behind the galloping mules toward the entrance of the racecourse.

Mabala had moved off and was shouting orders to the native mob, directing them toward the racecourse proper. He came back smiling broadly and saluted Bannock again.

"There is no trouble," he said. "Mabala speaks, my people follow. They know Mabala will lead them right."

Bannock asked him, "Mabala, how do you steal cattle? The Boers must have guards."

Mabala smiled, showing a massive set of pure white teeth. "They have guards," he said. "We go at night. Can a gun see at night?"

"Sometimes it can."

"That is right. Sometimes it is not easy. Sometimes it is easy. The Boers, they sleep at night. There are only one or two guards. When they are on this side, we go on that side." He gestured like a semaphore signaler. "When they are on that side, we go on this side. We talk very softly to the ox. And slowly, slowly, we say, Now walk, now slow, now stop, now walk again. Sometimes, when they make only a little noise, we can steal them. It is easy. But sometimes they say moo-ah, and we must run. Sometimes one or two men are caught. Then we never see them."

"When you bring the cattle in, you sell them to the army?"

Mabala grinned. "We sell two, we eat one."

"What do they pay you for an ox?"

"One pound."

"Is that what your life is worth?"

Mabala shrugged and stopped grinning.

Bannock went to unhitch Pot Pourri. Mabala followed

to help him mount, trying to take the reins, but Van Breda was there already and the big Zulu bumped into him.

"Sorry, small *nkosi,*" said Mabala, looking down at the jockey half his size.

"He can't speak," said Bannock, moving a finger across his mouth to demonstrate the fact.

Mabala looked down at Van Breda with great concern. Van Breda made the same motion with his fingers over his mouth, and Mabala did likewise, and they both nodded in understanding.

Bannock was in the saddle, smiling down at the big African. "You helped me this morning. I am grateful."

Mabala held onto the reins. "I am your man, *nkosi.* I will watch your horses. Groom, brush, clean leather, make them shine."

Bannock laughed. "But you are a chief," he said.

"I am a chief, you are a chief. I help you, you help me."

"Done," said Bannock. He turned his horse to go and called back over his shoulder, "We'll all work together."

Mabala stood, chest out with pride, a Zulu giant who towered above even the tall O'Flaherty.

O'Flaherty leaned against the stable wall trying to look nonchalant, but only succeeding in looking his most cunning.

"Now, Mr. Mabala," he tried, "there's a small question I'll be askin' you meself. It's about them diamonds."

"Diamonds?"

"Sure. Them little stones your people are always hidin'. That's the story I've been hearin'. The workers sneak them out, swallow them or whatever they do."

Mabala thumbed behind his thick leather belt and brought out a small pouch, which he shook into the palm of his hand. O'Flaherty and Van Breda leaned forward, staring. Mabala lowered his palm to allow them a glimpse of its contents.

"You're not sayin' that's a diamond?" O'Flaherty carefully picked up the biggest of three stones, about the size of a small pea.

"A-one stone," announced Mabala.

O'Flaherty frowned at the small, dull stone. "Looks more like a piece of broken glass."

"Pure white. Clear."

"You don't say? And where would you be gettin' such a stone?"

"You let me help you with the horses. I am a Zulu rider. The Zulu in the mountains ride like the Basuto. I had my own horse," Mabala said proudly.

"Would you be wantin' to sell this little stone?"

"No, *nkosi.* It is for my family"

O'Flaherty put the diamond back in the waiting palm. "Those fellows on the racecourse," he said, "they must also have stones."

"Someone, they got stones," agreed Mabala. "But another one, you must watch. They got stones, look like this but no good."

"How can you tell?" asked O'Flaherty, fascinated.

"Some got white quartz. Look just like this."

"This white quartz, is that no good?"

"No good. Just like other stones on the ground. You hold white quartz in the sun. Is like milk. And some got glass."

"Sure well, that looks just like glass to me, so how can I tell?"

"Glass is small weight." Mabala held up both palms as if they were the pans of a scale.

"Light?" suggested O'Flaherty.

"Light, yes. Glass light, Diamond heavy."

"But you didn't answer my question just now," said O'Flaherty.

"You let me help with the horses." Mabala's mind was on one thing and O'Flaherty's on another. "I bring good

Basuto horse boys. They clean stable, make feed, everything."

"Sure, that's good news, Mr. Mabala. But I'll be remindin' you of that question. Where would you be gettin' these stones?"

"Sometimes down the mine. You break the rock and there you see it."

"Don't they search you?"

"Right, Mabala head security boy. I catch mine boy. Give stones to security officer." Mabala smiled disarmingly. "Sometimes I not give stones to security officer."

"What a sensible idea," said O'Flaherty thoughtfully. "We must talk more about this, Mr. Mabala. There's a friend of mine and meself who are interested in the diamond business. An Italian chef, fine fellow."

"He is a chief?" asked Mabala.

"Yes, you could say that." O'Flaherty nodded seriously. "In a manner of speakin', he is a chief."

"Must I call my men for the horses?"

"I have a piece of bad news for you, Mr. Mabala. There are only three horses, and one of them is a mule and one of them is out. So two men will do. If you'd like to call one man now, we can be standin' here watchin' him get on with the job."

The saber struck the railing, and in grabbing for it Stevenson slipped and hung onto the banister, breathing heavily, trying to shake his head clear.

Slowly, he turned to face the last few stairs and the long, gloomy passage lit by the weak yellow glow of one lamp.

Even when he climbed slowly, the spur chains made their noise. They continued to ring quietly with every unsteady step of his boots along the passageway, past the family's private living room, to the door of his own room, Emma's room.

He stood there facing the door, breathing in slowly, straightening himself up. One hand went out to the door-knob, hesitated, and withdrew. Both hands began fumbling with the belt buckle.

He swayed back, leaning onto a picture frame, which crashed to the floor.

A door opened soundlessly farther along the passage and Stevenson was observed by Sarah through the narrow opening. She saw the tall figure swaying in the dim light. He remained where he was for some time, as if expecting to be discovered, then, tucking the belt and sword under one arm, he walked away, the spurs clinking faintly with each step until he turned and disappeared into the living room.

Sarah heard the door of the living room close. She watched Emma's door, listening for any other sound. But the handle remained still, and nothing else stirred.

Carefully opening her own door, Sarah stepped into the passage, where she stopped to throw a shawl about her shoulders.

There was still no sound. She clutched the wool together at her neck and crossed over to Emma's door noise-lessly on her bare feet to listen, ear to the join.

Satisfied that Emma was asleep, she went furtively on tiptoe to the door of the living room, turned the handle, and pushed the door open.

She could see Stevenson in the moonlight from the window, struggling to remove his boots. He stopped when he became aware of her in the doorway, the dim light from the hall exposing the shape of her long, slim legs through the thin nightdress.

"Geoffrey," she whispered in her smallest voice, "is anything amiss?"

"Only that I'm a little drunk. I need to rest, I think." He watched the shape of the legs he had never seen.

She hung on at the door. "You were in the field today?"

He sat, still holding one boot, his face hidden in the

dark. The tired voice answered, "You could say we went for an exercise canter. We went out with murder in our hearts . . . and ran into confusion . . . disengage and retreat. . . . It's fast becoming the order of the day. . . . As you say, we were in the field, but hardly in action."

"So you decided to drown your irritation?"

Stevenson watched the legs move gracefully one pace forward. The small voice again. "What would you like most in the world at this moment?"

There was no answer.

"A drink?" She whispered the invitation and waited. "Why not?"

The legs merged into shadow as Sarah closed the door behind her and leaned back on it. The room was left in darkness save for a shaft of pale light from the moon that silhouetted Stevenson at the window seat.

He still held on to the boot. He could see nothing, hear nothing, until she appeared in the shaft of light right in front of him.

"Let me help you," she whispered, going down and pulling at the other boot.

"Geoffrey, do you remember on day at Birchleigh when I was a child and you were already in uniform? I had those ridiculous ringlets and you looked at me . . . for a long time."

They both worked at the boot.

"Your hair was a miracle. You were very beautiful. Everyone looked at you."

"Strange that I should particularly remember the way you looked at me. And not just that one time. Do you remember dancing with me? Quite closely?"

"Sarah. My head is reeling."

"Lie down, my dear friend, lie down." She gently pushed at his chest until he lay back flat on the window seat. "Shall I fetch that drink for you?"

He sighed deeply. "I think not, Sarah. Maybe you

should go. It would not look right if someone came in."

"They are all asleep. And you need attending to." Her hands came to his neck and she began to unbutton his tunic.

Stevenson lay passive and wordless, watching the loose blond hair glinting above him in the moonlight.

"Your wife should be doing this," she whispered.

"Sarah, you must not misunderstand. . . . It would seem that I am at odds with everyone, but my problem is merely myself. I think you should make your way back to bed, my dear girl."

The small voice became teasing. "Who could you possibly have problems with? I will fight them all."

"It's come down to this, where old Thrumpton reads me a lecture."

"Oh, dear old man, why bother about that? Who else?" She had unbuttoned his tunic and laid a soft hand on the shirt over his chest.

"It's of no importance." His voice slurred with tiredness.

"Let me think of who could give you trouble. Bartholomew Bannock?"

"No, no. That matter is about to be settled."

"Emma? Is it Emma?"

"Sarah . . . I would rather you did not mention Emma. If you don't mind."

"When we were children, when you said I was beautiful, was I more beautiful than Emma? Mama always said I was. My hair was and is a little thicker and lighter in color, and I think it would be fair to say a little shinier. I always meant to be a better dancer and rider, and I was."

"Sarah . . . you don't need to compare yourself in those ways. Please, no more of Emma. You should be getting to bed."

The blond hair came closer. "What did you do for fun in all those years in India?"

"What do you mean?"

"I mean about love."

"I don't understand your question. . . . But I think the answer is nothing in particular."

"Then let me be more explicit. What did you do about sex? What did you do in Matebeleland? When you fought the native men, did you conquer the women in that way, too?"

"What are you saying?" Stevenson sounded shocked.

"How many natives did you lay?"

"Sarah, really."

"How did you let off emotional steam on all those sea trips?" She giggled. "How do you let off steam on a steamer?" She teased again, "Surely you're not some kind of military monk?"

His head rested in shadow, below the light from the windowsill; she could not see his expression.

Eventually, he answered, "No." A flat no and nothing more.

"There are those who would recognize that and those who would be too innocent, or should I say stupid."

"Please leave Emma out of this."

"I would be delighted to leave Emma out of this."

Sarah had her hands on his shoulders. She deliberately pulled herself into a sitting position over him. She sat astride the prone hero, smiling down into the inscrutable darkness, gently massaging his chest.

Her voice came to him barely audible. "You are not a military monk, you are a military man. I know you. You are the kind of man who would always demand satisfaction."

She had seated herself accurately; the thin material of her nightdress strained across his belt. She knew the effect she was having; she could feel it happening under her.

"Sarah?" The beginning of his question was left in the air.

Sarah crossed her arms and took down the straps of her nightdress, letting the shawl drop. "Shall I bare my heart to you?" Slowly she pulled down the bodice until her breasts were exposed in the moonlight.

"Sarah?" the unasked question again.

"I know what you're going to say," she challenged, smiling confidently down into the dark.

"We must lock the door."

"I locked it when I came in."

Emma held the bedclothes over her head and decided it was time for the next explosion to come. She heard the thud, and the long whine growing in volume, and then the crash, as if it was right there in the room; in fact it was some distance away—yet near enough to make the bed shake and rattle the bottles on the dressing table.

Then silence.

She had spent the night alone, sleeping only fitfully, and by the time real sleep had come, so had the shelling. Bed had merely become a place to hide from the awful nose.

The door handle squeaked. Emma pulled the covers off her face to see who was coming in. Stevenson stood there, glaring at her.

"Why are you not down in the cellar with your mother and Sarah? You are causing everyone unnecessary anxiety."

"Where were you last night?" asked Emma.

"I think that is beside the point."

"Why?"

"We shall talk presently, Emma. I shall go down to the cellar and wait for you there. We can talk privately in the passage."

"I am not going down to that cellar. If the building falls, that's where it will fall."

"Very well. I shall wait for you in your mother's living room. It is most important that we talk. I mean now."

He remained standing in the doorway, clearly with no intention of coming in.

"I'll get dressed," said Emma.

She watched him pull the door to and heard his spurred boots play their metallic music down the passage.

She got up and began dressing quickly. The sooner she could get there, the sooner this next scene could be over. Why had he slept out? But of course, there were so many possible reasons for that. Who would want to sleep in a bed where there was no rest? Where he fought his losing battles in nightmares from which he never expected to wake. Where he lost the battle for sex, while she lost the one for love or even affection.

She went to the middle of the room and held her ears as the next thud came and the next whine. But this time the explosion was distant, and the bottles on the dressing table only tinkled gently.

There was one further reason why Geoffrey should be so withdrawn, and if his obvious anger was an example, the reason was Sarah. She had threatened to speak to him. And the more Emma thought about it, the more characteristic it would be. Sarah would never let such an opportunity for spite pass her by.

She was ready. As she went into the passage, she decided she was ready for any attack Geoffrey might make.

The next thud; the next whine. Emma walked along the passage holding her ears, thinking that if this next shell hit the hotel it might solve a lot of problems—wipe out these incompatible attitudes, silence the intolerant accuser, and, at the same time, put an end to her hopeless confusion. But, again, the explosion was farther away.

When she reached the door, she paused. She realized that she felt no trepidation, only anger at the growing pattern of mistrust, misunderstanding, and sheer unbridled resentment.

Emma opened the door and went in, to find Stevenson sitting in her mother's armchair, legs crossed, elbows on the armrests, and fingers tapping together in front of his face. His eyes followed her as she crossed the room and sat down on the window seat facing him. They waited for the next shell. She resisted the temptation to put her hands to her ears, but there was no necessity; the explosion was in the far distance.

Stevenson waited for what seemed like minutes before he spoke.

"If you ever wish to do anything for me," he started slowly, "let it be something womanly that I can admire. I need no woman fighting my battles for me. It is a futile concept. But worse than that, it is in bad taste. Do you understand me, Emma? It is in bad taste."

"I understand what you are saying, but it is difficult to understand what you mean."

He seemed not to have heard.

"It puts one in the category of a loser," he went on. "Whereas I am perfectly capable of fighting my own battles, as you know."

"Why don't you simply say what you want to say?"

"Very well. Where did you get the impression that you could be responsible for my behavior, let alone my debts?"

"You have been talking to Sarah."

"Does it matter with whom I have been talking? We are not discussing my indiscretions, but yours."

"I think discretion has gone to the wind."

"Well, apropos of that, let us examine the facts."

"Oh, for God's sake, your imitation of a judge is grotesque. Just come to the point."

They were both struggling to control their anger. Stevenson looked away and pressed his shaking fingers together in front of his eyes until they were steady.

"I spoke to Sarah, yes. She was as discreet as anyone would be who was upset and humiliated. I also spoke to Bannock."

Emma froze at the thought that no one could have taken her integrity into account.

Stevenson hung on to the initiative. "I had to explain to this fellow that my wife was misinformed and generally quite beside herself. You should know better, Emma. One does not demean oneself by apologizing to someone who has been established as a ruffian. What really appalls me is that you should imagine there is anything to apologize for. You actually paid him money?"

"He refused to accept it."

"Ah. An honorable ruffian, are you suggesting?"

Emma sighed and reconciled herself to her husband's need for torture, his line of unreasoning recrimination. She leaned forward, determined to bring some sense into the situation.

"Please listen to me for a moment," she pleaded. "You have rushed around gathering evidence from other people. Now you are facing me with a final judgment on an issue where I may well be seen as innocent. Don't you see that I never meant to prejudice you in any way? All I said to that man was that you were under a great strain. That it was impossible for you in any normal circumstances to behave without honor—"

Stevenson burst out, "Who is judging who? How ludicrous to talk of honor to a man like that."

"May I go on?"

"No, you may not." The twitch had begun. "You know nothing of this type of adventurer. He may be able to pull the wool over your eyes, but he has come up short with me. That is where we stand at the moment, if we stand anywhere at all."

Emma slumped back on the window seat.

"We are far apart," she said.

Stevenson stood up and walked to the table where he had left his belt with pistol and saber. He picked them up as if he was going to put them on, then slowly put them down again, looking at Emma.

"I have come to the conclusion," he said, "that you don't care one way or the other."

She thought carefully about this. "Unless you could come to me first. Unless you could trust. No, it's simpler than that. Until you can fulfill some promise of love, then you are right, I don't care."

He remained where he was, leaning on the table looking at her. Emma became aware that the shelling had ceased.

"It is an extraordinary thing to admit," he said in a calmer voice, "my life seems to have little meaning. I have been warned not to be reckless. But somehow I am only alive when I am on a horse and when death is at stake."

"What a sad thing to admit," said Emma. "You are motivated by death."

"Who should be afraid of death in such an impotent life? Do I really want to be made into a businessman, by courtesy of your brother? Do I really want the honor of social acceptability, by courtesy of your mother? Do I really want the love you say you offer me, where even a simple thing like sex has its qualifications? Must I perform your curious charade, where to give credence to sex I must utter some wonderful definitions to your face and hope that what is happening down below, as you put it, is all taking place nicely and at a proper rhythm, with the proper hidden meaning—which is all frankly beyond me?"

"You are being most eloquent, but we have been over all this before. I know you, Geoffrey. Or at least I am beginning to know you. You have never spoken like this. This is rehearsed."

Stevenson put his hand to his mouth. The twitch was back, the fingers imperceptibly shaking, but his voice remained calm.

"Isn't it strange that I always believed that sexual satisfaction grew out of the activities of good old healthy impulses, and, of course, organs? And there we were, me playing the classical music of the organ while you sang some private song in your mind."

"This is rehearsed," she accused.

"Does that sound like harmony to you?" Stevenson's

voice was rising in pitch. "Surely mine is the natural music?"

"Oh, for heaven's sake."

"You must see it, Emma. Sex is simpler than you make it out to be. It's a simple matter of flattening out on the bed and getting on with it."

"At least that puts an end to your clever similes," said Emma. "You should never have brought up the matter of bad taste. You are in such bad taste."

"I have no choice. Music seemed a nice respectable basis of comparison."

Emma stood up, making a move to go.

She said, "You can bang out that rhythm with any whore, but not with me."

Stevenson swept the sword belt off the table, sending it crashing against the door in front of Emma. He came around, shaking all over, forcing her to stop in her stride, looking down at her threateningly.

"Damn you," he spluttered. "I never thought I would ever want to strike you."

He seemed to want to say more, but the twitch had become uncontrollable and he simply stared down at her, his face bent over slightly to one side, shaking.

Emma looked at the shining buttons of his tunic and waited. She felt only despair and compassion. She wished she could comfort him, but she waited.

· 5 · | THE WAKING NIGHTMARE

As an example of the fact that Masefield's thoughts could never be anticipated, for once the gold propelling pencil lay inert in front of him.

It could have meant that in the absence of any immediate need for notes he was thoroughly absorbed in what was being said. It could as easily have meant he was too bored even to doodle. Certainly the idea that he was riveted to whatever Colonel Kekewich was about to say was in keeping with the mood of every officer present. Word had gone around that tomorrow, the twenty-ninth of November, 1899, the day planned for relief, was to be a day of action, and that this meeting was to hear the orders.

The CO was saying, "If you train your ears when the wind dies down, you will hear heavy artillery fire to the south." For a moment, they all seemed to be listening. Even Masefield's double chin remained still.

The CO's voice again. "Last night the searchlights of the relief column could be seen clearly from the observation tower, I should judge somewhere in the area of the Modder and, if anything, closer to us than the signaled position of Klokfontein, which we picked up yesterday.

"The final evidence is possibly the best reason of all for optimism. You will have noticed that all enemy shelling stopped abruptly this afternoon, suggesting that the Boers will be concentrating to the south. Which brings me to the object of this rushed briefing.

"Considering the position of the relief column at this moment, and taking into account that it is a large force, a full division in fact, with considerable equipment, artillery, and infantry on the march, we can assume that no major push will take place before the early hours of tomorrow morning. And that, gentlemen, is where we come in.

"We must give Lord Methuen and his column every support. And for that purpose, we shall deploy the largest force we have put together to date. You will all be involved."

There was a murmur of approval. Masefield sniffed quietly, and Kekewich waited to continue as the room went silent. He turned and walked to a blackboard, where he surveyed a chalk-drawn map.

"We can assume that the relief column will come into view to the southeast of Beaconsfield, here."

Kekewich faced the room once more. "Now here is the overall deployment. Our combined force consists of eighteen hundred men, including the six guns of the Diamond Fields Artillery. The operation in the field will be under the command of Lieutenant-Colonel Chamier.

"We have two objectives." He went back to the blackboard and indicated. "The main column will demonstrate against Wimbledon Ridge here, which, as you see, is the nearest point of cover for a Boer resistance to the relief force. The main column will consist of one hundred mounted men, six guns, a section of Royal Engineers, six companies of infantry with six Maxims. This column will be supported on the right by six hundred mounted men under the command of Lieutenant-Colonel Scott-Turner, this in anticipation of any Boer activity from the direction of Carter's Ridge.

"Now here, on the other side of the approach, is the second objective, Alexanderfontein. Here I am given to believe that the tributary line is still in order, and we have decided to send the armored train, supported by three hundred men of the Town Guard. You will see my intention that the main force, proceeding as it does toward the enemy's established positions, is to divert attention from the approach route."

Kekewich came away from the map and stood facing the room.

"I think you all know where you fit into this scheme. And before we go any further, are there any questions?"

Masefield's eyes came to life, darting sideways as Colonel Scott-Turner immediately stood up on his right.

The CO reacted seconds later. "Yes, Scott-Turner?"

"Should we not divide the force and take Carter's Ridge as well?"

Kekewich shook his head. "It is not our intention to take anything," he said firmly. "Once again, we are demonstrating. Our best hope is that the Boers will have thinned out to concentrate farther south. Otherwise, we would be heavily outnumbered."

Masefield became conscious that Scott-Turner was still standing. He picked up the gold propelling pencil and only his fingers moved, agitating the pointed end on the surface of the table.

Kekewich looked up and saw Scott-Turner.

"You may speak."

"Sir, I contend that Carter's is the most strategic of the Boer positions, not Wimbledon. If we are to divert them, we should hit them at their strongest point."

"You are misunderstanding," said Kekewich. "Our priority is to harass and divert. We only fight when we are forced. There is no call for an assault on Carter's Ridge unless it is unoccupied or so slightly occupied that there is an absolute certainty of success." Kekewich frowned at his own seeming indecision.

Masefield's fingers worked the point of the pencil until the lead broke.

On the morning of the twenty-ninth, for the first time in three weeks, there were no enemy guns firing.

In the gray light just before dawn, the Market Square was alive with another sound, the neighing, snorting, and stamping of six hundred horses drawn up in their units and twelve teams of mules standing idle in front of the gun carriages.

But this relative quiet was short-lived, with shouted orders and the mule teams coming around in formation and heading off out of the square, their deadly freight rumbling behind.

On the steps of the Town Hall in the middle of the square, Colonel Scott-Turner was ringed by the officers of the mounted force. He was shouting to be heard above the noise.

"By the time you reach the reservoir redoubt, the infantry will already be on the march there and we can proceed without pause. Gentlemen, you are excused. Prepare to move off immediately."

They all hesitated, to allow Scott-Turner time to take the lead, then they went in a group, the elegant elite of Kimberley's defense striding across the square toward the head of the large formation of horses.

"Shall I give the orders, sir?" Major Peakman was going off toward the leading unit when the commander called him back.

"No, wait," Scott-Turner called out. "All of you, please. I have something to say." And as they all came around him again, he explained, "We have a little time. It will save us waiting in line for the rest of the column."

They crowded together in the swirling dust left behind by the gunners, and the officers waited to hear what their tough, nonconforming commander had to say.

"I asked myself in the briefing yesterday, what is meant by a demonstration? And then I had to ask myself, what kind of strategy ignores the predictable tactics of the enemy?" Scott-Turner hesitated and felt at the wound in his left arm from the sortie of the week before.

"I'm very much afraid that we have a muddled plan, like most of our plans. I call it taking the inoffensive. You will agree that an inoffensive attack is a contradiction in terms. Let's examine it quickly.

"If we attack Wimbledon, the weaker position, we are simply asking Carter's, the stronger position, to open fire or, if not, to attack in force. Agreed?" He addressed Peakman.

Peakman nodded a trifle uncertainly. "I can only agree," he said, and there was silence from the others.

Scott-Turner looked at them, frowning, and continued. "If while *demonstrating,*" he put a derogatory emphasis on the word, "we are attacked, we would be defending at a disadvantage. If we attack, our problems would be no greater. Who will tell me that the Boers will merely hold their positions and take no action? I am talking about Carter's, of course. It is a fortified place. Forgive me for using these strong terms, but to ignore Carter's Ridge is insane. I am prepared to go out as planned and take the decision later. But in the meantime, in principle, do I have your agreement?"

He looked around at his officers, and they all nodded and murmured assent. He was not entirely satisfied.

"Before we go, let me drive home my point. If there is no retaliation from Carter's—which would surprise me—it would mean they have withdrawn, and in that case I see no point in occupying the place. But if there is retaliation, it must be met, or this whole operation is a farce. Get mounted, gentlemen."

Stevenson was smiling as he walked down the line toward his squadron. His lieutenants remained very much at heel, no doubt as a result of his reputation with volunteers. He seemed aware that the eyes of the mounted troops followed him without their turning their heads. There was much exchanging of salutes with headquarters personnel coming from the Town Hall.

The waiting Parader looked magnificent as Stevenson strode to the front of his command. He was in the saddle before the trooper holding the horse's head could assist him, gathering up the reins and slapping the neck hard to bring the big, prancing animal under control.

There was a delay of about a minute before the shouted orders came back from one troop to another, and then the whole mounted column was on the move. The column wheeled and was soon proceeding at the trot through the streets of Kimberley in a haze of dust. They crossed the intersection of Victoria and Du Toitspan roads and took the shortest route past Newtown toward the southern perimeter, strung out in a neatly reticulated line that spread out at one stage all the way from the square to the reservoir redoubt.

At the redoubt there was a delay. The whole mounted column waited while the artillery went forward, followed by the mounted infantry, to join the main body of foot soldiers marching away into the distance.

Scott-Turner cantered across to the redoubt to speak to Kekewich, who had chosen to watch the proceedings from there. As he dismounted, the enemy batteries opened fire from the far hills.

The entire column of horses became restive and shuffled in their positions. Their riders worked to calm them.

Stevenson stood up impatiently in his stirrups, watching the dawn come up and the distant infantry disappearing into a cloud of red dust. Scott-Turner galloped back to take up his position. The bugler sounded the forward, and the column walked out into the open ground past the sand-bagged edge of the redoubt, magnificently conspicuous in the first bright light of dawn. The order was passed to trot, and they went forward in their long column-of-three formation, snaking ahead for the open ground to the right of the main force.

When the order came to canter, Stevenson had to cross the reins and take a double grip on Parader, who had been in a short, chopping canter from the time they left the redoubt. The big horse still could not understand these controlled paces. His rider laughed proudly at him as he plunged to one side, then the other, making a great spectacle of himself.

The enemy guns could be heard all the while above the noisy clatter of hooves. They moved fast, in a near perfect line, until they came alongside the main column on a parallel course. The order to halt came back, and Stevenson was forced to pull Parader out of the line to get him under control. He laughed again as he saw Scott-Turner and at least one other of the officers having the same trouble on their fresh horses up ahead.

"Signal, sir," the sergeant shouted. "Commander requests you to report."

But Stevenson had seen the signal even before he was told, and he was already galloping up the line, exhilarated; he overtook the captain of the troop ahead in his rush to report.

Scott-Turner looked grim as the officers pulled up one after the other and drew into a circle around him.

He shouted above the racket of the firing, "What did I tell you? If we wait long enough, Carter's Ridge could wipe the entire column out. Fortunately, their aim is not very good so far. Now listen to this: I intend to go under the ridge and take whatever action is necessary. Rejoin your men, please."

The words had the effect of a whiplash. The commander had spoken, and the result was electric. The officers turned like a band of wild horsemen and raced down the line to take up their positions. Parader skidded up the dust as he was roughly pulled up. Within seconds of being brought into position, the entire column moved forward at a fast pace.

Stevenson involuntarily ducked at the sound of shells screaming overhead. He turned in the saddle, to see the billowing clouds from explosions in the area of the reservoir redoubt. They were galloping at a pace being set from the front, when suddenly, the leading squadron wheeled to the right, away from the parallel course and directly toward Carter's Ridge.

Stevenson smiled his satisfaction. The so-called demonstration was turning into a day of action. He looked ahead and behind with confidence at the powerful galloping formations.

The ridge loomed in front, and it was possible to make out the fortifications along the top, with smoke pouring down from the enemy guns positioned there. A few more minutes and they were drawing up to shouted orders, overlapping formations in their excitement. Stevenson galloped forward at the signal to assemble.

Scott-Turner roared above the din from the guns overhead, "I want the first three squadrons to dismount and prepare to go up the ridge. The last four troops in line are to stand by to offer support."

Stevenson galloped back with his instructions, past troops who were already dismounting. The lieutenants and sergeants immediately took over, detailing the horse-holders, getting the men, who had drawn their rifles from the saddles and were fixing bayonets, into line at the foot of the ridge.

Marksmen were already on their knees in front, firing at the snipers on the edge of the ridge, where they could hardly be seen for the smoke that bellowed forward in a regular pattern from the guns. Stevenson looked around for casualties, but could see none. The sudden turn and fast approach had so far paid dividends.

For Scott-Turner there was no waiting. One after the

other the buglers took up the order to advance and attack.

Stevenson went up the hill with a sergeant bustling up beside him and one of his athletic young lieutenants actually going up ahead. They were near the top when the sergeant arched back and fell down out of sight among the men. They went right on to the summit where the Boer snipers had withdrawn. The troopers went to their knees and opened fire at the nearby fort, aiming at heads and guns that showed over the redoubt wall. Stevenson fired off a few rounds of his pistol, then ran recklessly for the stone wall. He lay against the wall watching his first troop running at him and the second scrambling over the summit and following their officer toward the back of the redoubt.

"Righto, gentlemen," he shouted. "Over the top."

They climbed over the low rock wall with its easy footholds and lay on the top, firing into a scene of pandemonium. Boers were running from their posts, some still firing from the back wall of the redoubt. Stevenson heard bullets rip along the edge of the stone wall. Some of the men fell in, hit, but the rest followed him into the redoubt. He stood leaning on an abandoned gun and, double-handed, fired off the remaining rounds in his revolver. A number of Boers were hit and lay wounded or dying at the far end of the redoubt, but the rest had evacuated and could be seen galloping away beyond the back wall. Stevenson walked across, reloading his revolver. He examined the big German gun carefully and the ammunition alongside. He walked past a Maxim gun, staring at it, then climbed the far wall to see what was going on all around.

The next redoubt, some one hundred yards on, seemed to have suffered the same fate; Mackeson's men were coming out and regrouping at the front. He looked around for his own casualties and groaned at what he saw. There were dead and wounded on the wall and on the other side of it, at least seven.

"Help the wounded, please," he shouted. "Take them down to the bottom."

He stood on the wall for a long time, watching the smoke from the volleys farther along the ridge. They had made a good start, but the Boers were still well entrenched over there in the third and fourth redoubts. Beyond the fortifications to the south there was nothing, just empty, rolling hills, with smoke swirling back and intermingling with the dust of the retreating horses.

He shrugged as he heard the bugles sound the recall. "Oh, well," he said aloud, "this is the way we fight. One step forward, one step backward, and another boring discussion."

A lieutenant shouted, "Special drill, keep the rear guard. The rest of you, down the hill and form up below."

Some of the men were still able to laugh at Stevenson as he walked an unstable tightrope along the top of the wall before he jumped off and followed on down the hill.

At the foot of the ridge, he mounted Parader, who was being held ready for him, and set off for the head of the column.

Most of the force had made their descent by the time he reached the meeting of officers. This time they dismounted, and some of them, including the commander, sat on convenient rocks, shading their eyes from the hot sun. Stevenson took off his helmet to wipe away sweat while Scott-Turner addressed them.

"We have put two of their forts out of action, and my congratulations to all concerned. Our objective now lies farther along the ridge, and it is my guess that we shall not have such an easy time of it. The procedure is as follows: The ridge gets steeper over there, offering better cover, I should think. So we continue along under the ridge until we are in the middle of their remaining positions, where the four last troops will dismount and carry the action. The six troops remaining will follow on after and give active support. It's as simple as that. I would be obliged if we could be on the move as soon as possible."

Stevenson galloped back, marveling at the inexhaustible energy of Parader, who was running with sweat but was as lively as when he had first mounted him early that morning. He looked at the wounded being tended in the hot sun. They would have to wait there until the action was over.

"Come on, come on," he muttered impatiently, watching the troops ahead get on their mounts and form up again.

The orders came, and they set off in three tight lines directly under the ridge. He could see the smoke blasting out just ahead and hear the rattle of the Maxims after each loud salvo. Once or twice the line parted up ahead, with riders spurring forward and pulling back to avoid rifle fire spitting down the dry gullies. Eventually they came underneath the main fire, with snipers' rifles crackling up above and bullets ricocheting off the rocky ground beyond. They halted, and Scott-Turner and Peakman rode back to watch the last four troops dismount.

"No bugles," shouted Scott-Turner. "Advance and attack as soon as you are ready."

The officers concerned had come together on foot, and immediately set off back to their respective positions. Orders were shouted, and the troops began to climb the ridge. It was a higher, steeper climb at this point, and they avoided the gullies, which afforded the enemy snipers a better view of them.

Stevenson sat on rock watching Parader at each report stamp and pull away from the trooper who was holding him. The veins were showing in his great arched neck and on his shoulders. His color had gone darker and shinier with the sweat. He could become the most magnificent cavalry horse of all time without ever losing that temper and sensitivity.

The attacking force reached the top of the ridge and there they stopped, flattened out by a ferocious barrage of fire. Stevenson stood up and walked backward to get a better view. Suddenly there was the loud, rhythmic blasting of a Maxim gun, and huge spurts of soil were seen flying off from the edge of the ridge.

Parader dragged his holder in a frenzied circle, observed moodily by Stevenson. He, in turn, demonstrated his own restlessness by pacing up and down on the hard ground, watched by his troopers, who were sitting and squatting, holding their bayoneted guns. He kicked a stone and stood, feet apart, staring up at the ribbon of men at the top where they lay helplessly waiting. There was no hope for them. If any one of them had stood up to advance, he would have been hit by a rain of bullets and Maxim shells. He could see the cavalry commander, Scott-Turner, farther along the right, standing hands on hips and looking upward. The firing lulled somewhat while the artillery continued its deep-throated salvos.

The commander was looking away at his right, and Stevenson realized that one of the sections was attempting to go over the top. There was shouting, and the effect rippled back as the other troops crawled forward into action. Immediately the enemy fire increased to a crescendo of rifle and Maxim reports. Where the line had first gone over the top, two men stumbled back and fell, visibly ripped through by Maxim fire. As their bodies rolled down, the rest of the troop scrambled back to take cover just under the ridge. And this was soon the pattern all along, with men crawling and falling over the edge, dragging themselves down. The whole line was swept back by the deadly fire. There were troopers sliding down the hill, some trying to run downward, some clutching their heads and stomachs, others dragging wounded men.

Stevenson watched Scott-Turner. The commander remained in the same position for a while, then turned and shouted for his horse. When the horse was brought, Scott-Turner mounted up and looked around with a wild expression on his face.

"Will you follow me?" he shouted one way and then the other. "Will you follow me?"

A few of the officers had anticipated his intention and were already on their horses. For a moment, Stevenson was immobile, the twitch at work, his eyes riveted on the new activity. Then, like a man who had suddenly awakened, he shook his head and came into action. He ran toward Parader. All around him, other men were going for their horses.

He gathered his reins in time to see Scott-Turner urge his horse forward, then jerk and go rigid in the saddle and slowly fall off. The commander was shot. In that moment, Boer snipers could be seen reappearing at the top of the ridge. Stevenson stared in disbelief.

A sergeant shouted, "Volleys, volleys! Ready! Present!"

There were immediately a hundred or more men on their knees aiming upward.

"Fire!" the sergeant shouted.

After that, everything was chaos. Stevenson galloped behind the line of riflemen to where a group of officers were gathering around Peakman.

Peakman called out, "Sound the retreat!"

A few of the officers shook their heads in disagreement.

"No!" shouted Stevenson.

"Do you hear me? Sound the retreat!"

As the bugle sounded, Peakman swung his horse away toward the confused crush of men arriving down from the ridge, where those who were able struggled to single out their horses from the handlers, drawing help from a diminishing force of riflemen.

Stevenson set his horse after Peakman, shouting, "No, no!" Then, suddenly, he seemed to change his mind, reining in to face the ridge.

"Will you come with me?" he literally screamed. The overexcited thoroughbred cantered on the spot against the tight rein.

Stevenson drew the saber.

"Will you come with me?" he screamed again. His eyes stared straight ahead and he ignored the shouts of the officers who rode up to stop him.

He loosed Parader's head, and in a second he was galloping toward the foot of the hill. Two officers galloped after him, shouting for him to stop, but they reined back on the lower slopes. By that time the powerful Parader was halfway up and beginning to struggle on the crumbling rise. Stevenson had chosen a slightly depressed gully, so that within another ten stumbling strides he was at the top. The rigidly held saber glinted in the sunlight as it disappeared over the top.

Stevenson was alone in a Boer shooting gallery, the nightmare a reality, the saber trembling at the prospect.

The first bullets struck Parader in the neck, in the chest, in the head. Stevenson's rein hand went limp as a bullet tore through his left shoulder. Another struck his stomach. And another. The momentum brought the great horse down in a sliding, crumbling heap. The saber remained upright as Stevenson went over, sliding ahead of the horse.

He got to his knees still holding the saber rigidly in front of him. He tried to say something but his mouth was full of blood. Slowly, he got one foot up and then staggered to his feet. He stared around as if he was having trouble seeing and began to stagger forward. The Boer riflemen in the vicinity had stopped firing and were standing in a wide semicircle watching him. His entire front, his cheek and chin, his shoulder and left arm, his whole tunic were red with blood.

Two of the Boers shouldered their rifles and came forward to assist him but he swung the saber at them. Then he seemed to make out the semicircle of men and stumbled toward them with the saber raised to strike. The Boers moved back to make way for him. He swiped out blindly from the shoulder, unable to move his chest. With his eyes closed, he stood swaying, lashing out with the saber again and again.

The Boers watched as he went down on his knees and

stayed like that, as if he were praying to himself. Then, slowly, he bent down, rolled over, and lay still.

A shadow came over him as one of the Boers leaned down, felt his temple, then, forcing his fingers open, took the saber.

The man held up the saber and other Boers came close to look at the shining blade.

· 6 · | EPITAPH WITH GUNS

Emma's eyes appeared enormous in the unflickering reflection of the candlelight. She had simply stared at each of them in turn and then abruptly gone off to her room.

Her mother and Mark had followed, leaving Colonel Thrumpton, who had brought the news, to spend a morbid half hour waiting in the living room.

When Lady Freestone-Grant returned on her own, he politely excused himself but was asked to stay. He had remained, uncomfortably sitting down at Lady Freestone-Grant's insistence. She had got up and gone to stand at the window seat, looking at the vague outlines of the moonlit town.

She kept him there with questions: "When will the relief column arrive?" She remained looking out, avoiding those old knowing eyes frowning through the fringe of bushy gray eyebrows.

He was forced to reply. "Difficult to say, m'dear."

"Will it be tomorrow now?"

"It begins to look questionable."

"The moment it ends I must take Emma away from here, back home to Birchleigh."

"We could be relieved at any time now."

Once again, the old man had run out of words. He was on the point of standing up when she spoke again.

"I laughed at Geoffrey, you know. He did insist this would be a proper war. Dear me, what a nice word for a war, "proper." I mean bloody, of course. I mean, we army people sacrifice too much. We kill our men."

The old head was nodding. "Our best men."

The ice was momentarily broken. Lady Freestone-Grant turned, smiling.

"No, not all of them. We need you old soldiers."

"You are being kind."

"Not at all. There is a reason why the best generals, like the best warhorses, are long in the tooth."

Mark had appeared, quietly going to the far corner to pour himself a drink. He made a sign of offering one to the colonel, who shook his head.

"Is she asleep?" his mother asked.

"I wish I could say that." Mark sipped at his brandy. "But she's calm enough. I don't think she wants to be watched over."

"I must go to her."

Lady Freestone-Grant was already on her way out of the room when Colonel Thrumpton stood up. He was left facing Mark, who held up the brandy bottle, repeating the unspoken offer. This time it was accepted with a nod.

Mark made a toast. "Here's to all the Geoffreys." He sipped, looked at the glass, and decided to swallow the whole thing. "We virtually grew up together, you know." He brooded. "He was like an older brother, really. I was very fond of him, but he was not easy." He looked up from his empty glass. "At times, just now and then, he was really quite difficult. That must surprise you."

The old man said nothing, and Mark concealed his discomfort by pouring another drink.

"Am I to understand that nothing was achieved by this action today?" Mark came slowly back until he was in a position to demand an answer.

"Nothing much. Nothing much was intended to be achieved. It was simply meant to divert some of the Boer forces away from the approach of the relief column. But of necessity the action involved almost half the entire garrison, and hence the serious risk. If they went into action, they would be hopelessly outnumbered. They simply could not afford a defeat, because in the event of a last, concerted attack on the town we would be left virtually defenseless."

"Then why, for heaven's sake, was Geoffrey killed?"

Thrumpton took it by stages. "I attended a staff meeting before coming here—"

"Post mortem," Mark interrupted.

Thrumpton frowned at Mark's belligerent tone but went on with what he was saying. "It appears that certain officers acted impetuously and against orders."

"Geoffrey was one of them?"

"Yes—and this is in confidence. There will be no blame. I've seen this sort of thing happen before. The waiting and the disappointments breed depression. The fighting spirit champs against the bit. What they did may have been foolish, but none the less heroic."

"They paid for their folly." This time Mark saw Thrumpton's frown of disapproval. "Don't misunderstand me, sir; we are going to miss Geoffrey desperately." His words were becoming somewhat slurred; his eyes stared, then came into focus on Thrumpton again. "Is the siege to last much longer than we expected? Did your meeting say anything about that?"

"Yes." The colonel nodded, as if relieved that the subject had changed. "We have been given no details yet, but I'm afraid to say the relief column has been trounced somewhere near the Modder." He ignored Mark's expression of shock. "The answer to your question is, yes. If they could check the column once, one assumes they could do it again. I would not want to be the one to explain that to your mother, that we could be trapped in the middle of a ring of artillery that has nothing to do but bombard us at their leisure. You realize that while it drags on, all the classical siege conditions apply. There are already shortages of food. We will soon run short of ammunition if the De Beers workshops cannot produce more. We will soon run out of meat, except for what the natives manage to steal and bring in."

"You make it sound as if the column will never get through."

"It might or it might not, my dear chap. Communications are almost at a standstill. Rhodes is raging with frustration and blaming the army. Our commander is beside himself and blaming everyone in sight. It is not a picture that inspires any confidence at all."

Mark had his attention now. "So Geoffrey died for nothing?"

"He died—" Colonel Thrumpton checked himself.

"He died for nothing." Mark said it quietly and downed his glass again.

"Well, that's good-bye to the old racecourse then, eh, Bart?"

Bannock and Charlie Watson were sitting on the grandstand looking over a sea of khaki army tents spread out across the course and on the other side of the rails to the east toward Beaconsfield. Between the closely pegged tents were swarms of natives, tending fires and cooking pots, carrying buckets of water from the pump, but mostly lying around doing nothing.

"It's all right, Mabala." Bannock watched the big Zulu order a group of young natives off the stand where they were sitting.

He shouted at them in his dialect, adding sternly for Bannock's sake, "Can't you see *nkosi* is talking?"

"Who's going to be sorry?" Watson was going on. "It's too short, ain'it? Now they can build a proper one."

Bannock was hardly interested. "They'll never get the going right. It's like running on stone."

"Whoever built this thing must have been racing polo ponies. Look at that turn at the end of the straight. You need skid-proof hooves to go around there, I can tell you. I've ridden around it."

"I thought you were a trainer these days," said Bannock.

Watson laughed. "I was a good jockey and I'm a good trainer. And I can still take up my stirrups if I have to."

The smaller man curled his toes in his lightweight boots, and Bannock thought, Once a jockey, those are the flimsy boots you'll always prefer.

"I want to get out of here, Charlie."

Watson looked around as if he had not heard, but he had. "I know that, I know that."

"What are we going to do about it, Charlie?"

"Just hang around, Bart. I told you, I've got the latest news. Brought it in last night in my saddlebags."

"One of these nights we're going to go out there and get our heads shot off."

"Just wait, Bart. The relief is coming."

"What did they say?"

"I don't read the letters, mate. But I spoke to a couple of chaps at the guard post."

"At the Modder?"

"At the Modder. You want to see what they're doing down there. You want to see the Modder now. I used to take a girl down there once or twice. You want to see it."

"I saw it coming through," said Bannock.

"Right, well. Ain't it like a bloody oasis in the middle of the veld? It was the only place—willow trees, grassy banks, hotels with proper pubs, swimming, you couldn't beat it. And now? It's like a great dug-up heap of shit. There ain't a tree in sight, mate, unless it's a stump. They had enough big guns firing to blow up the whole Boer army. But the way things look, they didn't do so good."

"How does it look?" asked Bannock.

"Well, mate, to judge from what those chaps at the guard post know and what I know, they don't know their arses from their elbows. It seems the worst of it is, the poor buggers are worn out. They've had three battles in just over a week. Poor sods had to march for fourteen miles nonstop before this last caper. Trouble is, they're trying to fight a straight fight and the Boers don't fight straight. Every time they think they've won, the Boers disappear, and every time they move on, the Boers come back. But they don't come back so's you can see them. They hide in the rocks, they lie in the bushes and the riverbed, and you can't see not one of the bastards. Kind of unsporting, you could say. And Bart, those Boers can shoot straight. They learnt it in the native wars, shooting natives on the run."

"What's happened at the Modder?"

"Oh, mate. That was a right fuck-up. You know the Grenadier Guards, bearskin hats, nice red jackets? You know them?"

"Of course I know them. Get on with it, Charlie."

"Well, you want to see them now. In plain khaki—except you can't see the khaki for the mud."

"What happened?" Bannock was becoming impatient.

"Well, them and the Highlanders and a couple of other brigades go marching toward the Modder River where all the Boers are waiting so's they can't be seen, even when they start firing. And Bob's your uncle, when they do start firing, our chaps all lie down flat on the ground, because if they raise one finger, it's going to get shot off. So they spend the whole day lying on their stomachs. Most of them went to sleep, but not for long. The Guards were all right, except for the heat and the ants crawling all over them. But the Scotsmen got the worst of it. First they got the backs of their knees sunburnt." Watson started laughing. "And there's worse to come," he said, breaking out into laughter again.

"Come on, Charlie, for God's sake."

"And the wind," Watson laughed, "the wind got up their skirts and gave their perishing positions away. Really, I don't know what I'm laughing at because they had a lot of casualties. And the horses. They've lost a lot of horses. Everybody's short of horses now, even the Boers. They're in even a worse state for horses."

Bannock turned and looked at Watson and wondered for a moment. "How do you know that?" he asked.

Watson looked at him open-eyed but blankly, as if he were thinking.

"Stands to reason, doesn't it?"

"No, it doesn't," said Bannock, forcing Watson to look at him.

"Oh, I remember now," said Watson. "That police rider, Coombes. The one who got killed going out. You remember Coombes?"

"I never met him," said Bannock.

"That's right," said Watson. "He was always riding around at night counting the Boer guns and the horses."

"Dangerous occupation."

"That's right. That's the way he must've got killed. By the way, Bart, did your horse come back?"

"No, he didn't."

"Sad about the major, whats'isname, Major Stevenson, ain't it?" Now Watson sounded as if he was trying to make small talk.

"Yes," said Bannock.

"He must have ridden right into it."

"No doubt."

"Well, it's his own bloody fault, ain't it?"

"What do you mean?"

"Well, you don't take a raving racehorse and try to go into battle with a bunch of cobs. Ain't that right? You're going to go in there and win the race. With a goer like your Parader, you're going to be fifty lengths ahead and on the other side of the enemy before the cobs get there." He looked seriously at Bannock. "Well, ain't it?"

"He had good hands, Charlie, strong rider."

"I don't care how strong he was. If you're going against a bunch of dogs and the racehorse is flat out, like up the straight, well, he ain't got brakes, has he? That's what I think. I think the enemy had to turn around to shoot him."

Bannock could not help laughing. But Watson had reminded him of Parader. "Do you think they might have captured Parader?" he asked.

"More like he's been shot, mate. Sorry, but maybe they captured him."

Bannock looked out across the tents. Mabala was standing below as if he was keeping guard on them.

"I'm going out this afternoon to see if I can see him there."

"You're going out this afternoon?" Watson showed his surprise.

"There's a body-collecting detail. It's been arranged. Flag of truce. I spoke to Masefield and he said I could go."

Watson showed his disgust. "Rather you than me. Don't do it, mate. They're not going to have the horse there for you to see."

"It's worth a try." Bannock felt more depressed than ever. "That relief can take a long time, Charlie. Are we going to get out of here? Why don't we all disappear in the night and go to Port Elizabeth? It's only twenty miles of heat and we're through the British lines. Then we're free."

"I told you, Bart. It's going to be in a few days. I heard it from Cecil John Rhodes himself."

Bannock gave him a smile of disbelief. "You've been chatting with Mr. Rhodes?"

"You won't believe it," said Watson. "When I came in with the dispatches, Rhodes himself came out to get them. Bloody this, he says, and bloody that, as he tears open the envelopes. And look at the bloody share prices, he says as he flips through the newspaper. He's a right tough bastard, I can tell you. They're coming, he says. They've taken a bloody long time about it, but they'll be here tomorrow or the next day."

"And what happened when you reported to the army?" asked Bannock.

"Oh, that was just one, two, three, well done; thanks, old chap, and take this chit to the pay office and cheerio for now."

Bannock thought about Watson and decided that the army had as much idea that he was working for De Beers as De Beers had that he was working for the army. He was the kind of man who could work for three different sides if they were available.

"Listen, Charlie, there's another problem."

"What's that, mate?"

"When the army gets here, they're going to grab every horse in sight."

Watson looked surprised.

"Well, you said so yourself, Charlie. They're desperate for horses."

"But Bart, you've still got two horses in pawn. You're not going to leave them here?"

"I'm getting them back," Bannock lied. "That's the deal with Masefield. If I go out on the body party, I get the horses back, and if I get the horses, we can leave."

Bannock was watching Watson carefully; Watson was looking hunted.

The small man suddenly stood up.

"I must think about this, Bart," he said. "Give me until tomorrow." He was already at the bottom of the stand looking up at Bannock, who remained sitting and watching him with great interest.

"I'll come back to you tomorrow," Watson called out, and strode off around the grandstand.

For a man who could outtalk anybody, Watson was suddenly reluctant to say anything further. Bannock wondered about that. What do you need to think about, Charlie Watson? Why this sudden confusion, when all you ever talked about was getting away from Kimberley? What could possibly keep the little man here? Had he decided to go on his own, for whatever reasons? Or decided to stay? In Charlie's case, the deciding issue would have to be gain. Bannock wondered what it was Charlie stood to gain that could change his mind.

"My lord." Mabala stood on the lower step of the grandstand attracting Bannock's attention. "Tomorrow you will have meat. I am fetching it tonight."

"I hope you come back safely, Mabala."

"Do not worry, *nkosi*. If they catch me, I am only a native. Here I am only a native, there I am only a native. When I am here I say *nkosi*. When I am there I say *nkosi*. To you, to them, I am the same. But, *nkosi* . . ."

"Yes?"

"When I am in the hills at Ulundi, my people call me chief. The men salute, the women come on their knees. In my land, I am *nkosi.*"

Heat and dust distorted the landscape. The horizon became transformed into a shimmering mirage of hills that did not exist. The dust blew in rising swirls, sweeping away and curving upward to disperse into the fine red mist that hung in the air.

Part of the mirage slowly emerged from what appeared as a ghostly prophet in the desert, to become a man sitting still on his short pony. This was the Boer doctor, unbelievably a Scotsman, dressed in felt hat and black frock coat, who had come in halfway to meet them. This stern little man had become an institution as the bearer of all truce messages from Boer headquarters. According to Masefield, he constantly appealed for and was given the chloroform and medical supplies he was short of. A wonderful irony for a town that was supposed to be running short of everything itself.

Bannock was riding well clear of the mule wagons.

They were the long, heavy variety with canted sides, which the army used for freight and the hauling of supplies. Five of them proceeded in line, the first two manned by six soldiers each, the other three with a like number of Town Guardsmen, but all driven by soldiers. There were two chaplains accompanying them; Bannock thought it was a little late for that.

He saw the leading party, a captain and three lieutenants, go up to the doctor and speak to him, the captain holding a lance with a somewhat dust-reddened white flag of truce fluttering from the top. The carts trundled on without hesitation, forcing the parleying group to trot ahead before settling down to a walk.

Bannock was bored. He had slacked the reins on Pot Pourri's neck and slumped into a riding posture that would never have done for the army. He looked fondly at Pot Pourri's head, still held high and attentive despite the hanging reins. He tried to think and plan, but only uncomfortable thoughts came, re-enactments of the arguments with Stevenson. The living hero was dead. That meant now he was a hero for all time. Rather think of escape. But how do you escape when the main object of the exercise is under guard in an army stable? Think of Charlie Watson. Now there is a curious situation. Charlie Watson was making no sense. Charlie Watson was lying the way all liars lie. They hesitate and frown slightly, then they lie. And in that instant you can see them looking in on themselves, checking the credibility of their own story. Then, just as quickly, they cheer up and expand the story that sounds good to them. But the story was wrong. No police dispatch rider ever went around at night counting Boer horses. You can't do that. Boer senses are trained for survival. They can sense an off-key cricket at night. They can see like owls in the dark. And what they can't sense, their chained-up dogs are there to sense. There was something funny about Charlie. For a man who stood to lose his horses to the army, he was balking at the perfect opportunity to get out. So why was he lying? Was it that a man who was a dedicated double spy might be a triple spy? Did he know about the Boer needs from firsthand knowledge? Were those strategic dispatches and copies of the London and Cape papers being read by the enemy? Bannock wanted to laugh at his own sudden feelings of loyalty.

Why did he need Charlie? Because he knew the route through the Cape, because he could introduce him to the racing fraternity in Port Elizabeth. He had decided not to tell Charlie about Marcus' being in army custody so as to put nothing in the way of persuading him to go. If he had agreed to go, it would have come as a bombshell. But he had not agreed, and plainly had no intention of agreeing. They would have to leave without Charlie. It was time to forget about the little man and think about how to get Marcus back. But how? Steal him?

At the sound of orders being shouted, Bannock looked up. Carter's Ridge was just ahead, looming out of the fluctuating mirage. The carts were being sent off in two directions. One party, of three carts with two lieutenants and the doctor, set off for a point farther along the ridge. The other two carts went straight ahead. The remaining lieutenant from the leading party galloped back toward him. He drew up in a flurry of dust, and they nodded to one another.

"Mr. Bannock," he greeted. "Lieutenant Masters. I have bad news for you."

"My horse?" queried Bannock.

"Your horse is dead, sir. He was shot. We've just had it from the doctor. Captain says it's quite in order if you wish to return now. But please take it slowly or the Boers might think something is up."

Bannock shook his head. "My agreement with Major Masefield was that I come to help, and I think I should do just that."

"Please yourself, sir. In that case, follow the two carts ahead." The lieutenant reined his horse around, then held back. "And Mr. Bannock." He hesitated. "Glad to have you with us, sir."

He galloped away, and Bannock was left wondering why he had not taken the easy way out of this morbid operation. In his heart, he had known his horse was dead. It stood to reason that if Stevenson was killed making a charge, the horse would have been brought down first. That was a feature of how they fought on both sides in this horse-starved war. He had actually heard the order quoted: shoot the horses pulling the guns. So how much more effective to bring down the horses carrying the leaders. You should say prayers for humans, not horses. But Parader was no ordinary horse. He was bred for winning races, not to die in battle. What might have been a glorious death for a cavalry horse was just a waste of hundreds of years of good breeding. The resolve came back: get out, get out of this slowly rotting situation. No brave officer was going to get the opportunity to die a glorious death on Marcus. That was all he had left, all he had started out with. If he could make enough in Port Elizabeth, he would take Marcus back to England. The family would never touch him. It would not be worth their while. They were interested in money, not meanings. And the money they had.

At that moment, he began to smell the bodies. He put his hand to his nose as the hot wind brought a miasma of decaying flesh into his nostrils. The stench combined with the smell of dust in the ghastly realization that those soldiers who had been alive and fighting just a few days ago were already wasting into oblivion.

The officers drew up below the ridge, the two carts pulling up behind them. The captain loosed the lance that carried the flag of truce from his stirrup and expertly speared the sharp base into the ground, where it stood and fluttered in the wind like a surveyor's beacon. At the top of the ridge, a large group of Boers stood and sat along the edge, idly watching them.

Bannock rode up to where the officers were standing

looking down at eight bodies laid out in a row. Five of them were uncovered, the other three had hessian sacks over the heads and shoulders. The reason for the sacks became apparent as they were removed. The men were unrecognizable, the faces partly or wholly blown away; what remained was alive with ants.

Bannock dismounted and followed the example of the others, tying a handkerchief around his nose. And like the others, he just stood there, immobilized by the horrible sight.

"Bring the covers," ordered the captain, and every man moved to shorten the time it would take to complete the operation.

Bannock wanted to help, but the bodies were being covered and lifted as fast as the soldiers could move. He eventually got his hands on the boots of the last remaining corpse and struggled along sideways to load it onto a cart.

The captain mounted up again, and Bannock wondered what he was doing urging his horse toward the foot of the ridge.

The lieutenant, who was also mounting up, pulled down his face mask and called to some of the soldiers, "You four men—yes, you and you, and you, sergeant. Follow us up, please." He saw Bannock's expression and explained, "Major Stevenson's body is up on top."

"On the double," the sergeant shouted, and they set off for the ridge, where the two officers were struggling with their horses higher up in the one convenient gully available to them. The Boers at the top remained where they were, except for a few who were forced to make way at the head of the gully.

Bannock found himself compelled by something stronger than curiosity to follow them up. There would be no last post for Parader. He had to see what had happened to his horse. The soldiers watched him as he mounted Pot Pourri and held her tight, waiting for the others to clear the top.

He whispered to her, "Now, show them how sure-footed a thoroughbred lady can be." Then he slacked the reins and set off at a canter for the base of the gully. The mare leapt at the gully with enough momentum to carry her to the top without slipping or hesitating on the way. The Boers jumped back as he reined in at the summit, unable to hide their surprise at a class of horse they had almost certainly never seen before. To his right was a stone wall with the muzzle of a field gun showing over it; ahead were the four soldiers, still approaching the spot where the officers had dismounted.

Bannock trotted toward them and arrived in time to see the hessian sacks pulled off Stevenson's body. And for the moment, he forgot about Parader.

The body lay on its back with one open eye, a nest of ants, gaping upwards. The captain leaned down and removed the chain of the helmet that lay over the blood-caked mouth, then gently pulled the helmet off. He showed his disgust as he tried to wipe away the ants from the side of the face that was still recognizable, but he knew he was wasting his time.

The sergeant waved the sack to chase away the flies, and the soldiers brought up the canvas cover. In the moment before they covered the bullet-ridden body, Bannock saw the shock of light, wavy hair and the prominent light eyebrow that remained. He remembered the eyebrows moving below the frown when Stevenson argued with him. The cover went over, and all that could be seen were the elegant boots with the spurs stuck into the ground.

"How many times must you shoot a man to kill him?" he asked aloud.

The captain nodded. "Extraordinary man," he said. "Apparently he just took off on his own. No one can account for it. It was against orders."

"They tried to stop him," said the lieutenant.

The body was being carried back, with the officers following, leading their horses, but Bannock remained behind. He had seen the drag marks and the carcass some distance away. The Boers had dragged Parader's body to a position where the carrion could clean up in peace. Bannock rode over, not wanting to see but having to see. A group of vultures fluttered away. They and the jackals had done much of their work. The belly was gone and the ribs almost picked clean, but the magnificent head lay prone, staring at nothing, and where there was flesh, the bullet holes could be counted.

Bannock choked on the stench and the sight. "What are we doing here?" he groaned, then turned Pot Pourri roughly and cantered back toward the officers who were waiting for the soldiers to negotiate their burden down the descent. The Boers watched his approach with curiosity, no doubt as much for the civilian rider as the fine thoroughbred.

When he came up to the two officers, the captain showed the way. "You go first, Mr. Bannock."

He was about to descend when he noticed something, a glint of metal. One of the Boers had a saber tucked into his belt. It was so obviously out of place, a cavalry saber, a curio picked up after the battle. It was Stevenson's saber. It had to be. He was the only officer to die at this point.

Bannock hesitated, then turned and rode over to the man, pointing at the saber. It was a threatening gesture, and immediately a few of the Boers brought up their rifles and cocked them.

"Give it to me," said Bannock.

The man frowned, said nothing, and made no move.

"The sword, man," shouted Bannock. "It doesn't belong to you."

He leaned out of the saddle and held out his hand, but one of the Boers kicked at Pot Pourri's leg, forcing the mare to rear and draw back.

"Mr. Bannock." The captain called out a warning. "Will you come along, please."

The rifles were pointed menacingly, but Bannock

cajoled Pot Pourri forward again, again pointing at the saber.

"Come on, hand it over."

"*Hou op, kerels.*" The man with the sword spoke with authority, holding up his hand in a restraining gesture. He pulled the scabbard from his belt and, walking out between the rifles, handed it up to Bannock. "*Hy is reg,*" he said to his comrades; "You are right," he said to Bannock and the matter was settled.

They considered each other for a moment without any sign of friendliness but with a hint of understanding. Then Bannock turned his horse to join the two officers, who had watched the proceedings in astonishment. Without comment, he took Pot Pourri sliding down the gully, shrouding the other two riders in dust as they followed down after him.

When he reined in at the bottom, he realized that the captain and lieutenant were smiling at him.

"You nearly had a fresh battle going there, Mr. Bannock," said the captain.

"Well done, sir," put in the admiring lieutenant.

"Can I hand this over to you?" asked Bannock.

"No," the captain replied. "I think you should hand that in yourself. That's Stevenson's property. It will go to his family."

"As you wish." Bannock shrugged and settled down to wait while Stevenson's body was loaded and the carts moved off.

He rode well to one side, taking the saber to put it in his belt. But he decided not to do that; that would be wearing it. Instead, he hung on to it clumsily with one hand.

It was sundown by the time Bannock reached army headquarters, and it only then occurred to him that Masefield might have left for the Club. But he was still there. He had abandoned his rolltop desk for the orderly's table in the middle of the room, where he sat poring over a pile of papers.

Bannock put the saber on the edge of the table and waited. He was in no mood for the fat major's tactical manners. He cleared his throat loudly.

Masefield looked up, not at him but at the saber.

"I know about that," he said. "Captain Norton came in a short while ago and told me about it. Shall I take it over?"

"Please yourself. It's not mine."

Masefield stood up still looking at the saber. He leaned across, then hesitated. "Maybe you'd like to hand it to the widow?"

"Whatever you say."

"Hmm." Masefield sat down, shaking his head. "No," he said. "I hardly think that would be right."

Bannock suddenly grabbed the saber in both hands and, leaning across the table, slammed it down in front of him.

"Here, you take it. And I'd like to make a suggestion about what you could do with it."

Masefield looked up at him for the first time. "Sit down, Bannock," he said quite calmly. "Please sit. There is something I have to tell you."

"What are you going to pay me for my dead horse?" Bannock fired. "If you had to pay by the bullet, it would cost you plenty."

Masefield seemed preoccupied, worried about something. "We can deal with that later. I'm afraid I have bad news for you."

"Bad news?" echoed Bannock. "Don't you think I've had enough? Is there ever any other kind of news in this lousy town?"

"Your two horses . . . I still cannot believe this myself."

"What about my two horses?"

"They are gone."

"What do you mean, gone?"

Masefield shrugged uncomfortably. "They have disappeared from the face of Kimberley."

Bannock froze in the chair, staring dumbfounded at Masefield. "Have they disappeared in Kimberley or out of it?"

"Or out of it, as you say." Masefield seemed interested in that comment.

Bannock was still in a daze, "What about Marcus?"

"He is still there safe and sound, and we've put an extra guard on the stables." He watched Bannock's impotent fury and went on. "It is quite inexplicable," he said. "Those two horses of yours and two of Watson's. They all went missing at the same time."

"What a useless army you belong to. You couldn't even guard your own horses. Now you can't even find them. You're supposed to be desperate for horses. Why didn't they take Marcus? Why can't you find them, damn you!"

Masefield took it calmly. "Your horse Marcus was shut up in a stable. The other four were put in the open on the picket line. I don't believe they were stolen for horsemeat. The thieves were most discriminating. They only took the racehorses and left the plodders, so to speak. To answer your other question, we have searched the town. They are gone."

Bannock got up, almost kicking the chair over. He walked up and down, shaking his fist in search of words. Masefield's eyes followed him expressionlessly.

"What do you mean, gone? Gone where?"

"God knows where."

"You mean outside the perimeter?"

"Mr. Bannock." Masefield took the wind out of Bannock's sails by smiling. "There are a few things I want to tell you. But first, you look pretty tired. What you need is a good stiff drink." He got up as he spoke and went over to the rolltop desk, where he fiddled in the drawers and came out with a bottle and two glasses.

Bannock slumped down on the chair and laid his arms

on the table. If ever he wanted a drink, he wanted one now. But he was suspicious. The fat, shrewd major was about to butter him up. But why this time? He looked at the double shot of whiskey that was put in front of him, took the glass, and gulped half of it in one mouthful.

"No ice, I'm afraid. This is not the Club." Masefield sounded more cheerful.

Bannock thought, I'm going to have this drink first and worry about being tricked afterward. He gulped the other half, drawing in his breath at the effect of it, and held out the glass.

Masefield smiled as he poured again.

"There are a few things I want to tell you," he said. "On the one hand, you have become a true credit to the garrison. On the other, there are still a few question marks hanging over your head."

Bannock looked upward for the supposed question marks, but said nothing.

"When we impounded your horses, I had the feeling that if there was some kind of retaliatory action you could take, you would take it."

"That's pretty obvious." Bannock took another gulp of whiskey and wondered where that was leading.

"Then I wondered if the opportunity had possibly presented itself."

"Do you enjoy being obscure? They should call you Sherlock Holmes in Wonderland. What particular opportunity are you talking about?"

"Your license to come and go as you please. You and Charlie Watson, the shadows in the night."

"Me and Charlie Watson? What's he get to do with me?"

"You both ride for Rhodes. You ride through the Boer lines. It would be easy enough to stop off on the way."

"What are you suggesting, that I'm dealing with the Boers?"

"Maybe Charlie Watson is."

"Oh, come on, Masefield, Machiavelli Masefield. Make up your mind which maybe it is you're suspecting."

"You don't understand." Masefield seemed pleased with Bannock's agitation. "Conjecture is the basic tool of investigation. You were right to cite Sherlock Holmes. What an apt analogy for this situation. It's all going to sort itself out by a process of assumptions. Clever assumptions, of course."

"How elementary." Bannock drained the last drops and slammed the glass on the table again.

Masefield poured a little more, eyeing the glass, willing it to do its job, but Bannock had calmed down. If anything, he looked more alert than when he'd arrived.

"So you suspect one or both of us of dealing with the Boers?"

"Maybe."

"You suspect us of stealing our own horses?"

"Maybe."

Bannock downed the next tot. "What else do you suspect?"

"Maybe you'd like another." Masefield held out the bottle.

But Bannock had his hand over the glass.

People in carriages, on horseback, and on foot were still converging on the cemetery thirty minutes after the late hour set down to avoid the shelling. Bannock followed along with them on foot. He had left the mare at Lennox Street, to pick her up later.

This time he decided he was being carried along by curiosity. Somehow, he felt related to Stevenson. But why? By the sharing of a horse? He even felt related to those dead troopers, the ones he had seen lying in the heat, the one he had touched. It seemed the sounds of bugles must be beginning to bend his mind, to work him into some state of loyal anger.

It had been a long, unsatisfactory day. First, hunting out MacGrath and holding him to his promise of special feed. Then fighting with the feed merchant, who, as it turned out, did not have the stocks to meet his promise. Then the afternoon at Lennox Street watching Van groom Marcus, watching Van exercise Marcus around the schooling paddock, and generally resenting the poor condition the stallion had got into. He had sent Van back to the racecourse on Lady Potter with the mule they had brought with them to carry the feed. And now he was going to the first funeral he had attended since his father's.

At the entrance to the cemetery, he had to pick his way through a crush of carriages and horses held by grooms. He could only see heads of thousands of people packed into the small military cemetery for the funeral of Scott-Turner, Stevenson, and the others who had died in battle. Over the heads were the steel points of cavalry helmets drawn up in line. He came closer to the sound of the brass band grinding out Schubert's miserable dirge, which mingled with the hushed murmur of voices all around. As he had wondered why he came, he wondered what he was doing there and why he was so determined to see it through. But so far there was nothing to see, except the backs of the military band and a squad of riflemen drawn up at ease.

He pushed his way through the aimlessly waiting crowd and, coming round the end of the troop, stopped, realizing he had come close to the graveside, unwittingly finding himself in front of the spectators on that side. He stood there, feeling self-conscious in his rough leather jacket and light breeches streaked with dust.

In front of him were the long line of graves and the long line of coffins with pathetic little bunches of grass and wildflowers from the parched town. Groups of clergy of different denominations were in their places along the line. Their prayers came back in a droning chorus of different resonances and pitches. Behind them were the dignitaries and the mourners. It was a scene out of England, with a proper old Church of England bishop bearing his mace, his deacons, acolytes, and cross bearer around him. There was a proper English mayor in robe and chains. For the first time, Bannock thought of Kimberley as a town, with the character of an English town and proud people who belonged to it. A place with committees and a Town Hall and drainage and a hospital. It existed in spite of the mines and the exploiters and the hangers-on, in spite of the siege.

Somewhere in the middle he could see the two familiar blonde heads disguised in black. It was a group like an ancient painting: the old woman supported closely on either side by Sarah and the brother, and the little blonde widow standing on her own; outstandingly on her own. He tried to see her face, but her veil was a mask.

The sun was at the horizon, throwing long, threatening shadows, giant shadows from the troopers and their guns. The prayers droned on. And then there came a deep thud, and another, and another. The crowds stirred as the flight of shells could be heard. Then everyone around Bannock automatically ducked as shells exploded about a quarter of a mile away. The service went on as the next series of thuds could be heard, and Bannock became conscious that some of the people behind him were quietly leaving. He watched with admiration the clergymen, who had not flinched at the noise of the explosions. He saw the young widow standing straight and still as a statue, and imagined the grief that would transcend any instinct of danger.

At that moment, Emma was concentrating on the back of the bishop's vestment. She counted the golden rococo rings down one panel and then the next. She heard the bishop's voice.

" 'When thou with rebukes dost chasten man for sin, thou makest his beauty to consume away, like as it were a moth fretting a garment, Everyman therefore is but vanity . . .' "

Emma thought, It's vanity versus communication.

Vain me, vain Geoffrey. If everyone is vain, how are we to make contact with one another? Is my problem vanity? Will I ever make contact? Her thoughts waited for a shell to explode. I will not react to those cannons or the bishop is a better man than I am.

The bishop was droning, " 'Hear my prayer, O Lord, and with thine ears consider my calling. Hold not thy peace at my tears . . .' "

Emma thought, My tears keep falling. Where do they come from? Grief is so natural. You don't have to try to feel it, it just happens to you. And this ghastly music, this gloating torture, this morbid ceremony helps. I must go back to counting rings and not think.

Emma concentrated on remaining numb. She tried to hear nothing, see nothing but the gold rings, but the explosions were closer. There was no way of ignoring them. If they came any closer, she thought, it will not only be Geoffrey who has passed on.

There was a huge explosion nearby, and as it cleared, the bishop's words came through without pause.

" 'The last enemy that shall be destroyed is death.' "

Is that what Geoffrey did? He knew he was going to die. He rehearsed it each night in his sleep. And then, oh God, then he did a brave thing.

Shells were falling and exploding only a few hundred yards away now, but they seemed to be coming no closer. Emma found herself shivering from the strain of it all, a curious condition, like the tears that were happening in spite of any conscious thought. At least, she thought, I must look very mournful to the others.

The coffin was lowered. Emma took sand from the spade held out by the deacon and threw it in. She bumped blindly into the bishop, who guided her back as the family queued past. The riflemen fired into the air, a puny gesture in the face of the ear-splitting shelling. The bugler played the last post unfalteringly through the interrupting explosions.

Only when they moved off did Emma realize how many people had fled for safety. She saw the anxious expressions of her mother and the bishop and began to emerge from the fearless trance she had created for herself. She wondered if they felt like running, too.

The servants had hung a long black ribbon above the mantel, where their own offering of a vase of dried veld flowers stood. The effect was only to expand the gloom that pervaded Lady Freestone-Grant's living room.

Emma sat in the chair normally reserved for Mark, facing her mother across the center table. Mark stood behind her, and she could feel his reassuring fingertips on her shoulders. Sarah sat apart on the window seat, her black bonnet and veil thrown down beside her.

Lady Freestone-Grant had read out the messages of condolence from Cecil Rhodes, Lieutenant-Colonel Kekewich, and other local dignitaries. Now she looked up at her son.

"I would be obliged, Mark, if you would read out the rest of the messages for me."

Mark crossed over and, standing beside his mother, picked up a handful of cards and letters from the tray in front of her.

Sarah got in first. "Mamma, is it necessary to go through each one of them? I'm quite sure Emma would like to retire, and frankly, so would I."

Her mother reacted sternly without turning her head. "I wish to hear these messages of sympathy, and I would like you to remain." It was a command.

Sarah went into the sulks, her lips tightening into the first sign of temper while Mark read out the messages, one after another.

Emma looked down at her hands lying limp in her lap. She felt she must look as if she were listening, but she heard almost none of it. The guilt was growing.

When her mother remarked of one of the messages, "That was very kind of them," Emma looked up and smiled, then looked down again into her thoughts.

The priority was guilt. What was it he had said? His life seemed to have little meaning. But how could any man say that, no matter what the faults of his wife? He said he only came alive when life was at stake. What secret despair made him fearless of death in the face of an impotent life? It was made to be impotent. It was always secret. Did he secretly love her with a tenderness he was unable to show? Did she have the right to demand the truth, to ask a man to expose his fears to her? Did she make enough effort to be loved? She would have to live with the question of whether she had known her husband at all. For that matter, did she even really know the boy she grew up with? The nervous boy. They had ragged him then. Was that a sign she should have seen? But all she saw was a handsome, growing horseman.

The worst question of all arose. Had Geoffrey by his own choice of action taken his own life? How many times had he shouted in his sleep "Die with me"? She shuddered at the memory, and realized that Mark had stopped reading and was watching her with concern.

"I'm quite all right," she said. "Please go on."

Lady Freestone-Grant was also watching her. "Emma, my dear," she said, "I think we must hear these messages. They are all from people who felt about Geoffrey."

Sarah sighed heavily. "Mother, can we leave this over until tomorrow? I think if Emma were to be honest, she would admit she was tired of the whole thing."

Lady Freestone-Grant turned around angrily. "We have heard enough from you, Sarah," she snapped. "Kindly stay where you are."

But Sarah was concentrating on Emma. "Come on, Emma, admit it."

"I'm quite happy, really." Emma knew her sister's temper and waited for it.

"I've been watching you and I don't believe that," Sarah shrilled.

Emma understood what was happening. She would not take it. "Why don't you keep quiet, Sarah? I told you I was quite happy."

Sarah was on her feet, raging. "You are about as happy as you were with your husband."

"How dare you?" shouted Mark. "Come back here and apologize immediately."

Sarah had reached the door. She held it open and fired back, "Is there a message there from a Mr. Bannock?"

"What are you talking about?" Mark stood glaring at her. "What has Bannock to do with this?"

Sarah smiled. "He was at the funeral today. I saw him there. He came to see his dear friend Emma. Everyone must sympathize with dear little Emma."

"You are talking nonsense." Mark was bewildered

Lady Freestone-Grant was not. "Sarah," she commanded, "kindly go to bed."

"No, I will not go to bed. Not until I have explained something to you about your precious little Emma. She went visiting Mr. Bannock when her husband was otherwise engaged."

"Geoffrey knew all about that," Mark intervened. "It was all explained and understood."

"Are you supporting that useless clod who sits around while brave men lose their lives? He had the nerve to show disrespect to Geoffrey."

Mark stopped her. "You are confusing your own emotional problems with the facts. You don't know that Geoffrey ended up feeling a little ashamed. He confided in me that he intended to settle properly with Bannock."

"So Emma had her way again." Sarah spoke directly to her mother, who remained tight-lipped, eyes averted. "What a clever little girl. Almost as clever as Mr. Bartholomew Bannock."

"You sound like a rejected woman," Emma retaliated.

She could not resist saying what immediately came into her mind.

Sarah strode across the room and looked down at her sister menacingly. "I have never been rejected," she shrieked. "I always did the rejecting. I even rejected Geoffrey. And I believe he lived to regret that."

"That is enough," demanded Lady Freestone-Grant.

Sarah tried to get hold of herself but she was beyond control, blurting out her feelings. "You never understood Geoffrey."

Emma shook her head sadly. "I am the only one who ever knew Geoffrey—that is, if anyone ever knew him. He had his own problems."

"What do you mean?"

"He was a nervous boy. He was a frightened man."

"Will you listen to this?" Sarah appealed to her mother in a voice too calm by contrast.

Emma went on quietly. "I am not denigrating Geoffrey. He had more honor than you would understand. I only want you to know that you do not possess the sensitivity to understand such a man."

Sarah smiled triumphantly. "A frightened man," she repeated. "A frightened man, do you hear that? Does the Empire grant its highest awards for courage to a frightened man? And with that preposterous thought, I will take my leave. Good night."

Sarah closed the door and Emma was left looking disconsolately at her mother over the table. She felt ashamed of what she had said. Mark came back into the middle of the room and gave her a sympathetic smile.

"I would like to tell you something Geoffrey said to me."

His mother said softly, "Not now, Mark, if you please."

But he persisted. "If you don't mind, Mother, I think this will help." Then, to Emma, "Geoffrey confessed to me the other night that, after all, he had no interest in our business venture. He saw himself as a supernumerary. He virtually implied that I had talked him into it. So if there was"—he tried for the right word—"depression, I didn't help."

"I certainly didn't help." Emma remained looking down. "And let's be fair to Sarah: I should never have approached Bannock on my own."

"Don't apologize for Sarah. She was not exactly being fair herself. We all grew up together and the idea of any romance between herself and Geoffrey would have come as a great surprise to Geoffrey. That's nothing more than spite on her part. Even her attack on Bannock is ridiculous. He is not sitting around. He has the most dangerous job of all, dispatch riding for the army."

"Did Geoffrey know that?" asked Emma.

"Yes, and I think he was impressed."

How strange, thought Emma, that he had not mentioned that.

"Did Geoffrey really say he would pay for the horse?"

"Yes, he did. He said that you had shamed him rightfully. Oh, I am sorry, Emma. I am upsetting you."

Emma wept silent tears. Her mother interrupted.

"If you don't mind, Mark, I would like to have a few private words with Emma."

Mark crossed over to his mother, bent down, and kissed her, but she kept him there and whispered in his ear: "You men are not subtle enough for moments like this. I know what to say to her."

He whispered back, "I have the greatest confidence in your wisdom. Good night, Mother."

He kissed Emma on the way out, and the two women were left alone.

"Come here, Emma." Lady Freestone-Grant held out her hand.

Emma went around the table, trying to contain her tears. She slumped down on the floor at her mother's knees and took the hand held out to her, holding it at her cheek.

"Emma," Lady Freestone-Grant started, "no matter what you thought of Geoffrey, you were married to a man who might well become a legend. He died a hero. Let him rest as he deserves."

"I regret what I said."

"Never mind." The old lady gazed into space, gathering her thoughts. "You may presume that I am bound by convention. You would be so short of the mark. Shall I tell you about us women? When you have outlived the age of romance by a few decades as I have, you can watch how it works, quite simply and quite critically. We are involved in marriages and maneuvers within marriages where we come to know every finite weakness in our partners, and they, of course, in us. The responsibility that rests with us for loyalty is so immense. We know things no man deserves to know. And here the woman's mind is more fragile even than her body. She can destroy so easily. It is such an awful force, and the man seldom recognizes it. He cannot understand how destruction can be such a delicate process."

Emma nodded, her cheek rubbing against the tightly held hand. "I think I have always understood that, Mamma."

"Said the flighty fledgeling to the old owl. You were not happy with him. If no one saw that—and I do not count Sarah, who is wise after the event—if no one saw that, and it is a credit to you that no one did, I did. I saw the sadness and the confusion and the loneliness and the resulting anger."

"I am not a very good actress."

"But you are, my child. You managed very well. And this is what I want from you. You managed very well as a wife; now you must continue that duty as a widow. And Emma, you must practice more wisdom with your sister. You allow her to provoke you."

"You allow her to defy you." Emma stopped herself. "Oh, I am sorry, Mamma. I should not have said that."

But her mother was actually smiling. "You were the

little tomboy with the strong mind," she reminisced. "Sarah was the strong one, I mean physically. She was always so much more robust than you. That was her only advantage, if you can call it an advantage. Yet, I have a certain sympathy with her. She is entitled to show spirit."

"I know that, and I know the fault lies with me. It's my gullibility, I suppose. I set my own traps. I rise to the bait every time."

"That sounds more a criticism of Sarah than of yourself."

"I can see my own selfishness as clearly as I can see Sarah's. Is the whole world selfish?"

"You do not believe that. I know you too well."

"Does the whole world just pretend to love?"

Lady Freestone-Grant smiled down at her. "You were a loving child and you were a loving wife. You did everything you could. That is one of the things I saw quite clearly. All that remains now is that you go on doing everything you can do," she added, "for Geoffrey."

·7· | SHADOWS AND KILLERS

"Mario."

"Yes, Paddi?"

"Would you be fetchin' our friend another beer from the bar? It's awful hot out here."

Pacelli made a pointing gesture at O'Flaherty, who smiled gratefully. "Sure, I'll be havin' one meself."

The large Italian got up off the edge of the stoep where he was sitting with O'Flaherty and Mabala and went off into the bar. Mabala sat holding the end of the halter rein of the big mule with feed sacks on its back, while O'Flaherty fanned his face with his hat and leaned back into the shade of the verandah to avoid the blistering afternoon sun.

"He's a great man, is Mario Paddykelly. He was one of the finest chefs in Europe, do you know that?"

Mabala nodded solemnly. "I can see he is a chief, *nkosi.*"

O'Flaherty registered a look of guilt. "There is somethin' I think we have to clear up, Mabala," he said. "Do you know this great new cook you have brought to make the food for Mr. Bannock and the rest of us, what's-his-name, Ndogo?"

Mabala nodded.

"That's the one," said O'Flaherty. "Now, if you had twenty fellers like that all cookin' at the same time and there was a chief cook tellin' them what to do, well, that's what Paddykelly does. We call it a chef. But I suppose you could call him a chief."

"Of course, *nkosi,*" said Mabala, seeing no problem. "He is a chief of men, like *nkosi* Bart."

O'Flaherty looked a little doubtful. "Yes, in a manner of speaking. He's a powerful man, you know."

Mabala nodded. "He is strong."

"He's not a man to pick a fight with. Every once in a while some tough character tries to push him around; then you've got to see him strike like a snake"—Mabala's eyes glistened—"with a punch like a fourteen-pound hammer." O'Flaherty dressed it up. "Ah, here comes the beer. And may the Pope himself remember you in his prayers."

Pacelli had to get rid of two mugs before crossing himself and sitting down. They clinked mugs, and big Mabala smiled shyly as he was invited into the great new custom.

"Now, Mabala." O'Flaherty became the chairman. "About this matter of the diamonds I was bringin' up to you the other day. Mr. Paddykelly and meself are extremely interested in the possibilities when it comes to those fascinatin' little stones." O'Flaherty must have felt that he had struck too hard with the subject closest to his heart, because he then remarked nonchalantly to Pacelli, "Did I tell you that Mabala supplies us with the finest beef you've ever tasted?"

"Beef!" exclaimed Pacelli, sucking froth off his large mustache and taking a new interest. "Where he'sa get the beef?"

O'Flaherty was displeased with the turn in the conversation. "He has a few connections out there." He pointed into the distance and tried to get back to business. "Now, about those diamonds."

Pacelli was not finished. "We have'a got the beef ration," he said. "Everything ee'sa short. The fresh herb, the fresh onion, the eggs. It ee'sa impossible."

Now O'Flaherty was really impatient. "Mario," he asked, "is it diamonds or food you are interested in?"

"Both. I would like'a to know where he'sa get'a the beef."

"That's impossible," said O'Flaherty. "He sells it all to the army."

Mabala reassured Pacelli. "Don't worry, chief. If you want beef, I bring it for you."

"Will you stop this?" demanded O'Flaherty. "Here is a wonderful opportunity to find out about diamonds and all you can talk about is meat. Now let's get down to it." He addressed the Zulu. "Mabala, you were tellin' me how they break the rock and there is a little stone on the one side."

"Yes, *nkosi.* Sometimes."

Pacelli leaned across. "It ee'sa only some of the cuts, Mabala. The hindquarters, the ribs." Pacelli put down his beer mug to describe the items with his hands in the air. "You know, you say'a the chops, the sirloin; you know, the big bone with'a meat under it."

"Will you stop this and keep to the subject!" roared O'Flaherty.

Mabala began to laugh, and even when O'Flaherty elbowed him to stop spilling some of his beer, he went on roaring with laughter in his big, deep baritone.

"Chief wants beef, *nkosi* wants diamonds," Mabala spluttered out.

"Forget it!" shouted O'Flaherty. "Who wants beef? You've heard what everybody is sayin'. The relief column will be here at any time. If we are to pick up some diamonds, it's now or never. Is that right, Mario?"

"Yes, Paddi, that'sa right." Pacelli smiled patiently.

O'Flaherty turned his attention back to Mabala. "It's a deadly serious man you're lookin' at," he said. "Where are we to find diamonds in a hurry? Is it down that big hole in the ground? Or can we climb down into the mine, which they'll not be usin' for a while yet?"

Mabala laughed quietly. "*Nkosi,*" he explained, "if you climb into the Big Hole, it will eat you up and no man will see you again. The Big Hole goes down, down, down deep. If you fall down, you are gone."

"And what about the mines?"

"If you go to the mine shaft, they will put you in prison."

"Who?"

"The security, *nkosi.* They are still there. Many men with guns."

"Well, it would be a sad day when Paddy O'Flaherty was worried about a few men with guns. Couldn't we be goin' in there on tiptoe and quietly as you like down the mine?"

Mabala shook his head. "No, *nkosi.* There is a cage, and the men stand in the cage. Then the big wheel turns and the cage goes far, far down."

"Can a man not climb down there?"

Mabala shook his head again. "No, *nkosi.* There is no place for the hands to hold. You will fall down and you will be dead." Mabala handed back his empty mug. "I must go fetch rations, *nkosi,*" he said, standing up.

"Sure, off you go then. We'll talk about this matter later."

O'Flaherty turned to Pacelli as Mabala led the mule away, saluting both of them. "He's a good man to have around. He'd do anythin' for Bart. He'll be standin' in the queues now to collect the rations." He looked at Pacelli unhappily. "It's a sad day when you discover that those diamonds they said were lyin' in the streets are beyond the reach of man. Come on, Mario," he said. "Let's go back in there and pour a drop of whiskey into the sea of beer."

The two large men got up and, wiping away sweat,

proceeded into the bar. The bar was full of men talking loudly about the only subject of the day, the coming of relief.

"Paddy, Paddy, over here." The voice that was shouting belonged to Charlie Watson, brought up to normal height by a high stool at the far end of the bar.

"Order the drinks, Mario, and I'll be right back." O'Flaherty edged his way through the crowded barroom until he reached Watson.

"Where's Bannock?" asked Watson.

For a moment O'Flaherty surveyed the two heavily built characters on either side of Watson. They looked like out-of-work miners at best, but thugs for sure. Watson made no attempt to introduce them.

"Do you hear me, Paddy?" asked Watson. "Where is Bart? I'm looking for him."

"The last time I saw him he was havin' a nice sleep."

"Well, I've got to see him." Watson leaned forward on the stool, beckoning conspiratorially. "Did he tell you about the plan for getting out?" he whispered.

"Does he ever stop talkin' about that?"

"Shhh." Watson put his fingers to his lips and leaned closer. He whispered, "The relief force will be here by tomorrow night, and they'll take every horse in sight. Now I've got to see Bart. It's got to be tonight. And the army must not see us together. Now listen carefully, Paddy. Bart must meet me tonight at the far end of Fenton Street, where the Claims offices are. Near the Big Hole, Paddy. The Big Hole. He must be there at ten o'clock sharp. Have you got that, Paddy?"

"Sure, I've got that. But why can't you be comin' to the racecourse?"

"I'm telling you, Paddy," Watson hissed. "No one must see us together or they'll be on to us. We've got to get the good horseflesh out of this town. Stop asking questions.

Bart asked me if I was ready to go at the off. And this is the off. Tell him I'm ready, and remember: ten o'clock tonight. Fenton Street."

An orderly had brought an extra chair into Major Masefield's office and left. The major looked around at the surprising deputation settling down on the other side of the table, and for the moment remained standing.

Sitting facing him was Sarah Freestone-Grant, sister-in-law of the late Major Stevenson. Facing him on her left was Captain Pendleton of the Buffs, whom he recognized as her regular escort. On the right sat old Colonel Thrumpton, who had ushered them in.

"Shall I order tea?" asked Masefield.

Thrumpton looked at the others for guidance and shook his head. "No, no, thank you. I imagine this will not take too long."

Masefield sat his large bulk down with a smile of anticipation, and Thrumpton cleared his throat to introduce the subject.

"We are here to put a rather delicate matter to you. Miss Freestone-Grant has confided certain information in me which I believe gives rise to the need for further investigation, if not steps to be taken. To this purpose, I have spoken with a certain senior colleague, without going too deeply into the matter, of course. It is the type of thing where the fewer involved the better, I think. My colleague in turn has put us on to you as being the right man to look into this matter." The old man smiled. "It seems you are the supreme sorter-outer."

Masefield smiled back. "I hope I prove worthy of that opinion."

Thrumpton continued. "I must tell you, Masefield, that we have had to overcome Miss Freestone-Grant's natural reticence in coming here. But I have managed to impress upon her that she has a duty to perform. Now let us mince no further words and get down to the subject of our problem, a certain Mr. Bannock."

Masefield's eyebrows rose a fraction but otherwise his expression remained unchanged. "I see," he said. "Please go on."

"To put it bluntly," Thrumpton continued, "Bannock has been bothering this young lady's sister. I'm sure you have met her—the widow of Major Stevenson."

"Of course," said Masefield, watching Sarah in her pretty bonnet frowning down into her lap.

Thrumpton warmed to his task. "In short, he is attempting to extort money from her, and we have reason to believe he is likely to succeed. We also have reason to believe that he is engaged in other suspicious activities which bear investigation."

Masefield leaned forward, interested. "What activities?" he asked.

The old man seemed momentarily thrown off his line of thought. "Well." He considered. "For example, he appears to go missing for days at a time, together with one or more of his horses."

"May I ask how you know that?"

Thrumpton looked around, disconcerted, and Sarah looked up at Masefield.

She said, "I have been to the racecourse on a number of occasions to see the horses, and his men were evasive on the subject of his whereabouts. I have seen his horse of an early morning sweating, and equipped as if at the end of a long journey."

"You are acquainted with Mr. Bannock?" asked Masefield.

Sarah reddened. "At one stage I imagined we shared an interest in bloodstock. But, how shall I say this . . ."

"He made advances," suggested Masefield.

"He is a common fellow." Sarah was becoming heated.

Pendleton intervened. "Let it suffice, sir, that she was forced to have nothing further to do with him."

Masefield turned his expressionless eyes on Pendleton. "Are you also acquainted with this man Bannock?" he asked.

"Never laid eyes on him," said Pendleton. "But he had better watch out if I ever do. When I think of poor little Emma Stevenson caught in that position."

"Ah, yes," said Masefield, "as to that."

Pendleton turned to Sarah. "I say, Sarah, I think you should tell him candidly what you told me."

Thrumpton nodded. "Yes, yes, brace yourself, my dear. You are the one to tell it."

Sarah looked nervously at Masefield and began. "First of all," she said, "I think you should know that Mr. Bannock's reputation as a fraud and a cheat has followed him from Cape Town."

"How do you come to know this, Miss Freestone-Grant?" asked Masefield.

"From Geoffrey—that is, Major Stevenson. He made certain inquiries."

Masefield kept his eyes on her. "Would you say the information was reliable?"

"Now hold on there," objected Thrumpton. "She didn't come here to be cross-examined, you know."

Masefield looked faintly surprised. "I must satisfy myself, sir, before I can form any opinion." He returned his attention to Sarah and smiled reassuringly. "Please go on with your story."

Sarah became more sure of herself. "Ever since Geoffrey's death he has been bothering Emma. He appears at different times and ogles her. He even had the temerity to attend the funeral. The worst of it is, Geoffrey found him despicable. Oh, I really don't know where to start with this. You see, my sister is really quite naive. She has been given the wrong impression that Geoffrey was under some obligation to pay a large amount of money for the horse he acquired. Would you say that was right, Major?"

"No, not really," said Masefield. "In fact, the horse

was commandeered, which means the army is required to recompense him."

"There you are," said Pendleton, and Sarah nodded her apparent surprise.

Masefield held up a finger for attention. "But one might assume," he said, "that there could have been such an undertaking on the basis that the army would never pay out the value of a thoroughbred racehorse."

"There was no such undertaking," Sarah said firmly. "I can assure you that Geoffrey impressed upon Emma that Bannock had no right to any consideration."

"Has she paid him any money to date?"

Thrumpton interjected, "Really, Major, I think we can assume that."

Masefield kept his eyes on Sarah, who frowned and said nothing. He asked, "But you say she now intends to pay him a sum of money?"

"I know that she has drawn a considerable amount for the purpose. She told me so."

Masefield kept her attention. "What about your brother, Miss Freestone-Grant? Is he aware of all this?"

Sarah looked worried. "Oh, no, Major," she said. "I should hate him to be involved. He would go straight to Bannock, and I would not like to be responsible for what might happen."

Masefield's eyes hung on. "But I am surprised he knows nothing about it."

Thrumpton came to the rescue. "I think we agreed in the beginning to keep this among ourselves. I must tell you that I considered going straight to the fellow and confronting him myself. But as Miss Freestone-Grant said, that would be giving things away, and in any event, Geoffrey got nowhere doing just that."

Masefield had not taken his eyes off Sarah, who was becoming visibly uncomfortable.

He asked, "Major Stevenson spoke to Bannock about this?"

But Thrumpton answered. "Indeed he did. Warned the fellow to stay clear of his wife, and apparently came away satisfied he had put him in his place."

Sarah fidgeted under Masefield's gaze.

He asked, "Major Stevenson told you that?"

She rallied. "Yes, he was awfully concerned for Emma."

"But he must surely have discussed all this with your brother as well?" He watched her look of consternation.

She replied, "No, I don't think so. I think he would have been too proud to admit it."

"Then he must have trusted you very much?" Masefield watched her carefully.

"Yes, he did." Sarah looked down.

Pendleton was watching Masefield suspiciously. "I don't quite see where these questions are leading."

Masefield ignored the remark, leaned back, and smiled at them. "We have come to the point," he said, "of how I can be of assistance. I think we must concentrate on the problem Mrs. Stevenson has created and treat your conjecture of Bannock's other suspicious behavior separately. In the case of Mrs. Stevenson, I ask myself whether it would not be enough to issue Bannock with a warning and take steps to recover any funds he may have wrongly acquired." He held up his finger at the signs of interjection from Thrumpton. "If you please, sir." He went on. "The alternative is to evaluate this as a police matter. But from everything you say, there would seem to be little evidence that could be of any real use. Unless"—he held up his finger once again to stop both men from protesting—"unless, of course, we could enlist the cooperation of Mrs. Stevenson." He saw the alarm on Sarah's face.

"That would be impossible," she said. "She is still in a state of shock over Geoffrey."

"Of course, of course," Thrumpton agreed.

"Well, then," said Masefield, "can I ask you to leave this matter in my hands for further investigation? Will you let me decide what the best course of action should be? And of course, I shall let you know as soon as possible what my findings are."

He watched Sarah stand up quickly, making little pretense of her desire to be out of the office. "Thank you, Major Masefield." She preceded the others to the door.

"Good day, sir." Pendleton looked dissatisfied as he followed Sarah.

Masefield got in before Thrumpton could shake hands, "Can I talk privately to you for a moment, sir?"

Thrumpton waved away Pendleton, who was waiting in the doorway. "Go ahead, my boy. I shall join you both presently." He returned his attention to Masefield. "Now what is it, Major?" he asked impatiently.

"A word in your ear, sir. Bannock is one of our most valued men."

"Valued?" echoed the astonished colonel.

"Any dispatch rider who stays alive at this juncture is valued."

"Dispatch rider? You don't say."

"We have also checked him out. He is no angel. But he has been honest enough with us. But one thing is certain: he is very tough. I would advise Captain Pendleton not to throw his weight around there, because he would come off second best."

Thrumpton slowly sat down, staring at Masefield in open-mouthed disbelief.

Masefield continued, "Bannock has had a bad time of it. Lost three of his horses, and in each case we were responsible. If he has problems with women, I suspect they arrive on his doorstep unannounced."

"What are you suggesting?"

"I am suggesting, sir, that Major Stevenson was in touch with me over the matter of his horse, and the evidence I know conflicts with what I have heard today. I also suggest that Miss Freestone-Grant knows, or I should say knew, Bannock better than you would suspect."

"Now hold on. Are you suggesting she is duping us? What about the money?"

"As to that, my impression of Major Stevenson's widow is not one of a gullible young woman. I have spoken to her, and she rather impressed me as a person of surprising intelligence."

"What is to be done?" asked Thrumpton helplessly.

Masefield was emphatic. "I cannot see my way clear to attacking Bannock without the direct evidence of Mrs. Stevenson herself."

"The point is, what do you intend to do?"

Masefield smiled grimly. "Nothing, sir," he said. "I intend to do nothing."

The light from the oil lamp on the bar made it difficult to read the letter. Bannock lay on his back on the straw bales and held the page close, angling it toward the light. He read the letter for the fourth time.

Shields Hotel
16th December, 1899.

Dear Mr. Bannock,

It has been reported to me that you performed a courageous act in retrieving my husband's saber from the enemy. For that I shall always remember you with gratitude. The saber will be given to his regiment to keep as a memento.

You will recall the occasion when I made an unsuccessful attempt to pay you for the horse Geoffrey took over. Now I am glad to be able to inform you that before he died, he told my brother that he intended to pay you the true value of the horse.

Therefore I am sending this by messenger with the best amount I can raise at present, and this time you must agree it would be wrong not to accept. The gesture comes from Geoffrey, not from me.

With kind regards,
Emma Stevenson

It was written in a strong sloping hand, difficult to relate to the pretty little writer. He tried to imagine her as she was writing it: the small face, the intense eyes, the coil of light curls hanging down. Could it be true about Stevenson intending to pay for the horse? It seemed unlikely, a too sudden change of heart and intentions.

This girl took some understanding. She was bent on paying him this money, despite, first, an irate husband and, now, almost certainly, her family, who would never approve. It had become a kind of relationship between them. He thought ironically that if he gave the money back, and continued to give the money back, he could be in touch with her for a long time. It could be the way of getting to know her. The day might come when he could say, Keep the money, I'll take you instead. Keep your sister, I'll take you instead. After all, she was single. Single and no doubt grieving. But you can't grieve forever.

"With kindest regards, Emma Stevenson." Emma. Is that short for a name or is it a name on its own? But Emma was not like Sarah, who had flounced past him in the street on the arm of a captain, carefully laughing and looking the other way. Emma was the name in a poem about truth. She was the true sister, who compensated for her sister's frivolity. True to her husband. True to the memory of a hero for all time. She is untouchable, Bannock. Keep the money and stop dreaming about her.

He looked at the ripped-open parcel of bank notes lying on his chest and thought, I'd rather have her there than you. Shall I count it? It looks like a lot. Maybe she thinks I'm starving to death here on the racecourse instead of counting those nice wads that come in from MacGrath.

There was a crack of a field gun firing in the distance; the echo traced it to the usual source, Carter's Ridge. The ear had become trained to follow the whining course of the shell and he knew the explosion would come a mile or two to the east. Another crack, and the same trajectory. Then silence. The Boer gunners were behaving erratically, firing desultory bursts at different times of the day, sometimes right through the night.

I am lying on my back and going nowhere, but we will have to get out before relief arrives. Forget about Charlie Watson. He has some strange plans of his own, and in a way he is not to be blamed. He knew the route to freedom better than anybody, and considering he had a large string to move, it had to be conceded that the smaller the party, the easier he was going to get away undetected. No, somehow they were going to have to get Marcus out of custody and make a break for it with their last three horses, leave the mule behind and head southwest the fastest way they could go. I keep saying this and we're still here. It has got to be tomorrow night.

He heard the sounds of Mabala and the cook talking and banging pots around, and wondered whether O'Flaherty had come back. He shouted, "Paddy, Paddy, are you there?" and throwing the letter and parcel of money on the bar, he got up stretching.

The door opened, but it was Van Breda, not O'Flaherty.

"Where's Paddy?" asked Bannock and watched the elaborate sign language.

O'Flaherty was not back. He was still in town.

"What is he doing there besides drinking?"

Van Breda lifted his elbow vigorously to show that was the only object of the excursion.

Bannock stepped out into the cool evening air and strolled across to the cooking fire, where Mabala and the cook sat in the middle of a ring of friends, talking animatedly. The drone of the chatter of thousands of native voices came from the racecourse behind. Mabala was on his feet, saluting.

"Dinner is served in one hour, *nkosi,*" he announced.

They hardly looked up at the sound of a distant gun going off. It was the same battery firing in the same direction, and clearly out of range of the racecourse.

"Smells good," Bannock remarked. "Are you going out tonight, Mabala?"

"Later, *nkosi,* later. When the moon is there." He indicated a point below the horizon.

Bannock watched the trail of gunsmoke hanging over the hills. "Those guns are strange," he reflected. "They don't seem to be trying very hard."

Mabala concentrated on the moon. "It will be easy tonight, *nkosi.* We get cattle tonight. Those people, they are all going away."

Bannock nodded. "I heard about that. They are going down to fight the relief column. Maybe that's why they're firing like that, to make it look as if there are more of them than there are. How many are there left, Mabala?"

"Not many, *nkosi.* Some fifty man here. Some fifty man there. They leave all the big guns. They leave the wagons, everything. The men and the horses, they go."

"Good," said Bannock. "I hope it stays that way, because tomorrow night we go."

Mabala brightened up. "I go with you, *nkosi.* Where you go, I go."

"I have no horse for you. Can you ride the mule?"

"I run on my feet, *nkosi.* This Zulu can run all night. I ride the mule. I make him go. Do I come, *nkosi?*"

Bannock laughed. "You come, Mabala." He grabbed the outstretched hand and they both laughed, Mabala exposing a great gash of gleaming teeth.

Van Breda was beside them, getting their attention with waving gestures. He gave the high hand-turning sign for O'Flaherty, then pointed. O'Flaherty was coming. By that time they could hear the clatter of Lady Potter's hooves and the raucous singing voice.

Bannock went to meet him and watched patiently as the great Irish rider dismounted to become a weaving, unstable drunk. Van Breda took the horse, and O'Flaherty straightened up into a dignified though unsteady posture.

"Don't snap me head off now. It's a fine afternoon I've been havin', and never a moment of it wasted."

"You mean you never stopped drinking?"

"That's enough of that now. I've been doin' all your messages. Directin' Mabala to where the rations are kept. And here's a fact that will interest you. I know the whole look of the diamond-diggin' possibilities."

"How does it look?"

O'Flaherty swayed and thought. "Not so good, Bart," he said, "not so good. And now I'll be takin' meself off for a short rest."

"What messages?"

"Messages? What messages?"

"You said you were doing my messages."

O'Flaherty's eyes lit up. "Oh, sure, and begorra. There was Charlie Watson himself sittin' at the bar with two big bruisers." He swayed toward Bannock, pointing at his chest. "You got to meet him tonight. Hey, what's the time? Look at your watch. You've got to meet him at ten o'clock. Fenton Street at the Kimberley Mine."

"What are you talking about, Paddy? Start again."

"It's the gettin' out of here. He said you talked to him. Now he wants to go. And it's all about the plan."

"Then why doesn't he come here?"

"That's what I was after sayin'. Why don't you go and talk to Bart at the racecourse, I said. But no." O'Flaherty put a finger to his lips. "Shhh, quiet, he says. People are watchin' him, he says, and watchin' you, too."

Bannock looked at his watch. It was after nine, and he

would barely have time to get there. So the army was after Charlie. Maybe this time he was forced to get out. In any event, it was worth hearing what he had to say.

"I'm going." He shouted to Van Breda, "Saddle up Pot Pourri quickly," then turned back to O'Flaherty. "Where did you say I had to meet him?"

"Fenton Street. It's one of them small streets on the side of the Big Hole. Sure, you know, leadin' off the market at that end. Will I be comin' with you?"

"No, I'm going on my own. You're in no state to go anywhere." Bannock was already striding off to help Van Breda, who had led the mare out.

They all watched as he tightened the girths, swung into the saddle, and cantered away into the dark.

O'Flaherty was offended. He stood swaying and staring at Van Breda and the group around the fire.

"Did you hear that?" he bellowed. "Did you hear what the man said? Paddy O'Flaherty is in no condition. Well, let me tell you all present here that there was never a time in the history of man when an O'Flaherty was in no condition. Forkin' cheek of the man. Not good enough to be a dispatch rider, am I? Well, I could teach him a thing or two about that. There's nothin', do you hear, nothin' that I'm in no condition for. I can prove it right now. Go on, draw a line. Draw a line and I'll be showin' you. And does anybody want to fight? Come on. I'll fight the whole lot of you. Come on, Mabala, you're a big fellow. Do you want to fight?"

Mabala came toward him, grinning. "*Nkosi*," he said. "If a man wants to fight you, I fight him. But you are too strong."

"You're a bloody liar," shouted O'Flaherty. "You're the strongest man I ever saw."

"You must rest, *nkosi*."

"Never in your life. I need a drink. Would you be after lookin' around and findin' me something to drink? Sure, I was drinkin' Charlie right under the bar."

"Charlie," echoed Mabala in a moment of recognition. "Piccanin man?" He indicated Watson's height. "*Nkosi,* you mean the small man, the jockey?"

O'Flaherty nodded impatiently. "The jockey, the trainer, the squint-eyed little shit."

"That small man, he speak to *nkosi* Bart there?" He pointed toward the grandstand. "He talk, talk, talk, and he go away?"

"That's himself. The squint-eyed little bugger with the big head."

"I see him there." Mabala pointed out into the darkness beyond the perimeter.

"Sure, sure, he's a dispatch rider too."

"No, *nkosi.* Not dispatch ride. I see him with the Boers. He take four horses to the Boers. Not army horses. This kind of horses."

O'Flaherty flicked his eyes and focused on Mabala. "What are you sayin', Mabala? Is it Charlie you're talkin' about? Little shitface Charlie? I never could stand the man. What are you talkin' about?"

"I see him there, *nkosi.* I stand in the cattle." Mabala squatted down to demonstrate. "I look through there. I see him come with one other man and those four horses."

"Is it racehorses you saw, like our horses?"

"Yes."

"Was there a gray one? Light color?"

"Yes. One light one, *nkosi.*"

"The bastard," said O'Flaherty, "the two-faced little bastard. And Bart is goin' in there to meet him not knowin' a word of this. Well, I'll be after him right away and make sure there's no funny business. Here, Van, get that saddle straight back onto the mare. Did you hear what Mabala said about that little rat?"

Van Breda was nodding and making indecipherable signs of violence with his hands. Then he went to the aid of O'Flaherty, who was staggering around the horse with the saddle.

"Now you all stay here," shouted O'Flaherty, "and I'll be dealin' with this little matter on me own."

They helped him into the saddle, and Van Breda made signs to be careful.

"Oh, I'll be careful," said O'Flaherty, pulling the horse around. "I'll be careful to break the neck of that connivin' little shit."

When the three urchins saw the thrower of coins, they wasted no time running after his horse, trotting quietly behind once they had caught up. He had almost reached the Market Square when he became aware of their presence, given away by the light patter of feet.

"I don't need you tonight, thank you." Bannock made appropriate signs and went on, but soon realized they were still there, pattering along behind on their bare feet. He turned Pot Pourri and they scattered away from the tall, impressive horse into the shadows, where they waited. Bannock laughed. There was nothing they would understand but the coin. He held one up and tried to think how Van would make the point with his hands. The coin was caught, and, at last, the negative message understood.

Bannock rode into Market Square and immediately reined back into an alleyway as an artillery troop rumbled past. Once they were gone, he emerged again into the deserted square. There was no time to waste with officials, who would try to apply the curfew in spite of his special pass.

There were a number of streets leading off toward the open mine from the left side of the square. One of them was Fenton Street. He kept close to the building, riding to the near corner, then working his way up the streets until he found Fenton. It was a street of Claims offices, closed up for the night, with no sign of life anywhere. The moonlight came in at an angle, lighting only the upper parts of the buildings on one side.

Bannock rode slowly into the narrow, gloomy street. Even at a walk, Pot Pourri's hooves echoed away like the sound of chopping wood. By the time he had gone halfway, he had neither heard nor seen anything. Then he thought he saw a movement in the darkness up ahead.

"Charlie?" he called, but there was no response. It had already occurred to him that he might be wasting his time. Charlie could have been talking a lot of drunken nonsense in that pub. He looked around at what he could see of the street and decided that if one had to choose a secret meeting place, this was it—one of those side streets that serve no passing traffic. He would ride to the end, then give up and go back.

Suddenly, Pot Pourri stopped dead and blew hard through her nostrils, and Bannock saw what she had sensed, two dark figures walking into the street a short distance ahead.

"Charlie?" Bannock called again, and heard his own voice echo into the darkness.

"Over here," came the answer. "Over here, mate."

Bannock began to dismount. His feet had hardly reached the ground when an arm came around his neck and one of his arms was twisted back in a powerful grip. He saw another shadowy figure grasp for the reins and pull the mare on one side.

"Charlie," shouted Bannock, but the arm pressed in, choking him, and he heard no reply as he struggled with the man behind him. Another two figures were converging on him, and he knew that if there was going to be any faint chance of getting away, he would have to take action immediately or be overwhelmed. He leaned backward until the man behind was forced to lean forward to balance his weight, then lurched forward down onto his knees, pulling the man right over him, driving his fists into his back at the same time. The man was forced to let go, and immediately Bannock was running as fast as he could along the dark street, using the moonlit tops of the buildings as a guide.

But there was a powerful runner behind him. It was an uneven match between his boots and his opponent's bare feet. He was being chased by a native who could have outrun him in any circumstances. He cursed himself, as he ran, that he had left the revolver behind. Then the tackle came, and he was brought down headlong in the dusty street.

Bannock was pulled up onto his feet by the man and swung around. But this time he was ready. He punched at the stomach and saw the head go down. The running footsteps were coming closer. He punched at the head and saw the man collapse as the others came on him. After that, he hit out blindly as the circle of figures closed round him, and in a short while it was all over. He went down, hit from behind by something heavier than a fist, groaning as he felt himself kicked once in the ribs and again in the stomach. The pain welled up through his stomach, through his chest, to his head, where it throbbed. Beyond that he was capable of little more than impressions: gruff voices, English as well as native accents. He was being dragged. He was floating. He could see nothing but the prickling lights that haunt the eyes when they close in pain.

Slowly, his senses returned. He could taste the dust on his lips and smell the leather of riders. Hands held his arms and legs. He was being carried, head hanging down, face down like a corpse on a battlefield. The ground moved past below, and he could see the bare feet of the two natives who were holding his legs, walking rapidly. He strained his aching head sideways and saw heavy, strapped boots marching there. He could hear their heavy breathing. Nothing was said; the action became monotonous. The pain also became monotonous, and he knew that he was virtually helpless in the grip of these four men.

The ground changed. There were stubbles of dry yellow grass, then neatly packed flintstones and a slab of metal, and another slab of metal. They were crossing the railway line. Plain gravel followed, scattered with stones. He watched the feet and their wild, walking shadows, thrown by the moonlight. He tried to think. That was Charlie Watson's voice, and he sounded cool as you like. No one was attacking Charlie, so what was his part in this? What was going on? What was Charlie Watson getting out of this? The pain came up and blanked out all thought, until he was brought up with a jolt. The marching feet had stopped. For a moment the ground stood still, then it moved again. They seemed to be edging forward slowly.

The ground came to an end and Bannock found himself looking down a precipitous slope. Suddenly, he knew where he was and knew what was about to happen to him. He struggled but he was being held tightly at each arm and leg. He was swinging. They were swinging him forward and backward, forward and backward. The movement brought waves of dizziness. The momentum killed all resistance. He heard a voice shout, "Now," and felt himself come free and fall into space.

He twisted and grabbed and fell headlong into the gloomy abyss. The descending wall of sand and rock rushed past. It seemed to be almost vertical at that point. His body hit what seemed to be a sandbank. A long, scraping sensation, and he was bounding away into space again. Another hit; this time an impact more like rock tearing at his clothes. He hit the side again and again, but none of it stopped the momentum of his fall. He began to roll uncontrollably, sliding and bouncing like a pebble going down a cliff. A sudden jar, and the wind was knocked out of him as he plowed into a bank of loose gravel that seemed to level off slightly from the acute precipice. The sand immediately gave way and moved, in a scraping avalanche that sucked in his legs, and then his torso. Bannock fought in a swimming motion to keep his head and arms above the surface. The moving mass of sand slowly came to a standstill, with only his head sticking out and the dust blinding and choking him.

He blinked until he could see. The sky showed above

the black edge of the crater, far above. The sandbank he had fallen into curved upward to a point, forming a long, ghostly glacier that stood out from the black surroundings. He struggled to free his arms, and the whole subsiding movement began again. There was a feathering sound of falling sand behind him. He looked back in horror as he realized that he was sliding toward the final drop, which went vertically down into a chasm nothing could come out of. The movement ground slowly to a standstill again, except that now his arms were free, his hands lying flat on the surface. He tried to move, but the smallest movement brought another inching of the subsidence. He had to keep still, control his breathing, or he would slide off the edge just a few feet behind him. He listened to the sand dribbling off the edge and concentrated on keeping absolutely still, hardly daring to breathe. Pain wracked his body and he became involved in the pain, lying there with his eyes closed for what seemed like hours.

Then thoughts began again, calmer thoughts. He knew where he was: partway down the crater dug by a thousand, how many thousand obsessions. From where he lay he could see the stars, framed in the black curve of the hole. He was in a vast, unturned megaphone that emitted only silence. But incredibly, there was a sound, hardly a whisper, coming in from above, a rustling noise that grew, a scampering like small animals climbing down the slope. He opened his eyes and strained to see upward. He could feel his heartbeat, pulsing from his buried legs through to his head, and knew his life was not worth much, suspended at that edge where he could drop into oblivion at any moment.

The sounds came down again, scraping and scampering, and this time he could see movements. Small movements, as if rocks on the slope had come to life. They were moving down slowly toward him. He closed his eyes as loose sand feathered down, stinging his face with flying showers of grit. The sounds came closer, scraping and sliding, a chittering of small voices. He opened his eyes again, and suddenly he could make out a small figure climbing down just above and to one side of the sand mass. Then another small figure just behind and, close behind, yet a third.

As they drew nearer they became three shadowy little boys, the flat, wiry ripples of hair catching the moonlight. The three little urchins, the three monkeys who hear and see everything. They came down expertly, sliding on their hands and flattened-out feet over the rocky surface alongside. They stopped almost in line with Bannock, who, in spite of his excitement at being discovered, kept very still, acutely conscious of the deadly three feet of sand that might move off at any moment.

"Stay off the sand," Bannock warned, but they huddled together and stared at him blankly.

One of them tried to approach on the sands toward him and immediately the movement started up, taking Bannock's body a few inches farther toward the edge before it stopped again. The little boy jumped back and stared down at the edge where sand poured over.

"Go fetch help," said Bannock, knowing as he said it that it was a pretty hopeless request.

"*Yebo, nkosi,*" one of the urchins answered without understanding.

The three of them chattered among themselves while Bannock waited helplessly. One of them produced a leather rein that served as a belt. They held it up and discussed it. It was the type of thin but tough leather cord used to tie the traces on teams of oxen. The one who held it up leaned over the edge of the sand and gently flicked the end toward Bannock's hands.

"You will never hold my weight" said Bannock despairingly. But they did not understand and began to chatter urgently at him in their own vernacular.

Bannock carefully closed one hand over the end of the rein. It was a chance where there were no other chances. He watched the three little boys all lean forward and take a grip on the short length of leather. Then they all put their heels down and pulled. Bannock got his other hand to the rein, and the sand began to shift ponderously down. He kicked with his feet through the loose, heavy mass, and for a while he was virtually climbing, just holding his own against the gathering momentum. But the little boys were stronger than he'd thought. They were pulling the upper part of his body toward them. He was nearing their side of the gathering avalanche when his feet felt the edge and slipped over into space. He looked upward desperately, one hand on solid ground. The little boys had caught their end of the rein around a jutting rock, and by that movement they saved his life. His knees were on the edge of the precipice and his fists gripping the rein flattened onto the solid rock face as the sand roared past on his right, falling into the silent, gaping mouth of the great hole.

Bannock crawled painfully upward, with one of the boys pulling at his collar. Once his feet were on solid ground, he lay still and laughed weakly. He patted the nearest boy on the arm, and all three crawled down and patted him on the head and back, chattering and laughing among themselves.

Slowly, he turned over and sat up, groaning at the pain in his ribs. The avalanche had passed almost noiselessly into the void below. The boys were already pointing upward and starting to climb. Bannock got onto his hands and knees and followed them. But he was shaking all over, and soon he had to stop and lie flat again. He rolled over on his back and unsuccessfully tried to remove his boots, sliding down slightly at each effort. The boys came scampering back and pulled the boots off for him.

"Leave them there," said Bannock, but two of the boys started off again, each with a boot under one arm.

He rolled back onto his stomach and began to feel better. The long, slow climb started. He found that by moving slowly, feeling with each hand, taking one foothold at a time, he was able to keep moving at a steady pace.

For a while he made good progress, until he stopped at the sound of a shout from above. The shouting came again, and the three boys let out piercing whistles in reply, which echoed around the crater. They listened to the shouting, but the words were inaudible. The three boys muttered together, and one of them went off darting up the slope on his own, while the other two waited for Bannock.

The pause for rest had only brought back the pain. He felt bruised and sore everywhere and utterly exhausted, but he knew that what had happened to him was done for a purpose. He had to find out that purpose and act against it as quickly as he could. The climb started again, with the two boys encouraging him at every moment. He could still hear shouting from above, and the boys paused once or twice to give their piercing whistles. He wondered how long it was taking, remembering the fast sensation of falling down to the edge of the lower precipice. It was all much darker. The moon must be going over the horizon.

Bannock lost all sense of time. He rested, panting, against the steep slope. He climbed, hand up, feeling, foot scraping up and holding, pulling up to feel with the other hand, groping and straining and stopping to rest again. He rubbed his sweating face against his sleeve, feeling the dust change to dripping mud. Now he could hear the voices above. O'Flaherty's voice and others. Sand trickled down, and the boy who had gone up ahead came sliding toward him at the end of a length of cable. They held the cable together as more of it came looping down.

A voice shouted from above, "Is that far enough?"

Bannock shouted, "Yes."

O'Flaherty's voice came: "Is that you down there, Bart?"

"Yes," he answered.

The first voice shouted, "Have you got hold of the cable?"

"Yes," he shouted back.

"Hold on, then."

The cable looped back and went taut. Bannock hung on tightly with both hands. He was dragged up slowly and by jerks for the final fifteen yards or so. He could hear men grunting and straining up above and saw the three boys climbing up alongside him. They went ahead and over the top, joining in to help with the pulling as he was hauled bodily onto the flat surface.

He rolled over onto his back and looked up at the night sky, thinking about how the mind takes over when it needs to survive. It makes things happen, ignores the impossible, it cries out in gratitude for life and becomes aware of what might not have been—the smell of the dust, the cool air, the sound of humans. But without the three little bobbing monkeys, nothing would have happened. Nothing but a long, falling path into death.

The men were bending over him. "There's blood on his chest," one said.

"What in heaven's name happened?" That was O'Flaherty's voice.

They tried to lift him up.

"Wait, give me a moment. Let me lie." Bannock felt as if he could go to sleep right there in spite of the pain.

O'Flaherty's voice said, "What grand little fellows you are. Come over here; don't be afraid."

"There are going to be a few questions asked here," came a gruff voice. Bannock opened his eyes to find himself surrounded by a group of Town Guardsmen. He sat up and looked down at his torn, blood-splattered clothes. O'Flaherty was holding one of his boots.

"Did you find Pot Pourri anywhere?" asked Bannock.

"The mare is missin' and Charlie Watson is nowhere to be seen."

"You'll both have to come with us," said the sergeant in charge.

Bannock could see a Cape cart with two horses in harness. "I've got a pass," he said.

"That's what your friend here said, but you'll still have

to come in for questioning. How the hell did you get down the hole, anyway?"

"Wasn't I just tellin' you?" said O'Flaherty. "He was pushed down. Would the man be jumpin' down for the fun of it?"

Bannock began to struggle to his feet, and they helped him. "Right now, I'd like to find Mr. Watson," he said.

"I've got somethin' to tell you about that," said O'Flaherty. "He was seen by Mabala handin' over horses to the Boers, one of them a gray."

"You can do your talking later," snapped the sergeant. "You're coming with us to Lennox Street."

"That's it," said Bannock as realization dawned. "It's the horses. He's planning to get out with our horses, the little bastard. Do you know what that means?"

O'Flaherty had caught up. "Marcus!" he gasped.

"That's right," said Bannock, already on the move toward the cart. You said Lennox Street?" he shouted at the sergeant. "That's where we want to go."

Three horsemen rode into the stable enclosure of the racecourse. They picked their way carefully in the moonless atmosphere, following the dull light of the carbide lamp held by the man in front. The lamp played across the closed doors of the stables. They stopped when they saw Mabala at the end of the stable block beside his small fire, laying out leather thongs, in preparation for his nocturnal sortie to the southern ridges.

"*Nkosi?*" called Mabala, thinking it was Bannock.

"Hey, you. Can you understand me?" It was Charlie Watson's voice.

Mabala stood up straight and suspicious. "Yes, I understand," he said.

"Where is Mr. O'Flaherty?" Watson was impatient. "Paddy O'Flaherty. Come on, man, call him."

"He is not here," said Mabala.

"Oh, there's Van." The light from Watson's lamp picked up Van Breda walking from the end stable rubbing his eyes and shaking his head.

"Where the hell is Paddy? I thought he'd be here." Watson dismounted and pulled his horse forward. "Van, my boy, you've got to do something for old Charlie. Which is Marcus' box?"

Van Breda stood still rubbing his eyes, looking blank and sleepy.

"Come on, son. Wake up. Come on, give us one of your clever signs. Is that the one? That's where you keep Marcus, isn't it?" He pointed impatiently. "Now listen, Van. Bart has sent me to fetch Marcus. We are putting all the horses at my place ready to move out."

Van Breda blinked and made no movement.

"Listen, boy, did you get the message? Come on now, look lively. Let's get Marcus out." He turned to the man behind him. "Mick, get down off your arse and check those stables."

The man dismounted and approached one of the stable doors, striking a match.

Mabala came up behind Van Breda, staring into the carbide lamp over the jockey's head. "Marcus is not here," he said.

The man who had dismounted called from the stables. "There's a mule here, Charlie." He threw away a match and struck another as he reached the next door.

"What do you mean, he's not here?" Watson began to sound really nasty.

"He is at Lennox Street," answered Mabala.

"The army?" Watson's voice rose to an agitated falsetto. "You're joking. Bannock would never agree to that. Lennox Street? What's he doing there, anyway?"

Van Breda and Mabala remained obstinately still. Watson lowered the lamp and Van Breda stared in amazement when he recognized Pot Pourri being led by the man who was opening the stable doors one after the other.

"You're lying," shouted Watson. "Has Paddy got Marcus? When's he coming back?"

Van Breda turned and walked quickly toward Bannock's quarters in the grandstand bar.

"Where the hell are you going?" shouted Watson. But he was more interested in the stables. "Look in every stable," he ordered. He kicked the ground and shone the weak light toward the two stable doors still to be opened. He waited. The stalls were empty.

Van Breda's footsteps were coming back. Watson shone the lamp on him, then moved quickly around to the other side of his horse. Van Breda came on with Bannock's revolver. He stood with his back to Mabala and pointed it.

"What do you think you're doing, Van? Have you gone off your nut? Put the gun away, there's a good man." Watson used his horse as cover, holding on tightly to the reins and the stirrup leather.

Van Breda and Mabala ducked as a shot rang out, ricocheting off the ground beside them. They were facing three guns: Watson's revolver aimed from under the neck of his horse, another revolver in the hands of the mounted man behind, and a carefully aimed rifle held by the man at the stables.

"Put the gun down, you stupid dumb midget."

Mabala whispered, "Please put it down, small *nkosi.*"

Van Breda put the gun on the ground and Watson walked forward to retrieve it. The man at the stables reholstered his rifle, and suddenly Van Breda was running. Before Watson could bring the lamp round, the little jockey was past him and racing toward Pot Pourri. He literally climbed up the mare's near side onto the saddle and smacked at her neck with his flat hand. Pot Pourri reared back, pulling the man who was holding her off his feet. But the man held on, skidding after the backing horse.

"Get off that horse," Watson shouted, juggling wildly with the lamp and the revolver and the reins he was holding.

Van Breda spurred at the mare's flanks, slapping her hard behind the saddle. She whipped around furiously and flung the man clear. There was the crack of a revolver. Van Breda spun off the far side, falling, as Pot Pourri went off at a gallop.

Watson uncocked the hammer of his revolver, cursing to himself. He hardly had time to hear the heavy footfalls from behind when he was grabbed roughly by the back of the neck and swung around. The lamp fell to the ground. The revolver was snatched from his hand and he was helpless in the grip of Mabala, the two massive hands around his throat choking away all sound, choking him.

Charlie Watson died with his feet clear of the ground before the other two men knew what was happening.

"Charlie," shouted the one who was mounted.

"Let's get out of here," said the other, who was still on his feet.

But they were too late. They were surrounded by a mob of natives, shadows who came quickly out of the dark.

The man on the horse fired into the air and shouted, "Get back," but was immediately pulled from his horse. The crowd closed in, taking hold of the horse, snatching the weapon away.

Mabala called to them and they went quiet, holding the two men, who were speechless with terror.

The big Zulu crossed to where Van Breda lay still. He leaned down, felt the blood on the small jockey's chest, and supported his head in one big hand. Van Breda opened his mouth in a painful smile. He made slow movements with his hands, the one held upward, the other pointing sideways. Mabala nodded furiously, pretending to understand. Van Breda's eyes closed and his arms went slack.

Mabala felt the chest and shook his head slowly. He picked up the small body and walked back to the stables.

* * *

The pale gray light, part night, part morning, gave shadowy form to the activity in front of the stables. Hundreds of Africans stood and squatted, watching impassively.

Masefield sat on his shooting stick in front of the flat open wagon watching the troopers bring out the two prisoners and load them onto the back. He turned, scooping up the shooting stick in his hand in a surprisingly agile movement for such a fat man, and walked slowly back to the stables, tapping the stick thoughtfully on the ground. He stopped in front of Bannock, examining his torn dusty breeches and shirt with its patches of dried blood. Bannock ignored him and remained leaning on a stable door, staring unseeingly.

"You look awful," said Masefield.

The doctor came walking quickly from the end stable, where the two bodies lay.

He said, "Watson looks as if he was hung by hand."

"What a curious diagnosis," remarked Masefield.

"Well, it's difficult to express one's findings in a case like this." The doctor tapped his chin. "The cause is undoubtedly strangulation, and the only logical deduction is that the act was carried out by hand. But it's an interesting case, I must say. Very unusual. You see, death must have been instantaneous, and in a case of strangulation that is unusual. No signs of violence on the body except the severe contusions at the neck. If I were asked to identify the kind of hands that did it, I would have no hesitation in suggesting a giant, or something approaching it."

"Interesting you should say that." Masefield was looking at Mabala, who was sitting leaning against the stable wall a short distance away, beside O'Flaherty.

"Do you need me for anything further?" asked the doctor.

"Thank you, Doctor. You may leave. But kindly regard this as confidential for the time being."

The doctor went off to his horse. "The bodies are for

the morgue and I am for my bed," he remarked cheerfully.

Masefield called after him, "This is not for the *Diamond Fields Advertiser,* you understand."

"My lips are sealed," he called back.

The light was growing, and Mabala got up to turn off the storm lantern that was left in the open.

"Coffee, *nkosi?*" he asked. Bannock nodded.

"What a good idea," said Masefield, who was considering Bannock with the expressionless eyes of an interrogator. "You were walking along in the dark and you fell into the deepest man-made hole on earth. Come along, Bannock, we must get to the bottom of this. Oh dear me, excuse the pun."

Bannock continued to stare into space, but Masefield kept at him.

"I could call in the police now and you might all go to jail. Admittedly, there are investigations I wish to complete myself. The choice is open to me. Martial law is a wonderfully flexible state of affairs. I could arrest the lot of you. But for the present, let's just kick off with a few answers. Come on, old chap, I know you've had a hard night."

Bannock spoke without looking around. "If Charlie Watson was alive, I would find him and kill him."

Masefield looked at the two horses, Pot Pourri and Lady Potter, tied at the hitching rail. "Those trappings on your mare—campaigning saddle, rifle holster, saddle pack? Not your sort of style, I would have thought."

"He wanted my horses. He thought Marcus was standing here."

"Surely he could simply have stolen them and gone off?"

"You don't know anything about racing," said Bannock. "You can't race somebody else's horse. And Charlie Watson knew that as long as I was alive, he would never get away with it."

"Ah. So in other words, Mr. Watson wanted you out of the way?"

Bannock said nothing. Four troopers walked from the wagon, looking expectantly at Masefield. He gave a sign and nod, and they went down to the end stable.

"Let's go back to the Big Hole." Masefield opened his shooting stick and settled down. "That must have been a dreadful experience for you. The question of course is, did you fall or were you pushed?"

Bannock slowly slid down into a sitting position on the ground. "Stuff your questions, Masefield. Come back tomorrow," he said wearily.

"Let's start at the beginning," Masefield suggested pleasantly. "You were out for an evening ride in spite of the curfew."

Bannock sighed. "I got a message from Charlie Watson to meet him. It was about the missing horses. I was met by four characters, who threw me down the hole."

"Was one of them Charlie Watson?"

"No, but I heard his voice."

Masefield smiled. "You've heard the stories about drunks falling down that hole. No one has ever come out alive before. You seem to have managed very well. What happened next?"

"I assumed he was after Marcus, and I went to Lennox Street to find out."

"As I heard it, you were taken there by force, with O'Flaherty. Which brings us to O'Flaherty. What was he doing up so late? Why was he not also tossed down the hole?"

O'Flaherty looked around at Bannock and shrugged.

Bannock said, "He came after me. He found out something about Watson and wanted to warn me."

"That sounds interesting," said Masefield. But Bannock's attention was elsewhere. The troopers were carrying the bodies, wrapped in horse blankets, back to the wagon. Some of the watching natives ran forward to help. Bannock's eyes followed the procession all the way.

Masefield tried O'Flaherty. "What was it you found out about Mr. Watson?"

"I found out . . ." O'Flaherty paused. He was watching the bodies being loaded on the wagon. "There goes a double-crossin' little shit for you. He was takin' our horses to the Boers."

"Amazing," said Masefield.

"You knew that," snapped Bannock. "You warned me about him."

"We suspected him."

"Well, you were right."

Masefield was still looking at O'Flaherty. "Yes, but how did you find out about it?"

"Say nothing, Paddy." Bannock was still watching the wagon.

Mabala came with mugs of coffee.

Masefield smiled again, took a cup of coffee, and nodded to Mabala. "I know the way you work, Bannock. Silently and efficiently, and you do it because you are forced to. You would never spend the time of night spying on the Boer camps. We pay native runners to do that type of work. But ours saw nothing of the sort. However, there is something else we do know. We know of those enterprising natives who bring in cattle, supposedly for sale to the garrison. We also know that rather than sell them, they are sharing most of them with their hungry brothers. A praiseworthy idea, if against the regulations." He was letting Bannock see that he was keeping an eye on Mabala, coming back with mugs of coffee for O'Flaherty and himself. "The Boers keep their cattle pretty close to their camps, do they not?"

"Why don't you say it outright?"

"Because you are so slow at answering questions."

"I want my horse back," said Bannock.

Masefield shook his head. "Patience, my dear chap," he said. "It will take a day or two to complete the red tape over this business. But for the moment, there is still one awful gap in the evidence. Who killed Charlie Watson?" He was sitting at an angle where he could clearly see the expressions of Bannock, O'Flaherty, and Mabala, who were studiously watching the troopers bring around the mules in preparation to leave with the wagon. They seemed to have not heard his question. The whip cracked, and the wagon began its somber journey.

Masefield took a sip of coffee and repeated himself. "Who killed Watson?"

Bannock turned on him aggressively. "Charlie Watson killed Silky Van Breda. He was our friend. Everybody around here knew that. You want to know who killed him, but we're not interested in that. No, listen to me, Major; I'll tell you how it happened. There were hundreds of natives here at the time. They all look on us as friends for some reason I can't quite fathom. But when Charlie killed Van, everybody had one idea in common. They were elbowing one another out of the way to get at him. The point is, we don't know who got there first."

Masefield pondered. "Where was Mabala at that time?"

"All right," said O'Flaherty loudly. "All right, I'll be givin' it to you straight. It was meself who did it. And I'd do it again, you may be sure."

"I could believe you," said Masefield, "almost." He smiled. "Almost, but not quite."

"We don't know who did it," said Bannock flatly. "But whoever did it, you should be grateful to him."

"Oh, dear me, I have no strong feelings about this sort of thing. I told you, in time of war the army tends to shoot people who go against them. But even in terms of that, there is still a thing called justice. British justice, my dear chap. I'm sorry to carp. Maybe I should ask Mabala himself?"

"All right, Masefield," Bannock broke in. "In view of what you said earlier, I was trying to avoid the issue.

Mabala has been out all night on one of his cattle sorties. He didn't make out very well. They were surprised and had to crawl back. He wasn't here, you see."

"Oh, what a pity." Masefield stood up and walked around Bannock until his back was toward O'Flaherty and Mabala, then settled himself down again on the shooting stick. "This is just for your ear, old chap," he said quietly.

"You're always being so confidential." Bannock leaned his head back against the stable door and closed his eyes uncooperatively.

Masefield thought a moment before he spoke. "This matter cannot be swept aside. We are still interested in Watson's late activities. We are going to have to question your men, and I am still quite aware that you will prime them carefully. But remember, I still have two prisoners to question. However, I believe you are the one who can really help us. Do you know something, Bannock? In spite of all the overwhelming evidence, I am beginning to like you in a vague sort of way."

"You amaze me."

"No, no. You're an interesting character. A bundle of trouble, an attracter of disaster, but interesting."

Bannock smiled without opening his eyes. "Maybe the description fits, but do you think I'm enjoying it?"

"I don't know, I don't know. All I know is that you've got the prettiest females in the town either liking you or hating you." He noted Bannock's frown. "I meet all these people, you see. Considering our state of siege and privation, there are still gatherings and get-togethers of the most elegant sort."

"You should be watching your weight. I thought we were all supposed to be on short rations?"

"Oh, there are still a few fair vintages and tin of pâté and so on. But there are these two pretty ladies who seem intent on you, the one animated by recriminations, the other by admiration for your courageous retrieval of the saber and other matters."

"That reminds me," said Bannock. He suddenly came to life, stood up from the stable door, and limped off stiffly toward the bar without another word.

Masefield watched him for a moment, then lifted up his bulk and strode out into the dawn light, where he stood looking south. There was a faint rumble from that direction, and he listened attentively. He looked toward O'Flaherty and spoke.

"I would be fascinated to know how you managed to get through those barriers at night without a pass."

O'Flaherty leaned back and sighed. "There was many a time in dear old County Kilkenny—that's where I come from," he reminisced. "There were times when a young man had to get home and his mother was waitin' up for him and it was him not crossin' the river but instead takin' a stroll into the hills and round the other way . . ."

"Yes, yes." Masefield impatiently turned his attention to Bannock, who was coming back from the bar.

Bannock held out the partly open package of money that had been sent by Emma Stevenson. "Since you are in touch with these people and I am not, I'd be obliged if you would return this to Mrs. Stevenson. There was a misunderstanding."

Masefield took the package and fingered the open edge to check its contents. "It would seem to be a considerable misunderstanding. What shall I say to her?"

"Oh, nothing. She'll understand, I think."

Masefield pointed at the southern horizon. "Do you see that smoke on the horizon? Some of it is smoke from the artillery, some of it is dust from the relief column in action, about twelve miles southeast, don't you think? It's the wrong direction, of course. It looks like the hills at Magersfontein. Wrong direction altogether. We expected them from slightly west of the line. Listen carefully and you can hear the guns."

"I can hear them," said Bannock, his heart sinking at the thought of Marcus.

"But there it is, old chap: relief at last. We are all going to be relieved, don't you think?"

· 8 · | HORSE `A LA MODE

THOMAS BRAITHWAITE, *DIAMOND FIELDS ADVERTISER*. Masefield examined the visiting card as if he had suddenly become shortsighted.

He became even more massive on his side of the table in contrast to the small, thin man in thick spectacles glaring at him from the other.

"There is only one newspaper in this town, sir," the visitor was complaining, "and I am the senior journalist on the permanent staff."

"I can't see why you should have been referred to me." Masefield was making much of being puzzled.

The thick spectacles expanded the dislike in the visitor's eyes. "It should be quite obvious. Apparently you are known as the Communications Officer, which I would have thought implied you were in charge of all communications."

Masefield smiled malevolently. "Nothing so general as that, Mr. Braithwaite. You see, my title applies specifically to strategic communications, those pertaining to and of help to the army—and not your newspaper."

The magnified eyes narrowed. "I must remind you, sir, that any suppression of the free flow of news is against all

246

tradition. Being censored by the army is bad enough, but when you give us insufficient information to make a rational announcement—"

"Ah." Masefield maintained his smile. "You mean the signal?"

Braithwaite blustered, "Do you call that a signal? 'I am checked.' Are we to believe that General Lord Methuen, given the opportunity of sending a heliographed signal, decided to be tantalizing?"

"We did wonder about that."

"Oh, you did? Then you agree that 'I am checked' is hardly a way to describe the fact that an entire British army division was defeated, and then what? Did they sit down to dinner in sight of the enemy? Did they retreat? Did they come forward? 'I am checked'; what kind of statement would you call that?"

"An understatement."

"I see, I see. Then you admit it has been a disaster."

"Mr. Braithwaite, I don't believe much of what I read in newspapers, so I suppose it's fair that you don't believe me, but all we have got to go on is what you know. Three tantalizing words, as you say. You should embroider on that in the way you are accustomed to doing. How about a magnificent headline: 'TANTALIZING MESSAGE,' or 'THREE LITTLE WORDS SPELL DISASTER,' or how about 'THE BIG CHECK,' or 'GOOD GRIEF NO RE-LIEF'?"

A very unamused Braithwaite had gotten to his feet, but Masefield was not giving him a chance to speak.

"Why don't you concentrate on the other interesting things that are happening? I understand Mr. Rhodes is footing the bill for a soup kitchen to make the rations go further. If it's the truth you want to print, tell them they'll have to pull in their belts. Tell them we're going to run short of everything."

Masefield was around the table and so close to the small man that he had to move his chair to clear his path toward the door. But Masefield followed him with more suggestions.

"Why don't you tell them about the vast piece of artillery Labram is building in the De Beers workshops? Mr. Rhodes would like that; he may even give you a bonus. He does own your newspaper, doesn't he?"

Braithwaite never looked back. He was through the door and the anteroom and gone. Masefield spoke to the empty doorway as if Braithwaite could still hear him.

"How would you like to print the shocking truth about the soup kitchen, about the curious smell coming out of the soup? And it's no good saying that's a lot of horse, because it is. We're running short of bull, you see, so we'll have to munch our mounts instead."

Pacelli's disapproving face pressed down on his double chin. He disapproved of the arrangements; he disapproved of the ladies. In general, he hated the atmosphere of disorganization. In particular, he could not approve of the idea of mass-produced soup. The greatest banquets of Careme, Di Capo, and Escoffier were not mass productions. They would turn in their graves at the idea of vegetables and meat reduced to this humiliating English concoction called soup. Not consommé, not potage, not even minestrone—there were not enough tomatoes for that.

He followed around after Perkins, the army catering officer, and Tyson of the Kimberley Club, who together had organized the arrangements for the soup kitchen. First he was shown the long trestle tables in the Town Hall itself, standing ready for the queues. Then he was taken through to the long corridor at the back that served as the kitchen. There the officer proudly pointed out the line of large coal-fired boilers contributed by the army. Against the opposite wall were positioned the combined kitchen staffs of the Sanatorium and the Kimberley Club, all busy cutting meat and peeling and chopping vegetables.

Pacelli startled Perkins by shouting, "Julienne! Not'a chop, not'a smash, just'a julienne."

"What was that all about?" asked Perkins.

Pacelli demonstrated with his hands. "Julienne ee'sa fine cut. Long and'a thin. Not'a chop like'a this and'a that."

"What do you think of the arrangements, chef? We're depending on you now."

"I think," said Pacelli, waving his hands around for the words, "I think I never live to the day when Pacelli ee'sa cooking horsemeat."

The two men froze, catching each other's eyes. Perkins held a finger up to his lips. He leaned toward Pacelli, whispering in his ear.

"You are not to say that word. Nobody is to know. The whole idea of the soup is that people won't know the difference. It is meat we are serving. Meat, do you hear, chef?"

"I hear," said Pacelli solemnly.

Perkins spelled it out. "M-e-a-t, meat."

"All right, all right." Pacelli waved an impatient hand. "This'a m-e-a-t"—he spelled it out—"for Pacelli ee'sa insult."

The catering officer leaned in, looking a little superior. "The Belgians eat it, you know. They adore the stuff. Didn't you know that?"

Pacelli pulled his lips down and made a circle with his hand. "The Belgians, they eat it," he said. "The Italians, they ride it."

"Shhh." Perkins tried to quiet him.

"Not'a chop," roared Pacelli.

One of his assistants in the vegetable line held up a potato as a query.

"Also," shouted Pacelli. "Everything'a julienne, nothing'a chop."

"Shall I call the ladies together?" asked Perkins.

"Right." Pacelli nodded.

"Ladies, ladies." Perkins smiled as he called the twenty or so female volunteers together. They all came in their aprons and stood around attentively while Perkins addressed them. "I would like to thank you all for your generous assistance. Head Chef Pacelli of the Sanatorium will now explain your duties."

Pacelli surveyed his small army of amateurs disapprovingly. He pointed to the men at the boilers. "On your'a left," he said, "ee'sa chef, one, two, three, four, five, and'a so forth. On'a your right ee'sa seconds for the onion, the vegetable, and'a the m-e-a-t." He spelled the word out.

The ladies looked surprised, and Pacelli went on.

"That'a stands for meat," he explained. "You must'a stand in the middle and when'a they shout you must'a run. When the people they come, you must'a run in there with the pots. If'a you can carry the pot, I don'ta think so."

Pacelli thought about his latest doubt, and Perkins broke in with a nervous smile.

"I think what Chef Pacelli means, ladies, is that you will be assisting by fetching and carrying during the cooking period and serving during the serving period."

"That'sa what I say." Pacelli glared at Perkins for being repetitious.

"Take up your positions," called Perkins. "Down the middle, if you please."

The women spread themselves out for their unaccustomed field of battle. Among them, Emma Stevenson decided that she felt no more strange in the circumstances than did any of the others. They were all strangers to her except for one or two women she had been introduced to at parties. But she was rather proud of herself being there. Proud of the first long apron she had ever worn, and proud to be one of that eager band of whom there were far too many for the amount of work they were required to do.

She waited in the middle of the big noisy corridor, grateful for the noise that softened the jar of the shelling from the perimeter. But no amount of noise could drown out the explosions nearby that set everyone on edge with the rattling follow-on of the shrapnel doing its destructive work.

The head chef was shouting. "First'a the fat. Seven minutes. Remove'a the pieces. Next'a the onions. Five minutes. Next'a the m-e-a-t. Why you look'a at me like'a that? M-e-a-t ee'sa meat. Ten minutes. Next'a stock. Next'a the carrots, turnips, beans, the legumes—julienne, not'a chop. Next'a wait twenty minutes. Then'a potatoes, julienne, not'a chop. Then'a shut up and'a wait long time, thirty minutes. Then ask'a Pacelli to taste."

Emma waited to be useful. Soon, a man in a long white apron on the julienne side held out a huge colander full of onions. She rushed for it. The man indicated a chef in a white hat at the far side, waiting at one of the big boilers. She struggled across with her load, handed it over, and dashed back to the middle to wait again. But it was going to be a slow process. She exchanged smiles with her neighbors and waited.

At least she was doing something human, even useful. Not having to prove what a good little widow she was capable of being, how sad she could look, how properly uninterested in life. If it was only a matter of mourning the loss of Geoffrey, she knew she could have done that with all the feeling and all the sadness that came naturally. That should have been enough for anybody. But her mother wanted another quality of grief, something everybody could see. The black clothes, the bowed head. As long as the appearances were right, that was all that mattered. Emma had tried to conform.

But how do you reconcile grief with guilt, when it is mostly guilt you feel? How do you explain to your mother or your sister, who are so involved in appearances, that your whole married life became a facade of appearances, that all you have inherited are feelings of failure? There was no one she could tell that to. She had to live with it. But is that all there is to live for? When she heard volunteers were required for the soup kitchen and her mother and Sarah had objected, she rebelled. And she was glad. The apron covered some of the blackness; the activity, some of the guilt.

The head chef was shouting again. "Stock, stock, put'a salt, taste'a for salt." Then everyone jerked and became tense as a shell exploded nearby.

Emma liked the huge head chef, with his thinning hair and thick, floppy mustache. She imagined him as the director of the opera, with his principals the shouting chefs along the cauldrons, his male chorus the vegetable brigade, and the shrill chorus of sopranos in the middle.

She was being left out, with only one vegetable or meat chopper to every three women, and leapt forward gratefully when she was again given a chance to struggle with one of the huge dishes of julienne, not chopped, vegetables to the chef opposite.

Then she was in the middle again, waiting. She sighed and thought of having to go back to the hotel after this diversion, to an atmosphere of solemn recrimination. If only she could tell her mother what she felt. She had tried last night, just begun to try, when she sensed the usual wall of rejection, the immediate transformation of wise, understanding mother into keeper of the myths. But she should have known; myths have a way of never changing, and neither would her mother ever change.

Emma closed her eyes and felt her own private rebellion welling up. They could make a saint out of Geoffrey if they wished. They would never know about him, that he had lived in a trap he could not free himself from. Her mother also lived in a trap of her own making. Sarah hops in and out of that family trap as it suits her, and dear Mark inhabits it as if it didn't exist. But Geoffrey should have set me free. He should have become my family, just he and I. Instead, he left me in the trap and he left me this confusing legacy. I do not belong in it anymore. I want to be free. I cringe from the thought of going back tonight and having the door sprung on me and being alone again.

Perkins was calling out, "We are opening the main doors. Ladies, if you would like to go through and arrange the queues, we will call you back when we are ready to serve. There will be six queues as indicated on the tables, and I must depend on you to arrange an orderly distribution of those present."

Emma filed along with the other women, and as they went through the doorway to the main hall, she saw the big Irishman who worked for Mr. Bannock making his way in, looking around as if trying to find someone. He seemed to see her and look away quickly, then apparently saw who he was looking for and waved.

Pacelli sniffed when he saw O'Flaherty and waited for him to come up.

"Good afternoon, Mario." O'Flaherty beamed at his friend. "It's glad I am to see you again."

"What do you talk good afternoon?" Pacelli glared at O'Flaherty. "You come here and make'a big diamonds business."

"Shhh." O'Flaherty tried to quiet him.

"What you talk, shhh? Everybody say to me, shhh. You come here big talk, I turn around you gone. What ee'sa going on?"

"Now wait, Mario. If you'll be givin' me a chance, I'll explain. When I was here an hour ago I saw this young lady, the one who was givin' Bart the money and he gave it back. But there was no message and I know he wanted to speak to her. And there she was before me very eyes."

"What you talking, Paddi? What'a lady, what'a money?"

"Now don't you be worryin', Mario me boy. You wait here and I'll be back in a minute."

Pacelli waved a few circles in the air with his hand. "Come, go, come, go; diamonds, ladies, money. What do I know, what do I care?"

O'Flaherty dashed back through the door into the main hall, past the tables where the volunteer ladies made pacifying signs to the long queues. He negotiated his way through the waiting throng and eventually found Bannock leaning against the wall near the door.

"She's there, I tell you," he said. "Up behind those tables. No, you can't see from here. But she's there, you may be sure of that."

Bannock shrugged and remained leaning against the wall, "Forget it, Paddy, it's a waste of time. I thought I could see her for a moment to explain, but it's hopeless in this mob, and she's obviously busy."

"What are you talkin' about, what are you talkin' about? Now you go right up there and say, miss, I mean ma'am, here am I tellin' you about that money. And you needn't be pretendin' with me. It's plain you like the little lady. And you know how to talk to them ladies."

"Don't be ridiculous," said Bannock. "She has nothing to do with me. I told you, it's just about the money I've got to explain."

"Well, what are you after comin' all this way for anyway?"

"Because I want to hold on to you, Paddy. You can forget about your diamond hunting now. I've got plans for tonight. We have to discuss them. We're getting out tonight."

O'Flaherty looked at him askance. "Without Marcus?" he asked.

"With Marcus," said Bannock.

"With Marcus?" O'Flaherty echoed the words as if Bannock had lost his senses and needed to be humored. "So you're goin' to go in there, shoot the sentries, and take the horse?"

"If I have to."

"And that's tonight, you say."

"You can stop looking so amazed, Paddy. Are you getting nervous?"

"Nervous?" O'Flaherty's chest expanded. "All right,

Bart." The challenge was met. "In that case I'll be wantin' to say good-bye to me dear friend, Mario."

"Don't say good-bye to anybody. Do you want the whole town to know we're going?"

O'Flaherty nodded as the meaning dawned on him. "Well, I'll be havin' a few words with him anyway, and I'll see you back here."

Bannock waited for O'Flaherty to get away, then made a decision. He was going to feel foolish doing it, and he was going to feel foolish if he went away again without having done it. So he set off up the side of the hall, squeezing past the waiting queues. There were murmurs of impatience that grew to outright objections as he forced his way up to the front.

When he reached the tables, he stopped and weathered the curious glances of the women sitting on the dais and standing around waiting there. Almost the only one not looking at him was the one he wanted. It was a ridiculous moment. The small figure with the perfect blond curls sat facing away at the far end of the dais, and to get there he would have to make a loud-booted spectacle of himself. For a moment, he considered going back. He was going to make a spectacle of himself either way. He thought, Damn them, and set off between the women.

A shell exploded nearby as he reached his objective. Everyone jumped and there was nervous laughter. In reacting to the noise, she had turned around, and she saw him.

"I came to explain something to you." He tried to say it softly, but felt that every woman in the vicinity had heard him.

She stood up and they faced each other awkwardly, both conscious of the audience of eyes. Bannock looked around for somewhere to go, but Emma acted first.

"Please follow me, Mr. Bannock."

She took hold of her apron and skirts and set off decisively toward a side entrance to the hall, a passageway with pillars. Bannock followed her, and they stopped together in the middle of the passage, where only a few of the curious eyes could follow them.

Emma got in first. "Mr. Bannock, I am afraid you have made me feel a little foolish about the money."

"That was not my intention." He tried to remember what he was going to say. "Please understand, I must have the choice of accepting or refusing any offer that is made to me. No, that's not very well put."

"I understand what you mean." Emma could not meet the intense eyes gazing down at her. She looked at his chest. "You have put the money in its place . . . I mean, the money is not the real issue . . ." she faltered, "but I still feel you have made a wrong judgment. Oh, now I am not expressing myself very well."

"Let's start again," said Bannock, and they both laughed.

Bannock started. "I think your gesture was magnificent." He sounded ridiculously formal to himself.

"I was only worried that I would have underestimated the value of your horse." Emma spoke to his chest, despising herself for not meeting his eyes.

"I never counted the money. By the feel of the parcel, I think you were overgenerous."

"Why did you have to refuse?" Emma was surprised at the intimate sound of her own voice. She hardly knew this man.

He replied, "For the same reason you insisted I accept. We both share the same problem. Your pride, my pride."

"You mean somebody's pride has to suffer?" Emma was surprised again. She had never traded thoughts with a stranger like this, yet she went right on. "Is that really what it is, my pride? I recognize your pride, Mr. Bannock. I've seen it in action. But my pride?" She paused, staring at his chest. "Yes, you could be right. I suppose I try to compensate for my own inadequacy."

"You are not inadequate." Now it was Bannock's turn

to be taken aback by his own hot response. He had raised his voice, and they both looked up the passage at the curious watchers, who immediately turned away.

She stared back at his chest anxiously.

"You are too intelligent to be inadequate." Bannock couldn't stop himself.

Emma felt the color in her cheeks.

"You are too beautiful to be inadequate."

Bannock knew he had lost control of the situation. He turned to go and marveled at his own confusion. He should be saying good-bye, but he was walking off toward the prying eyes of the women, who quickly looked away.

"Mr. Bannock," she called him back.

He turned and went toward her as if drawn by a magnet.

This time she looked straight up into his eyes. "You are a dispatch rider, are you not?" she asked quietly.

There was an explosion nearby, but neither of them flinched.

"How did you know that?" He immediately thought of the day he had told Stevenson.

"My brother told me," she said. "You ride through the enemy lines again and again and you come back safely each time. The relief column is so close now, they say twelve miles. Is that correct?"

"Yes." Bannock smiled at the ease with which she was talking now. "What are you leading up to?" he asked.

"When will you go again?"

"Now hold on, Mrs. Stevenson. You are cross-questioning me. It's a very confidential matter."

"Take me with you." She stared at him and took advantage of his confusion. "I mean, just show me how to get beyond the lines. I shall not be a burden to you."

"Now hold on, please," objected Bannock, but she was not to be stopped.

"I assure you, I can ride quite well. As soon as we are through the lines, I'll be responsible for myself."

"Hold on, hold on." Bannock spoke in an urgent whisper. "You cannot imagine what it's like. It is really dangerous out there."

"I am not afraid."

"This is ridiculous. You must know I would never agree to it. What's put an idea like this in your head? The town could be relieved at any time."

Emma frowned up at him. "I cannot wait."

Bannock studied her in a state of complete exasperation. "You must know I would do anything for you. I don't know why I say that, but I feel it. But in this matter you have a flat refusal. I'm sorry, it's impossible."

"Will you only think about it and speak to me about it tomorrow?"

Bannock found himself locked into the intense eyes that merely flickered when an explosion came close, rattling the doors and windows.

"I suppose we have made enough of a spectacle of ourselves." She smiled at him.

He found it difficult to go. "Good-bye," he said, and set off up the passage into the main hall, conscious of every thump of his boots and jingle of spur chains in spite of the loud, murmuring atmosphere of the hall.

The volunteer women made no further attempt to appear uninterested. They watched him every step of the way as he marched between them and passed behind the queueing crowd.

Looking back through the heads of the crowd, he got glimpses of Emma standing on her own, red-cheeked and frowning, staring blankly in his direction. What a wrong word she had used. Would an "inadequate" woman be prepared to ride off into the night, risking her life? What would make any woman wish to do a thing like that? There was something very wrong with her. Something far more wrong than could ever be attributed to grief. He wished he could go on talking to her, and the more he recognized the urge, the more it amazed him. It was a natural urge; nothing intended, nothing rational. But such thoughts must be put away, Bannock. The lady is untouchable. She is under an enormous strain of some kind, and confused as a result. She is an aristocrat, born, bred, and trained for her own kind. Be a good chap and forget about her.

He found O'Flaherty waiting at the door, giving him an ironic smile.

"So it's no use and a waste of time, you were sayin', and she'll be too busy, you were sayin'. And then I find you hidin' in a corner with the little lady and givin' it to her as fast as you can go. Oh no, he says, it's the money, I'm not carin' about her. And there he stands gazin' in her pretty little eyes."

"That's enough," snapped Bannock. "Come outside; we've got to talk."

O'Flaherty followed him, wedging his way past the queues that wound outside into the hot afternoon sun. They walked around the side of the building to where the horses were tethered.

"We're going to get out tonight," said Bannock.

O'Flaherty came to an abrupt standstill, forcing Bannock to walk back to join him.

"What's wrong, Paddy?"

"You're lookin' at a man who never has a choice. A man who is not good enough to be a dispatch rider like yourself. You say we're goin' to do this, we're goin' to do that, but never have I heard you say, What do you think about this, Paddy me boy?"

"I'm sorry," said Bannock honestly. "But there are reasons why we must go tonight. Will you listen to me first?"

O'Flaherty nodded and looked away, in a pose of dignified attention.

"This town is running out of forage. Now we can't even get crushed corn from De Beers, and the situation is worsening by the day. If the horses slip any further out of condition, you know yourself it's going to take us months to get them right. Have you looked at the condition of Marcus lately?"

"Now, that's an interestin' point you're makin'," said O'Flaherty. "How do you think you're goin' to get the great horse away from the army?"

"I'll think of something."

"Sure you'll be explainin' to the guard that you're just takin' him for a nice walk."

"I haven't thought about the sentry yet, but I told you, I'll think of something. Now just keep quiet and listen. The relief column is desperately short of horses, and if they arrive here, they'll be no respecters of pedigree. If they come in tomorrow, they'll grab everything on four legs including Marcus, do you understand? If the relief column doesn't come, there are two other nasty alternatives. Either the horses starve, or the Boers come in and take over, and they need horses just as badly as the army does."

O'Flaherty shook his head sadly. "Mario and I have been talkin' about those mines. It's empty they are, and there must be some way of gettin' in there."

"Will you listen," said Bannock. "Mabala knows what's going on out there. The Boers keep bringing in people and strengthening the fortifications. A few days more and it will be impossible to get through."

"But why tonight? Why not tomorrow or the next night?"

"Because everything is right. There is no moon until the early hours of the morning, which gets us through the lines in the dark and helps us to see our way and move along in the open country. We need those hours of dark, because we won't be able to leave until we get our hands on Marcus."

"Do you know somethin', Bart? Considerin' the awful cost of whiskey, I was just beginnin' to enjoy this place. Do you know Mario? You should talk to him. It's a grand man he is, with a fine voice and a great knowledge of all the hotels of Europe. You should hear him about the princes

and fine ladies. I love that great fat Italian. I'll be missin'
Mario. And you'll be missin' that little lady."

"You're crazy. She has nothing to do with me."

O'Flaherty laughed rudely as they went to untether the
horses, but not Bannock. He seemed preoccupied as they
mounted up and cantered across the Market Square.

O'Flaherty looked down at the siege in miniature.
There was a complex of little mud buildings a few inches
high, already drying off, with the damp showing darker at
the higher edges. On one side was a small neatly dug hole
to represent the Kimberley Mine; on the other side, small
constructions made of rusty wire with rough wire wheels at
the top, to represent the shaft-heads of the Du Toitspan
Mine; and in a wide ring right around, primitive but cunning constructions of wire, to represent the guns at the
perimeter.

The creators of this small artistic miracle sat on the far
side of it, looking round-eyed at O'Flaherty.

He looked back at the three little African boys, who
had become part of the racecourse scene, and suddenly
called out, "Hear no evil."

Two of the little boys put their hands to their ears. But
one put his hands to his mouth and looked sideways uncer-
tainty.

"Hear," said O'Flaherty sternly and repeated, "Hear,
hear." He demonstrated with his own hands to his ears, and
the little boy who had got it wrong switched from mouth
to ears.

"Speak no evil," boomed O'Flaherty. This they got all
right, clapping their hands to their mouths.

Bannock was sitting against the stable wall in earnest
discussion with Mabala. He called, "Paddy, come over
here; we've got to sort this thing out. There isn't much
time."

O'Flaherty smiled at his three little monkeys. "See no

evil," he shouted, and they all put their hands to their eyes and peeped through their fingers at him.

"Paddy," Bannock insisted, and waited until he got up and came over, followed by the boys.

"Take a seat and listen," said Bannock. "According to Mabala, there is only one sensible way out of here and that's due west. We can't go east because that's the Boer route to Bloemfontein and Jacobsdal and they're in and out that way all the time. We can't go directly south because they've fortified every inch of the way against the relief column. And even if we do go west, we have to keep north of Carter's Ridge." He pointed at the map Mabala had drawn on the ground. "If you look here, just north of Carter's Ridge is Dead Man's Vlei. They keep cattle there, that's how Mabala knows it. It's a big, damp pan that the Boer riders avoid. And on the far end of it is open country, beyond their fortifications. From there we go due south across the Modder and carry on until we strike the Orange River, well west of the bridge. There should be no particular activity in that whole area. Which means our worst problems are right here on the way out."

O'Flaherty appeared skeptical. "How are you goin' to get through the perimeter after curfew on the other side of town?"

"We're not," said Bannock. "We leave from here, ride out a mile away from town to the south. Then we'll also be a mile closer in from Carter's Ridge. From that point, we ride round on a parallel course to the perimeter, hopefully too far from the reservoir searchlight to be seen in the dark. In that way we'll bring ourselves round to a position a mile away from Kimberley Mine to the west, and be ready to ride due west toward Dead Man's Vlei. Mabala says it will work, and I believe him."

O'Flaherty was still doubtful. "I've been havin' a thought that truly fascinates me," he said. "I was askin' meself, how will he be gettin' his hands on Marcus? With all them guards and after the curfew and all?"

"We're not going after the curfew, we're going now," said Bannock, squinting at the red ball of the sun on its way to the horizon.

O'Flaherty cocked a questioning eyebrow at him. "I was also askin' meself, how is he goin' to be gettin' his hands on Marcus anyway? Is he goin' to be sayin' to the guard what I've just been sayin' to these little men? Kindly close your eyes and your ears and your mouth all at the same time and pretend there isn't a great gallompin' horse goin' out the gate that shouldn't be."

"I've got a plan for that, too," said Bannock.

"Well, it's all ears I am to hear how you're goin' to get past that one."

The three little boys reacted as one, concentrating on whoever was speaking, following every movement. But Mabala's attention was elsewhere. He was staring intently upward like a great brown statue, and Bannock followed his gaze to the bunching of clouds, vast cumulus storm heads, a promise that the heavens would open sometime during the night. He wondered whether a storm would be an advantage or a disadvantage. The flashes of lightning could give away one's position. But on the other hand, the rain could provide a perfect screen of camouflage, just so long as one knew where one was going. It all depended on Mabala.

"Will there be a storm?" Bannock asked him.

"Later, *nkosi*. Late tonight."

"Will we find our way in the rain?"

Mabala smiled. "We will find our way."

Bannock asked O'Flaherty, "Would there be anything strange about you taking forage to Lennox Street before eight in the evening?"

"I can take feed there anytime I want to. I've taken it early, I've taken it late. Why do you ask?" O'Flaherty knew that expression. Bannock was scheming.

"I've got a plan that might work and might not work, but if we don't do this, we'll do nothing, so here it is. The whole thing depends on the dark. The sentries on the outside at Lennox Street know nothing about what's going on inside; they keep changing them. And in any case, they wouldn't know a horse from a mule. It's the sentry at the stables we have to worry about. Now here's what you do: you go up there leading the mule with our last two bags of forage on its back, and you exchange the mule for Marcus."

"What are you talkin' about?" exploded O'Flaherty. "Are you tryin' to say anybody in his right mind is goin' to be mistakin' Marcus for a mule?"

"Don't worry about that for the moment," said Bannock. "I'll also be going in there with my pass, and I'll look after the sentry."

O'Flaherty gaped in horror. "What are you goin' to do to that sentry? Do you want the whole British army after us?"

"I may not have to do anything to the sentry. I may or I may not," he said grimly. "I'll explain the whole thing to you on the way. So get out the mule and the backpack and the forage and let's start getting ready."

"What about Mabala?" asked O'Flaherty.

"Mabala waits for us. He is the most important person of all. He has to lead us out of here."

"And what about poor Macushla? Is it in your mind to just leave her behind?"

"We get Marcus," said Bannock, "and the army gets the mule."

It was dark by the time they reached Lennox Street.

Bannock dismounted and looked at his watch again. It was a little after eight, which meant that they had about an hour to be back at the racecourse, where Mabala was waiting. The shelling had become sporadic, and concentrated somewhere over toward the Bultfontein Mine. He waited at the corner of Du Toitspan Road, watching O'Flaherty riding Lady Potter and leading the mule with the bales and sacks on its back toward the vehicle entrance at the far end of the army headquarters buildings.

The street was still fairly busy, with men coming off duty and heading for their billets. Lights flickered from storm lanterns at the sentry posts and at the outspan area, where mule teams were being unhitched and led away. He could hear O'Flaherty whistling a tune and saw him tugging at the mule's rein as he reached the sentry post at the yard entrance. O'Flaherty seemed to be managing well, leaning down to joke with the sentry, who was trying to laugh and stay at attention at the same time.

Bannock waited almost fifteen minutes before getting back into the saddle. He kept Pot Pourri at a walk as he approached the entrance. The sentry, whom he remembered from a previous occasion, unshouldered his rifle and stepped forward, and after examining his pass nodded him through. So far it was a normal enough occasion. There was no reason to expect it to be otherwise considering that every day one or the other or both of them arrived to attend to Marcus.

Bannock rode through between the gaunt buildings, past the lines of open stalls, where the animals neighed and blew and shuffled at the mare's presence, and eventually reached the two long rows of loose boxes with the paddocks beyond. He could see the sentry and O'Flaherty, leaning against the hitching rail that ran parallel to the stables, talking animatedly, a lamp on the ground between them, the horse and the mule waiting alongside. They were positioned halfway along the line of stables, which gave Bannock hope for his plan. He began to feel the tension rise as he rode toward them, thinking of the alternatives, all desperate ones, if his plan went wrong. As he dismounted, the sentry was lighting a lamp for O'Flaherty.

"Good evening, sir," said the sentry. "I'm just giving this mad Irishman a light so the stallion doesn't stand on him."

"Sure, it's the mule I'm worried about," said O'Flaherty. "Have you seen the size of his feet?"

"Move along, Paddy," said Bannock. "We've got to get back before curfew." He leaned against the rail beside the sentry and took out a halfjack of whiskey, holding it up toward the man.

"Keep some of that for me," O'Flaherty called back as he led the two animals down toward where Marcus was stabled, the second loose box from the end.

The sentry eyed the bottle longingly, and Bannock held it poised. "Come on, nobody's going to know," Bannock said.

The sentry took a gulp and handed it back.

Bannock took a gulp and said, "They move you fellows around, don't they? You were out front the other day, if I remember rightly." Bannock watched O'Flaherty out of the corner of his eye. The stable doors were open and he had led the mule in, leaving a faint spillage of light that showed Lady Potter tethered to the door.

"They keep moving us," the sentry was saying. "But I'd rather be here than on the street with all the shoulder arms, stand at ease, shoulder arms, march, about turn, march. Drives you mad, I can tell you. It's so boring. It's better here, where you can do anything you like except take a kip. You can hear the sergeant coming a mile off."

Bannock held out the halfjack again. He could hardly believe his eyes when he saw Lady Potter also being led into the box, and wondered how all three big animals were going to fit. He watched the sentry take another gulp and said, "I would judge you come from Manchester or thereabouts."

"You're wrong." The sentry laughed. "Try again."

Hurry up, Paddy, thought Bannock.

At that moment, O'Flaherty felt slightly hysterical, leaning against the back wall of the stable with the lamp set up on the corner manger, looking up at the three heads of the tightly packed animals. He pointed a stern finger at

Marcus as he leaned across to bite Lady Potter on the neck. "Now, you're all goin' to be good," he whispered, "while meself does the change-overs." Then he went to work ferociously.

First, he unwrapped the bales of sacks from the mule's back, dumping them against the back wall of the stable. He took the halter off the mule and held it on his arm while he got the bridle off Lady Potter. He put the halter on Lady Potter, and spoke soothingly as he put the bridle on Marcus. Now the saddle. He was beginning to sweat as he hurriedly unbuckled the girths, squashed between the two tall horses. Bustling his way around under Marcus' head, he threw the saddle onto the stallion's back. He hooked up the girths and adjusted them quickly, bent down and shuffled back under the heads again, pushing himself between Lady Potter and the mule.

Now for the backpack. He had never handled that big structure on his own, but he quickly loosened the corner straps and, taking hold of the side slats firmly, applied his powerful arms to the task of lifting it up, cradling it high above his head, and slowly heaving it across from the mule to Lady Potter's back. The mare immediately became restive under the unaccustomed feel and weight of the backpack, stepping around, bumping into the mule on one side and Marcus on the other, and threatening to start an equestrian riot in the overcrowded loose box. O'Flaherty whispered, patted and stroked, and eventually managed to get them quieted down, wondering what the sentry must be thinking.

But the sentry was involved in memories of home.

"That's right," he was saying, taking another sip of whiskey and handing the halfjack back. "Seven children, if you can believe it, in that small place. All boys but for two girls, and them two the youngest."

"Are any of the others in the army?" asked Bannock, swinging up the halfjack but drinking none of it.

"Two of 'em," said the sentry. "The others are all in the factories. Good jobs, mind you." He looked around. "What's happening with that Irishman? I thought he was only dropping the feed off."

"He's very fussy about the stallion," said Bannock, holding out the halfjack again and wishing O'Flaherty would hurry up.

O'Flaherty was addressing the three animals. "Now, we're goin' out there, and you, my dear," he told Lady Potter, "you are goin' to behave like a mule. No hoppity skippity from you, do you hear?" He looked sadly at the mule. "Good-bye, Macushla, me darlin'," he said and, switching off the lamp, prepared himself to work in the dark.

He backed Lady Potter out of the box, squeezing her from between the other two animals. "Now keep calm and step slowly, like a mule," he whispered.

The activity outside the box caught the attention of the sentry, who looked around. But it was too dark to make out more than the faint outline of an animal.

Bannock tried to keep the sentry's attention. "And what happened to your oldest brother after that?" he asked.

"Oh, it was all over," he said. "He came back home and nothing more was said. But my mother never spoke to him for weeks."

Now there were two animals outside and O'Flaherty was closing the stable doors. Even though there was little to be seen, Bannock went cold as he saw the chestnut glint of big Marcus, embarrassingly conspicuous, prancing around with the joy of being in the open again. O'Flaherty was on his back struggling with the lead rein from Lady Potter, who was chopping down with her rear hooves in resentment at the uncomfortable backpack.

"Good night, see you tomorrow," shouted O'Flaherty, his voice giving him away as he struggled with Marcus and the unhelpful halter on the mare. Together they disappeared as an unruly team around the far end of the line of stables.

"Why's he going round that way?" queried the sentry, turning around and staring into the dark.

Bannock tensed, his fists ready to strike. The test was now. The alternatives might have to be put into action.

The sentry shouted, "Hey, you, it's this way round."

"Leave him," said Bannock. "He's been at the bottle all evening. He's sure to find his way out."

The sentry shook his head. "He must be drunk, all right," he said. "He'll break his neck in the dark trying to get between those open stalls."

Bannock relaxed again. The sentry had not recognized Marcus. For the moment, the crisis was over.

"Would you like to finish this?" said Bannock, handing over what was left of the halfjack and looking at his watch. "We'll have to hurry to beat the curfew."

"You should come earlier in the day," said the sentry. "What are you coming so late for?"

Bannock swung into the saddle and turned the mare to go. "I'll make a point of that tomorrow," he said. "I hope you'll be here. I'd like to hear the rest of that story."

"Good night, sir," said the sentry, watching Bannock ride into the darkness.

He rode back the way he had come until he saw O'Flaherty up ahead, silhouetted in the weak light of the storm lantern at the sentry box. Pot Pourri stood waiting while Bannock held his breath. He heard the "Good night" from O'Flaherty to the sentry, and the sentry's friendly response, and breathed out with relief as he realized they were clear.

Bannock walked Pot Pourri through into Lennox Street, waving to the sentry and keeping at a walk until he turned into Du Toitspan Road. Then he went at a steady trot for almost half a mile before he caught up with O'Flaherty. He decided that Paddy was having trouble or he could never have gotten that far ahead. And he was right. He found the Irishman dismounted and struggling with two cantankerous horses.

"Let's get that backpack off," said Bannock, dismounting and taking hold of all three horses' reins. O'Flaherty unstrapped the pack and manhandled it to the side of the road, where he dumped it in the dark cover of some bushes.

"You can ride this thoroughbred maniac," said O'Flaherty, coming back and taking over both mares' reins.

Bannock felt a thrill of recognition as he took Marcus' reins to the high withers, leaving O'Flaherty to hold the head. Characteristically, the great horse swung away, quarters going down and vibrating with excitement, forcing Bannock to run in a circle before he could mount. He felt the saddle surge under him in prancing waves of power. O'Flaherty handed him the lead rein for Lady Potter. Bannock circled, pulling the rein in a dancing tug of war, while O'Flaherty got up on Pot Pourri and came forward to take over the mare.

They moved on slowly, with Marcus sniffing suspiciously at the dark and shying at the rustling noises of a hot wind that was coming up. There was little to guide the eye beyond degrees of blackness. The silhouette of trees against the sky gave some idea of the direction of the invisible road. O'Flaherty followed quietly with the other two horses, and Bannock was left with his thoughts.

The wind had a smell of moisture in it, the typical introduction to another violent storm, but there were no distant signs of lightning, so it would be a while yet. How would Marcus behave out in the open in a storm that crashed and flashed in a manner that made gunfire seem insignificant? The answer was obvious: he would behave hysterically. He would have to be managed. And how would Mabala perform? Did he really have some magical instinct that could guide them through a wall of rain? At the point where they penetrated the lines, their direction would only have to be a few degrees off for them to walk straight into a Boer encampment. But Mabala had survived thus far; there was no choice but to believe in him.

They saw the lamps of the perimeter post ahead, and took advantage of the guiding light to move along at a brisk trot.

Two of the Town Guards waited for them with rifles at the ready. They relaxed when they saw the familiar figures.

One of them called out, "Cutting it a bit fine, aren't you?"

Bannock leaned down, holding his pass close to the man, hoping he could not tell one horse from another, as if the great gleaming chestnut could be compared to any horse in Kimberley. But the guard nodded, and Bannock wasted no time riding on through the opening in the barricade. Then he really worried. You could mistake one horse for another, but you could never mistake a racehorse for a mule.

His worst fears were realized. He heard a guard ask, "Didn't you come through here with a mule earlier? What's going on with you? You go in with a mule and come out with a horse?"

"It's very observant you are." O'Flaherty sounded quite calm. "This horse you see was at the farrier the whole day, which is where you will now find the mule. It's a troublesome beast that, let me tell you. Refuses to take a single step in the dark."

He could talk his way out of hell, thought Bannock as O'Flaherty came through.

Marcus was free. They were free of Kimberley, outside the perimeter, continuing their slow, groping journey to the racecourse.

The wind had grown stronger and hotter, blowing waves of dust that had them both coughing. The pace was infuriating. Bannock's instincts shouted for action. He wished he could gallop to the racecourse, pick up Mabala, and gallop straight out, in a race for stayers at a pace that would lay the risk of anyone being able to stop them or catch up with them. But it was not a time for risks. Too many risks had been forced on him. This time, they would have to go carefully and make sure. Every detail of their plan must be followed.

He suddenly thought of a detail that could undo them.

"The lamp, Paddy, the storm lantern. You left it in the stable."

"All right, I'm sorry," said O'Flaherty. "I should have brought a light."

"That's not what I mean. You put out the lamp, but you left it in Marcus' box. The sentry will go to fetch it."

"My God." O'Flaherty realized. "The mule."

"We might have more than Boers to worry about."

"Let's keep movin'," said O'Flaherty, and they set off at a jog without exchanging another word until they came to the racecourse.

Mabala was waiting for them with a fire and coffee, and hundreds of dark faces watching from the shadows. Bannock noticed the small feedbags, blanket rolls, and saddlebags, all packed and laid out in a neat row beside the fire.

"You've done well." He patted the huge shoulder. "We must leave immediately. Paddy, keep an eye out toward the barricade. Listen for anything you can hear."

"We'll be hearin' nothin' in this wind," said O'Flaherty, but he nevertheless went off to the far end of the stable block.

As soon as the horses were watered, Mabala gave the orders and willing hands came forward out of the shadows to strap on the equipment. The horses were ready, and O'Flaherty came back with the three little boys, who had found him.

"We'll walk the horses into the open," ordered Bannock, and they each took their reins and started walking.

Mabala made a sound that was more of a grunt than a word, and hundreds of voices replied in a deep, resonant salute.

O'Flaherty called back to the three little boys, "Hear," and the three covered their ears; "Speak," and they covered their mouths; "See," and they covered their eyes. But he knew they were peeping.

They walked abreast of one another, Bannock leading Marcus, O'Flaherty leading Lady Potter, Mabala leading Pot Pourri.

"Did you hear a bugle?" asked O'Flaherty.

"I can only hear the wind," said Bannock.

"You are right, *nkosi*," came from Mabala. "It was a bugle."

They watched the searchlight to their right sweeping from the reservoir redoubt. It swept to the left, picking up waves of scurrying dust, stopping just short of the direction they were taking, then swept away to the right, falling well short of Carter's Ridge. The edge of that long, sweeping arc was the path they would be following, and judging by the force of the wind, the searchlight would soon be rendered ineffective by rain.

They were almost a mile out and beyond the sweep of the searchlight when the thunder began, distant at first, with a flickering pattern of lightning along the horizon, each flash showing the banked-up clouds. Not only was there no longer any doubt that there would be a storm, but it was certain that it would be a bad one, with heavy showers.

Mabala indicated that it was time to turn west and follow the edge of the light.

"We'll mount up and keep going slowly until the rain comes," ordered Bannock. He took back the reins over Marcus' high head and followed in the inevitable circle to mount the restless stallion. O'Flaherty laughed at his efforts. Bannock struggled to bring Marcus under control, wondering again how most animals who lose condition lose their high spirits, but not Marcus.

They rode on slowly, staying just clear of the light, watching nervously in the direction of Carter's Ridge. It was like a sea of darkness with a lighthouse flashing at them from the shore. Bannock felt lonely and threatened on behalf of all of them. He knew that if there was a sharp watch from Carter's Ridge, they would have no hope. He tried to visualize the small, momentary silhouettes that could be seen from there each time the light flickered past, and imagined the deadly Maxims coming on to target at perfect range.

The first drops of rain came, with their promise of relief from the danger, huge spots striking the earth, bringing up the smell of wet dust. Marcus pranced with his head high, blowing impatiently at the unaccustomed dark, shying at every gust of wind, going down at the quarters in a tremulous dance at the first loud crack of thunder.

The rain began to splatter down. The lightning spread into a pattern of forks that covered half the horizon and lit up the veld around them in brilliant flashes. The thunder came at shorter intervals, and all three thoroughbreds showed their temperament.

Mabala rode up alongside Bannock. "We can move faster now, *nkosi.*" He pointed in the direction of Carter's Ridge. "Those men are in their tents and wagons. They are not watching."

But faster was not fast enough for Marcus. He plunged and fought against the bit, reacting violently to every flash of lightning, every roll of thunder. Bannock doubled the rein, leaned down on a grip that bowed the long neck, and spoke to him. "We're not racing, Marcus. This is an exercise canter. Slow down, boy; we've got a long way to go."

He thought about that as he held Marcus in a tight canter, watching Mabala on Pot Pourri just ahead, going almost two paces to his one. They were three lone men with animals that had to trust in them to take them a thousand miles to Port Elizabeth. It all depended on what happened now; just four or five miles of real danger and they would be riding free.

He strained his eyes against the gray screen of rain and

realized they had come the full sweep of the reservoir searchlight. They were riding into pitch darkness, and without a word between them, they pulled up to a walk again. Bannock would have judged they were far enough north, but Mabala stayed in front and kept going without hesitation.

The rain grew heavier, coming at them in gusting waves. It created the illusion of a ghostly gray light around them, a sandblasted screen that blocked out all visibility. Mabala pulled back, his bare head streaming wet, and pointed to the northeast. Bannock strained his eyes in that direction and saw the faint, swinging orb of the searchlight at the De Beers mine redoubt. But the rain came down and the gray screen became denser as he watched, taking the last sight of the searchlight with it, obliterating the last sign of Kimberley.

Mabala was going away to the left, looking back for the other two to follow. They turned west, heading directly away from Kimberley toward, if Mabala's instincts were right, Dead Man's Vlei. So far the Zulu had done them proud, choosing a flat, featureless route with no bushes and little in the way of loose stones.

Following Mabala's example, they moved at an orderly trot, except for Marcus' caperings as he was restrained from canter to trot again and again, Bannock forcing him to remain behind Pot Pourri. The forks of lightning could no longer be seen, only great fluorescent flashes that seemed to light up every drop of rain. The thunder became almost incessant in a deafening cannonade from above. Bannock was wet through, the water coursing down inside his collar, into his boots, saturating every inch of his clothing, but he began to count his luck. The weather, no matter how uncomfortable, was on their side. Karoo storms seldom lasted that long. If the cover of the rain could get them through the vlei and behind the Boer lines into the vast semidesert beyond, there was still the promise of an open moonlight ride to freedom.

It began to seem like a reality. Good-bye, Kimberley and utter frustration and waste and loss; the useless waste of time, the loss of three good horses. Good-bye, all the problem people there. He saw Sarah with the riding habit pulled up around her waist. She was worth remembering. She was worth forgetting. He thought of fat Major Masefield; a pox on his sardonic verbal crappery. And Major Stevenson. He had never given Stevenson much thought beyond the anger of losing Parader, but somehow, in spite of himself, he could not think of the man as evil. Twitchy, yes, and obsessed. And brave? He must have been brave to let a galloper like Parader carry him into action. He left a lot behind him—a heroic reputation for all time and the most beautiful widow on earth. So good-bye, one more thing: "With kind regards, Emma Stevenson." He saw the words written down and the eyes of the writer. If I were to miss anyone in that godforsaken town, it is you. I would like to make love to you, not in a pulled-up riding habit but in a big, soft bed.

The rain began to thin, the thunder and lightning coming at longer intervals and with less intensity. They kept up a steady trot, the hooves slapping noisily on the hard, wet ground, the smell of wet horse and wet leather filling their nostrils. Slowly, the sound of the slapping hooves changed. They were going into softer ground, on a slight downward incline.

Mabala forced them all to a walk and pointed ahead. "The vlei, *nkosi*. We must go slowly."

As they rode on in the steam of the horses, the rain stopped. They could see stars up ahead of the black edge of the clouds and hear the faint rumbling remains of the storm behind them. There were also other sounds, frogs and crickets and, somewhere off to the right, the mournful lowing of cattle. Then Mabala pointed again. Over to the left there were the pinpoints of storm lanterns. They were uncomfortably near the Boer position.

"This is one end of the vlei, *nkosi*. We must go more to that way."

They set off at an angle from the lights into Dead Man's Vlei, a vast, normally dry pan turned to thick mud by the rain. Bannock was apprehensive about the amount of noise they were making. The hooves sloshed in and sucked out and the wet leathers creaked and the horses snorted in long, rattling breaths. He looked anxiously at the horizon, where a pale glow announced the coming of the moon. That would make it about midnight, which meant they had taken much longer than they anticipated to get that far. They had lost the storm too soon for comfort. He wished they could have remained in total darkness until they had cleared the vlei.

From the distance came the whinny of a horse, and there was no stopping Marcus as he lifted his head and proclaimed his virility with a call loud enough to be heard back in Kimberley.

Bannock groaned, and O'Flaherty's voice came in a loud whisper: "Did you hear that?"

They stopped and listened, and realized O'Flaherty was right. There was a distant sound of shouting. The moon had begun to show at the horizon. It reflected off the wet surface of the vlei. It reflected off the three horsemen, picking them out by contrast almost as clearly as if it was day.

"Keep still, *nkosi*." Mabala stood up in his stirrups listening attentively as the noise over to the left grew louder. There were agitated voices, there were horses' hooves, and the guttural language came down to them.

"What are we waitin' for?" complained O'Flaherty. "Let's get out of here."

Mabala held up a restraining hand. "When we move, *nkosi*, they will see us. When we move, we must go fast."

Bannock considered the soft mud with trepidation and said, "I agree with Paddy. Let's get cracking straight ahead."

"Be careful, *nkosi,*" warned Mabala. "There are holes and deep places."

Bannock was ready to go, taking up the reins tightly like a jockey under starter's orders. Mabala reacted quickly, slapping the reins down on Pot Pourri's neck, and O'Flaherty was with them. All three jumped off together, galloping away into the long stretch of wet, thick mud.

Marcus forged ahead, finding his own mudlarking pace, the four legs rising high and digging in deep and pulling out high again. They were moving faster than Bannock could have imagined possible in such soft going. Suddenly, Marcus's long neck went down in front of him, and water came splashing up. The saddle came over, sending Bannock flying forward with incredible momentum. He hit the mud, squashing into it with an impact that took his breath away. All the horses had galloped into a deep watery depression and gone head over heels, sending their riders sprawling and helpless in the dark.

Mabala was first to get to his feet. He ran clumsily through the mud after Pot Pourri, but she had pulled herself up and was making off fast in the direction of Kimberley. He turned and tried to catch Lady Potter, but he was too late. She had also struggled to her feet and galloped off after her stable companion.

Bannock was being dragged through the mud by Marcus. He clung to the reins, still stunned from the impact of the fall. Mabala splashed through the pool after them. He got to Bannock and tried to dive for the reins, but by that time Marcus had backed frantically out of the pool and reared up on the firmer ground, flinging Bannock aside and ripping the slippery reins from his grasp. Mabala helped Bannock to his feet, and they both slipped headlong into the mud again.

O'Flaherty came groping up to them, spitting out mud. "Let him run," he spluttered. "Let him run and settle down or he'll just keep runnin'."

But Marcus was galloping away from Kimberley, in

the opposite direction from the mares, his great flying torso glinting in the moonlight. Then, just as suddenly as before, he was down again, flailing, trying to kick his way out of a deep pool of mud. Bannock struggled to his feet in a stupor. He started walking, sliding like a drunk toward the struggling stallion in the distance. Then he felt Mabala's heavy hand on his neck and he was pulled down flat into the mud.

"Keep still, *nkosi*," came the urgent whisper. "Keep down, my *nkosi*," he whispered back to O'Flaherty.

Bannock struggled against the restraining hand, surprised that he should feel so weak. Then, slowly, he became aware of what was happening. He could hear the sound of horses galloping at the edge of the vlei. There was rifle fire and soft, plopping sounds in the mud nearby. The Boers were firing in the direction of the pool where they had come down. He listened to the sound of the galloping and realized they were going after the two loose horses. But there were other sounds of horsemen. And then he saw them, about a half a mile up ahead, picked out by the moonlight, stepping warily over the vlei toward Marcus, who had dug himself deeply and helplessly into the mud.

Bannock wanted to shout. He reached for his revolver. He wanted to get up and go after them, but all he could feel was the restraining hand of Mabala, and his consciousness became clouded. Even the picture of Marcus fighting in the deep mud and neighing angrily began to fade.

"We must get to the cattle," Mabala whispered to O'Flaherty.

They turned Bannock on his back and, each taking an arm, they crawled, dragging him through the mud toward the far edge of the vlei.

Bannock was muttering in a slurred voice, "Marcus . . . wait. . . . Get Marcus."

They stopped to rest, lying flat in the mud just long enough to get their breath back. The noise of the cattle was very close, and the slow movement of the animals could be seen nearby. O'Flaherty pulled ineffectually at Bannock's arm and realized that Mabala was still lying there.

"Are you all right, Mabala?" he whispered.

Mabala crawled closer and, leaning on an arm, looked back. A small group of Boers could just be seen, dismounted and handling Marcus out of the mud.

Mabala whispered, "They are not looking. We must pick *nkosi* up. We must get to the cattle."

"I'll carry him," said O'Flaherty, lifting Bannock by the collar of his leather coat and sliding himself under his chest.

Bannock complained as he was lifted, "What's happening?"

O'Flaherty whispered, "Quiet, boy, quiet."

"What are you talking to me like a horse for?" Bannock slurred.

"Shut up, or you'll have them all on us."

Bannock struggled. "Let me down, you bloody fool."

"Shhh," O'Flaherty warned, letting him slide to the ground.

Bannock staggered backward, staring across the vlei. "What's happened to Marcus?"

"The cattle, *nkosi*." Mabala pushed him in that direction. "We must hide."

Bannock allowed himself to be led toward the tall silhouettes of Afrikander cattle, their long, curved horns showing menacingly against the sky. They went in among them, and the huge animals moved lugubriously aside to make a dark pathway. Bannock shook his head and felt full consciousness coming back. He heard Mabala making soft noises like the cattle, and covered his nose and mouth with his hand at the overpowering stench of fresh dung and wet hides. He tried to see what was happening at the vlei, but the big forms converged together, leaving them in a black stockade of horns. Bannock went down on his haunches, still trying to shake away the feeling of dizziness.

"Can we get out of this stinkin' place?" O'Flaherty felt his way blindly, eventually bumping into Bannock.

They heard a moaning sound from the ground in front of them. Bannock reached around until he found Mabala, who was lying out flat. He felt at his head and his torso, felt him jerk as he touched his shoulder, and knew immediately that the warm, sticky substance on his hand was not mud.

"You've been shot," he said.

Mabala groaned as he began to pull himself up. "I'm all right, *nkosi*. We can go now."

Bannock got his hand inside the Zulu's shirt and felt for the wound. It was high on the shoulder, but he was bleeding badly. He felt around the back of the shoulder. The bullet had not come out.

"We've got to get back as quickly as we can," he said. "Come on, Paddy, you take the other side."

"What direction?" O'Flaherty looked frantically round for the moon.

"This way," said Mabala, trying to take the lead. But they both hung on to him, stepping warily toward the closely packed cattle.

Mabala made the necessary sounds and the cattle parted again, objecting noisily at first, then forming up again peacefully behind them. The deep chorus of mooing and shuffling of hooves drowned out all other sounds as they struggled forward, sliding in the dung, reaching out to slap the high rumps as they turned away. Bannock marveled at the size of the herd, which seemed to extend far beyond the vlei and onto the flat plain below the ridges where there were still low stubbles of bush. Eventually, they reached the end and stopped just clear of the herd, suddenly feeling threatened and exposed in the open moonlight. There was nothing to be seen of the Boers, but they could hear the slapping hooves in the distance as they galloped back through the vlei.

Mabala looked better. He was standing straight and

alert, but Bannock knew the wound would be bleeding.

"We have to get back and fast," Bannock said. "There's no point in trying to get to the racecourse. We go back the shortest way. If we are seen, we are seen. If we stay here, we have no hope anyway. Let's get going."

"We're goin' to be in real shit if we go back to Kimberley," said O'Flaherty.

"We've got to get Mabala to a doctor."

Bannock found himself faced by Mabala. "You go on, *nkosi*. You will get through. I will go back. My people are there. I will see your face again."

"I'm not going anywhere without Marcus. I'll get him back, Mabala, I swear, somehow I'll get him back." Bannock was adamant.

He began walking, and the others followed. They could still see faint flashes of lightning in the distance and that, combined with the moonlight, showed an outline of the town. They walked directly toward the middle of that dark shape, with its pattern of mine heads and low buildings. To the left of it, the De Beers mine searchlight swung away to the north; to the right, the reservoir searchlight swept toward them on the flat plain and away again; in the center lay their dark objective, the Kimberley Mine redoubt.

Bannock watched Mabala, who was plodding heavily ahead. This was a proud and powerful man, who would shrug off any offer of assistance as long as he was conscious and could move on his own. What a man this was, who had helped him when he came off Marcus, kept his head, and dragged him through the mud with a Mauser bullet in his shoulder.

The sounds they had heard behind, the horsemen and the cattle, became faint and indistinguishable. They were making good progress, and the moon was not so bright that they could be seen from a distance. The dizziness was gone, his head was clear, and the implication of their position began to dawn on him. He had taken Marcus out of custody and they would come down on him for that. They had been stopped from escaping before, and they would come down on them for this attempt. He was about to face the consequences, but he was past caring. All he could care about was Marcus. Those Boers would have a hard time managing him. The anger came up as he thought of those long black whips they trailed in their hands as they rode. He thought about the two mares, wondered if they were off on a run home; if they were, no Boer horse could have gotten near them. I am wet and cold and covered in mud and dung. Is this the way my life has got to be? Is there anything worse that can happen? I am stripped of everything that means anything to me.

Mabala stumbled to his knees, but immediately got up and walked on faster than before.

Bannock thought about the irony of the cool success of each of his dispatch rides and the absolute failure of his carefully planned escape attempts. He tried to imagine what would have happened if he had agreed to take the Stevenson girl. They would have strung him up or shot him if anything had happened to her. As it was, he knew they were heading for jail, and he didn't care. Masefield would be after his blood for stealing his hostage and spoiling his clever plans. MacGrath would be gunning for him for taking the money and reneging on the dispatch riding. There would be no help and no sympathy from any quarter. There was little reason for caring about anything.

Kimberley was coming closer, slowly and threateningly. Then Mabala stumbled and fell. The two of them were at his side in an instant, and he laughed and shook his head as if he were embarrassed by his weakness.

"I am all right, *nkosi,*" he said. "We must go on."

"Lie still for a while, my friend."

But Mabala pulled himself to his feet and laughed again as they tried to help him. They struggled on, supporting him as best they could. The Zulu looked down at his trembling legs, seeming to will his feet to move one in front of the other, keeping up the excruciating pace right into the shadow of the high redoubt.

They heard shouts and the squeaking of a Maxim gun coming around on its mount.

Bannock shouted, "Friend, do you hear? Friend. It's Bannock; I have my pass."

Town Guardsmen came down from the redoubt and they struggled toward them until they could see the rifles held up and aimed in their direction.

"It's Bannock," he shouted again, and the Guardsmen moved round them in a circle.

A lieutenant stepped through the circle and shone a lamp on them. "We've had our eye on you for some time," he said.

"Then why didn't you come out and help?" Bannock glared around at the Town Guardsmen, who had begun to laugh at their condition.

"Have you been wallowing in the mud?" The lieutenant began to laugh himself. "You don't smell too good, you know."

"This man has a bullet in him. He needs a doctor," shouted Bannock.

The lieutenant stopped smiling. "Keep your voice down, please," he ordered. "We have instructions about you. You are under arrest." He turned to his men and ordered, "Take the native through to the hospital, and put these two heroes on the cart."

"The cart again," said O'Flaherty. "Every time we run into these characters they put us on a cart."

Bannock woke up and saw what he might have expected to see: vertical iron bars. They had been taken to the detention barracks at Lennox Street, and he had fallen asleep on the hard bunk as easily as if it had been a featherbed. He and O'Flaherty would still have been asleep but for the clanging of the bars as two troopers came in with a basin and jug of hot water and mugs of tea, which they placed on a small iron table.

"You've got a few minutes to clean up." The one who was a corporal roared with laughter as he looked at them in the clear light of morning. "You'd need ten jugs like this to get that muck off, but the orders are to be ready to march off in five minutes."

The troopers went out still laughing, slamming and locking the gate behind them.

O'Flaherty sat up on the edge of his bunk, and Bannock looked at him in amazement. He was an even tone of reddish gray from the top of his head to the tips of his boots. He had not only taken on the color of earth, but large caked pieces of it seemed to have become part of his clothing. As he bent over, the caked areas cracked and pieces fell off onto the floor. Bannock began to laugh at the ridiculous picture. For a moment, O'Flaherty glared at him morosely.

"You want to see yourself." O'Flaherty pointed, and promptly began laughing himself.

They pointed at each other and carried on laughing. Bannock looked down at his mud-caked boots and breeches. He felt at the dried mud in his hair and adhering to the stubble of his beard.

O'Flaherty went to the table and held the jug over the basin. "One splash and this water will be mud," he observed. "I think we had better be doin' it together."

They stood on each side of the basin. O'Flaherty poured half the jug over Bannock's head, then waited for Bannock to do the same for him. They shook their wet heads, and Bannock took of his leather coat and beat it against the bars, bringing back streaks of the original color. By the time the guards returned, they were confronted by the same two mud-colored figures, but with fairly clean faces.

The gates squealed open and the corporal waited outside accompanied by two troopers with rifles.

"Look lively there," he ordered cheerfully. "You are

summoned to the presence of 'is nibs, who will deal with you as your 'orrid behavior deserves."

Bannock and O'Flaherty went out with the troopers along a passage and out into the familiar lane beside the headquarters building. The troopers positioned themselves in front and back of them, with rifles shouldered.

The corporal snapped, "Prisoners! Quick march!" but the prisoners spoiled their orderly routine by walking too slowly.

"Move along there," shouted the frustrated trooper behind, and O'Flaherty promptly stopped and turned around, forcing him to a standstill, staring down at him from a head taller.

The trooper looked confused as the corporal came back. "Look, mate," he pleaded, "we 'ave to do it like this. It's orders. Be a good man and move along or we're all in trouble."

"Come on, Paddy." Bannock pulled him around and they compromised by walking a little faster.

O'Flaherty had a face like thunder as they entered the building, with the nailed boots marching noisily in front and behind.

"I knew it," said Bannock as they approached Intelligence and Communications.

"What are you talkin' about?" asked O'Flaherty, who had not been inside the building before.

"We are about to have the pleasure of the company of big-lip Masefield."

"The fat major?"

Bannock nodded as they were marched through the outer office into Masefield's office. The troopers stopped on either side of the door, banging their heavy boots down to attention, crashing the butts of their rifles on the floor, and standing at ease.

There was a moment of waiting before Masefield came in. He looked at the troopers. "You are dismissed," he ordered.

The troopers looked surprised, and went through their usual routine of banging heels and noisy stamping on their way out.

Masefield walked slowly round his desk curiously examining the mud-covered figures standing on the far side. His laughter came out as a deep wheezing that animated his double chin and his stomach. Then he sat down, assuming a mock-serious expression.

"Shall I begin by reading you a few extracts from the book of military regulations?"

Bannock and O'Flaherty said nothing.

"You may also be interested in a few of our current emergency proclamations, which now apply to you."

"Is there any news of Mabala?" asked Bannock.

"We will come to that later."

Bannock insisted. "That is all I am interested in," he said. "That, and whether my two mares got back safely."

Masefield leaned back on his chair and put on a wide-eyed look of disapproval. "You have your priorities wrong," he said. "You are in an awful lot of trouble. Your right to ask questions and your rights in general have become strictly limited."

"My priorities are my own affair. I'll reserve my own rights, and you can do what you like."

Masefield tilted his chair back lazily, but his expression left no doubt that he was angry. "Now you listen to me, Bannock. If I have any more clever talk from you, I'll hand you over to the civil authorities, who are handling emergency cases on our behalf. There are serious charges involved, and I would hate to imagine how both of you could end up. You have stolen property from the army. Let me make the point: *commandeered* property. You were involved with one Charlie Watson, a suspected spy. You were both somehow involved in that same man's death. Say nothing and listen. I am telling you what the court will hear. You have misused your official pass, broken curfew on various occasions, and twice you have attempted to exit from Kimberley illegally. All of this will be seen in the context of your already established bad reputation. I wonder how you would plead."

"I would plead that I have risked my life enough for this stupid situation, which is none of my making. I have lost my horses and with them my livelihood, and there is nothing here that interests me. Why should we not be allowed to go? It gives no risk to anyone but ourselves."

Masefield shook his head. "You are an Englishman, Bannock. Everyone here has volunteered, and many of them have lost far more than you. The court will say better men than you have given their lives and you are still alive."

"You make it sound like some special benefit that's been conferred on me."

Masefield leaned forward and tapped the table with his fist. He stared at Bannock. "I find your attitude incomprehensible. Why do you imagine you can do as you like, flout all regulations, consistently challenge authority, and expect to get away with it? Is there no way of impressing upon you the gravity of the situation, that every man has a duty in this siege?"

"I expect to get away with nothing. I have got away with nothing. My life is buggered."

"You are an obtuse fellow. You are still unable to see that you have brought it all on yourself."

Bannock raised his voice. "I am tired of this silly lecture. Why don't you get on with it and do your duty, whatever that is."

Masefield sighed. "Very well," he said, and then surprised them. "Why don't you both sit down?"

They took the two available chairs and slumped down on them.

"What about Mabala?" Bannock asked obstinately.

"Ah yes, your priorities. Mabala. They took two Mauser bullets out of him."

"Two?"

"Lucky fellow. One in the shoulder and one through

the flesh at the hip. He lost a lot of blood, but it doesn't seem to matter to him."

"The mares?" asked Bannock.

"Your horses arrived back full of spirit, and from what I am told, there are about two thousand natives tending them with loving care. My men couldn't get near them. They were also mourning the death of their great Zulu chief in very noisy fashion. Now may I ask a question? I assume you have lost your stallion."

"Yes," said Bannock.

"Dead or captured?"

"Captured."

"Interesting," said Masefield. "I expect you will now go out and attack the Boer army single-handed to get it back. That is the sort of thing you do, isn't it, Bannock?"

"Have you got a cigar?" asked Bannock.

"Would you be havin' two cigars?" asked O'Flaherty, looking longingly at the cigar box on the table.

Masefield ignored the requests. "Now, once again, will you listen to me and hear me out? I have been studying certain options that are open to me in your case. I know it is illogical at this stage that I should have to bargain with you, but I take into account, Bannock, that you have that curious type of convoluted brain that cannot think rationally without a bargain, because you are a bargainer and a gambler by nature. So I am going to offer you a bargain and gamble, with no option implied. You have no option, as you will soon see."

"For God's sake, Major, come to the point."

Masefield cleared his throat and looked up as if nothing had been said. "First the bargain," he continued. "You will do something for us and we in turn will do something for you. You will ride out on a special mission I have in mind, and we will review the charges that should be made against you. The mission is a fairly dangerous one, and thereby hangs the gamble. But the bargain, you will admit, is more than generous."

Bannock laughed ironically. "What kind of dangerous mission?"

"Some highly strategic equipment has to go to Mafeking. We are sending a small force of regulars part of the way to deliver this equipment into the hands of another like force from Mafeking. Where you fit in is that we need a couple of scouts on fast horses."

"That's specialized work?" asked Bannock.

"The only specialist ability required in this case is speed. You will be required to simply ride ahead and check the lay of the land. We are prevented from using the usual volunteers, and as you two can no longer be described as volunteers you may consider yourselves appointed for the assignment."

"You call me a bargainer," said Bannock. "You're bargaining with our lives. That's no bargain, that's blackmail. You know as well as I do that the days of getting through the Boer lines easily are over. It's impossible for one man, let alone a 'small force,' as you call it."

"It's not quite the way you think," said Masefield. "The Boer fortifications to the north are relatively weak. And if you knew the whole plan, you would understand that it is quite feasible."

"Can we reduce the gamble, then, and leave O'Flaherty out of it?"

O'Flaherty glared at Bannock. "You see, sor, I am not even good enough to be a dispatch rider."

Masefield gave a wicked smile. "Dear me, do I detect a note of resentment? Personally, I think that if you're good enough to escape, you're good enough for this. Quiet, Bannock, the bargaining is over. But let's get the terms clear once more. If you try to disappear, you'll be found, thrown into jail, and faced with the full issue. If you try to disappear on the sortie, there will be instructions to shoot you without further ado."

"Does that mean we are free to go?" asked Bannock.

"You can go but you are not free. You will both report

here at noon tomorrow, and every day thereafter until the sortie takes place. In the meantime, you will accept no commissions from your contact at De Beers, and you will not leave the perimeter, except to go to the racecourse and back."

Bannock and O'Flaherty got up to leave, but Masefield was not finished. "One last thing," he said, coming around the table and picking up the cigar box. "Merry Christmas." He opened the cigar box and offered it.

"You mean today?" said Bannock in real surprise.

"Tomorrow, my dear chap. This is Christmas Eve, the twenty-fourth of December, eighteen ninety-nine. And we shall have Christmas pudding tonight, by courtesy of Mr. Cecil Rhodes."

They both took a cigar and thanked him, and he struck a match for them.

"There is still hope for your stallion," Masefield said on a surprisingly kindly note. "The cavalry sorties have been going out well beyond the Boer lines, and as you can imagine, they are after horses more than prisoners. The point is that once the relief column marches in, our chaps will be straight out rounding up every horse they can find."

"They won't hand over Marcus," said Bannock.

"You carry out your end of the bargain and we could give you an undertaking to that effect."

Bannock was impressed in spite of his mistrust. "That's the first reasonable thing you ever said to me."

Masefield put down the cigar box and smiled at them benevolently. "By the way," he said, "that mule you left here got into the feedbags. He has colic, I'm afraid. I believe the vet is having a look at him. Maybe you can help?"

"Colic?" O'Flaherty was horrified. "The poor beast will be needin' help, if he's not passed on already." He turned and went straight out of the room without another word.

Bannock stopped at the door and looked at Masefield. "You're a cunning devil, aren't you, Major?" he said. "You would have had problems putting us into court. You know I had nothing to do with Charlie Watson's business. You're the bargainer and I'm the gambler. That's about the measure of it, isn't it?" Bannock thought of something further. "What equipment are you talking about that has to go to Mafeking?"

"There's no need for you to know that." Masefield was returning his attention to matters on his desk.

"Is it heavy? What size is it?"

"The weight is immaterial. It runs on its own wheels. I should say 'they,' not 'it.' Two field guns, my dear chap."

Bannock went out wondering if they were the same two pieces of artillery that had put them off the train two months before.

Masefield remained watching the doorway, speaking to himself as if he were still speaking to Bannock. "You keep surviving in spite of yourself. But this time you're riding with a deadly target. And the Boers are out there waiting for you."

Bannock walked into the lane in time to see O'Flaherty disappear around the end of the stable block at a run. He was sorry for the mule. It was the old story of mules never knowing when to stop. There was little hope for the animal if it had gotten the feedbags open. The crushed corn especially would have swelled to many times its bulk once it got trapped in the stomach.

As he approached along the line of stables, he could hear more than one Irish voice raised in argument.

O'Flaherty was bellowing, "I don't give a damn about your fancy Trinity College degree, the mule must be got on his feet and that's that."

Bannock's arrival interrupted the argument. He looked at the mule, slumped in the straw with its eyes half closed and its stomach badly distended.

"That looks bad," he said.

"It's gone too far, I'm afraid," said the other Irish voice, and Bannock examined another big truculent-looking Irishman, in a baggy jacket with a bald head and bunches of graying hair above the ears. Standing behind him were two native assistants leaning against the wall, waiting.

"This is Mr. Michael O'Dowd, the vet," announced O'Flaherty. "I reckon he needs a spot of help the same as the mule does."

"I need no help," protested the other big man. "I've dosed a thousand mules in my time, and this one is pretty far gone. Too far gone, if you ask me."

O'Flaherty pointed at the stirrup pump, with its hose and bucket standing on one side. "Will you look at that ungodly piece of equipment?" he said. "Do you want the poor mule to explode? The only good use for it is to water the vegetables. And will you look at that great bottle of linseed oil? It's too late for linseed oil."

The vet scowled. "I know it's too late for linseed oil. It's too late for anything."

"And will you look at all this beer standin' here?" O'Flaherty kept at him.

"That's not a bad idea," said Bannock, as he saw the crate of black stout with a few empty bottles lying alongside. "But you'll choke him before you dose him where he's lying. We'll have to get him on his feet."

The vet shook his head. "He'll never be getting up again."

O'Flaherty looked knowingly at Bannock, then said to the vet, "It's our mule and we'll be dealin' with him."

Holding the cigar between his teeth, Bannock took a halter from the open canvas bag belonging to the vet. He threw a length of rope to O'Flaherty and went to the stable door, doubling up the head of the halter. O'Flaherty passed the rope through the mule's halter and took a double grip on it. The mule's head drooped, and O'Flaherty gave it a few rough tugs, then he shouted, "Now." Bannock leaned back with his improvised whip and lashed forward at the big rump at the same time O'Flaherty pulled at the head. The mule hardly reacted, and only flicked its long lop ears at the second lash. But at the third, the legs suddenly became mobile, and so did the vet and the native assistants, who rushed forward to help the great lumbering beast to its feet.

O'Flaherty looked smug as he busily knotted the end of the rope to the mule's halter. The mule began to stumble and looked as if he would go down again. "Keep him up," shouted O'Flaherty, whacking at the thick neck, and the others leaned in from both sides, propping him up from all around.

"Ah," said the vet, "we'll be getting his head up for the dosing. Ezekiel, get some of those bottles open."

"What would we be doin' without you?" O'Flaherty said haughtily to the vet. But they were all in action now. O'Flaherty climbed up by way of the manger with the end of the rope over his shoulder, pulling himself into the rafters and climbing across to a position directly above the mule's head.

"Lift the head," he shouted as Bannock joined him in the rafters, and they both pulled on the rope, doubling it over one of the beams. Slowly, they got the mule's head pointed up toward the roof, and O'Flaherty took the bottle of stout that was handed up to him and jammed it deep into the mule's nostril.

"Ah, I see what you're up to," said the vet, looking upward.

"Oh, do you now?" jeered O'Flaherty.

"I would have done the same myself if I could have got her up," said the vet. "You obviously know the animal well."

"We know all animals well," shouted O'Flaherty from above. "That's why we do our own dosin' and doctorin'. It's the trouble with vets that they know all them fancy diseases without knowin' the handlin' of animals."

Bannock laughed. "Come on, Paddy, I'm sure Mr. O'Dowd knows his business."

The beer glugged in and the mule snorted and struggled, in its first slight sign of animation. But the body continued to lurch around below, and the animal half struggled and half sagged from weakness. The native assistants leaned on either side of the rump, while the vet doused water over the steaming back.

"He's beginnin' to enjoy it, poor darlin'." O'Flaherty pulled out the empty bottle and slotted in a fresh one. "Look at you, Macushla, you're enjoyin' your drop of stout."

Bannock watched in wonder as O'Flaherty took the next quart of stout that came up and downed it swallow for swallow, almost without a breath.

"Hurry up with it, Paddy." He sweated as he hung grimly onto the rope held around the rafter.

Down below, the vet was leaning backward against the mule, gurgling down a bottle of stout himself.

The mule burped up beery froth and bubbles.

"The colic is beginning to break," shouted the vet.

"That's it," shouted O'Flaherty, as he threw away the fourth empty quart and dropped down from the rafters. "Let his head go, Bart. Come on, Macushla, you're goin' to have a great big fart, and you're goin' for a walk. You're goin' to walk, me darlin', and you're goin' to keep walkin' until there's no more chance of you droppin' dead."

O'Flaherty manhandled the big head around and pulled the staggering mule toward the door, forcing her out by sheer brute force while the natives pushed from behind.

"Get me another bottle of that stout," he shouted, and the vet rushed to open another quart and hand it to him. But the extra bottle was again for O'Flaherty's consumption, and he drank as he pulled the mule along.

Bannock came down, and he and the vet leaned in the doorway.

"Now I've seen everything," said the vet. "Today I'll

have to go home and tell my wife that when it comes to saving a mule, a strong arm is worth more than a medical head." He went back in and fetched a bottle of stout for each of them.

They watched O'Flaherty glugging his stout while he pulled the mule.

The vet shouted, "I'll be congratulating you, Mr. O'Flaherty."

"Not a bit of it," O'Flaherty shouted back. "It was the stout that did it."

"The mule would be dead but for you," shouted the vet.

"All right, then," shouted O'Flaherty. "It was half and half."

Bannock called to him, "Come on, Paddy, bring your mule. We've got to get to the hospital and find Mabala."

Mabala walked wearily toward the racecourse stables, his khaki shirt slung over one bare shoulder. The other shoulder was heavily bandaged, the arm tied up in a sling. He had spoken to no one when he was discharged from the overcrowded hospital, setting off smelling of chloroform and sweating in the midday heat.

He was at the stables, looking at the heads of the two mares pointing out, before anyone saw him. Then the self-appointed grooms came running and touched him, laughing with joy. They rushed beyond the grandstand, shouting, and Mabala followed, walking calmly and smiling at the excitement he had caused.

By the time he reached the side of the grandstand, there was a mob coming toward him. They converged around him, all trying to touch him, those in front struggling to pull back to make space for him. But the crowd kept pressing in, banking up into a swarm of more than a thousand.

Mabala looked up at the sky, laughing. He called out, "*Ngibuyile*, I am back."

The crowd answered in a deep chant, "*Ubuyile*, you are back."

Mabala shouted, "*Ngiyaphila*, I am alive."

The crowd chanted in chorus, "*Uyaphila*, you are alive."

Mabala let the tears flow without shame. They crowded forward to touch him and withdrew, allowing others to touch him.

The deep song of salute began and Mabala's resonant baritone joined in the harmony.

· 9 · | THE DISAPPEARING GUNS

The smoke from the armored train rose in bright red curls like garish fireworks, reflecting the setting sun against the darkening sky.

Bannock led Pot Pourri up the ramp into the truck, already crowded with restless horses all bridled and saddled and ready for action. He squeezed her into the middle and handed her over to an army groom who was holding all the reins at that end. O'Flaherty was on the way in with Lady Potter as Bannock felt his way back through the crush of crouching hindquarters and out once again onto the open platform.

Their new colleague, Patterson, was waiting for him, and Bannock examined the tall, wiry man with interest. He was a permanent scout attached to the Cape Police, who knew intimately every bush and stone of the route they were taking. What really interested Bannock was the horse he had led into the truck, a bay gelding, obviously a thorough-bred.

"Was that your horse?" asked Bannock.

"No, it's one of Charlie Watson's. The late Charlie Watson."

"How did you get your hands on it?"

"The army supplied it. Major Masefield arranged it. What's so strange about that?"

Bannock was laughing. "I wondered what would become of Charlie's string."

O'Flaherty came back down the ramp and together they watched the feverish activity around them. Hundreds of natives were coming across the tracks of the yard, crossing the low platform, and climbing onto the flat, open trucks behind. Two teams of horses in their traces were being maneuvered with great difficulty into the closed trucks ahead.

There was a shout from the signal tower nearby. "You three, over here, please."

They walked toward the signal tower, where the officers had assembled. Masefield waited for them at the top of the ladder, resplendent in a dress uniform of red jacket showing a heavy curve of stomach, and tight black trousers with gold stripes.

Bannock climbed up first and smiled appraisingly at the major's outfit. "I didn't realize this was a formal send-off. What are you all dressed up for?"

Masefield smiled smugly. "While you are out facing risk and privation, I shall be attending a rather elegant regimental do."

"Sarcastic shit," muttered O'Flaherty as they followed him into the signal tower.

Masefield was not the only one in dress uniform; there was also Colonel Peakman. They both stood out brilliantly from the other three officers in drab operational khaki. The scouts stood out in their own way: Bannock in his usual leather coat with a bandolier slung loosely over his shoulder, O'Flaherty with his bandolier proudly done up, and Patterson in a battered felt hat, the very image of what a scout should look like, the bandolier tied over a khaki shirt whose sleeves were removed to expose wiry shoulders.

Peakman, commander of cavalry and newly promoted to colonel, made the introductions.

"Ah, the scouts," he said. "I want you to meet Captain Rennie, Royal Artillery, who will be leading this party; Lieutenant Porterfield, Royal Artillery; and Lieutenant Masters, who has volunteered from the Imperial Mounted Infantry."

"Good evening, Mr. Bannock." The fresh-faced young Masters beamed at his recent acquaintance.

"Oh, yes." Bannock remembered. "You were on the body-collecting detail."

The colonel was impatient. "Very well, you are Bannock, I take it, and you are O'Flaherty," He acknowledged their nods. "Let me explain briefly why you're here and what's expected of you. Bannock, you have some experience of getting through the enemy lines, and the two of you must have what are virtually the last of the fast horses available to us outside the garrison. You will ride point for this mission, under the strict supervision of Patterson, who is our most experienced scout."

Colonel Peakman turned to a map on a small table. "Will you gentlemen crowd round while I attempt to answer all your questions in advance. You will understand that for reasons of security we have had to leave some of you in the dark until the last moment.

"This is what we are about. On the one hand, we have an exodus; we are transporting a swarm of natives up the line to where it is torn up. On the other hand, you will be taking two field guns to a point near Mafeking. I shall explain presently how the two things coincide. The background to the natives is briefly as follows: Chief Lerothodi wanted to take his two thousand-odd Basutos back to the Malutis, and for once, everyone agreed—De Beers, the CO, even the Boers.

"Now this is where we are at present." The colonel drew attention to the map. "So far we have had three trips up the line, with no problems and no incidents. There are fifteen hundred Basutos waiting up there near Riverton, where the line is broken, and the Boers have long since lost interest in the proceedings.

"The plan is as follows: As this consignment of Basutos is disembarked, the whole Basuto party will set off to the north before turning east. Concurrently with that happening, the two guns will be detrained, and the detail will form up and move off, taking up station near the Basutos. I must explain that the gun carriages and limbers are disguised with hessian and canvas stretched across the hitches so that they appear as some sort of supply wagon. Instead of mules, we are using fast teams of half-breds borrowed from De Beers. Two drivers will be mounted on each limber, with four mounted men accompanying each unit. The idea is that as the natives turn east, the gunners will proceed northward at a fast pace until they reach the Vaal River.

"We are keeping open an option of two crossings at the Vaal, both deep fording points but with plenty of rock so there should be no trouble in getting through. Patterson will make the choice at the time, depending on the circumstances. Once you have got clear of the Vaal, I believe your troubles are over. You will be heading northwest in virtually empty territory toward your destination, Salpeterpan. There you will meet the Mafeking party and hand over the guns. By Patterson's reckoning, it should be three days out and three days back, riding mostly at night.

"Finally, you must understand that this is not a normal artillery force. It is a transit-and-delivery operation, pure and simple. There is no circumstance envisaged where the guns could be brought into action. Everything depends on the position of the enemy at the time you part company with the Basutos. If the enemy is there in force, you are to beat a fast retreat to Kimberley. Your precise orders will come from Captain Rennie, who is in command of this operation as of now."

The colonel turned to Rennie. "Good luck, Captain.

Don't keep the train waiting," he said. "Are you coming, Masefield?"

"I'll see them off, sir," said Masefield, joining in the saluting.

The sun had gone by the time they all descended from the signal tower and headed toward the train. The open carriages were alive with noise and movement: the shifting heads of the natives on the trucks, the horses seen through the slats stamping restlessly, the engine up front hissing loudly, venting steam out sideways and smoke upward. The natives were singing in superb harmony, their hymnlike chant blending with all the other noises to create a sinister orchestral effect of suspense.

Bannock walked beside Masefield. He eyed the shiny buttons of the tunic, hanging slack on the large midriff. It made him feel better that the clever, conniving major who had led them into this was going short of his usual gastronomic share. He wished he could attack him with words, but that would be like a dog barking at a thorn tree. Masefield could talk his way around anything. He was like a fat, spiteful spider, using words to trap and destroy; all words and no meaning, the meanings in each case tailored to the desired result. He was one of those quiet, unruffled people who in their own way were really more deadly than any man with a weapon in his hand.

"Just don't forget about our bargain," said Bannock. "Remember what you said: I take the gamble, you honor the bargain. I'm referring to your undertaking about Marcus."

Masefield nodded absently. "Yes, yes."

Bannock watched the bouncing curve of the gold buttons. "And try not to choke on all that food tonight."

Masefield took no offense. "It's not a dinner, you know."

"What a pity; you'll be fading away." He pointed rudely at Masefield's stomach.

Masefield laughed. "Oh, it's not that bad. There will

be wine. there's still whiskey in the mess, I believe. There will be snacks of a sort, and if things go true to form, Rhodes will send over a case of port or sherry."

They walked to where the officers, with Patterson and O'Flaherty, were climbing into a closed cattle truck. Lieutenant Masters stretched out a hand to help Bannock, who tried to have the last word, shouting down to Masefield.

"If you eat too much tonight you'll blow up. That's your gamble."

But Masefield had the last word. "I'll worry about my digestion if you worry about stray bullets." He knew Bannock could not hear him over the hissing and dashing sounds of the engine. "That's your gamble . . . and this time the odds are against you."

"What did you say?" shouted Bannock.

"*Bon chance,*" Masefield called back, smiling warmly.

The officers beside Bannock saluted Masefield as the train began to move off.

Captain Rennie shouted above the noise, "My apologies, gentlemen. It's standing room only. Rather like tramming it to the city, don't you think? And about the same length of journey."

They all leaned to one side of the rocking carriage to make room for the three officers' horses and the trooper struggling to keep them out of their way.

Lieutenant Masters spoke up beside Bannock. "I've gone and volunteered myself right out of a good party tonight. It's a mounted affair, you know. And by the way, talking about myself being there, I really think you should have been there."

"Me? What on earth would I be doing there?"

"Well, they are presenting that sword, you know. You know, Major Stevenson's saber. They're presenting it to the regiment—or I should say the few representatives of the regiment who are in Kimberley."

"Who's presenting it? Not Masefield?"

"I really don't know. I suppose Mrs. Stevenson. But I

really think they could have given credit where it's due. They would never have gotten it but for you."

"And Masefield is going to take a bow on our behalf?"

"No doubt."

"The fat shit."

The pink-cheeked lieutenant looked puzzled and had nothing further to say.

Bannock thought about the unaccustomed anxiety he had seen on Masefield's face as he shook his hand. It was like a good-bye, and it made him wonder. There was one opinion he needed, an expert opinion, and he groped his way along the dark interior of the truck until he found Patterson.

"I'd like to ask you a question," he started. "According to the briefing, this is going to be a pretty straightforward operation. What do you think?"

"You want my honest opinion?"

"Yes."

"I think it's going to be a disaster."

"But you heard all the nice assurances. Don't you agree with them?"

"No, I don't."

"What are you getting at?"

"You don't know the Boers, my friend. They'd be likely to leave Peakman and his large mounted force alone, but they're not going to stand back for a small party with a suspicious-looking cargo."

"Did you tell them what you think?"

"I did."

"But the army knows better. You think they'll spot us?"

"They don't miss anything within a ten-mile radius these days, day or night."

Bannock looked through the slats and saw the faint outline of the flat horizon. They were clear of the town and steaming out into the veld.

He asked Patterson, "You think it's going to go wrong on us?"

"It's going to go wrong."

Colonel Thrumpton looked like some elderly diplomat waiting for an audience, in the cocked hat and flowing cape of his dress uniform. He walked stiffly up and down the reception hall of the Shields Hotel, brushing past the potted plants as if they had no right to be in his way. He ignored Captain Pendleton, who had saluted him on his arrival before slumping back into a chair with a magazine.

The old man continued his pacing, glaring self-consciously at the people who came through. Eventually, he opted for the privacy of the garden, continuing at the same slow march through the French doors and out onto the gravel walkway with its dry border, where flowers had once grown.

He stopped on his return march as Emma appeared in the doorway. The stern mask was instantly transformed into smiling wrinkles at the sight of the beautiful girl in black.

She called out, "Mother sends her apologies," then came toward him, smiling. "You must understand you are dealing with a family of women, with due respect to Mark, which means that even though you are exactly on time, you are early."

The old eyes twinkled. "Shall I go away and come back again?"

"No, Mother's instructions are explicit. You are to come up to the living room and sip a sherry with me because I, as you can see, am a unique type of woman. I am entirely ready."

They went back through the hallway, where the colonel raised a questioning eye toward Pendleton, who still seemed engrossed in his magazine. Emma shook her head.

She took the old man's arm and steered him firmly up the wood-paneled staircase. He seemed amused at being rushed up the stairs and along the passage.

"This is very kind of you, Mrs. Stevenson." He stood back for her as she entered the living room.

"Why do you call me Mrs. Stevenson?" she teased. "You call Mark Mark and Sarah Sarah. Am I so much less of a friend to you than they are?" She brought him a glass of sherry and he smiled and nodded.

"You are quite right," he said. "I called Geoffrey Geoffrey."

Emma went and sat at the window seat, concentrating on the glass in her hands.

"I called him Geoffrey," she said softly. "I called him, Please Geoffrey. May I, Geoffrey? Do you mind, Geoffrey? And nice person that he may have been, I'm not sure that he ever really noticed."

The colonel sighed deeply. "My dear, my dear, you are upset. It's my fault."

Emma looked up at him. "Your only fault is that you have become a friend of this family, and you must know that true friendship is always abused by the truth itself. The nice truth and the ugly truth."

"I consider that a privilege."

"I am not afraid to talk about Geoffrey. I need to talk about him."

"I think I may have come to know him fairly well."

"I have never met anybody who knew him even fairly well. I didn't. Maybe you can tell me about him."

The colonel walked slowly across the room, taking a chair and pulling it along with him so that he could sit in front of her.

"Emma," he said, waiting to get her attention. "Why are you upsetting yourself?"

"Maybe you can tell me whether he committed suicide."

The old man's shock was expressed in silence. The gray

head shook slowly. "No, my dear, you are wrong. How shall I explain this to you?" He paused. "I think there must be a separate definition for the brave. Their very braveness must be seen as potential suicide. I have never held with men being called reckless in battle. To be brave, especially to lead with courage, is to be reckless. You see, the term is wrongly used. Sadly, there are two points of view here: the way it must be seen by a military man, and the way it must be seen by a wife. It all goes to put an old soldier like myself in an even sadder context. One feels that to survive implies a lack of bravery along the way."

It was Emma's turn to shake her head. "I will not believe that of you."

"We are exchanging truth, as you said," he mused. "Oh, yes, I have seen plenty of action in my time, but on reflection, I must admit I am here by virtue of caution. I could have been braver."

"And dead."

"Ah, no doubt. But here's the irony: today I am too old to die in that way. I just vegetate and feed on the glory of the heroes."

"Were you ever married?"

"Yes. There you are, I have something in common with you. My wife died of yellow fever in Egypt a long time ago."

"Do you have any children?"

"No, but there were nieces and nephews who looked forward to my homecomings. It was the largesse, you know. The magnificent uncle returned from the wars, bearing exotic gifts from foreign parts."

They both looked up as Sarah entered in a rustling gown of pale blue satin. The colonel stood up.

"Good evening Sarah," he greeted her.

"Good evening, Colonel." She surveyed the room expectantly. "Where is Pendle? He sent up a message."

"He is waiting downstairs," said Emma.

Sarah frowned. "Didn't you invite him to come up?"

"I thought I would leave that to you."

Sarah glared at Emma and rustled away through the doorway.

"Oh, dear," said Colonel Thrumpton. "My friends are really showing their feelings tonight."

Emma gave him a mischievous smile. "Never mind, have another sherry."

"I think I am beginning to need it. Ah." He turned to greet Lady Freestone-Grant, who had entered the room tall and regal in a black dress with a single decoration of pearls.

"Good evening, Simon." She said it with a warmth deserving of the first time she had been heard to call him by his Christian name.

All three smiled and the colonel said, "You look most distinguished, my dear."

"I feel less than distinguished. I feel defeated. I need your help to put down a revolution."

He caught Emma's eye. "And I thought I was finished with action for all time. What revolution?" he asked.

"My children. They are each determined to go against my wishes. Emma here would like to get out of going to this party."

The colonel's eyebrows went up. "But surely she is the guest of honor?"

"Of course, of course." Lady Freestone-Grant took the sherry Emma held out to her. "She understood that. But happily, she is dressed and ready."

Emma said nothing as she handed the colonel another sherry.

"I cannot imagine what has gotten into them," Lady Freestone-Grant went on. "Sarah has broken out into blue at a time when we should all be wearing black, but Sarah makes her own rules. There is nothing I can do with her. Then there is Mark. He has become my greatest anxiety. He has simply gone off and joined the Town Guard, and nothing I could say would stop him. He is out there tonight. I do feel that having waited this long, he could have waited a little longer for relief to arrive. You must excuse my attitude, Simon. We are a military family, with a proud record of leadership. Mark is the exception. He knows nothing of military matters, let alone of the ranks. I believe he will have difficulty in coping. Do you understand? He knows nothing of danger."

The colonel tried to restore calm. "He will be involved at the perimeter. I think you must realize that most of the shelling is aimed into the town. He is in no more danger than the rest of us."

"That is what he said to me. You are all reassurers. You say he is at the perimeter, and what then if the Boers attack?"

"That seems more and more unlikely. Although I must confess that I am hardly in the confidence of the Commanding Officer and his colleagues these days. You see, the old horse was out to grass, and it is natural for them to forget that he could once perform."

Lady Freestone-Grant was indignant. "They should be drawing on your experience."

"Oh, they do, they do. But I'm afraid that war is becoming a young man's game. There is no lack of respect, mind you. They are simply very busy, and they leave it to me to make myself useful where I can."

Emma felt close to tears. She felt responsible for the old man's confession. She thought of other old military men connected with the family whom she had grown to love, each a seeming anachronism. And here was the most telling example of all, of how the art of war, the very craft of destruction, can produce a soul as gentle as a monk. She wanted to say something that might help, but the opportunity was lost with the sound of Sarah's laughter in the passage.

Sarah led Pendleton into the room, still laughing and gushing. "Pendle says that in spite of all, we are going to have a brilliant party tonight. There is to be a bar and buffet that breaks all the emergency regulations."

Pendleton went forward, cap in arm and hand on saber, to greet Emma and her mother.

Sarah's smile faded as she examined Emma's dress. "I thought you were remaining behind tonight?"

"I have decided to go," said Emma.

Sarah appealed to her mother. "I do think Emma was right in the first instance. Surely she should not be going out yet?"

Emma's temper flared, but her mother anticipated her.

"You are under some wrong impression about this affair tonight. It is not a party so much as a gathering to pay respect to two deceased officers and to present their sabers to their regiments. It is essential that Emma attend and she has agreed to do so."

Sarah was not finished. "Geoffrey's saber?" she asked, without turning round. "You didn't mention that, Pendle, although you did mention how the brave Mr. Bannock retrieved it."

"I didn't say brave," said Pendleton.

"Does that mean Mr. Bannock is to be there? Because if that is so, I shall not be going."

"No, no," Pendleton insisted. "This is purely a military affair."

Colonel Thrumpton had listened disapprovingly. He addressed himself to Pendleton. "Surely you were told what was intended for tonight?"

Pendleton was flustered. "Yes, yes, of course, sir."

Sarah broke in sweetly. "It's my fault," she said. "I've so longed for some real entertainment that I created a party in my mind."

"Are we all ready?" asked Lady Freestone-Grant.

"I must fetch my cape," said Emma, going to the door.

Sarah was bubbling again. "Shall I fetch your stole, Mother?" She called out as she followed Emma, "Pendle, tell them what you said about my dress."

But then she was in the passage and her expression changed as she took long rustling strides to overtake Emma.

"I suppose you were hoping for Bartholomew Bannock to be there?"

Emma stopped in her tracks and looked coolly at her sister. If there was to be a scene, there would be a scene.

"Do you know, Sarah, that the one thing that never occurred to me about Mr. Bannock was that one could feel any kind of emotional response to him? While Geoffrey was alive, I never allowed myself even to see another man. But now I am a widow. Do you understand? I am a free agent."

"What do you mean?" Sarah was suspicious.

"Simply that you are putting ideas in my head. I can see now what you saw in him."

"He is a pig."

"He has quite amazing eyes, has he not?"

"You don't know what a pig he is. He attempts to make love in a wild, savage way."

" 'Attempts'?"

Sarah stared in silence and Emma knew the expression. She waited for the rage to explode.

"How . . . dare . . . you." Sarah spaced out the words. "You little prig. What are you suggesting?"

"Oh, come now, Sarah. You got handled, seduced, and tossed out in record time, even for you."

Emma turned and walked into her room to fetch her cape, expecting her sister to storm after her, but she heard the rustle and footsteps going toward her mother's room. For a while she stared into the mirror, her mind wandering away. She thought about Birchleigh; how she wished she were there. Anywhere but in this siege of ghosts.

Her mother had come out of the living room to call, "What has happened to you two?"

"Coming, Mother," Emma called back. Only then did she really see herself in the glass. The young widow in black.

Yet if black were meant as an appropriate disguise for a female, it didn't work. The plain dress was really quite flattering. The pulled-back style of the yellow hair, insisted on by her mother, contrasted very well with the color and gave a lift to her eyes. At least this widow looks attractive, no matter how she feels.

I must stop these arguments with Sarah about Mr. Bannock. It does make me think of him. It would have been interesting if he had in fact been there tonight.

The wind came in gusts out of the blackness, bringing unseen dust that took their eyes and noses by surprise.

Bannock rode beside Patterson, who could only be seen as a dark image of head and shoulders, moving with the action of his plodding horse, against the sky. They were on their own, far ahead. The sound of the chanting Basutos had faded into the distance in the east. While there was nothing to be seen except the demarcation of sky and earth, deep blue and black at the horizon, there were still sounds. Some way back could be heard the hoofbeats of the teams, the rattling of the chains on the traces, and the wheels of the two gun carriages and their limbers grinding across the veld. The cries of jackals and nightbirds were no louder than those sounds behind, which set Bannock to wishing that the whole Boer army might be asleep and that if they were, they would stay asleep. He looked back longingly at the one feature that stood out in the dark landscape behind them, a small flickering pinpoint of light, the far-distant searchlight of the De Beers Mine redoubt.

Patterson had set this pace with the reluctant agreement of Captain Rennie. It was to be dead slow, with stops every ten minutes to listen for any suspicious sounds before proceeding. Yet it was obvious that Rennie had confidence in Patterson's scouting ability. He had taken all his advice and satisfied himself with organizing his troop in its readiness to take off at a fast pace in case of emergency.

The unloading of the seven-pounders off the train had been done when it was already dark, the Basutos providing a camouflage of noise, singing loud and true in a rousing chant.

O'Flaherty had been posted at the rear to hang back within hearing of the gunners and to listen when they stopped. The instructions from Captain Rennie and Patterson had been clear: If there was a Boer attack before they reached the Vaal, the scouts were to withdraw and hot-foot it back to Kimberley, with the artillery detachment following after and taking their own chances—hence the fast horses instead of mules. Once they got past the Vaal, there was only one destination: Salpeterpan, to the northwest.

They were riding away to the east of the direction taken by the teams, Patterson having decided that the only possible trouble might come from the cover of the low hills in that quarter. It was also the direction of the coming moon, which, however, would give scant light, being in its first quarter.

Pot Pourri had become a true night owl, stepping along quite calmly, feeling out for the low bushes and loose stones, cleverly holding off and sidestepping at the slightest obstruction. The reins were hung loose to allow her to do her work, and the pace and the darkness became utterly monotonous. Bannock began to wonder whether the army was right and Patterson was somewhat of an alarmist. Yet the creaking, grinding noises from the teams some hundreds of yards behind were uncomfortably loud.

There was nothing to be said riding beside the taciturn Patterson; there was nothing to do to add to the mare's bouncing efforts. Bannock retreated into thought. He tried to give order to his feelings of frustration. He was risking his last two horses, and that brought back a resentment of Masefield that bordered on hate. If the reason for using his horses was speed, why had Masefield not provided two from Charlie Watson's string? Why should Patterson be offered a mount and not themselves? There was something peculiar about Masefield. A cruel streak, a need to torture, maybe a need for revenge against a man who refused to bend to his will, like a fat, spoiled prodigy who had to have his way no matter what. Yet that made the fond farewell of a few hours earlier seem out of character. It had the ring of a final good-bye, suggesting the most positive form of revenge of all.

When he thought of it now, Masefield's behavior had been strange from the beginning. At first he had seemed predictable, a more than normally clever officer with an uncanny ability to detect and handle trouble. But then he became too clever, an exploiter, bargainer, manipulator. There were other ways to get a man to do things than by threat, but even that hardly described it. It seemed more of a game than anything else, with Masefield holding the bank in a game of roulette where the chips had Marcus on them, and instead of red or black, it became life or death for the players.

My mind has become preoccupied with this fat man and what he can do to me. It's almost impossible to fight a man like that. It's not a question of fighting fair or otherwise, because Masefield gets what he wants without fighting at all. I would rather be a fighter than be like him, meet whatever comes along headlong and fight it out to its conclusion.

But how do you fight games and clever words? What kind of game has no end . . . or has to end in death? You can never use the analogy of poker or chess, because both games come to a logical conclusion. Masefield only sounds logical. But when logic gets mixed up with cunning, the results are unpredictable. It's impossible to reconcile the flashes of friendship and the calculated torture.

Yet I must concede that no man could be expected to understand my attitude about Marcus. It seems insane even to me that I should go on believing that the Boers have no right to Marcus, that somehow I shall get him back. That is the insane idea that keeps me locked into Kimberley and Masefield's schemes. I'm dealing with a man who has some extraordinary insight into that, who must suffer from some like form of insanity to recognize the same condition in me.

But there was something Masefield didn't know:

Mabala had managed to trace Marcus to a Boer camp behind Carter's Ridge. Driven by feelings of guilt at the loss of the stallion, Mabala had done a brave thing, crawling up the ridge at night and waiting almost until dawn to identify the stallion in the picket lines, coming back with the news that the camp was heavily guarded. In that way, the position seemed hopeless. There was virtually no chance of stealing the horse, only the glimmer of a chance based on Masefield's seemingly empty promise. He would be kept to that promise. On the next mounted raid on Carter's Ridge, Bannock would ask to have himself included, and if there were any military objections, he could put himself forward as a scout. If he could scout for the gunners, he could scout for the troops. He would try it on Masefield as a bargain for a bargain. It was a far-fetched idea, but the only one he could think of at present. It depended on many things, the immediate one being staying alive for six days in enemy-occupied territory.

"Hold up," said Patterson, and they stopped and listened. His veld instincts were better trained, and Bannock realized that the sound of the teams had stopped. There was absolute silence, except for the wind humming off the stony ground, then the bark of a jackal, over to one side, that seemed to be keeping track of them.

Patterson stretched in his stirrups, saying nothing as he looked to the north, then around the hills to the east. He lit his lamp and signaled back, covering the weak beam with his hand, uncovering it and covering it again, then turning it off. They remained sitting still, listening to the sound of the teams starting up again.

Patterson brought his horse in closer. "We're coming to the river at an angle. I want you to ride straight across the front of the gunners until you reach the river. Then work slowly north along the bank until you meet up with me. I'll be waiting there for you. If you see or hear anything, head back for the guns and report."

"How will you know if I do that?" asked Bannock.

"I'll be able to hear what you're doing."

"Right."

Bannock turned Pot Pourri and headed away to the west at a fast walk. The mare perked up and he had to apply the reins to stop her from setting off at a gallop. He had not gone far when he heard Patterson call.

"Bannock!"

He stopped the mare and waited.

The voice came again more urgently. "Come back here."

Bannock rode back and pulled up beside the dark figure.

Patterson pointed at the hills. "Do you see any movement up there?"

"I saw something move," said Bannock, uncertainly staring at the black dome of the hill where its summit became outlined against the sky.

"Keep looking."

"Yes, the whole of the top of the hill. Are those riders?"

Patterson sighed. "Thirty or forty of them," he said. "And they can hear everything we can hear. They must be wondering what's going on. Come on, Bannock, follow me. Keep in trot, and let's hope we get to the guns before those Boers stop and listen again."

They trotted back, heading at an angle toward where they had last heard the noise of the teams. The two horses sensed the excitement, fighting at the bits, Pot Pourri jumping low bushes when she brushed into them.

The dark forms of the teams became visible and Patterson called out.

"Captain Rennie, sir, pull up your guns."

Rennie rode forward to meet them. "What's up, Patterson?"

"Enemy, sir. Bunch of horsemen coming over the hill."

"Halt," called Rennie. "Halt and keep quiet."

The orders went round and some of the troopers dismounted to quiet down the shuffling teams.

"Officers here, please," ordered Rennie. "And dead quiet, everybody."

The two lieutenants rode up and brought their horses into the circle.

Rennie addressed Patterson. "I thought you said the Boers slept at night? Their lookouts are obviously wide awake."

"Come now, Captain." Patterson was irritated. "There are no lookouts on those hills. There's nothing to look out for."

"Then what woke them up?" Rennie was equally irritated.

"You want my opinion? They saw the unloading at the train. They've checked out the Basutos and come on a shortcut over the hills. I say we turn and run for Kimberley."

"No, sir," retorted Rennie. "I'm in no mood for running unless it's forward. Dammit, man, the whole idea of this fast unit is that we can get away in the dark."

"Listen, please," said Patterson, and they all went quiet.

There was a soft sound like drums played out of rhythm, from the direction of the hills. Then silence. Then the sound again.

"They are listening for us," said Patterson.

"You haven't answered me," snapped Rennie.

"It's no good giving me a lecture on what kind of unit this is, Captain. I think it's a joke. I thought it was a joke from the start, and said so. As far as I'm concerned, you're about to give the Boers a gift of two seven-pounders."

Rennie raised his voice. "Listen, Patterson, and stop being negative." He checked himself and spoke more quietly. "I reckon we've been on the road for nearly an hour.

It's still before nine and the moon won't show for another hour yet. If we go on at a gallop to the river, how long will it take to make a crossing?"

"Forget it." Patterson was scornful. "If you gallop, you'll bring the teams down. If we get to the river and take the first crossing we come to, it will take twenty minutes or more to get across. And even then, we would have to be lucky. Crossing that river in the dark is going to be a risky business."

"Well, if you don't like my suggestion, I don't like yours. If we gallop back, they'll alert their garrisons on the ridges. Have you any other suggestions?"

"Yes," said Patterson. "Sit tight, keep quiet, and don't move."

"What are you talking about?" demanded Rennie.

"You stay here and I'll ride to the river and bang off some rounds, and when they come following, I'll take them on a wild-goose chase to the north."

"There's something in that," Rennie allowed.

"Then you have only one choice, because every Boer in the district will wake. You turn tail and go home. That way you might save your guns. Repeat, might."

Rennie said nothing. They all remained silent for some time, listening for the noise on the hills and, ominously, hearing nothing. Eventually, Rennie spoke.

"Very well, Patterson. And by the way, when we get back to town, we'll have a drink together and a discussion, not an argument."

Patterson laughed. "Understood, sir. I'll be in position in about five minutes. I'll fire off a round to let you know. Once I've emptied off a magazine or two, I suggest you make your move."

"I'll come with you," said Bannock.

"No, you won't." Patterson was emphatic. "It's a one-man job, and you don't know the countryside. Anyway, you're going to have to lead the way for this lot. It's a long ride back."

"You stay here," ordered Rennie. "Good luck, Patterson."

Patterson turned his horse to go. "We're all going to need luck, sir," he called back as he set off at a trot.

Porterfield asked, "Shall I bring the teams round, sir?"

"No," said Rennie, still staring in the direction Patterson had taken. "Leave them where they are. You can pass the word that anyone who wants to get down and stretch their legs may do so. But no striking of lights, and no talk."

Bannock asked, "Can I go back and tell O'Flaherty what's happening?"

Rennie shook his head, but remained watching in Patterson's direction. "No, Mr. Bannock. O'Flaherty will either wait or come on of his own accord."

But Bannock was not satisfied. "I just thought that if we turn and gallop in that direction, he's likely to start shooting at us. I could go on foot."

"You will stay here, if you please." He turned to face Bannock and Masters. "I believe Patterson has given us an option. We will sit here for a few hours, if need be, and if all is still quiet by that time, I may well decide to go forward after all." With that, Rennie walked his horse toward the teams.

Bannock dismounted and looked up at Masters. "Did you know there was an option? How does he expect to get across the river without Patterson?"

Masters dismounted before he answered. "Yes, well, I'm sure Patterson intended no option, but then, on the other hand, the captain knows the orders."

"Do me a favor, Lieutenant, you heard the orders as well as I did. Run for home is the first alternative."

The next gust of wind brought the distant sound of a galloping horse. Patterson had chosen to make himself conspicuous before he ever fired a shot. They waited. And then the report came echoing back. They listened to the silence before the storm. Then the storm broke, in a rumble of galloping hooves that seemed about a mile ahead, heading across their path toward the river. The rifle fired and echoed again, and the echoes kept coming, report after report.

"I hope Patterson knows what he's doing," remarked Bannock grimly.

"He's quite a man, Patterson," said Masters. "He was one of the last people out of the post at Vryburg at the beginning of hostilities. He's become quite famous, really, for getting all the way through to Mafeking and back. I believe he'll lead them a good chase and come back smiling."

"I can't imagine him ever smiling," said Bannock.

Rennie came back, leading his horse, and they listened to the almost inaudible sound of firing in the distance. The wind whistled dust through their boots and the legs of the horses. The only other noise came from the blowing of muzzles and stamping of hooves behind them.

Suddenly, rifles clicked and slammed as they were loaded from the direction of the gun carriages. They all took their reins, ready to mount, then Bannock blew out his breath in relief at the sound of O'Flaherty's voice.

"What in the name of creation are you all doin' standin' around as if there was nowhere to go?"

"The moon will be up soon." Bannock watched the light glow at the horizon.

"New moon," reminded Rennie. "It's not going to give much light, and there's no choice of cover around here, so kick your heels, Mr. Bannock, and resign yourself to the idea that we shall be waiting here for an hour or more yet."

O'Flaherty came up, still mounted on Lady Potter. "Is that you, Bart?" he called.

"Will you keep your voice down," ordered Rennie.

O'Flaherty hissed in a loud whisper, "If somebody doesn't tell me what's goin' on around here, I'll be goin' right back and joinin' Major Masefield's drink-up."

* * *

Emma looked around and made some calculations. There must have been more than two hundred people in the Town Hall that night, the ratio of men to women more than six to one. It was difficult to imagine the place as the daily venue of the soup kitchen where she worked in her long apron. Not that there were any decorations beyond a few regimental flags, but the uniforms with their shining buttons and braid and the women in their best dresses created a feeling of decoration in themselves, while the brass band of the Loyal North Lancashires blew away quietly on the stage.

She was trapped in a select circle under the watchful eye of her keeper. Lately her mother had contrived to be with her all the time, more, she felt, out of intentions of surveillance than sympathy. Her mother had become the keeper of her propriety, the watchdog over her widowhood, the stern mother fowl poised to peck at the fledgling who dared to flap its wings before the proper time. She had even taken to attending the soup kitchen, not to help, but to watch.

It seemed that Geoffrey was to join the ranks of the family deities, with Emma a permanent fixture at the lower end of the shrine. But Emma could only remember the Geoffrey who could not even cope with his own fears. She believed her mother worshipped nothing but recognition. As for herself, she could think of nothing she wished to worship. She thought, I am in this room of rousing voices and I am not.

Colonel Peakman was giving them a pedantic account of the military problems of the siege. Her mother listened beside him, and next to her a self-consciously handsome captain was covertly ogling her daughter over the rim of his glass. Emma looked directly at him with an expression she felt should put him off, but he seemed to take it as a positive reaction and ogled all the harder.

A lieutenant came up and whispered in Peakman's ear. The colonel excused himself and climbed up to the stage, leaving them with the captain and Colonel Thrumpton, who had joined them. The band stopped playing. The hall went quiet, and Peakman's voice boomed out.

"I've waited to make this announcement in the hope that it would not be necessary, but according to the message I have just received, I must announce as follows. Colonel Kekewich extends his compliments and begs to be excused from this gathering, which he would have wished to attend. Unfortunately, there is a situation which will occupy the commander throughout the night. He wishes you all a pleasant evening, and so do I."

The band struck up again and Peakman came back to join them.

Lady Freestone-Grant remarked to him, "We were looking forward to at least seeing Colonel Kekewich. He is a bit of a ghost, isn't he?"

Peakman found that amusing. "You would not find him a ghost if you attended his briefing sessions, Ma'am. He holds the floor, he provides both the questions and the answers. But don't misunderstand me: the questions are pertinent and the answers extremely analytical. He is a stern man, you know. There is very little humor. Works harder than any of us. We have a sound man in command, make no mistake."

Emma's mind withdrew again. Her mother was providing the questions and the colonel obliged with a long dissertation on the present and expected situation of the siege. But he soon found himself avoiding the issue of the Kekewich and Cecil Rhodes quarrels, which were becoming common knowledge. Other officers joined in to listen behind the circle, and an offered tray of drinks was subtly denuded.

Lady Freestone-Grant persisted in her questions, and Peakman smilingly, adroitly fenced with her. No, there was no question of any contention between the General Staff and either Kekewich or Rhodes. She smiled icily at his refusal to open up. No, they were not precisely friends. No, there was no confusion he knew of in the exchange of official messages. No, it would not be correct to say Rhodes in his position as a Privy Councillor of the realm should have the veto in military as well as civil decisions. There should be no question of how a most difficult situation is being handled.

Peakman's warning frown put an end to the questions; his good humor returned in a flash; the lecture continued in its previous affable style. The newcomers appeared to be listening, but, like the captain, they occupied themselves in staring at Emma. She looked carefully toward her mother, to be ready with a reassuring look when the old lady's eagle eyes came around to check, but she could still feel the other eyes boring in.

She wondered whether she appeared resentful and gauche. I must put on a smile or I'll be putting a damper on this affair. But how much of a smile? At the age of twenty-five, I still have not learned how to cope in a crowd. There are men looking at me, and as usual, I cannot judge a friendly look from a lascivious one. I may have this problem, but Sarah certainly does not. Is that the price of experience with men? Her eyes are like two seductive signal lamps saying, "Yes, yes," "Come here," "Here I am," "Why not?" and they flock around her. Is that the way to handle it and still keep one's poise?

The colonel went on talking. Emma smiled politely in his direction, but went on thinking.

I have never been a candidate for seduction. Maybe that's why I don't relish the idea. She thought of her first instincts of sex. I had hardly stopped being a tomboy when I became a wife. With all these men in the world, I have only made love with one. And now for the first time in my life, I seem to be wondering what it would be like. Will I meet a man who is worth experimenting with? I am not innocent, merely inexperienced. I think I must be sexless, because I am not wondering too hard. I shall be terrified if it happens again, when it happens again. Because that first belief in the promise of passion with Geoffrey was such a precious and powerful thing that to not realize it might be to never realize it. Were all the poems of love and passion just the frustrated longings of people who never properly achieved it?

She tried an experimental smile in the general direction of the oglers, and they all smiled back enthusiastically, as if they were not listening to the colonel at all. She wondered what it was they were seeing—a fragile little widow with jet buttons all the way up to her throat, a vulnerable little female, attractive enough and unattached? I hate this siege. It ties me to my mother, it exposes me to foolish, grinning eyes, it subjects me to a role I cannot bear. I feel like burning this dress.

"Emma." Colonel Thrumpton was leaning down to get her attention, and in the moment she looked up she realized that the old man's eyes were flicking around under the bushy gray eyebrows, observing her admirers critically, then coming back to rest on her. "Are you all right, my dear?" he asked. "Shall we go and check on your sister?"

"Yes, I would like that." Emma took his arm gratefully and looked at her mother, who nodded her permission but was not altogether pleased.

They took their leave of the group and began to make their way through the crowd. Emma clung to the arm and rested her head on the gold epaulet at his shoulder like a child.

Thrumpton whispered, "I venture to repeat my question."

"I am really quite all right," said Emma. "Just glad that you are here."

"I suspect you are not really enjoying this."

"Oh, it's an easy enough duty."

"Shall we promenade through the crowd? If we keep moving, they won't bother us."

"Good idea," agreed Emma.

The old colonel walked proudly with the beautiful girl on his arm, nodding to acquaintances but steering her past all possible engagements. Eventually, they stopped in an open space, where the colonel took a drink off a passing tray, Emma having declined. She looked up to make a remark and realized her partner's attention was fixed on something nearby.

He said, "There is a brain locked up in this siege."

Emma followed the direction of Thrumpton's gaze. Standing on his own with a drink in his hand, glaring around as if he dare anyone to speak to him, was the large, rotund figure of Major Masefield.

"I don't know whether you have ever spoken to him, but he is a brilliant fellow."

Emma was inclined to agree. "I had the same impression. I'm glad you think he is clever."

"There are those in Kimberley who regard me as an old fool, but even old fools are listening and observing. No, don't protest; age is a foolish condition. It slows up the body, but the mind goes on perceiving on the basis of a lifetime of critical experience."

"Does Major Masefield remind you of yourself?"

"No, my dear, never. He will never become an old fool. He is altogether too shrewd for that. I suspect he has only one weakness. They say he is a gourmet, an expert on the epicurean subtleties. I suppose that accounts for it; there is nothing subtle about his waistline."

Masefield glared around in a full circle, one hand behind his back like a mop-haired Napoleon, the big brown penetrating eyes eventually coming to rest on Emma, who smiled in recognition. He came toward them with the same intense expression, nodding in return to Thrumpton's greeting and confronting her with the gesture of a smile that came and went, while the eyes never let go.

He said, "I'm sure that widows are not supposed to look ravishing."

Emma laughed at his solemn manner, but she wondered about that stare. Surely it was innocent and friendly. She must stop imagining that every look implied an ulterior motive. The stare went on, and she waited for him to speak again.

"I visited your soup kitchen the other day."

"I saw you."

"It's a noble occupation you have found."

"Oh, there is nothing noble about it. It's my escape—" Emma stopped herself from saying what she might regret.

Masefield seemed surprised, as if he might pursue the thought, but instead he said, "By all accounts, the soup is very good, although I understand it doesn't appeal to horsemen."

"You should be able to taste the prejudice. Even our chef is a horse lover."

Colonel Thrumpton cleared his throat for attention and addressed himself to Emma. "Can I leave you with Major Masefield for a moment? I must check on your mother."

"By all means," said Emma vaguely wondering whether the old man had engineered this meeting with Masefield and vaguely pleased, in spite of her doubt, that Masefield was someone worth talking to.

They watched Thrumpton wend his way through the crowd toward the stage. Then, as if by some intuitive agreement, they watched Sarah, past the heads in front of them, holding court among a group of officers that included Pendleton. Emma felt her sister would have looked more attractive if she could have been a little less animated. She decided firmly that that style was not for her. But Sarah had their attention, eyes for eyes and every gesture aimed.

Masefield said, "Your sister is not your friend."

Emma looked at him in amazement. "What has given you that impression?"

"She is jealous of you. She is the jealous type of female, and you are the type females are jealous of."

He was going too fast, confusing her. "Jealous of what?"

"Your amazing beauty."

"You are making me blush."

"I would rather make you smile. You are looking a little too serious even for a widow."

Emma could not help laughing. "And why should I be smiling when you are looking so serious?"

"Because"—Masefield exaggerated his gloomy expression—"because on these occasions we must put on the expressions that do us the most good. You must try to look pleasant. I must contrive to look stern and intelligent."

"Is glaring at everyone a sign of intelligence? They say you have brains. Are you blushing now, Major?"

Masefield was actually smiling, but he said nothing.

Emma saw the ogling captain making his way through the crowd some heads away. "Will you take me to see the presentation?" she asked, slipping a hand into Masefield's arm and almost pushing him into action.

They moved slowly away.

She asked, "You seem to me more like a distinguished lawyer than an army man. Are you in the right profession?"

"Are any of us in the right profession?"

"You are supposed to answer, not question."

"Very well, let me start at the beginning. I left school and joined the army and presently gave it up because I saw no real future in it. I resigned and went away to read history at Oxford, and when I graduated, I decided that all the opportunities open to me would see me live and die and never be involved in history again. So I made a truly historical decision and went back into the army."

She laughed. "And now?"

"I think I should like to be a farmer."

"You seem to be unable to make up your mind."

"Making up one's mind is an exaggerated virtue. Making up one's mind is an interim condition to changing it."

"I like that," said Emma as they reached the table with the two gleaming sabers, one of them Geoffrey's, and the laid-out decorations with two illuminated scrolls. She stared at Geoffrey's saber. "You have taught me something that makes nonsense of all the grand maxims we were brought up on."

Masefield had to smile. "I think you are mocking me, but I am quite serious."

"No, I am impressed with what you said. I think cynicism finds things out."

"I am not a cynic, I am a realist. What I actually meant was that why we believe is more important than what we believe."

"I've heard that preached."

"It's not a doctrine, it's a strategy."

Emma leaned over to examine the saber. She thought, I somehow take exception to that. Those are only clever words. I am not going to ask what they mean.

She read the scroll above the saber, then turned to Masefield.

"May I ask you a question about this saber?"

"By all means."

"Has Mr. Bannock been properly recognized for bringing it back?"

"He was thanked." Masefield's eyes showed doubt. "I think he was thanked."

"Shouldn't he have been asked here tonight?"

Masefield blinked uncomfortably. "No, I don't think he would have expected that. In fact, he is otherwise engaged tonight. You might say he is out of town."

"I am not a spy, Major. Do you mean he is out riding dispatch?"

"Something like that." Masefield showed his reluctance to say more.

"I have decided that I like Mr. Bannock," said Emma. "One way or another I think he has behaved extremely well. You must value him very highly."

Masefield frowned and made no pretense that he had to think about what he was going to say. "How do I put this? Bannock is not the kind of man you would easily understand. Frankly, I like him, but if you want my true opinion of him, I think you would be surprised."

"I might also be interested."

Masefield took a slow sip from his glass before speaking. "He is a kind of brute. He has no fear of anything, and whether he means it or not, he is bent on destruction. He invites violence the way some people are prone to accidents. I should say that apart from a few primitive symbols he has created for himself, like a stallion that he regards as the whole meaning of his life, his life has little meaning. He has intelligence, but on that primitive side, he is really no more than a stallion himself."

"From what I have seen, this sounds harsh."

Masefield appeared not to have heard. "In that way, he is attractive to women, I think. He is the kind of man who can fascinate another man without harm, but if he fascinates a woman, I believe there is only one senseless purpose in it."

"You are not the first person to have warned me about Mr. Bannock. My sister also called him an animal. But does an animal have honor?"

"My dear lady, what a question! The average dog is prepared to die for its master, and a stallion as good as Bannock's will gallop as far as it is urged. Does an animal have honor? Oh, yes, I think this one does, and honesty, even sensitivity of a sort. He gives back money."

"Twice," corrected Emma. "He gave it back twice."

"A stallion's pride. He moves like a stallion, stands like that with his head up. A stallion's stallion, and that's the fault. He would kill and die for a mere horse, and a man who is prepared to do that is not to be trusted."

"I've seen that horse. It is a truly magnificent animal."

"It's in the hands of the Boers now."

"How on earth did that come about?"

Masefield took a sip of his drink before answering. "Bit of carelessness on Bannock's part."

"You admire him and you denigrate him in one voice."

"You have misunderstood me." Masefield avoided her gaze. "I am not an admirer of stallions."

"I still misunderstand you."

Masefield assumed an obstinate smile instead of answering.

Emma looked at the saber again and hoped Bannock had better weapons for survival. She felt she had reacted to everything Major Masefield had said like a typical woman. She thought, Something quite contradictory is happening here. Is it that I can be influenced by my own need to defend? Does a normally attractive man like Mr. Bannock become singularly attractive by defending him in a situation where one is constantly reminded of him? I am being foolish, she cautioned herself. I am losing all sense of proportion in this whole stifling situation.

She saw her mother bearing down on her through the crowd. The mother fowl was fluttering in, and Emma frowned down at the saber again.

"Major, may I ask you something?"

"Anything."

"You are in charge of dispatch riders—you send them out?"

"That is not a question, and if it is, you should not be asking it."

"Get me out of Kimberley."

Masefield was flabbergasted. "You are not serious?"

"Can't you arrange for me to leave at night with one of those men?"

He whispered, "That's preposterous."

"I asked Mr. Bannock, but he would have none of it."

"Of course not. You have no idea of the risk. We have had seven of our messengers killed or captured in just over two months. What you are suggesting is insane and impossible."

They both looked up and fixed smiles on their faces. Lady Freestone-Grant was upon them.

Bannock crouched down in front of Pot Pourri, resting an elbow on a knee in order to have a clear sight through the field glasses. He could see the fires more clearly; three of them; spaced out over a few hundred yards near the river, and, in their reflections, the dim shapes of Boer horses and dismounted men.

He realized, looking around, that it had been wishful thinking that the weak light of the new moon would be in their favor. Scanning toward the hills, he tried to judge how far he could see the shapes of the low bushes, to have some idea of the extent of natural cover the night would provide for them. It was uncomfortably far, and he cursed Rennie for wasting more time by sending him out. He immediately mounted up and began riding back at a trot.

The teams were gratifyingly quiet as he approached. He whistled the agreed signal.

Rennie was waiting with the two lieutenants and O'Flaherty for what he felt would be yet another indecisive discussion. It began to seem as if Rennie was bent on dying a hero's death, but if Bannock could have seen his expression clearly as he dismounted, he would have known that the captain had lost some of his resolve.

"What can you report?" asked Rennie.

"I only got a closer view of what you can see from here. It's a big commando, and they're spread out having a coffee break, as far as I can see."

"There are more of them coming over the hill," said Porterfield.

"Right," said Rennie wearily. "We go back, but not necessarily to Kimberley. If we follow the river south and give Barkly West a wide berth, we might be able to make a crossing farther west and head north from there."

Bannock fought back his irritation. "Assuming that

you get that far without being attacked, are you going to attempt a crossing without Patterson?"

"Why not?" Rennie appealed to Masters. "You know the area. What's your opinion?"

"Frankly, sir, we have never been into the Barkly West area, partly because there was no reason to, but also, I happen to know that Colonel Peakman felt it was too heavily infested with the enemy. They are very active around there."

Rennie was adamant. "We have come this far undetected, and if we can remain undetected, we must stay with our objective. I agree that we are poised on a boiling pot and that we must go back, but I intend to turn and try again if there are enough hours of darkness left and if conditions seem right for it. There is no hurry; we'll turn and go quietly and calmly. So get the men mustered and take up your positions, please. Bannock and O'Flaherty, I suggest you ride ahead at the two quarters and signal if there is anything urgent."

Bannock and O'Flaherty mounted up and rode through between the teams. The troopers were getting up from where they had been sitting huddled around the guns holding onto the reins of their horses. Bannock noticed with surprise that in his absence the canvas and hessian wrapping had been removed and that the two new pieces of artillery gleamed a shining gunmetal blue in the moonlight.

He looked back at the first sound of restless hoofbeats, depressingly loud even though the teams were being led around slowly. The harnesses creaked, the chains clanked, and the metal hitches of the limbers squealed for as long as the turning action continued.

"It would be a miracle if they don't hear all this commotion," said O'Flaherty.

"Let's hope for a miracle."

"I'll be prayin' for that."

They set off at an angle to take up their lonely positions, Bannock to the left, nearer the hills, and O'Flaherty to the right, toward the river.

"Try to stay in sight of me," Bannock called.

"Right," O'Flaherty's voice came back, and they both began to trot to get ahead of the teams, which could be heard making a lively walking pace.

Bannock kept up the trot for longer than was needed to take up the quarter position Patterson had shown him. Then he pulled up to a stop, taking advantage of the extra ground to scan with the field glasses. The glint of the railway line showed to his left, and he was relieved to find that the hill beyond seemed deserted. That hill would lead into Dronfield Ridge, with its heavy gun emplacements facing Kimberley. He scanned ahead where there was nothing but a void of darkness. But the trouble was not going to come from ahead. Any troop movement coming toward Kimberley between the Boer posts could almost certainly be assumed to be made up of Boers. If there was to be an attack, it would be more likely to come from behind.

He rode on for what seemed a long time, listening to the noise of the hooves and the gun carriage wheels and imagining how the troopers were holding their breath. Every minute that passed became a gift of time and space that brought them closer to hope of survival. If the Boer garrisons ahead at Dronfield on the left and from the Pumping Station and Kamfersdam to the right and forward of them were alerted, this small force would be helpless.

Bannock wondered about Patterson and felt hopeful. That was a man of the veld, who knew the surrounding area like the back of his hand, and he had a particular advantage in riding that stringy stayer of Charlie Watson's. He would be able to use the gelding's speed to get away, then conserve its stamina to gallop again when necessary. There was just one flash of a nightmare, of the horse tripping or coming down or being brought down by a stray bullet. But men like Patterson lived by those terms of chance. His chances were little worse than theirs. Bannock felt the odds against survival were shortening as he recognized the steep, low ridge of Dronfield and even made out some details of the rough stone walls of the Boer forts through the field glasses.

The reality of its proximity was brought home by a flickering campfire at the top of the ridge. He remembered Patterson's words about the Boers' sense of hearing in the veld, and became aware that the muscles in his face had gone tense. Should he signal back, or was it obvious enough? They had come too far. If they veered to the right at this stage, they would run into the Boer garrison at the Pumping Station. There were only two choices: to risk the noise and keep going the way they were, or to stand still in silence and pretend they were invisible, and that was no alternative. To stand still would be to waste hours of darkness, which they could not afford.

It seemed inconceivable to Bannock that the sound he could hear from the teams had not been picked up. He waited for the first shots to come from the rear, but they never came.

Then he heard something over to the left, and stopped to listen. There were sounds audible from both quarters: the noise of the teams filling his right ear from behind, and, unmistakably, another noise coming from the left, horses' hooves some distance away, but more likely at the bottom of the ridge than at the top.

He swung the mare around to signal but decided it was too risky, the lamp could be detected from any other angle. O'Flaherty could not be seen in the gloom, and Bannock felt the urge to shout a warning to his friend and to the oncoming unit. But the sound had changed, and he realized that the hoofbeats he could hear, no matter how many of them, were moving at a cautious pace. The only alternative was to ride back and report.

He turned and cantered toward the teams, deciding that the faster pace would make no more noise than a trot. Again he was heading into the dust-laden breeze that amplified the sound of the gun detachment. He gave the whistle as softly as he could as he approached.

Rennie rode out to meet him, followed by Porterfield, and he reported.

"There's enemy activity over toward Dronfield, riders on the move, quite a few of them."

The captain swung his horse around and Bannock barely heard him give the command to halt. The teams were pulled up and held, and they took a few moments to shuffle themselves into a calm state and settle down. By this time there was nothing cautious about the sound coming from the direction of the ridge. There were horses galloping, and they even heard a shout.

Masters cantered his horse between the teams and pulled up beside them. "There's activity behind us, sir, if you'll listen."

"That does it," said Rennie. "We are about to go for a gallop, gentlemen. We will go in column for about a half a mile, Porterfield with number one gun leading, then cross the railway line south of Dronfield. This will leave us about a mile and a half to cover to reach the fort at Kenilworth. If anything stops us on the way, one of the gunners—you select one, Porterfield—will go straight on to the fort and report our position. We'll leave one driver on each limber and the other two men will ride lead. Get it all ready quickly."

The lieutenants moved back, giving the orders, and the two men came from the limbers to mount the leading horses of the teams.

A low whistle sounded, and O'Flaherty arrived just in time for the action.

The orders were shouted and the teams came to life. This time there were whips cracking and shouts urging and no inhibitions about noise.

Bannock and O'Flaherty went ahead together, holding back on their reins, easily maintaining a lead with their horses' superior speed. The stubble of bush had disappeared and they were galloping on flat, arid veld. The noise that followed them was terrific—blowing horses, crunching wheels, and shouting men, drowning out any possibility of hearing the enemy activity.

Out of the corner of his eye, Bannock watched the ridge receding fast behind them. They were well ahead when they heard the teams turn and go for the railway line, and turned themselves to cross on a parallel course. He wondered how the heavy gun carriages would manage over the low rise and the railway tracks, and he held his breath as they approached. But the horses clattered over in fine style, urged on by the lead riders. The wheels of the limbers and carriages banged and leapt and banged again, giving off sounds like a series of enormous gongs, and they were over.

The teams were just back into their stride when an enormous flash came, and an earsplitting report, and straightaway another. They were being shelled, and although the first two rounds were wide of the mark, Bannock realized that from the elevation of the ridge it only needed the new moon to pick out any movement against the veld below. He and O'Flaherty had to take firm measures with their thoroughbreds, forcing the two nervous animals to cross the rails. They both reluctantly jumped and scrambled over. But once across, they were back into a gallop, following the detachment on a closing course.

The next two volleys of shells came, one well ahead of the teams and the next even closer to Kimberley. The teams took fright and parted company, the number two gun on the far side veering off almost at right angles to its destination. Bannock knew he had the speed to help and galloped through behind the near team and after the other, which was heading away from him.

The lead rider was shouting and leaning over on the traces, dragging at his horse's mouth. Then the horse fell over under him, vaulting him into the air, and the whole team crashed, piling into one another, with the limber coming on into the melee, doing terrible damage to fallen horses. The heavy gun carriage keeled up on one wheel and crashed over beside the milling, whinnying animals. Bannock saw the driver plummeting onto the ground and going under the wheel of the limber as it tilted over.

As he reined in, he heard Rennie shouting, "Bring your team around. Pull up here."

Bannock dismounted and called to O'Flaherty, who was coming up, "Hold the mare. Give me your sheath knife. Hurry up, damn you."

He grabbed the knife and ran toward the struggling team. He passed the lead rider, who was stumbling around holding his head, and the next moment he was in among the struggling, grounded horses, furiously cutting at the traces to release those who could still get up. He had cut the leathers in six places when he came upon the driver under the wheel of the limber. But even before he touched him, he realized he was dead.

The next flash came and then the next, and Bannock was lying flat as he heard shrapnel rip in amongst the horses. But there was a farther flash and a lesser report, and the shell exploded away toward Dronfield. There was a flash from the direction of Kimberley. The Kenilworth redoubt was firing at them.

Rennie and Porterfield dismounted nearby and he heard Rennie shouting at the lieutenant, "What happened to your bloody messenger?"

"He went straightaway, sir. He should be there at any minute."

After that, the sky became a pathway for howling missiles. On the one hand, it was a relief to see the Kimberley volleys stretching out toward the Dronfield Ridge, though with no hope of making the distance. On the other, the Boer volleys, fired in strict sequence from two guns on the ridge that had them in their sights, were coming closer by degrees.

Orders were still being shouted and Rennie was setting

up the intact gun for firing. The unhitched team plunged
and fought where it was held by the gunners behind.

Bannock went over to find out what Rennie intended.
As he reached him, a shell whined in and exploded some
fifty yards beyond the gun, sending back a rain of deadly
shrapnel into the second team of horses. Bannock and the
officers had gone down flat at the moment of the explosion,
and as they stood up, they saw three horses of the team
pathetically trying to drag away their dead and maimed
companions. The two gunners who had been holding them
were down and obviously dead.

"Check on those men," shouted Rennie. "Is this
bloody gun ready?"

"Is there any point in staying here?" shouted Bannock.

"Kindly keep out of this," Rennie shouted back.
"These guns have to be spiked."

The first of the next two salvos exploded nearby, and
Bannock saw Lady Potter rear straight up and go over
backward, with O'Flaherty still on her back. Pot Pourri got
loose and galloped away, and when the next explosion came
he saw her legs fly up, and in the instant of the blinding
flash, her body was ripped apart. He shouted, "No!" as the
image of flying legs stopped in the air, leaving him blinded,
his vision blurred with light-distorted versions of that
image. He went on swearing, unaware of what he was saying. Then he heard Rennie's voice, matter-of-fact, beside
him.

"Get a grip on yourself, man."

The next two shells exploded off to the other side. They
had all ducked, and as they straightened up, Porterfield
stayed down. For a while he remained on his knees, then
he fell flat. Bannock helped Rennie turn him over, but he
was already dead, with a wound in the upper chest that
looked too neat to be shrapnel. This evidence was immediately confirmed by spurts of dust and the spark of a bullet
off the gun shield.

"Snipers." Rennie pulled Bannock by the shoulder. "Behind the gun," he warned. "Fire off a few rounds," he ordered Masters, now in charge of the number one gun.

"What range?" asked the lieutenant.

"Forget about the range, bring her down and fire along the ground."

Masters gave the order: "Range, five hundred yards. Load."

Bannock watched the professional crew come together like an extension of the gun, one man turning down the elevation to a low trajectory, another snapping open the breech, another ramming in a shell. He looked around for O'Flaherty and saw him for an instant silhouetted against the sweep of the Kenilworth searchlight, unloosing the traces on the second team of horses.

"Number one. Fire one round," came the order from Masters.

"Ready," came the gunner's response.

"Fire!" came the order, and Bannock felt his head would split as his hands came up too late to cover his ears.

The smoke still billowed as the next command came.

"Run up. Halt. Number one, fire one round."

"Ready."

"Fire!" And they could see nothing but the repeating flash from the barrel.

"Hold your fire," ordered Rennie. "Prepare to spike the guns quick as you can."

The spiking rod was carried from the hitch to the muzzle and rammed in as a shell went into the breach at the other end.

Rennie went forward himself with three men to carry out the same procedure on the gun that lay on its side.

The rifle fire seemed to have stopped. Bannock listened for it, hearing only the singing in his ears from the previous explosions. But he did hear the next thud of a shell being fired from the ridge, followed by the second thud a few seconds later. He was standing with Masters and the three gunners who remained in their positions, wondering whether there was any point in going down flat. Those shells might explode in front or behind or right on them. And the fear became a reality as the first explosion shook the ground and filled the air with brilliant light. The metal of the gun rang in a splattering of shrapnel, and Bannock felt something strike him in the face as he went over backward. Masters stepped over him and ran around to the front of the gun. The next shell burst, and Masters came tumbling back, to lie still on the ground beside him.

Bannock crawled over to help him, feeling at his own painful face where the flesh was broken along the left side of his jaw, feeling up to the ear where the lobe was torn loose. But Masters had fared worse. Bannock groaned when he saw the blood showing on his jacket and the breeches torn away to reveal one of the legs badly shattered. He lifted him into a sitting position, and found the young lieutenant staring at him blankly.

"Up you come," Bannock said, holding up one of Masters' arms and getting his shoulder into his stomach. In a moment one of the gunners, a corporal, was helping him to get on his feet with the lieutenant on his shoulders.

"What about Rennie?" asked Bannock, lumbering round and looking beyond the gun.

"Captain's dead, sir, and the other three."

Bannock yelled, "Get your men out of here. If they want these guns back, they can come and fetch the damn things themselves."

O'Flaherty joined him as he staggered away in the direction of the searchlight.

"Let me carry him," he offered.

"It's all right, I've got him."

They made a few more yards before they heard the next two reports from the ridge. Bannock could feel Masters' shallow breathing as he went down on his knees and slowly lay on his side, with the torso still over his shoulder.

O'Flaherty was also down, and they waited for the missiles to whine in and explode. They came and went like two great peals of thunder, spitting out their ricocheting shrapnel like scattered stones.

O'Flaherty helped him to his feet, recoiling as he grabbed at the smashed leg of the lieutenant. Bannock looked back toward the destruction. All he could see was a dark milling of dust and the shadowy forms of the remaining gunners coming to join them.

They walked on into the sweep of the beckoning searchlight, and Masters began to moan and talk on Bannock's back.

"The guns," he said. "Have they spiked the guns?"

"They're doing it now," said Bannock.

The searchlight began to light them up as they walked, and when the next reports came from behind them, nobody bothered to lie down, they just kept walking. The explosions produced a clanging of metal that echoed on after the blast.

"Let me carry the poor man," asked O'Flaherty.

Bannock shouted, "I'm carrying the bloody man," and he plodded on, realizing that O'Flaherty was holding Masters' shoulders to steady the pace.

"What about Lady Potter?" he asked.

"She got away, Bart," said O'Flaherty. "She galloped off home in fine style. Bart, I'm sorry about—"

"Shut up," Bannock said hoarsely. "I'm sick of everybody being sorry. I'm sick of being sorry myself. Shut up about being sorry, do you hear?"

They walked into the blinding turn of the searchlight. O'Flaherty could see the blood on Bannock's face, but he knew him too well to say anything further.

The shelling from the ridge had stopped.

Bannock knew he had been dreaming. He had seen Pot Pourri rise into the air and begin slowly to disintegrate, with pieces of anatomy breaking away in the form of sections of a jigsaw puzzle. A hind leg and quarter, a shoulder and neck, the head, each neatly finished off by the clean delineations of the puzzle. It all came together and disintegrated into sections again, came together and shattered into individual pieces.

His eyelids tremored. He tried to keep them closed and go back to sleep, but the pain was too real, burning up his cheek and into his ear. He thought, Why should my dreams make excuses for reality? The sound of hoofbeats was also real, and the straw rustled as he turned on his back, looking at the ceiling, wide awake, hurting.

There were voices. Masefield's voice. The devil was on his doorstop, back for the next round of torture. He remembered his parting phrase, *"Bon chance,"* and his smile. What was there to smile about? And before that, something about "stray bullets." He couldn't hear the words, but the malicious eyes had given away the smiling mouth. He struggled to hear the words, but the sounds of confusion and Masefield's distorted shouting faded away, as if he no longer existed.

But the voice was still there: Masefield was still there, outside, standing in a circle that included O'Flaherty, Mabala, the three small boys, and the heads of Lady Potter and the mule looking out from the stables.

Masefield was bending down to examine the large collection of Boer shell fragments laid out on the ground in front of the stables by the boys.

"They're doin' a great trade," remarked O'Flaherty.

Masefield shook his head disapprovingly. "It's typical of the hysteria building up in this town. Why anyone should rush to collect pieces of burst shell, and why they should pay large sums of money for them, is beyond me."

"They got a pound the other day for one of them big ones."

The three monkeys offered pieces to Masefield, but he shook his head again and walked off toward the bar entrance of the grandstand.

Mabala went after him quickly, getting ahead and positioning himself in front of the door to block his way.

"*Nkosi* Bart is sleeping," he announced. "He say nobody go in."

Masefield frowned at the imposing black man blocking his way and turned around indignantly when he heard O'Flaherty laugh.

"I wouldn't step in there if I were you, sor." O'Flaherty was still laughing at the sight of Mabala guarding the door. "Bart has been sayin' some terrible things about you, and I'm thinkin' he means it. Take my word, it might be dangerous goin' in there."

Masefield called out, "Did he go to the hospital?"

"Would you mind keepin' your voice down? The poor man needs all the rest he can get."

Masefield hovered in front of Mabala, looking toward O'Flaherty. "Did you get him to the hospital?" he persisted.

O'Flaherty put on his philosophical air. "Some horses you can lead to water and they won't drink, and some you can't even lead to water. There are times when you don't tell Bart Bannock what he should be doin'. But it's on your own head if you want to wake him up. Let the major go in, Mabala."

Masefield looked at them as if they were mad and went in through the door. He crossed the room and stood at the bar looking down at Bannock, who was wide awake and glaring up at him.

"You were supposed to have that wound seen to."

Bannock sat up, feeling the crust of dried blood along his jaw. "What are you doing here?" he asked wearily. "Have you got some new deadly plan cooking in your head? Because if you have, you'd better keep quiet about it. I'm not part of your plans anymore, do you hear?"

"I came to see how you were getting on."

Bannock laughed mirthlessly, gingerly feeling at his jaw. "I see nothing very clearly anymore, but you I see clearly. I'm beginning to understand what you're all about,

Masefield. You are the devil in this hell. You've really buggered us up this time, haven't you? You're responsible for that mare's death, you bastard."

Masefield tried to speak, but was forced to listen.

"Masefield—"

"Yes?"

"If anything happens to Marcus, you'd better not be around after that."

"Listen to me." Masefield had lost some of his usual poise. "I've said this to you before, but you don't seem to understand. We are at war, and we all have a duty to perform. I know you volunteered, no matter how reluctantly, but look here—"

"You're talking rubbish," Bannock interrupted. "I never volunteered, you forced me into it. And you know what you forced me into, don't you? Action, the deadly kind, where men disappear in the night and men rush to fall dead when the bugle sounds. And what do you do, Masefield? You sign orders for suicide missions, you fill out requisitions for coffins. What do you do in that little office of yours? What kind of soldier are you?"

"Some of us are paid to think. You must understand that war—"

"I think you exaggerate your ability to think. What's the point of you skulking in the background thinking, while the men you send into action do everything by numbers?"

"I was not in favor of this operation."

"What's the good of Rennie sacrificing half his men and giving his own life for the sake of two lousy cannons?"

"Nobody dies on purpose."

"It doesn't matter how they die, they're all dead. Scott-Turner, Stevenson, Rennie—they're typical. You spend ten years training them for five minutes of glory. Is that what you think about when you're thinking?"

"You're not being very rational."

"What about Lieutenant Masters? Is he dead, too?"

"He is going to be all right."

"With one leg missing."

"I don't know about that."

"And your cannons, your precious cannons? Did you get the bloody things back?"

Masefield met the questioning eyes. "What cannons?"

"Oh ho, you're about to say something fucking clever, aren't you Major? What happened to the cannons?"

"Let's say they disappeared. There was nothing when the light came up except a few dead horses. Nobody can understand it. And Bannock, there is never going to be an explanation forthcoming."

"Two cannons and a mess of bodies can't disappear."

"They don't exist, my dear chap. They never existed."

Horses were arriving outside, and Masefield went across to the door to look out. Bannock could see him over the top of the bar from where he sat. He marveled at Masefield's game-playing, wondering what those cryptic remarks meant, whether the guns had been captured or brought back and hidden for some strange official reason. Either way, he thought of the irony of so much destruction for a result that could only be accounted for with a riddle.

Masefield called from the door, "I had another reason for coming here. If you're feeling up to getting on your feet, there is something outside I'd like to show you."

Bannock got up and followed him toward the door. "If you think you can talk me into another one of your schemes, you're wasting your time."

They went outside, and Masefield watched Bannock as he blinked in the harsh sunlight, taking in the scene of an army wagon drawn by mules and a horse being untethered from the back by an African groom. A trooper was handing down a saddle and bridle to O'Flaherty, and it dawned on Bannock that it was light racing tackle and that the horse was a thoroughbred, somewhat thin and rundown in condition, but a thoroughbred nevertheless.

"What's this all about?" Bannock was suspicious.

Masefield looked away noncommittally and said,

"Apropos of what we have just been discussing, things and people have a way of disappearing in times of war, like a certain racing trainer together with his horses."

"Charlie Watson," said Bannock, looking at the horse again, a black gelding of good height.

"The name is immaterial, my dear chap. To all intents and purposes, this racing trainer, who has no known next of kin, does not exist. Nor do his horses."

"You gave one to Patterson."

"I told you, I know nothing about them. They were brought in to H.Q. but never requisitioned, and one or two were indeed handed out. This particular one remained in my care, so to speak, and I have come to the conclusion that it is not suitable, and because it is a thoroughbred, I felt it might be of use to you."

"You mean you are giving it to me?" Bannock was still suspicious.

"I am saying nothing official, Bannock, but yes, it is yours for the taking."

"What's the bargain?"

Masefield roared with laughter.

Bannock kept watching him. "With you, there's got to be a bargain."

Masefield walked away around the wagon, still laughing to himself. One of the troopers from the wagon unhitched his horse and brought it to meet him.

Bannock shook his head in disbelief and went after him as he was about to ride away.

"Patterson didn't come back?" he asked.

Masefield stopped laughing and sighed. "Patterson didn't come back."

·10· | MOONLIGHT RIDE

The cavernous metal interior of the De Beers workshop exaggerated every sound—the low voices, the shuffling of boots, the atmosphere of expectancy appropriate to the occasion.

In the center, rising above the machinery, the great gun called Long Cecil, after Rhodes, was on show for the first time, a private viewing for the CO and some of his officers.

Masefield loomed, following his own shadow from the glare of the entrance, strolling at first with the shadow elongating away into a ridiculously thin silhouette until it crossed swords with the equally long shadow of the gun. He moved faster as he became aware that a speech was in progress.

As if it had been intended, the De Beers engineers and their assistants, with George Labram at their head, stood apart from the military men, giving the impression of a handing-over ceremony.

Masefield tried to merge into the background, but no one seemed aware of his late arrival, all showing signs of elation, all eyes on the gun.

O'Meara of the Royal Engineers was in mid-lecture.

"The fact is, there would be no gun at all were it not for the existence in the De Beers stocks of one vast piece of shafting of the appropriate dimension. Ironically, were it not for the lack of suitable metal for the inner tubes, George Labram would have been able to make further such pieces of ordnance."

They looked toward Labram, who made no reaction.

"Tell them the specifications," prompted Kekewich, who was standing slightly apart from the rest.

"We can fire off a shell halfway to the Modder."

There was an impressed silence as the meaning sunk in.

"The specifications, the specifications," the CO insisted.

O'Meara spread his arms like an exaggerating fisherman. "Twenty-eight pounds, gentlemen. Long Cecil has a barrel of four-point-one-inch bore, capable of throwing a twenty-eight-pound shell to a range we have yet to determine—but it is a vast range, you may be sure."

The CO took over in his flat, booming delivery. "Gentlemen, this unique cannon will go into action tomorrow, and I believe that once it starts spitting out its hellfire—especially now that the Boers are paying less than usual attention to their shelling—we are going to give them the shock of their lives."

Some of the men cheered. Masefield sighed.

The CO droned on. "The venue for the first firing has been chosen. We have decided on the number one searchlight redoubt in the northern barricade. The target has also been selected. The objective is to strike the main Boer laager at the Intermediate Pumping Station. Quite apart from their garrison, if we can damage their water supply we will damage their morale, and that will make a nice change."

Masefield couldn't resist it. "That sounds rather a long shot, sir."

O'Meara, as much as the CO, took the point literally.

"It is, Major, four and a half miles, in fact. I have Mr. Labram's assurance that Long Cecil can do it."

Labram gave the ghost of a nod. Masefield sniffed.

The open carriage made its way toward the northern defenses, traveling slowly so as not to tempt the dust, converging with the track that led alongside the railway lines, then following its winding course between the high sand dumps of the Kimberley and De Beers mines.

The entire family, with the exception of Lady Freestone-Grant, were off to see the first experimental firing of Long Cecil, the great gun that, by all accounts, would swing the balance of the bombardment. It was to be a gala occasion with all the town's dignitaries attending. Yet Emma had as little enthusiasm for it as anything else in her life at present. She had vaguely believed in Long Cecil's invincibility until Colonel Thrumpton had raised the chilling point that all it might achieve, at this time of light shelling by the Boers, could be a sharp increase in the enemy fire.

Emma sat beside the old colonel, facing forward, with Sarah and Captain Pendleton opposite, facing back at them. Every once in a while Sarah leaned forward and waved to Mark, who followed out of range of the dust wake in a borrowed trap drawn by a thin pony.

Emma watched the hot air dance and vibrate over the top of the dumps. She felt red-faced in the heat of the late-afternoon sun. She was wearing Sarah's riding habit, the only black garment suitable for going out in the daytime apart from her soup kitchen dress. Both she and Thrumpton were reduced to silence by the noisy attempts at jolly conversation taking place opposite them. Pendle—Emma decided it was an appropriately silly name for him—was holding forth on the imaginary dinners they would have once they had put the hungry experience of the siege behind them.

"And on the following night we shall dine out yet again. This time we shall start with select Colchester oysters."

"No we won't," called out Sarah. "To begin, we shall have shrimp canapés with a sprinkling of caviar."

"But I loathe canapés," protested Pendleton. "And it was your turn the previous night."

"You shall choose the wine," squealed Sarah.

"But I haven't chosen the main course yet."

"Chateaubriand. You may choose a burgundy."

"But you are choosing everything."

"Well, never mind, Pendle, you may choose the vintage."

Emma glanced sideways at the grand old man looking like the earl of something in his impeccable red jacket, gleaming brass, and brilliant white helmet. He also seemed to be making a determined effort to retire into his own thoughts in the face of the rather forced peals of laughter from opposite.

She watched them without listening. Pendle was an ideal partner for Sarah. They had much in common. His good looks were an ideal match for hers and so was his fatuous humor. They behaved like a couple of asses. They were not funny. They were not even particularly nice, and Emma would have liked to have been anywhere but in their company. However, she knew what her choice was. It was them, which included Sarah's subtle and sometimes not so subtle attacks, or it was her mother, or it was both together.

She thought, Once again am I inviting depression, breeding it, wallowing in it? Am I creating my own private siege here?

The carriage slowed and the driver maneuvered his way through a crowd of other conveyances drawn up in a wide circle in front of a wall of sandbags. There were gleaming landaus, coaches, and carts, and a picket line for the saddlehorses. Emma looked sadly at the animals. They all had one pathetic characteristic in common: they were all visibly thin and underfed—far more so than those they served.

A sergeant saluted up at the officers. "I'm sorry to say, sir, that everyone is to proceed from this point on foot. They don't want the animals taking fright."

Mark pulled in alongside as they alighted. Other vehicles were queuing in and raising dust all around. The sergeant marched ahead of the party to point the way through the barricade. Once on the other side, they got their first sight of Long Cecil, gleaming new and blue above the heads of the crowd.

Mark caught up with Emma and took her by the arm as they walked toward the gathering of townspeople in their Sunday best surrounding the gun. "You're looking like a small storm cloud about to explode. Are you all right, Emma? Whatever you say, I'm glad you've come."

"I wouldn't have come if you could not have gotten time off. You look like somebody else's brother in that uniform."

"Oh, I don't know." Mark looked down appraisingly at his drab khaki tunic and field boots. "I'm really quite enjoying this, in spite of Mother's horror. I'm quite proud of being a private volunteer, and it does pass the time. Instead of sitting at home dreaming about food, I can dream about food out on the barricades."

They reached a point at the edge of the crowd where chairs and mess benches had been set out for the ladies.

Thrumpton addressed them. "If you'd like to come with me, we can attempt to get through that crowd and take a closer look at this remarkable piece of machinery."

"Not I," said Sarah. "I'll wait here, if you don't mind. Pendle can give it two looks to make up for me."

Pendleton laughed, appreciating the joke so much that it was a while before he realized the others were waiting for him.

"I'll wait with Sarah." Emma smiled at Thrumpton, who led the other two men away into the crowd.

All Sarah's enthusiasm vanished when they were left alone, and the two glum young women sat down and said nothing. But they had become the focus of some attention. Three older women who had put their heads together in recognition of Emma came forward, and one of them introduced herself.

"I am Mrs. Fellows; my husband is Captain John Fellows of the Buffs. I don't think you would have met him, but he knew your late husband. I'd just like to say . . ."

Emma saw the eager eyes enjoying their morbid involvement. She saw the other two pairs coming in closer, queuing for their turn. She thought, you are torturing me. You are shiny-eyed old birds of prey. You enjoy sorrow too much, you could never understand how I feel. You are torturing my guilt.

The large lady behind came up alongside. "Is this Mrs. Stevenson? I had no idea you were so young. My poor, dear child, I was only saying the other day . . ."

Emma thought, Oh, God, what am I doing here? How long will this go on? Why must I live in a black shadow for a man who didn't know how to love me? I never knew a husband the way you women do. I lived with a man who was not there. I slept with an animated saber.

"You must come and see us. Please say you will."

Emma turned around, nodding blindly. She was already walking away when she realized Sarah had followed quickly and put a hand on her arm to stop her.

"I wish I had not come," said Emma.

But there was no sympathy in Sarah's eyes. "Poor Emma," she mocked. "It must be so tiresome having so many people trying to be nice to you."

"I'm sorry if I upset them."

"Oh, don't be silly. You never do anything wrong. They think you are a brave little person overcome with grief."

"I do not pretend to be distressed, Sarah."

"Whatever you do, right or wrong, you give a good impression."

"I really don't feel like arguing with you. You are the one who bothers with impressions."

"Yes, but I am a little fussy about whom I impress."

"Let me save you the words, Sarah. You are going to bring up Mr. Bannock."

Sarah was caught off guard and she came back angrily. "He hadn't crossed my mind, but he seems to have crossed yours. You really should forget about him."

Emma sighed. "You are being very insulting."

"Well, the real problem is not that you may be thinking about him but that he had you at the top of his list of conquests. He was quite clever, really. He recognized your susceptibilities. He knew that you were incapable of judging the type of ruffian he is."

Emma decided not to take the bait and to let Sarah go on.

"But once again, everyone was bothering about you, and you can be thankful to the colonel for sorting out the matter of Mr. Bannock."

Emma took the bait. "What are you talking about? Which colonel?"

"Our Colonel Thrumpton, who else?"

"Sorted out what?"

"He merely arranged that Bartholomew Bannock should be put in his place. People like that are quite easily put in their place, you know."

Emma stared in disbelief. "What on earth has Mr. Bannock done that he should be put in his place?"

"Oh, my naive sister—"

Emma swung around and walked away. She heard Sarah call out, partly in confusion and partly in anger, "Emma, come back here."

But she held her skirts and almost ran toward the crowd, searching for the three men, eventually realizing that the heads were too tall and the shoulders too tightly packed for her to see anything. She stood still at the edge of the crowd and raged impotently to herself. Why don't I just walk out of this town? Wait until nightfall, step over that barrier, and keep walking until I get somewhere or something happens to me, I really care not what.

Directly to one side of her was the sandbagged wall of the redoubt, with three steps leading up to a vantage level. Mounting the steps, she looked back over the heads and was soon able to identify Thrumpton's white, silver-pointed helmet. She knew by this time that she was very likely beyond the limits of rational thinking, or rational behavior for that matter, and she didn't care. If she was going to make a fool of herself, there was no help for it. But if Colonel Thrumpton had done what Sarah suggested, he was going to have to explain himself.

She set off into the crowd, aware that the anger boiling up in her must be showing. How could anyone have the temerity to take it upon themselves to protect her in a situation where there was no apparent threat? How many of them were acting on her behalf without her knowledge? I will rise above this collusion. If that man who gave me back the money, who hurt no one, is attacked, I will take his side. I wouldn't care whether he were a thief or a criminal in the normal way, he has done nothing to me, he has stolen nothing from me, and against this sort of unjust attack I will take his side.

Emma went to force her way through the crowd, but they parted and let her through, and each way she turned they parted again, until the crowd became a maze with all sense of direction lost. She was becoming desperate when she suddenly came upon Mark and Thrumpton. Her brother saw her first.

"Emma, where have you sprung from?"

She ignored Mark and got Thrumpton's attention.

"Colonel, I must speak to you. Will you come with me, please?"

The old man was taken by surprise. "Well, yes, of course," he muttered.

Mark saw her agitation. "Is there something the matter?" he asked.

"You must excuse me. I have to speak to Colonel Thrumpton. It is most urgent." Emma made to go.

"Of course, of course." Thrumpton looked at Mark questioningly and followed after Emma.

They got clear of the crowd, but Emma went ahead and waited for him at a point where they were out of earshot. She saw Mark emerge as well, with the look of anxious concern she knew so well, but he waited for them some distance away.

Thrumpton folded his arms and looked down at Emma. "Well, my dear," he said, "I recognize a situation where one of the family has a problem and an old friend of the family has been appointed to adjudicate. You are upset, you have a problem?"

"Yes, I have."

"Can I help?"

"Yes, you can. I suspect you are the problem."

Thrumpton frowned. "I think you had better explain that, Emma."

Emma rushed in. "Did you or did you not take some official action to protect me from a man called Mr. Bannock?"

"Oh." Thrumpton looked away and nodded to himself. "Someone has been talking out of turn."

"Colonel, I will not mince words with you and I hope you will not mince words with me. It was Sarah who told me this."

"Hmm." Thrumpton hesitated uncomfortably.

"Are you prepared to tell me about it or are you not?

"Emma." Thrumpton raised his hand in a gesture of truce. "I know what you are talking about, and you must understand right away that whatever I did was done in good faith and with your best interests at heart."

"What did you do?"

"I am not sure that I did anything at all. But I know I was put in that position where the question arises of where one's loyalties lie. I suppose it is natural that when you subdivide loyalties, you lay yourself open to attack from the very ones you wish to protect."

"I don't understand you. Why do you have to subdivide your loyalties? Why do you have to use these surreptitious methods? I mean dealing on my behalf without telling me. It was you who told me all about truth the other night, so why can't you just tell me what you did?"

The old man frowned down at his folded arms, and Emma decided to get a grip on herself.

"I'm sorry," she said. "I am being disrespectful."

"Oh no," he said. "You are quite right. If you ask a straight question, you deserve an honest answer. But you understand, I was in a sense put on my honor to do something in confidence. However, if Sarah has thought fit to mention this, I will tell you whatever you wish to know. But before we waste our time with a lot of irrelevant questions, let me tell you in a few words what happened." The colonel shifted from one leg to another awkwardly. "Because it was believed that you were being hounded and possibly exploited by this fellow Bannock, I was prevailed upon to make inquiries with the authorities about him and to suggest, if need be, that some action be taken to restrain him from bothering you."

"You were prevailed upon by whom?"

"Let that be, my dear."

"Shall I assume, my mother?"

"No, no; oh, no."

"Then it was Sarah?"

"Whoever it was is of little importance, since it seems nothing is to come of it. Although I must admit there was a point which shocked me and really was the reason that caused me to act. A suggestion of extortion, which I never understood. It was never explained."

"It can never be explained because it never happened."

"You are making me feel no more foolish than I felt at the time."

"Let me be very clear on this: did you bring the accusation to whoever it was in the army, that Mr. Bannock was extorting money from me?"

"I acted on what I was told."

She spelled out the question. "Did you tell them that?"

"I told them merely what I was told."

Emma glared up at Thrumpton, forcing him to look straight at her.

"Thank you, Colonel," she said icily. "I am sorry that I have attacked you in this way. I apologize for my behavior." She knew he wanted to say more, but swung away and left him standing. She also knew that there had been no tone of reconciliation in her apology, and that had only heightened her anger.

Mark was still there waiting, looking somewhat apprehensive as she walked quickly up to him, giving him no chance to speak.

"Mark, I wish to leave. Do you mind very much if I borrow your trap?"

"For heaven's sake, there's no need to drive yourself. I'll take you," he insisted.

"No, I wish to go on my own. Please just let me go."

Mark was adamant. "I'd never hear of it, and Mother would hardly be pleased at the idea of your driving around on your own."

Emma stood her ground. "I'm becoming very tired of what Mother thinks proper and what Sarah thinks convenient and what you . . . Oh, Mark, I must be honest, I'm even tired of your genuine concern. Will you let me take the trap, or I'll set out and start walking back on my own right now."

"Oh, very well." Mark took her hand and they walked toward the inner barricade of the redoubt.

She caught sight of Sarah laughing at something Pendleton had said, quite unaware of what was happening with her.

Mark was fussing. "Please be very careful. That trap is extremely light and unstable. And please, Emma, go very gently with my poor half-starved animal."

They reached the trap, where one of the troopers on duty brought the pony around to face the road. Emma climbed up. Mark arranged the reins for her and had his last say.

"You must calm down, Emma. It is not just me who is genuinely concerned for you, we all are. You must stop this anger. I hardly know what it's about, but I believe you would fare better if you were not to operate so entirely on your own. Will you think about that?"

She waited with the reins gathered. "I'll think about that," she answered gently and nodded to the trooper, who steered the pony out between the high coaches and carriages.

Once on the road, she let the pony find its own trotting pace. The low trap raised the dust, adding to the choking impression of heat, and she felt the perspiration begin on her forehead as she settled down to cover the short journey into town.

Her thoughts were not so gentle. What do people do when they have lost all the things they hung on to? Not just the meanings and values, but the very instincts that make them right. Like the duty to do this and the duty to do that. Like the love of family. The past family smiling out of oil paintings, and the living ones, whose aliveness is about as much identifiable as the carefully posed expressions of those on the wall. What do people do when they see the past in blurred terms and the future as a blank? Is that when they commit suicide? It would be so easy to take that course. Her great aunt had walked into the sea at Brighton. Geoffrey had ridden into a rain of bullets. Did he feel as I do now? He seemed to behave in that way, angry and remote and proud—about who knows what? Yet for me, somehow the instinct to survive is still there. It endures in spite of everything, and yet it is not everything. I reject the need to survive in these conditions. I must make my own conditions. I will just walk out of Kimberley. The army is only fourteen miles away. I could walk there and possibly get through somehow. Isn't it strange how danger becomes secondary when one makes this kind of decision? Is that how it was for Geoffrey? Did he lack imagination so much that the glory bugles drowned out the sound of the guns? Maybe he was not as self-destructive as he seemed, maybe no less than she was at that moment.

She had passed along the side of Market Square without noticing it and had almost reached Victoria Road by the time the booming report came from Labram's new gun. It was the loudest explosion she had ever heard. As it echoed through the streets, men came out of the bars to check on their tethered mounts, and soon people were rushing from the buildings cheering excitedly.

The pony hardly reacted and neither did Emma, holding up the reins to sustain the steady pace. She realized she had passed her turn-off and was heading toward Newton, but she kept the reins up and let the pony go. This was an instinct at work, and she was going to allow it to carry her to another destination. She was going to the racecourse to speak to Mr. Bannock.

What was it she was going to say to him? Was he going to be particularly interested? She doubted that, yet the need, the duty to speak to him was compulsive. There had to be an apology, another vague, compromising apology on behalf of her family. But why blame the family for Sarah? It was obviously Sarah who was motivated by some private argument with Bannock. Emma knew her inclination for treachery too well, those attacks that were seldom based on any truth. She also knew that if Sarah had evidence that would damage Bannock, she would bring it out in the open and not bother with the usual course of whispering vague accusations to a third party.

And in the case of Colonel Thrumpton, the only evidence that had impressed him was that of Bannock's extortion of money from her.

All that mischief based on a false accusation. She blamed herself for ever letting Sarah know that she was sending the money. But the damage, whatever damage it was, was done, and if Bannock was the kind of man Major Masefield had described, he would react badly to an apology. An apology for what? What action could have been taken on the colonel's request? What cruel injustice had given Sarah the satisfaction she was looking for? What is it that makes women continue to seek hurt and revenge in a situation that, on the face of it, has long ceased to concern them in any way?

Emma was brought back to reality more by the next reverberating report from Long Cecil than by the vague realization that she was approaching the perimeter defenses. Some of the guards had gone up on the barricade, no doubt hoping to see the smoke from the gun. As she reined in, two sentries on duty at the post looked surprised to see a woman on her own.

"Can I see your pass, Miss?"

"Pass?" Emma was baffled. She had never thought of the need for an official pass. Her mind raced back to Geoffrey on one occasion and the driver from the hotel on another, and she could not remember a pass. "Do I really need a pass?" she queried.

The sentry grinned. "I'm very sorry, Miss, you most certainly do."

"But I am only going to the racecourse for a short visit. Surely you can allow me through?"

The sentry laughed, eyeing her up and down, and looked suggestively at his sidekick. "For you I would like to change the rules, Miss, but we've got strict orders. If you'll drive back to Lennox Street and ask for a pass, there'll be no problem."

Emma sized up the sentry and impatiently summed up

the situation in her own way. She asked, "What if I were to simply drive through? Would you shoot at me?"

"I don't think so, Miss." The sentry was enjoying the argument. "But you'd be reported, you'd be in trouble."

Emma made her decision and flipped the reins so that they slapped the pony on the quarters, shocking it into instantaneous action. The small, hungry pony, which had hardly been out for a walk for weeks, was away at a gallop, leaving the two sentries shouting in the background. The light trap veered and skidded from side to side, and Emma forgot her irritation for a moment while she struggled with the reins. The frail animal soon came under control, first trotting, then slumping into a heavy-footed walk.

Emma blinked in the dust, trying to regain her composure. She was alarmed at the realization of how late it was. The sun was down and disappearing, setting up a widespread glow of red on the fine dust that hung all round. She became conscious of the hubbub of a thousand voices and was disconcerted to see the vast tent town that spread right across the center of the racecourse. She began to have misgivings. Had Bannock been moved from here? But then, as she drew nearer, she saw a horse, a thoroughbred, tethered outside the stables, saddled up and dry, waiting to be ridden off. It could only belong to Bannock.

She drove the trap right up to the hitching rail beside the horse and immediately got down to tie up the pony, which stood tamely for her. There was no one in sight, except for a few passing natives who ignored her and went around the far side of the grandstand.

She looked around helplessly, feeling ridiculously nervous. What was she going to say to the man, if he was there at all? She remembered going into the room beneath the grandstand, and wondered whether to go there and knock. But it was not to be that simple. The crunch of boots warned her—running men, apparently. Then she saw the two Town Guardsmen across the end wall of the grandstand coming from the direction of the barricade.

There was a moment of indecision. Should she run for the grandstand or try to hide? The second alternative suggested itself when she noticed that the stable door behind her was slightly ajar.

She fled into the stable, almost falling over, her heavy skirt catching in the bedding, and immediately recoiling, trembling as she confronted a startled horse. This was no time for nerves. She leaned out and pulled both halves of the door almost closed and waited.

The boots crunched past. There were inaudible mutters and curses and she thought she heard Bannock talking to the sentries. She felt ridiculous, standing there with the horse snorting its confusion behind her. Why should she feel like a fugitive? Go out there and deal with those fellows. But the boots were coming closer again, and she hesitated and waited in a state of hopeless indecision.

One of the sentries was being purposely insolent. "Nobody is going to come and visit you if you don't know them. And nobody is going to just leave their cart standing here."

Bannock's voice came sharp and angry. "I've never seen that bloody rig in my life. Listen, you two, why don't you go back to your hole in the wall and leave me alone?"

The sentry's voice: "The lady is here somewhere and we're going to find her."

Bannock's voice: "If all you've got to do is chase after some woman, go right ahead. But keep out of my way."

"Can we look in your room?"

"All right, come and look in the room."

The boots moved off. Emma peeped through the narrow opening and saw the tall figure of Bannock striding away toward the door in the grandstand, followed by the two sentries. She became immobilized by an instinct that said, Wait for a moment, then run and get away from here; followed by a more sober one that said, If you wait long enough, they will go away. I am too confused to make a good fugitive, she thought.

The two sentries came out of the door, and Bannock

followed. All three of them went off around the grandstand and out of sight.

Emma put her hand to her skirt and firmly pushed both halves of the stable door open. She went out and looked at the empty area between the stables and the grandstand, at the sad, thin pony in its harness and the strong thoroughbred saddled and ready to go. It took just a moment to walk toward the horse, marveling at her new impulse, and the decision was made. She unhitched the reins, flipped them over the thoroughbred's head, and danced on one foot as the other went into the stirrup and she reached up for the pommel, pulling herself up onto the tall animal. The decision was a mad one, but there was no going back. Her hands trembled at the reins. She was conscious only of drumming and thumping—her heart, the hooves, the thumping hooves coming round in a dancing circle. The stirrups hung loose far below her feet. The skirt cut into her side where it was caught up in folds but she waited for nothing, slapping down the end of the reins onto the horse's shoulder.

The horse was away and galloping and she knew, as she gathered the reins and leaned back on them to balance herself, that she had never ridden such a horse. The red ground flashed by underneath, and the southern rail of the racecourse passed and disappeared to one side. She was flying away into the graying evening and the endless veld.

The feeling of exhilaration began and rose with the violent action of the horse. There was some great reckless purpose in this. She felt free for the first time in all memory. As Geoffrey had ridden into his fate, she would ride into hers.

She had to hold her head back as the long brown mane flailed up at her, and she laughed at the sight of the black skirt billowing up around her waist. But there was no control, her hands had no effect. She crossed the reins and tried sawing at the lunging mouth the way she had done on the

hunts at Birchleigh. There was no response. This was another kind of horse, a bigger, stronger, longer-striding version of the best she had ever ridden.

Emma's thoughts raced like the horse. I don't know
what I'm running away from but I know I have got to get
away from it. Everything in Kimberly and everything about
Kimberley. The ghost of Geoffrey, the ghost horror and the
real horror, the prison my mother built. Just now I can't
define it. I must simply get away, even from Mr. Bannock,
poor Mr. Bannock, who has lost another horse.

Bannock heard the rush of hooves and saw his horse
leaving from the other side of the stand. For one brief
moment he watched, incredulously recognizing the blond
hair and black riding habit, assuming it to be Sarah. In the
next moment he was running, shouting for Mabala, who
seemed to be nowhere around. He ignored the two sentries
who were running after him as he considered the choice of
harness for a horse he had never ridden, whose name he had
never been able to establish. He grabbed the first saddle that
came to hand, a light racing one, and pulled down the right
bridle.

The two sentries watched him dash to the stable and
bring the horse out. The bridle was on with the throat-lash
still hanging loose, the saddle banged into position, the
girths brought under and roughly tightened. Bannock was
up and out on Watson's big black gelding, praying that it
had enough pace even to stay with Lady Potter, let alone
catch up with her.

He cursed the short racing-length stirrups as he
hunched over the excited gelding, urging him into the best
effort he could make. He was riding a race against time and
the dying light, and for a while he just rode as hard as he
could, straight out into a piece of territory he knew was
dangerous enough in the pitch dark. In this light, it was a
direct invitation to trouble.

It was going to be a chase and a long one, if he knew his own mare, but he swore to himself he would find that female if it took all night—and if the idiot didn't ride straight into the Boer defenses in the meantime. He stood higher on the stirrups to see ahead without relaxing the pace. The gelding was doing better than he had thought possible. The dust trail plumed up ahead, catching the scarlet and violet afterglow of the sunset. He tried shouting, ending up with a stream of breathless curses. Sarah had taken leave of her senses, gone mad, or become suicidal to take the risks she was taking. She was riding headlong toward the heavy fortifications of Wimbledon Ridge. She was also approaching the railway line at an oblique angle, and there was every chance she wouldn't see it in the poor light before she was upon it.

Bannock felt the big horse flagging and watched hopelessly as the dust trail continued straight ahead toward the ridge. But suddenly, it changed direction, veering off to the left, and a second later the deadly rattling sound of a Maxim gun reached him. He swung around to follow, and for the first time saw Lady Potter at the head of the dust throwing down her hooves and literally skidding into the front of the railway lines. She was over with a clumsy jump, almost unseating her rider. The Maxim sounded again, sending up spurts of dust, banging and splintering wood on the railway tracks. Lady Potter had turned and was coming back, still going at an impressive pace. Bannock could hear the hoofbeats as he closed toward her. They were racing back on either side of the railway line, with Lady Potter well ahead once again.

He heard the gun and saw sparks fly off the tracks. The dust trail was becoming lost in the darkness, but Bannock was still able to see Lady Potter hanging in toward the railway line, then shying in sharply to her left and repeating the skidding run up to the line and making another clumsy jump. This time, the rider was unseated. She went over beside the neck and clung there for a while, helplessly slipping down, finally falling and tumbling over and over behind the galloping mare.

Bannock watched Lady Potter high-tail off into the darkness. He took a hold on the gelding, which immediately slacked off and jolted to a walk, blowing out in huge exhausted breaths as they approached the prone figure of the girl.

A new horror occurred to him as he dismounted. She lay absolutely still, her feet turned in and her face slumped into her arms. He put his hands to her neck and whistled through his teeth with relief to find she was breathing, deeply but normally. He swore as the Maxim rattled again and the gelding pulled him away to one side, taking fright at the bullets cracking across the line, ricocheting and whining away into the dark. The burst was over, leaving them in absolute silence.

The girl moved. She leaned up on her elbows and shook her head. Bannock loosed the girth on the blowing horse and looked into the growing darkness toward Wimbledon Ridge, wondering if they would continue to spend ammunition on a target they couldn't see. He watched her slowly sitting up on her heels, hands leaning on the ground, hair hanging down over her face. To judge from the way she was moving, there were no broken bones.

His mind began to clear, and there was only one question: Why? What insane impulse had set her off on this destructive course? Anger began to take over. He went toward her, pulling the gelding along.

His anger found words. "I knew you were a stupid bitch, I didn't know you were a dangerous lunatic into the bargain. What in hell has got into you?"

She stayed as she was, head down. The blonde curls began to shiver, her back shook in spasms as she began to weep.

Bannock felt sorry and went to help her. "Sarah, are you hurt?"

Her arms went limp and she flopped down again in the

dust. She was muttering. "I should have known. . . . I'm no good at this sort of thing. . . ."

The doubt began in his mind as he took her shoulders to turn her over. They were small, delicate shoulders. The head came around, leaning onto the sand, and the hair fell away from the small face. He leaned closer and the doubt became a shock of recognition.

"You?" he said. "Good God," he stumbled. "You, uh, Mrs. Stevenson."

The Maxim fired another burst, this time going well wide of them. Instinctively, he went down beside her in a shielding gesture. The reins pulled away, jerking their two heads together, and he leaned up reluctantly from the warm, shivering cheek.

He took her by the shoulders and gently pulled her into a sitting position. She swayed, but he held on.

"You took a bad fall. Are you hurt anywhere?"

She brought her hand up past his arm to her forehead and he followed her fingers, feeling until he found a bad graze in her hair.

"Just sit still for a while. Are you hurt anywhere else?"

"I feel very stupid," she muttered.

"Do you think you can stand up?"

"I am very stupid."

"Why did you do it? What were you trying to achieve?"

"I was leaving. I told you I wanted to leave. I know you told me it was impossible, but I had to try."

"I must get you back." He felt her shoulders shake and her body convulse.

She gasped out, "I don't want to go back. You can leave me here. I won't . . . I won't . . ." She struggled for breath, and when he took hold of her, she clung to him and wept uncontrollably.

Bannock's mouth was at her ear. "All right, all right," he whispered. "We're not going anywhere. We'll stay here for a while." He felt the small frame shivering in his arms, the coughing breath on his neck. His hands clenched and stretched behind her back, longing to embrace and fondle her.

She also whispered. "Can I tell you something, a confession, what I've just done? It's the only thing I've ever done in my life that could be called taking action. In one mad moment I have broken every rule I know. I've broken away, committed outright mutiny. I should feel hopeless, but I feel elated. I'm not sure I know what I feel. Will anything ever be normal again?" She released her arms as if she had suddenly realized what she was doing. "I'm sorry; you're dealing with an hysterical woman. I've stolen your horse, and now it's run off."

Bannock sat down next to her as close as he could get. He could feel her breath and had to resist the impulse to put his arms round her again. "Don't worry about Lady Potter," he consoled. "She's becoming quite accustomed to this sort of thing. She knows that when the guns fire it is time to unseat her rider and rush back to the stables. She's very sensible that way."

"You are reassuring me. That is one of my problems. It is so confusing for someone who wants so much, yet doesn't know what she wants. I so need to talk to someone who might understand."

"I'm listening."

"But no one can understand another's selfishness, and when it is self-pity, it only deserves to be humored. What am I trying to say?"

"Take your time." Bannock was waiting for the next burst of Maxim fire, but it never came. He leaned forward to see her eyes, and found them staring at him.

"I have these selfish instincts. I am destructive. I am involved in destruction like you."

"Like me?" He frowned, but the wide eyes remained staring.

"Someone said that."

Bannock knew who it was. "Sarah."

"Not just Sarah. Someone else, jealous like Sarah. A person who is jealous of you said you created situations of destruction but that you were without fear."

"Who said that?"

"Are you really without fear?" The wide eyes challenged. "Do you know what I believe? I believe that everything we don't do that we should do is dictated by fear. Even the things we do are determined by fear."

"I don't follow you."

She looked away. "How would you understand a frightened human being? I have never met a man who could overcome fear."

"Your husband was a brave man."

"My husband was a brave man. My husband was a frightened man. He was two separate men in that way. I never discovered which was real. I never really discovered anything about him. I could never tell this to anyone." She was shivering again. "I really should not be talking about it."

"You're upsetting yourself."

They both reacted when the Bultfontein searchlight came on, pale at that distance but with enough light to show their expressions for a brief moment as the beam arced round.

"Why am I telling this to you? No, please listen, I want to tell you. I have only been related to one man in my life and I couldn't relate to him. I was a useless wife. I couldn't project love. There was no love, do you understand? A wife who was not perfect was expected to be a perfect widow, and a widow who lives with guilt cannot cope with anything. I am shocking you, Mr. Bannock. I so desperately need to tell this to someone. Can I tell you?"

"Yes." Bannock waited for the sweep of the searchlight to see her face. It was frowning and wet-cheeked, and utterly beautiful to him.

"Do you want to know how ugly I can be?"

"I told you, I think you are beautiful."

"It's quite extraordinary. With every word I say that I shouldn't be saying, I feel better."

"I think you are the most beautiful woman I have ever met in my life."

Bannock came very close to her. She stared at him, and blinked and looked away, and stared at him again.

"Don't stop," he said.

Her lips moved silently as she tried to find the words. "You see, guilt is only part of the punishment. There are people who encourage the guilt."

"Sarah?" said Bannock.

"Sarah is not a problem. She is not so effective. It's my whole family." She was past any point of restraint; it was just pouring out. "It has to do with our military history. We march together, with my mother in the lead. She waves the flag and keeps the ghosts alive, and to all the military mediocrities of the past, she has at last been able to add a hero. If she has her way, this ghost will live forever. And it's as simple as this: I cannot live with the myths my mother creates for me. The one about the perfect man, the hero, the one about a perfect wife, and the one about a widow who will mourn for eternity. It is not just expected, it is defined for me. And all the time she didn't realize that I was not a machine with an ON switch and an OFF switch."

Emma gulped for breath. "She said a strange thing to me the other day. It was meant to help, but I think it only made things worse. It was about women and how unpredictable they are, that they compensate for their weakness by practicing destruction. And I questioned that. It occurred to me that women practice their art of destruction by necessity. If they don't fight, they are nothing. I believe that at that moment I became a rebellion about to happen. If I go back now, there will be a new guilt, shame in the face of my mother. But in my heart I can never go back, not to stay. I'll find a different way to live, or I'll die in the attempt." Emma sighed and hung her head. "I thought I had so much to let out, but it doesn't sound like much, does it?"

Bannock took her hands and she let him hold them.

"You have said nothing," she said.

He still said nothing.

"You must say something. I think I need to know what your opinion is of me."

Bannock stopped himself from blurting out his opinion of her. "I feel as if I've always known you." He could hardly believe the emotion that started up in him. "I think you are a dream I had. I think . . ." He groped for the words. "I think you are like me in a way. I think your dreams let you down." He felt the small hands tighten their grip on his. "I'll tell you something about me that you might understand. My dreams were pretty simple, yet somehow I believed they would come to pass. But I was brought up in the racing business, where you learn at an early age that most men are bastards, soft bastards and hard bastards. And you soon get to believe that most women are bitches of one degree or another. The strange thing was that the dreams were still intact. I want to tell you about one that came true. I have a horse called Marcus."

"I know. Your stallion."

"Marcus Aurelius. It was not just that he had the breeding, he was my idea of a great horse. He fitted the dream, you see . . . and made the other dreams possible."

"What other dreams?"

"Oh." Bannock felt embarrassed and exposed by more than the searchlight that came around on him. In the moment when he felt it on his face, he saw the beautiful eyes again. "I can't think of anything when I'm talking to you."

"What other dreams?"

"You. You are the other dream."

There was a silence between them. They waited for the pale light to come back. Her eyes still stared unwaveringly.

"You hardly know me," she whispered. But something had happened between them. Their hands were locked together tightly.

He whispered back, "Every time I saw you, you stayed in my mind. I dreamed about you. It only got worse."

The next sweep and she was looking away. "They've stopped shooting." She still whispered, still clung to his hands.

"I know your name is Emma. I know all about you, things even your own family don't know."

"That's true."

"I know your secret fears. I want you more than any woman I've ever known. No, that doesn't describe it."

What he wanted to do, she did. Slowly and deliberately, she put her arms around him. Bannock felt as if he was in a trance, unable to speak. His fingers felt across her shivering back, and they clung together for a long time.

She spoke into his ear. "My life is a whole development of longings."

"And mine."

"Longing to come out of loneliness. And even then, it's not as simple as that. I was brought up on so many slogans of honor, and they were too simple for me. I wanted a better kind of honor. Something you cannot get from people. It had to be one person. One's faith is nothing in a crowd. It is too precious and too vulnerable to be put at risk by being put at large. It is for one other and one other only. I am rambling."

Bannock held her very close and lowered her to the ground, with her head on his arm. The rein slipped from his hand, and he vaguely wondered whether the gelding would stray. He kissed her ear and she kissed his cheek, and they stared at one another in anticipation of the searchlight.

"You have a reputation for being a seducer."

Bannock kissed her and she responded with a strength in her small body that took his breath away.

"Are you going to seduce me, Mr. Bannock?

He knelt and took off his shirt, and in the next sweep of the light she saw the powerful man she had found. He put the shirt under her head, and she lay quite still while he slowly undressed her.

She whispered, "Take it all off, please, I want nothing between us. I want it all off."

He knelt in front of her, naked, and watched her small perfect body as the light came around again. There was no more speaking as he bent down to her. They lay clinging to each other for a long time, then slowly came together.

It began slowly. A slow, powerful rhythm that beat in Emma's mind, relating itself to everything: her gasping breath, the sweep of the searchlight, the moving of Bannock's viselike grip on her body.

He whispered urgently, "I dreamed of doing this. I love you, do you hear? I dreamed of loving you."

She became acutely conscious of every movement, of a passion she had never felt before. Each turn of the searchlight showed his eyes staring into hers. It was the dream. Sex had become love. The genitals were doing their violent work without prompting. It became wilder, more urgent.

"I want you to belong to me. I want to make you pregnant," he blurted out.

The words shocked her. She was shocked by her own response. At that moment of final, lunging ecstasy, she wanted what he wanted.

Emma ended up crying. And when the sweep of the light showed Bannock's anxious expression, she laughed and cried at the same time.

"Mr. Bannock," she blubbered, "don't you know that women can weep when they're happy?"

They stayed close together, seeing each other in the moments when the light came and went.

"Will we be together?" she whispered.

"Oh, Mrs. Stevenson, we must be together."

They laughed and rolled over together ridiculously, until Bannock realized what the hard ground must be doing to her and pulled her gently on top of him. He lay like that, looking up at the sky.

"Mrs. Stevenson, did you realize there were star above this siege? I didn't. I've ridden out in the night, fel my way in the dark, looked behind, hid from shadows, and I don't think I ever took the trouble to look up."

"Do you know, Mr. Bannock, I don't think I knew they were there either." She gently fingered the scar at hi chin.

"Are you my lover?" Bannock sounded very serious "Are you really my lover?"

"I am your lover."

"Shouldn't lovers get onto Christian-name terms?"

"Yes, Bartholomew."

"Will you do me a favor? I don't like people who cal me Bartholomew."

"Yes, Bart."

"How did you know that?"

"I heard that Irishman call you Bart. I've known you a long time. We met on a train, do you remember? Or we almost met on a train. My bottom is getting cold."

They laughed, and Bannock reached for her clothes

Emma stood up and felt the night air on her body reveling in her nakedness, laughing at the thought of he own lack of shyness.

"What are you laughing at, Emma?"

She stood limp and let him dress her, holding out arms lifting up a foot obediently.

She said, "This should all be so wrong, but it isn't. Thi has changed everything. It's not just a feeling of reckless ness, it's something I know. I don't even care how much trouble there will be. Am I talking too much? I can do that." She tried to help him with the skirt.

Bannock embraced her, fastening the skirt behind he at the same time. "I undressed you, I'll dress you again."

Both heads jerked sideways at the sound of hooves.

"Are those the Boers?" asked Emma.

"No, I very much doubt it. It's coming from that side." He pointed toward Kimberley. He caught sight of horses i the distance, their long shadows fleetingly thrown forward by the searchlight.

"Come, Emma." Bannock took her toward the gelding, who had stayed there in spite of everything, munching at some dry stubble.

"You wait here," he said, and mounted so quickly that by the time the next sweep came, he was in the saddle, lengthening the stirrup leathers.

"Come," he said, holding down a hand and lifting her by the arm. "Up you come." She used the free stirrup as a step, and he propped her sideways in front of him.

They heard the horses again, working parallel to the perimeter at a canter.

"Are they searching for us?" asked Emma, settling herself onto Bannock's chest.

"They're searching for you." He put his arms around her, holding the reins in front, and the gelding set off at a bouncing walk.

"I've caused a lot of trouble."

"I'm glad you did."

She laughed into the hairs of his chest where the shirt hung open. "I suppose I shall be in a lot of trouble."

"I wouldn't worry about that."

"I don't just mean the authorities. I'll have to deal with Mark now. Poor Mark, I stole his trap as well as your horse. And my mother. If I can't get away from her, I'll have to deal with her. Quite apart from the guilt and the resentment, there is sympathy. Can you understand?"

"Of course."

She hung on to him, bouncing comfortably against him.

"You didn't mention Sarah," he said.

"I told you, I'm not bothered about Sarah. She will jeer and attack when she hears about you and me, but jealousy is such an impotent weapon. I think it strikes back more than forward."

They were riding across the beam of the searchlight

and farther into its influence. Bannock listened for the horses, who had stopped somewhere nearby, and heard them start up again. They were coming in their direction, and he began to consider whether to make a break for the perimeter or let things take their course. As it happened, he had little choice. The horsemen came into the end of the beam of light, and it was clear that they had been seen.

"Is that you, Bannock?" came a shout.

"Yes," he shouted back.

"I'm not looking forward to this," said Emma, curling herself up closer to Bannock.

"We will go down together," he clowned.

Emma began to shake with laughter.

"We will go down fighting if need be," he shouted.

Emma was convulsed with laughter.

"What did you say?" came a voice from the approaching group of riders.

"Nothing," Bannock shouted, and whispered to Emma, "I was talking to this girl."

She put an arm around his neck and tried to see his face. "I'd forgotten how to laugh," she said, still laughing. "I think I do it too hard. It's giving me a pain in the chest."

They were surrounded by troopers. Bannock counted ten of them.

"Is that Mrs. Stevenson?" It was a sergeant speaking.

"Yes," said Emma.

"We've been searching for you, Miss. The major's waiting at the racecourse."

Bannock spoke. "The lady's horse ran away and I went after her."

Emma whispered upward, "You're an awful liar."

The sergeant turned his horse and shouted, "Johnson, ride back at a gallop and report we found the people." He turned to Bannock. "Will you follow, if you please," and they set off for the racecourse, only a short way off by this time.

Emma ran her hand over Bannock's chest and said

quite seriously, "You don't have to lie on my behalf. I did what I did and I will take whatever is coming to me. It may be quite irresponsible of me, but I am worried about nothing. I am happy, do you hear, Mr. Bannock? I am very, very happy."

They rode on in silence with Bannock's arms more tightly around her than necessary. The troopers kept their distance and hung back as the rail of the racecourse came into sight in front of them. They could see paraffin lamps at the stables, throwing a dull light on uniforms and horses.

Mark Freestone-Grant came from the darkness, with O'Flaherty behind him. Bannock lowered Emma to her white-faced brother while O'Flaherty took the horse's head. He heard Freestone-Grant say, "Emma, are you all right?" and Emma say, "Yes, I'm fine now."

O'Flaherty came beside him and looked up to heaven with his half smile. Bannock leaned down to him and said quietly, 'If you make one smart comment, I'll smash your face in."

O'Flaherty grinned. "I never said a word."

"Did the mare get back?"

"Sure, she's back in the stable where she belongs."

Bannock watched Emma's silhouette going away toward the stables with her brother.

Mark was saying to her, "I can't believe it. I don't know what could have gotten into you. But not now; you don't have to bother now. You can tell me about it on the way back. Mother is beside herself."

"She blames you, of course."

"There was no keeping it from her. We must get back there immediately."

Emma could see Masefield's rotund figure in the light of the paraffin lamp.

"What about Major Masefield?" she asked.

"He is no problem. He wants to cover the whole thing up. You don't have to speak to him. It's all been arranged."

But Emma had made her own decision. "Will you give

me a moment? I must speak to him." She left Mark with no choice and walked straight toward Masefield.

The troopers were mounting up and moving off as she reached him. She cut him off before he could greet her.

"Major, I must have it quite clear with you. You know I wanted to get away. Well, I tried. I stole Mr. Bannock's horse and tried, and if it were not for him I would be in far more serious trouble now."

Masefield pursed his lips and looked down as if he would rather have avoided the issue. "There is no need to explain. We can go over it at some later stage if need be."

Emma said formally, "Thank you," then took hold of her dusty skirt and turned away toward Bannock, who had dismounted.

She went across and stood directly in front of him, staring up at him. "I've got to go now. I have to deal with those things I told you about. Will you trust me?"

"Of course." He hesitated. "But you owe me no trust."

"I owe you more than you can imagine. I think I would do anything for you."

"There is only one thing I want."

"What is that?"

"Stay with me."

"I can't do that. I've caused too much trouble as it is. You know about my mother; you know almost everything there is to know about me. I'm going now. But Bart, if all you want is me, you'll get me."

She went quickly; Freestone-Grant was waiting to help her into the trap. Bannock watched her as they drove out of the light, but she never looked back. His attention was drawn to Masefield, who was strolling toward him swinging a paraffin lamp at his side.

Masefield put down the lamp and folded his arms, fixing Bannock with his most incriminating look. "Well, you've certainly excelled yourself this time, and once again, judging from the girl's comments, we're never going to get to the bottom of it."

Bannock shrugged.

"Do you know, Bannock, I'm getting to the point where when I'm awakened at night, I know where the trouble is coming from. You're a living emergency."

Bannock shrugged again. "Major, why don't you go home and back to bed."

"When I heard that girl had run off, they didn't have to tell me you were involved."

"Should I have let her ride off on her own?"

Masefield's eyes remained riveted on him. "To think I could have simply had you shot as a spy the first time I ran into you. Think of all the trouble I could have saved myself, let alone the garrison and the community in general."

"I don't quite see what you're complaining about, not this time."

"I was watching Mrs. Stevenson talking to you. She is a very upset young lady. Confused, wouldn't you agree?"

"Not entirely."

"Don't confuse her any further, Bannock. She is not accustomed to dealing with a man like you."

The usual fencing was over. Bannock was angry. "Just what are you suggesting?"

"That you have nothing in common with her. And as I said, she could be easily confused by you."

"I suggest you mind your own business."

Masefield nodded thoughtfully. "So be it," he said.

Bannock had had enough. "Good night, Major."

"Oh no, I am not quite finished with you. A curious thing happened while you were out on your latest adventure. Another quite separate visitation from the outer veld arrived here unannounced."

"What are you going on about?"

Masefield picked up the lamp and beckoned him to follow, and they came across Mabala, looking rather sheepish, with a group of his night raiders hanging back in their blanket cloaks.

For a moment, Bannock was really worried. Then, as

the light went forward, he was relieved to see that the booty piled up in the background was not beef but fresh-cut grass in bundles.

"What's the problem?" asked Bannock.

Masefield held up the lamp to see his face. "These people are not at liberty to walk into the veld on their own account or yours. The whole garrison is short of fodder."

"That's not feed, that's just bedding for the stables."

"Oh, come on, Bannock. I know sweet grass when I see it. You've got the only well-fed animals in Kimberley."

"You can't prosecute anyone for cutting grass off the veld," said Bannock. Then he thought, Thank God it wasn't beef-raiding night, and began to laugh.

"There's no good grass within miles of here and you know it."

Bannock was still laughing, and for once Masefield looked as if he was losing the initiative. But he took it well. He was actually smiling.

Mark had tried to persuade Emma to change her soiled clothing before going in to her mother, but she refused. She also refused to sit once she entered the living room, and stood stolidly beside her brother while he gave the most diplomatic report he could manage of the night's events.

Lady Freestone-Grant sat straight in her chair, looking pale and tense. She had never taken her eyes off Emma's dust-streaked clothing and bruised forehead.

When Mark ended his apologetic description, Emma said nothing. They both waited for their mother to speak.

"I think you should explain better than you have. I would like to hear it from you, Emma. You have obviously held a lot back from us. What did you hope to achieve by going off on your own?"

Emma answered firmly, "I had to get away from Geoffrey."

The old lady's expression hardened with disapproval.

"You are being a little melodramatic. In your case, there is so much pride to carry the pain of loss. Where is your pride?"

"I will not answer that."

Her mother judged her in silence for a moment.

"How did this man come to find you?"

"I fell off the horse."

"I don't understand. Was he with you?"

"No, he was following me."

The old lady tapped her fingers together impatiently. "I will never understand this. How you could do such a thing. And how you could involve a total stranger, and Major Masefield, and God knows how many others."

"Bart Bannock is not a total stranger."

"I remember that name. There was an argument about money."

Mark tried to help. "He was a friend of Sarah's."

Emma came in defiantly. "He is a friend of mine."

Lady Freestone-Grant turned her attention from Mark to Emma. "How can that be? Sarah was most critical of him."

Emma replied, "Sarah didn't make out very well with him."

"What are you implying, Emma?"

"His name is Bart. I have come to know him very well. In fact, I am in love with him."

Mark was first to react. "Emma, really, do you have to—"

"I'm sorry," Emma burst out. "I shouldn't have said that. I'm sorry, Mamma, there is no crisis anymore. I am quite under control."

The normally statuesque face of Lady Freestone-Grant was animated with shock. She spoke slowly. "I wish to remind you that Geoffrey has only just died."

"I've only just come to life." Emma could not help herself. She was conscious of being cruel, but she had begun to be honest and she couldn't stop. She looked at Mark, who shook his head in disapproval and exasperation. They waited for their mother to continue.

Her tone was imperious. "You will not go into that foolish state of infatuation that young girls seem to suffer. It becomes out of control, infatuation upon infatuation."

"It is not like that, Mamma."

Her mother seemed not to have heard her. "You are beyond that stage. It is a humiliating weakness. I've had to watch it on occasion with Sarah, but you were always above it. I know you were. And now you will remain above it. I have seen myself in you, Emma, you must see yourself in me. If you are to marry again one day, it must be on a level you understand. It must be an affair—how can I put this— it must be developed and understood within the terms we know. I must protect you in this. I must find a way to convince you."

Emma thought, I'm sorry I told you I loved him.

"I must threaten you if need be."

Emma thought, I'm sorry I spoke at all.

"There will be no compromise, Emma."

Emma thought, Poor Mother, how can I help you and help myself?

"I forbid you to see this man, do you understand?"

Mark spoke up. "I'm sorry, Mother, you are bullying her. She must be exhausted. I don't think this is the time."

His mother issued a quiet threat. "You will leave this to me, Mark, if you please."

But Mark was not backing down. "Emma has had a bad time. I don't care how she has brought it upon herself, she's had a bad time. Please don't torture her, Mother."

Emma thought, I have become immune to this kind of torture.

Lady Freestone-Grant slumped in her chair with a hand to her mouth, seemingly defeated. Emma felt truly sorry for her.

"Go to bed, Emma," she said softly.

Emma went forward, kissed the unyielding cheek, and

left the room, returning Mark's smile of sympathy as she went.

Mark watched his mother sit up straight again, determined and alert.

"We must put our heads together and have an end to this nonsense," she announced. "I shall speak to Simon Thrumpton, and I suggest you speak to Major Masefield. I think he is the sort of person who would know what to do. I've also noticed that he is quite friendly with Emma, which puts him in the position of an ideal arbitrator, don't you think?"

Mark was already shaking his head before she finished. "I loathe the idea of involving all these people."

"I disagree. They are friends, Mark, and people who can be trusted. Rely on my judgment."

Mark shook his head again. "I have seen something of this Bannock. He is not the kind of person you can merely tell what to do."

"If you have listened to Sarah carefully you will realize that, allowing for some hysteria, she must have judged the fellow well. He is the type who is a fortune hunter. Having failed with one sister, he is trying with the other. Have you stopped to think, Mark, of how much money Emma is worth in her own right? Her grandfather's legacy alone—"

"Yes, Mother, I know."

"And Geoffrey's estate—"

". . . will be considerable," Mark echoed. "But Mother—"

She ignored him. "I grant you, Emma has not even thought of money. With all her strength of purpose, she has always been too giving, the altruistic angel who wouldn't know the devil if she saw him."

"I do think you're underestimating her."

"I am not underestimating *him*. However, these sort of people can be dealt with; they have their price. Find out what his price is, Mark, and pay him off. If you can't manage it, I'm quite sure Major Masefield can."

· 11 · | THE COLOR OF THE COUCAL

The blast of a shell nearby postponed Braithwaite's exit. He stood ready to leave, thin and sagging in his loose jacket, the thick glass orbs menacing. Seeing Masefield sitting there like a self-satisfied bullfrog seemed to inflame him again.

"You've wasted my time," he blustered. "I really thought you were ready to cooperate."

"Oh, I am, I am."

"That is not true. You refuse to answer my questions, questions the whole town is asking. And all you can offer is a rumor."

Masefield smilingly fanned the flame. "My rumors are reliable."

"Nothing but a damned rumor. You're not even sure whether this dreaded cannon is the Long Tom."

"It's the only big gun the Boers have available."

"Rumors, secrets, ha ha." Braithwaite was beside himself. "Do you think we can print that sort of thing? Good day, sir." And he was gone.

Masefield frowned at the ceiling as if he could see the shell whining overhead. The explosion came from farther south, and he nodded, as if that was what he expected. He got up from his rolltop desk and went to the table, where

384

he picked up some papers in order to assume an official pose. He allowed his next visitor to arrive in the office before he looked up.

"Ah, good morning. I'm sorry to have kept you waiting." He busily pulled around a chair for Sarah and put the papers down again.

"Good morning, Major. I'm so glad you could see me, but I am afraid it is the same dreary subject as before." She sat down on the straight chair, arranging her wide skirt around her.

Masefield went around the table and assumed another official pose. "How did you manage to get here, Miss Freestone-Grant?" he asked.

"Captain Pendleton brought me. He is waiting outside. He insists on waiting there and I am terrified that a shell will fall in the street."

"There is every chance of that. I think you have taken a great risk coming out. You really should get back and under shelter as soon as possible."

"I must speak to you about this matter."

Masefield sat down and directed his disconcerting stare at her. "Very well," he said. "Please proceed."

This time, Sarah was better prepared, more sure of herself. "You know, of course, about my sister's extraordinary behavior last week."

"I do know about that."

"It was a ghastly and embarrassing experience, and at the time I was not aware of the full implications. But the worst of it is that my mother is in a state of collapse over the whole thing." Her expression had tightened and her eyes went upward nervously as another shell whined over.

"You don't have to worry, that will land a half a mile away." His tone was offhand.

They waited until the explosion sounded in the distance, and she smiled faintly, acknowledging his judgment.

"You were saying."

"As I was saying, my mother is in a terrible state."

"I am sorry to hear that," said Masefield. "But your sister suffered no harm, as far as I know."

"That remains to be seen, Major, and that is why I have come here today. Oh, no." She caught his expression. "She suffered no physical harm. But what has emerged is that the threat we anticipated on the last occasion I was here has now become very real. When I tell you this, you will wonder how you can be involved, but please be patient and let me explain."

"By all means."

"Only yesterday, my poor mother, who is usually our main pillar of strength, well, she just broke down and let it all out. Some things that I hadn't realized until then. The fact is that Emma, my sister, has become emotionally involved with that man Bannock."

Masefield listened with only a glimmer of expression.

Sarah ignored the whine of the next shell and continued. "You may remember, that was our worst fear, and now she has openly admitted it, and worst of all, to Mother herself. I have never seen Mamma so distressed. She questioned me at length about Mr. Bannock. Unfortunately, there is little she can achieve on her own. You see, I'm sorry to have to say this, but in order to have the situation properly understood it must be said: my sister is a perfectly intelligent person in every way but one. She has had no experience of men save for her marriage, and she is by the evidence, I'm afraid, emotionally gullible, you could almost say unstable."

"You mean this present evidence?"

Sarah frowned suspiciously. "Not exactly," she said carefully. "One knows her, you understand."

"Please go on," said Masefield.

"Well, now an awkward thing has happened. My mother is under the impression that my brother has come to you for help."

"That is a wrong impression."

Sarah nodded knowingly. "Of course I realize that," she said. "You see, Mark has spoken of offering Bannock money to keep him away, but if you know Mark, you'll know he is almost incapable of doing that sort of thing."

"Do you believe Bannock would respond to an offer of money?"

"Not really; I think he would be too clever for that. I don't believe he would accept an outright offer, but I suspect that if any offer was made, it might be the beginning of a blackmail situation."

"You think him capable of blackmail?"

"Oh, that and more. He could just as easily get money directly from Emma, who does have private means. And that is the worst fear, that Emma will run off with him. It's very much in the cards."

"Then she has indicated as much?"

"She has implied it, and her behavior has implied it even more. It's obvious that Bannock put her up to running away. It was just that the plan failed."

"I was under the impression she had decided to go of her own accord."

"I think in the circumstances you must expect her to cover up for Bannock."

"He is seeing her, is that what you are suggesting?"

"I'm quite positive they are. If there is the slightest opportunity, they will be seeing one another."

Masefield folded his hands at his chin. "Miss Free-stone-Grant." The hard eyes demanded her attention. "I am at pains to see how I could possibly be of any assistance in this matter. Frankly, I doubt it."

Sarah looked astounded. "The man must be stopped." She became shrill. "He should be arrested."

"It is simply that this is not a military problem."

"Major Masefield." Sarah was threatening. "My mother could have taken this to the commander, or even to Mr. Rhodes himself. The last time we were here you were given both evidence and well-founded grounds for suspicion, on which we had your word you would carry out investigations."

Masefield remained absolutely still, with his chin leaning on his hands. If there was anger, it was hidden behind the expressionless eyes. His reply was delayed as a shell came over, but neither of them looked up or away until it reached its point of explosion.

"Well, did you investigate?" she challenged. "And if so, what conclusions did you reach?"

Masefield had watched her temper rise. He kept her waiting.

"Miss Freestone-Grant," he opened slowly, "today is the twenty-second of January. Did you notice all those flags in the streets when you came through?"

"What has that to do with the issue?"

"Those flags are to celebrate the hundredth day of the siege. It follows that in a hundred days of worsening siege conditions, the inmates become a little edgy."

"I am not interested in a lecture on behavior, Major. I asked you a question."

"You asked me whether I investigated. I did investigate. And my findings, then and now, are that your evidence is faulty and your suspicions misleading."

Sarah's mouth came open dumbly. She spluttered, "I beg your pardon?"

The eyes kept hold and the mild voice continued. "Let me explain to you in each case, if I can remember the complaints in their correct order. Your brother: he is a capable and intelligent person, as I know. Whatever he has decided, I should rely on his judgment if I were you. In the case of your sister, you have said she is emotionally unstable and clearly implied a loss of judgment and responsibility. I know your sister quite well; I have spoken to her at length. She is clever and she is quick, and she in no way fits the description you have given of her."

Sarah had jumped to her feet, but before she could speak, Masefield did.

"As to Bannock—you will wish to hear this part—the idea that Bannock enticed your sister to run away is untrue. I have cast-iron evidence for that. On the first occasion you came here, you mentioned an amount of money your sister had sent Bannock. He returned that money to her in my care. I suspect you didn't know that. On this occasion, you have mentioned blackmail, and I suggest you are in danger of being accused of slander. The only point on which I might agree with you is that Bannock and your sister are a mismatch, and I fear that the only people who could break up that match are Bannock and your sister herself."

Sarah came forward and leaned over the table, white-faced and furious. "You don't understand this matter at all." Somehow she was restraining her temper. "You cannot work by evidence the way you are doing. You don't know him. He could dupe anyone. He has an uncanny charm. I will even admit he is in no way a fool. But you must believe me: behind all that, he is shifty and unscrupulous."

"But I do know him. I know him very well." Masefield's patience was at an end. "He is a friend of mine."

Sarah took a pace backward. Her lips tightened before she spoke. "If you are a friend of a man called Bannock, you were entirely the wrong person to consult."

She all but ran out of the office, leaving Masefield staring into space. He drew a deep breath and slowly stood up. He frowned and said out loud, "I think you would have liked me to have said I hate Bannock. Very well, I'll say it."

Emma felt like a little girl being taken for a walk by her grandfather. She had to take long, slow steps to match the short, slow steps of Colonel Thrumpton's long legs. By the time they reached Du Toitspan Road, more and more people were coming into the open after a morning of heavy shelling in the center of town.

There were still the distant bangs and thumps of shelling over at Beaconsfield. But in each quarter, the Boers still followed their normal pattern of firing, only more intensely. They seemed to stop for a rest once in a while and sensibly close down to sleep at night.

"I hate that cellar," said Emma. "And I'll never feel the same about dinner gongs. That gong has two uses. It calls to anemic little meals called lunches and dinners, some with a small portion of horsemeat and some of a starch content impossible to identify. At any other time, the gong means shelling and get down to the cellar fast. I refuse to go and have to be dragged. Every time they sound that gong, I swear I will run into the street and keep running until I find a place where there are no shelters and no dull, apathetic people crowded together."

The colonel's stick tapped a steady rhythm in the dust. He was smiling and concentrating on the road ahead. "Rebellion seems to be your constant problem."

Emma swung her folded parasol in time with her stride. "Surely if you can hear those shells coming, you can see them coming? So all you have to do is run and hide each time."

The old man chuckled to himself. "Not quite, not quite," he said. "You can't see them so easily. The sound is deceptive, and the shrapnel has a way of getting around."

"I'd still rather take my chances with the shrapnel than die of slow boredom in that cellar." Emma pointed to a burnt-out house on the Belgravia side and asked, "Is it the shrapnel that does all that damage or simply the fire?"

"Bit of both, my dear."

"Do these shells explode in the air, or only when they hit something?"

"Good question, good question. The artillery chaps tell me there are both kinds. It's mostly to do with the fuses. There are percussion fuses and time fuses. We only get the ones with the percussion fuses, which explode on contact, as you say. They call them ring shells, from the ring segments which break up and scatter with the explosion. The ones with the time fuses are apparently too heavy to reach the town. They save them for poor old Peakman, and anyone who has the temerity to go riding out of town on sorties."

"If the mounted forces can go out of town, why can't they reach the relief column? I suppose that's as good as asking why the relief column can't reach us."

"My dear, we are short of numbers, and between us and the relief column there is a whole Boer army. But I can tell you, if we had two thousand regulars instead of seven hundred, there would be no siege and no shelling."

They stopped beside a house where men were filling sandbags to add to their shelters.

"It's given everybody something to do," remarked the colonel. "I think it's become socially competitive to see who has the best shelter."

"Do you know what it's like in that cellar at the hotel?"

"I'm sure it's very boring."

"It's worse than that. There is not enough light to read or write by. There is nothing to do, and nothing to see except dissatisfied faces. It is becoming a sick siege, and the sickness is called indifference."

"Surely that is the symptom, not the sickness? They are all hungry, tired of threat, and tired of queuing for their meager rations. They are all waiting. But never mind; we will not have to wait long now."

The colonel looked surprised when Emma swung around and walked backward for a while beside him. She was looking south, toward where all her feelings lay. The racecourse was there, and Bart. She wondered what he was doing and thinking. She wished they could go in that direction, but knew their present direction was planned and approved. She could not wait too long, she would have to see him soon. There would have to be a solution to all this. Somehow, coming out into the air was a relief. A momentary part-freedom, with the promise of wholeness soon, very soon.

She turned again and walked in step with the colonel, mischievously imitating him, tapping the parasol and swinging it like his stick, keeping in time and looking up at him while he smilingly pretended to be unaware of what she was doing.

"This is part of a plot, isn't it?" she teased. "A scheme on the part of Mother and yourself to allow me out for some fresh air without getting into mischief."

"I have my instructions. I will admit your mother steered me in your direction and I have been gently nagged into talking to you."

"What about, or should I guess?"

"Oh, there is nothing to guess about. I quite like the role of family adviser, the ancient all-seeing eye. Although I do believe that no one can presume to understand another's problem."

"My problem is my family."

He didn't seem to hear that. "I took it upon myself, with Geoffrey once, to give him fatherly advice. Do you mind my mentioning Geoffrey?"

"Not at all. I'm glad when people speak openly."

"Did he ever tell you about my lecture on risk?"

"He never told me anything about himself. Not consciously, that is."

"When you made that outburst about Geoffrey to me, I was shocked."

"I know."

"I thought, What kind of young woman is this who can bring down a hero, no matter what relationship she had with him? Then I remembered Geoffrey, the sword in the hand and the reflection of the blade in the eye." He cleared his throat, embarrassed by what he had said. "I am only trying to tell you in my clumsy way that I've become aware that things might not have been as simple as they seemed."

They walked on without looking at one another, and Emma said, "Thank you for saying that."

They turned off into a side road that headed north. Emma decided to sound more cheerful.

"Where are you taking me?" she asked.

"To the Botanical Gardens."

"I can't believe it. Do you mean to say this dusty town has a garden?"

"It has what is euphemistically termed a botanical garden. It never was much of a garden, and all that remains now are a few half-alive aloes and succulents, some apologetic roots and stumps, and a clump of indigenous bushes. The bushes are my objective, and I hope to show you why presently."

"I like mysteries," said Emma. "But I also suffer from acute curiosity. What is behind the bushes?"

"Ah, yes, but before I tell you, I must tell you what else there is in the garden. There are a few worms dying of thirst. There are ants and termites, which seem to survive in any conditions. There are spiders and other insects. There are moles and there are rats."

"I wish to go home immediately." Emma was enjoying the old man's performance.

"And the whole community of crawlers and pests is ruled over by a coucal." Thrumpton smiled smugly, having delivered his mystery word.

"Coocul?" Emma had trouble with it.

"Coucal."

"That sounds like a monster, a garden with a monster. This is beginning to sound fascinating. Does the coucal breathe fire?"

"The coucal, my dear, is a bird. There are in fact two coucals here, a mating pair. I discovered them before the siege began, and I fully expected them to leave once they became aware of the hostilities. But they decided to stay, and I have been fortunate enough to see them on a number of occasions, including once yesterday evening. Now I am hoping you can share my good fortune."

Emma saw the old military man in a new light. "Are you an ornithologist?"

"No, no, never an ornithologist. Nor an expert on anything, for that matter. I am merely curious and, I hope, observant about things I see. When an exotic bird or flower takes my interest, I look them up and find out more about them. I believe my enjoyment of these little discoveries would be spoiled by knowing too much."

They had reached the edge of a wide area of almost barren ground. Dust swirled thinly through a stone-based pergola running down the middle, and at the far end, with the railway line passing behind, was a wide cover of thick, dry bush, tinted in places the red color of the earth. They both looked sadly at the long line of splinters and gaping holes where the fence had been removed for firewood, and at the sun-baked curves of the once cultivated beds.

"Come, Emma, we shall walk down that passage, and if we are very fortunate, we will see the coucal."

He helped her over the broken ground and they entered the long pergola.

Emma began to wonder again about the true purpose of this outing. "You were telling me about your instructions."

"What instructions?"

"Mamma's instructions. You were to talk to me. She must have discussed the whole matter of her difficult daughter with you."

Thrumpton stopped and considered Emma's determined expression. He nodded thoughtfully, the bushy gray eyebrows almost concealing his eyes.

"Emma, you are a most intelligent girl. You know your mother is very concerned about you. Trouble is, you look so damned defenseless and delicate. Your family believes you are confused, whereas I am fast beginning to believe they are under a wrong impression."

"The ancient all-seeing eye."

The old man laughed, but stayed with his subject. "It seems to me that as their anxiety over your confusion increases, your confusion is growing less."

"You are most observant."

"You know, I began to understand decades ago that the last person to ask about any member of any family is another member of that family."

"Why is that?"

"When they are together, they are too close to judge. They see what one another do without seeing the motives. They presume to judge by the subtle prejudices they form along the way. And in this way, each one of them reaches a point where they can only be assessed and understood by others who see them as they are, not merely as a development of their faults and foibles."

"How true."

"In other words, what family familiarity breeds, quite apart from love, are assumptions of knowing."

Emma said quietly, "Thank you. You are helping me."

Thrumpton sighed. "My child, my child. Your mother has put me in a difficult position, just as you did when we last spoke."

"I feel badly about that."

"Accepted. But now I must protect your mother's feelings. She is a true friend, and of an age I can identify with. As to the rest of the family . . . Mark? Mark seems to have managed to stay in the frying pan while I have slipped into the fire."

"The crossfire." Emma sympathized.

"Sarah? I thought I detected a streak of courage, and I still believe it is there, be it somewhat misdirected. She has unusual force for a woman, admits openly her frustrations with the role of the female. Yet everything she purports to be and needs to be, you are without even trying. I wish Sarah all the happiness she intends grabbing for herself. I am a little cross with her. You see, she rather took advantage of my friendship. I have the impression she was suffering from a case of sour grapes."

"I should say nothing. Maybe I am too close to her, as you said."

"The story she told me was so credible, so incriminating . . ."

"You mean about Bart Bannock?" Why split hairs? thought Emma.

"Yes." Thrumpton looked away, as if forced to discuss something he would rather have avoided. "I was given a very bad account of him. I later heard some good things about him from a more reliable source. The two stories bore little resemblance. I see a movement in those bushes. Quiet, Emma. Come along quietly."

She felt a rush of affection for this elegant old man. He had carefully chosen his moment to change the subject, but he had said enough to show that at last someone was on her side.

They had not gone far when he signaled her to stop, holding up a finger and raising his eyes to draw attention to the bird call, a descending roll of notes, a beautiful trilling sound like a flute. Rustling noises came from the bushes, and Thrumpton touched Emma on the arm, nodding in that direction. She saw a glint of copper and shining brown that fluttered to a higher branch and settled, to reveal a large and robust bird with bright eyes and black beak.

Thrumpton whispered, "He lives in a siege of his own making, never moving without his mate. He stays mostly under cover, always goes back to cover. It's a siege within a siege. Anything that threatens sends him back. He will not leave Kimberley while the shelling is on. There is no cover to go to, you see."

She whispered, "What does he live on?"

"The rats and mice and moles. He destroys his prey on sight and survives all his enemies. That is his secret. The predators won't attack this bird. He has the body of a small eagle, the beak of a buzzard, and the claws of a fighting cock."

Emma thought, That part is like Bart.

The old man whispered, "Shall I tell you what I said to Geoffrey that night, that night of the fatherly advice?"

"Yes?"

"I told him about the coucal, and I said, be like the coucal. I meant it so well, and yet I am not sure he understood."

"I'm sure he did." Emma reassured him and thought, Would Bart understand? He would understand that to be brave and yet survive takes faults and fears that are honest and acknowledged. He would understand that passion must start with love. But would he accept anything so simple as the self-preserving instinct of the coucal? If only he could be like the coucal.

The coucal bounced down onto another branch, waving it up and down with its weight, glistening copper and brown in the sunlight.

"I think the coucal is magnificent."

The colonel beamed. "I am so glad you share my opinion."

The coucal's mate appeared and gave the trilling call, before gliding down, with amazing grace for such a heavy creature, to an even lower branch. Then they both disappeared into the bush, and the performance appeared to be over.

"If that coucal were Bart and I were that mate, we could live out this siege and fly away when we were ready." Emma was miles away. She seemed unaware that Colonel Thrumpton was watching her, somewhat mystified.

While the real shelling sounded above, a small game of destruction was taking place below.

The three monkeys were destroying their own replica

of the siege. They became the guns and the shells, each holding a stone high in his upstretched hand, each running forward in turn, imitating the scream of the shell and throwing in the missiles. The little siege was going the way of Kimberley, but worse. Stones smashed the carefully constructed barricades, the miniature buildings, and the delicate wire guns.

The booming sound of an exploding shell reached them in a series of echoes, and the echoes continued in the imitating cries of the three children.

O'Flaherty called to them to stop molesting their handiwork, but by that time the damage was almost complete.

On the far side, Bannock sat on the ground leaning against the hot wall of the grandstand and staring toward the town center with a hand shading his eyes. He tried to judge the position of the target. The smoke rose again. It was somewhere in the area of the railway station, so Emma at least was safe.

The pattern of firing was typical of the preceding days, the shells coming in at a rate of about one a minute, ten to fifteen rounds aimed at about the same spot, before a lull. After a rest of some ten minutes or so, the firing started again on a new target, with the same procedure adopted by the guns from the north, east, and west. At the moment, only one gun in the south was active. The deep-throated reports of Long Cecil could be heard returning the fire from its position on the reservoir redoubt, and from time to time, the seven-pounders at the barricades set up their high-pitched banging.

O'Flaherty and Mabala had settled down in front of Bannock, who had called them over from where they had been supervising the brushing of the three animals, Lady Potter, Watson's gelding, and the mule. The native grooms had become experts under the watchful eye of O'Flaherty.

They both waited, but Bannock said nothing. They were conscious of his mood and careful with him after days of living with those smoldering eyes, his constant pacing up and down and rushing into town, only to come back more disgruntled than before.

O'Flaherty sat on an upturned tub, Mabala squatted impassively. There was all the time in the world, and they waited.

Bannock was frustrated in more ways than one. He wanted to get to Emma and he had tried. She was not at the soup kitchen. The hotel manager and porters had clearly been given instructions to put him off. He was told twice that she was out and once that she was not available, and on that third occasion he had left a note, asking her to at least leave a message for him. But nothing.

Was it possible she was purposely avoiding him? What was happening to her? He had thought about that night, that incredible night. What she had set out to do was like suicide, a desperate impulse. Was making love with him another desperate impulse? No such thought had occurred to him at the time. He had believed in that moment of truth, and come away convinced that she also believed in it. The world was going mad when the only thing you ever touched and felt and then wanted above all else was withheld from you. He wanted to go to that hotel, go up there and break in if necessary. And demand. Demand his mind back. The force of his own impulse was unbelievable, and with every passing hour it was getting worse. He saw her face, felt her breath. If the shelling fell near there, he could not stay away. He would go and find her somehow.

O'Flaherty dared to speak, making it sound as if it were more to himself. "It's a large pot I'm lookin' for. Somethin' about this size." He held his arms wide to demonstrate. "Maybe Mario Pacelli can let me have one. And then it's to Finnegan the farrier I'll be takin' meself, to have that long snoot put on."

"What are you on about?" Bannock was dragged out of his state of introspection.

"It's a still I'm thinkin' of. The true Irish still, to make the true Irish stuff, poteen. All we'll be needin' after that is potatoes and we'll soon be forgettin' we were ever worried about the lack of whiskey and brandy."

"There are no potatoes."

"Sure, there's the market garden at Wesselton. I'm thinkin' I might pay a visit there, in the dead of night, of course."

Bannock remained skeptical. "Have you ever had a still, Paddy?"

"Sure, I've seen them at work. And in these hard times it's worth the experiment."

Bannock leaned his arms forward on his knees and got Mabala's attention.

"When you saw Marcus the second time, was he tethered in the same place as before?"

"Yes, *nkosi.*"

"How far back from the forts was that?"

"You see the racecourse, *nkosi.* From that side to that side, it was that far."

"So if we went in between Johnstone's Kopje and Carter's Ridge and kept going south for a while, we could come round and approach their picket lines from behind?"

"You're mad to think of that," said O'Flaherty.

Bannock kept his attention on Mabala. "Let Mabala speak."

"It is no good, *nkosi.* Behind the horses is where the Griquas sleep. There are guards, plenty. Every week there are more Boers. Sometimes they stand guard. Sometimes they ride round and round all night."

"But you said they are guarding the cattle now, yet you still got some oxen the other night?"

Mabala shook his head ruefully. "It is different, *nkosi.* The cattle are far from Carter's. Now they are far, far back. Sometimes there are guards. Griquas. When there are too many we say, *hau,* no good, and we come back. Next time there are one, sometime two beasts away from the herd and it is very dark. And next time also the night is warm and the Griquas they are sleeping. But *nkosi,* the beasts must be quiet. If they are not quiet, we come slowly, slowly, quiet, quiet, all the way back. If they are not quiet, if they make noise, then we hide and wait and the Griquas they take them back and say, '*Hau,* why are these beasts so far away?' "

"I understand all that," said Bannock, "but maybe the guards at the fort also go to sleep sometimes."

"They no sleep, *nkosi.* They sit with guns."

"Well, what's wrong with me dressing up like a Boer, walking in there, and untying my horse? By the time I was on his back and away, they'd have no hope of catching me. They wouldn't even see me in the dark."

"You're mad," said O'Flaherty softly.

Mabala was shaking his head emphatically. "They say stop, *nkosi.* They know everyone how he looks. This time when I go to look, I see nothing. There are more people. Like all those there." He pointed at the tents on the racecourse. "Three times more, four times more. For the beasts it is the same. We can still go tonight and maybe we bring one beast. But for Carter's, it is no good. It is too much."

"I'm sick of sitting around here doing nothing," said Bannock. "I'm going out there tonight and get my horse. You can come with me as far as the kopjes and bring the horses back. I'll do the rest on my own."

They were looking at him rebelliously.

"I can only try," he shouted.

O'Flaherty opted out of the tense situation. "I'll be seein' to the horses." He got up and went to do just that.

Mabala was braver. He waited until Bannock looked at him, and then shook his head meaningfully.

"All right, all right," Bannock conceded. "We'll see what the night looks like. I'll decide then."

O'Flaherty called from over by the horses, "Here comes trouble again."

"What trouble?" Bannock was unable to see around

the corner of the grandstand, where O'Flaherty was looking.

"You should have gone when you got the message. It's him, himself."

"Who the hell is himself?" But Bannock remembered the note brought down by the Town Guard, a peremptory order to see Masefield at Lennox Street.

"It's the fat major on a thin horse."

"Get some coffee going, Mabala." Bannock leaned his head back against the wall and closed his eyes. He quite looked forward to an argument with Masefield. It would pass the time.

The hoofbeats clipclopped in, and he heard the greetings.

O'Flaherty's voice was saying, "Good afternoon, sor."

Masefield's voice came: "You've got the only fat horses in Kimberley, do you know that?"

"Sure, we give them the food out of our own mouths, Major."

The boots crunched toward him, and still he kept his eyes closed. The boots stopped in front of him. There was a pause and then the sarcasm.

"I can only assume that the message I sent to you did not get through."

"What message?" Bannock opened his eyes, to see Masefield's enormous bulk already settled on the precarious shooting stick.

"There you are," said Masefield. "The message you received from me did not get through to you."

It was Bannock's turn, and he allowed a typical Masefield pause before he spoke.

"I feel like setting up my own siege here. I should get in the middle of that racecourse and fire at anyone who comes from any direction, especially that one." He nodded toward the town. "Because every time someone comes here, they're after my horses or my head or my reputation."

Masefield was unimpressed. "You left something out."

"What?"

"Your irresistible charm."

"Very funny, Major. What are you being so amiable about? What is it you want this time?"

A shell whistled past overhead and Masefield looked up, frowning. "I find it extraordinary," he muttered, "that they never fire on the perimeter or the fortifications. It's always into the middle of town. This must be the safest place in Kimberley."

"Outside of Kimberley," corrected Bannock. "And as I was saying, what is it you want? Would you like me to ride through fifteen thousand Boers and drop a message at the Modder?"

"If you can manage to shut up for a moment, I'll tell you what I'd like you to do. I'd like you to get out of Kimberley right now and stay out. I mean right out, far away, where you can cause no more trouble."

"That's a switch. You try to keep me in, then you want to throw me out. What's this all about?"

"It's about your irresistible charm and a family you seem to have an unnatural attraction for. I'd like you to keep your hands, if not your mind, off Mrs. Stevenson."

Bannock came off the wall and sat up rigid with anger. "Who do you think you're talking to?" It came out hoarsely. "Damn you, Masefield, what are you getting at?"

The normally unwavering gaze flickered for a moment in the face of Bannock's hot reaction, but Masefield stayed on his shooting stick as Bannock unwound onto his feet like a leopard about to strike.

"I warned you once to mind your own business," Bannock said slowly.

Masefield's arms hung limp on his thighs in a passive challenge. "Calm down, Bannock," he advised. "This is not simply my idea. It is a combination of advice and orders that have been given me."

"Orders?" Bannock's fury was tempered by curiosity.

The eyes hardened, and Masefield was immediately himself again. "I've had it from up the line, old chap. Influence has been brought to bear. The girl's mother has been pressing buttons." He could see Bannock was uncertain and he wasted no time. "The mother has whispered to a few colonels and, I gather, threatened them with Rhodes and the CO. They, in turn, have passed the threat on to me. I am supposed to investigate you."

Bannock spat out each word. "You can go to hell."

"I think you should listen. You have come up against a situation here which I believe you are incapable of handling. This family has been ranged against you and the mother is going to use all the influence at her disposal to wipe you out if necessary. And she can do it, Bannock. Let me assure you, she can do it."

Bannock said nothing. He shouted at himself to say nothing. The argument was postponed while Mabala and one of his men brought coffee. Masefield raised his eyebrows at the proffered sugar, but didn't comment.

Bannock watched him unbutton one of his tunic pockets and pull out a bent-over envelope. The envelope was held out to him and he took it.

Masefield said, "This letter was delivered to me at the Club by a porter from the Shields Hotel. It was inside an envelope addressed to me. I suggest you read it. It may throw some light on what we are talking about."

Bannock put down his mug of coffee and studied the envelope. His excitement rose as he recognized the same hand that had written, "With kind regards, Emma Stevenson." He ripped open the envelope and read the single page. It went:

Bart,
     Everything I said, I meant. There are difficulties. It might take a little time.
     Trust me. I love you,

Emma

He read it only once. Once was enough. He let his arms hang down, the envelope in one hand, the letter in the other. His heart pounded and his mind danced with Emma, but he looked at Masefield unsmiling, as if nothing had happened.

"You were saying?" he said.

Masefield looked down at the letter hanging in the hand, then his hard eyes bored in on Bannock.

"I suspect the letter is from Mrs. Stevenson, Emma Stevenson. I know her quite well, you know, and please understand that whereas I am ordered to help the mother, I would be much more interested in helping her. I think she is a wonderful person. I also tend to agree with one of the raised points of contention, that she is almost certainly in a susceptible state. I mean by that that she could easily become subject to an emotional situation."

Bannock said nothing, staring back, neutralizing the interrogatory eyes.

Masefield was ruffled. "I don't know what happened that night," he said. "I don't know what you've been up to with this girl, but I think you're a damned fool to go on seeing her the way you have."

"The last time I saw her was the last time I saw you."

"That is not what I've been told."

Bannock recognized the confusion he had created. "I'll admit I tried to see her, but the barricades were up. I left a note for her, which I now realize she never got."

Masefield began to look like a man who was hiding his confusion. "There's a logical way out of this," he suggested. "It will make it easier for her and easier for me and, I can assure you, a lot easier for you. Leave her alone until after the siege. You should know from your own experience, the siege breeds emotional nonsense. Relief is going to mean what it says. Wait for relief, Bannock. It could give us all what we want." Masefield was talking to a stone wall. He tried another way. "One wonders how Emma Stevenson would feel if she knew about your affair with her sister."

"You're way behind. She knows about that. She knows everything there is to know."

Masefield had lost the initiative. Bannock held the initiative in his hand, and very deliberately, he held it out. Masefield took the letter, read it, and sighed, and Bannock now knew him well enough to be able to see his attitude change. He held onto his advantage.

"In the normal way, I will admit that you are quicker than I am and a lot more cunning. You have tricked me, outwitted me, and given me a hard time, but this time you're wasting your breath. I'm going to give you a warning for a change. You had better not assume anything. She may be infatuated, I may be infatuated, we may run away to China together. She may be matching herself with the kind of man she doesn't know, and the same goes for me in reverse."

Masefield tried to interrupt, but Bannock was in full flight, doing an emotional thing unheard of for him.

"Listen to me, Im tired of listening to you. I'm not sure whether you understand this term, I'm not sure I always understood it myself. I'm in love with that girl, and if I'd risk my life for a few lousy messages, I'll risk anything for this. I'll take on the mother and the sister and the brother and you and the whole bloody army, if necessary. If she wants to be with me, I'll fight for her, I'll kill, do you hear, I'll fight for her the way you've never seen me fight."

At last, Masefield gave up. "I was offering advice and nothing more. Shall I tell you something?"

"Will anything stop you?"

"I don't really believe Emma Stevenson is in any way gullible. I think she knows precisely what she wants. In fact, I think that young woman has more character than the whole lot of them put together. And by the way, I shall be seeing her the day after tomorrow."

Bannock couldn't stop himself from showing his fury. He had to take it out on someone. "Get on with the work," he shouted to O'Flaherty, who was trying to edge himself away from the horses and into earshot.

Masefield stood up, put down his mug, and closed the top of his shooting stick. He moved off around the edge of the building, forcing Bannock to follow him.

"All right," Bannock demanded. "You're going to see Emma. What does that mean?"

Masefield was quite himself again. He leaned on the outer rail of the racecourse and waited for Bannock to come up.

"There is a gathering at the Sanatorium on Friday evening. It's Rhodes and his crowd making a gesture of appeasement for his arguments with the military staff and Town Council. There will be a lot of people there, including the Freestone-Grant family, and to my surprise, I have been asked to accompany them." He paused, looking at Bannock. "You should ask me why I am surprised."

Bannock was still sore. He aped Masefield's superior manner: "Why are you surprised?"

"Because I had a sharp brush with Emma Stevenson's sister the other day, which leads me to believe that she was acting on her own nasty initiative. I somehow doubt she reported the outcome to her mother. I think I might have worried her a trifle."

"I don't know what you're talking about. Are you leading up to something?"

"I was going to suggest that you come along to the Sanatorium on Friday evening."

"You're mad. I can't go to that party."

"I wasn't suggesting you go in, but wait outside."

"What for?"

"You're being rather dense, old chap." Masefield was smiling for a change. "If you lurk in the bushes outside, you might just see your Emma. And don't ask me how. I told you I know her quite well. I might be able to arrange it."

Bannock leaned on the rail, keeping his attention on

the hive of tents to hide his astonishment. Masefield kept surprising him with his mixture of threat and friendliness.

"Well, what do you say?" asked Masefield.

"I'll be there."

"I can't promise anything."

"I'll be there."

Masefield sniffed the air and cast an eye on the tents. "I believe I can smell beef cooking," he said.

Bannock wanted to turn around to see if Ndogo was at work at the cooking fire behind the stables, but he remained facing forward toward the tents.

"Beef?" he said innocently. "You must be mistaken. Maybe they caught a rabbit in the veld. Oh, no, very definitively, that's not beef."

Masefield sniffed again. "I could tell the smell of cooking beef anywhere. I've taken to dreaming about beef."

"Your nose is fooling you."

"I think this racecourse bears investigation. My nose never fools me, nor do my eyes deceive me. Where did you get the sugar?"

"We get odd small luxuries from the Sanatorium; there's no shortage there."

"The Sanatorium?"

"Paddy has a friend there, the head chef."

Masefield straightened up and started off toward the horses. "In that case, I shall look forward to Friday night. Maybe I could sneak you out two kinds of morsel."

Bannock followed him back to his horse and watched him heave his great bulk into the saddle. He waited for the parting shot, but it never came. Masefield glanced down at him with his usual disdainful expression as he turned the horse.

Bannock called after him. "Masefield."

Masefield paused and looked back at him. "Ah," he said. "You wish to thank me."

Bannock nodded. "I wish to thank you."

* * *

O'Flaherty arrived at the Sanatorium at a bad time. It was late morning, when the vast kitchens were busy preparing for lunch. He could hear Pacelli's booming voice as he made his way through the yard. His friend was shouting above a hubbub of voices, clattering of plates, and clanging of pots and pans.

He went in through the open door and inhaled the thick steam, with its superb aroma of cooking food. The smell was excruciating to him. Even the small portions of beef Ndogo cooked for them when Mabala brought it in were nothing by comparison to this smell. This had herbs, the scent of great cooking in it. He saw Pacelli between racks and canopies standing tall and round, waving an arm to conduct his white-hatted orchestra. Cellini, standing across a counter from Pacelli, waved to O'Flaherty, and the big chef turned around to look.

"Paddi," Pacelli roared. "Where you've been? Why you not'a come see me?"

O'Flaherty made his way between counters and iron ranges where cooks were busy at work. "Hello, Mario. Hello, Mr. Carloleeni. What have you got cookin'?" he asked with feeling. "What's that beautiful thing in jelly? It looks good enough to eat."

Pacelli looked at the aspic mold and nodded skeptically. "That'sa galantine."

"What's in it?" O'Flaherty was licking his lips.

"It'sa secret, Paddi. It'sa so much secret I won'ta eat it myself."

O'Flaherty was disappointed and Pacelli went back into action, lifting a heavy metal spoon and crashing it down on a nearby piece of equipment. He roared, "Bain-marie, bain-marie, where ee'sa everything? Where ee'sa consommé?" He rattled an empty pot in the bain-marie with the spoon. "Hey, you, you consommé." He pointed the spoon menacingly at one of the men, who nodded nervously. "Bring a bleddy consommé, dammit. Where ee'sa béchamel?" He rattled another empty pot, then waved the spoon for O'Flaherty's attention. "Have'a you ever heard of'a béchamel with'a stock and'a no milk?"

O'Flaherty, who had never heard of béchamel, shook his head reassuringly.

Pacelli by this time was holding up an earthenware jar, looking in it, and holding it up again. "What ee'sa this rubbish?"

Someone called, "Demi-glace, chef."

"This ee'sa demi-glace?" he jeered, holding the jar aloft. "This ee'sa bleddy fat with'a nothing in." He slammed down the jar and waved the spoon toward O'Flaherty again. "How do you make'a demi-glace with'a tins? Everything ee'sa tins." He came back through the bustle of the kitchen suddenly smiling, speaking sweetly to Cellini like a grand organ with the soft stop out. "Cellini, please watch'a the bain-marie and the sautés." He gave his attention to O'Flaherty. "*Si*, Paddi, what ees you want'a see me about?"

"There's two things I want to talk to you about, Mario. One is the diamonds. I've been havin' a few ideas about them diamonds. The other is a big pot for makin' poteen."

"What ee'sa pocheen?"

"It's a kind of liquor that blows off the top of your head when you take a small sip."

"Like grappa?"

"Now there's a fine drink you introduced me to. Sure, it's a little like grappa. But with a bit of dynamite added, if you're followin' me."

"Sounds'a good, Paddi."

"Blow your eyes right out of their sockets."

"Sounds'a very good."

O'Flaherty's attention was distracted by three gleaming pies that slid along the counter and stopped in front of them.

"What a wonderful-lookin' pie," he said, leaning down to smell the rising steam. "I wonder what's in it."

"It'sa pigeon. Not'a tin. Pigeon, number one, *autentico*. Paddi, what you say about the diamonds?"

O'Flaherty smelt the pie blissfully. "Pigeon pie." He sighed. "Sure, it was always one of me favorites."

"There ee'sa man here, the saucier, there he ees. He says he know about diamonds. We speak'a to him later."

O'Flaherty saw nothing but the pie. "I've never smelled a pie like this one. Where did you get the pigeons?"

"Cellini," shouted Pacelli, and when the chef came up, all three looked at the pie. "Cellini, you make'a these pies?"

Cellini nodded proudly.

"Paddi, ask Cellini if you can taste'a the pie."

O'Flaherty gave Cellini a sweet, imploring smile.

Cellini was shocked. "But chef," he protested, "these ee'sa for the special today."

Pacelli brandished a large carving knife, pretending to stab the pie, but instead put the knife down again, roaring with laughter at Cellini's horrified expression. "Hey, number three," he shouted to one of his assistants. "Fetch'a the red wine."

"The red wine?" Cellini seemed surprised.

"And bring'a two glasses," roared Pacelli like an opera singer, one moment bellowing it out and in the next quietly and with feeling to Cellini, "Cellini, you can'a keep'a your pie, special today. The pie it ee'sa for Meester Rhodes, not'a for Meester Flerriti."

Cellini looked worried. "Let him have'a one piece, chef," he suggested grudgingly.

Pacelli gave a superior smile. "No, Cellini, the pie ee'sa not'a for Meester Flerriti, he'sa my guest. The wine ee'sa for Meester Flerriti. Cellini."

"Yes, chef?"

Pacelli roared, "The bain-marie, watch'a the bleddy bain-marie."

Cellini went away trying to look dignified, while

Pacelli grabbed the two-thirds-full bottle that was slid to him across the counter. He poured into the two glasses as they were slid along, and the two big men smiled as they toasted one another.

"Here's to the diamonds, Mario."

"And here'sa to the big'a promises. Where ee'sa the beef you promise me?"

O'Flaherty's eyes darted around furtively. "Shh," he cautioned. "It's been difficult. Tomorrow, if God is willin' and Mabala gets through, there'll be a fine piece of meat for you."

They emptied the goblets and Pacelli filled them again, leaving a little in the bottle. He took the bottle and dropped it, letting it smash on the floor. He shouted.

"Hey, Cellini, who ee'sa break this bottle of kitchen wine? Go speak'a to Meester Henderson in the bar. There'sa no red wine in the kitchen."

Cellini flung the spoon he was holding into an empty pot and beckoned to one of the men.

Pacelli became serious, conspiratorial. "Paddi," he said quietly, "I think'a you must forget'a these diamonds. The saucier, he say you can only get'a the diamonds from the natives. They all got'a diamonds. The mines they are closed. You can'ta go down the mines."

O'Flaherty whispered, "But Mario, I've been lookin' at those mines. There's hardly a guard in sight. You can walk in there anytime you like."

"Si, si, but you can'ta go down the mine."

"Sure, that's a problem all right."

"Hey, Signor Saucier!" Pacelli shouted across the kitchen, brandishing the carving knife for attention.

The saucier came running. "Yes, chef?" He faced them from across the counter, smiling apprehensively.

"Theese is'a Paddi I was telling you about. Tell him what you told me. He'sa brother," he explained to O'Flaherty. "Tell him about your'a brother." He waved the knife at the saucier.

"My brother is an underground foreman, now in the Diamond Fields Artillery. I also worked the mines for a while. I told chef, you're wasting your time, Paddy."

"Is it the security, you're meanin'?"

"No, it's not the security." He and Pacelli both shook their heads vigorously, and the saucier went on. "There's almost no security. All the able-bodied men are in the garrison. No, it's just that the mine heads are closed, the headgear is all shut down."

"That'sa what I was trying to tell'a you." Pacelli slammed the knife down.

"But wait a minute." O'Flaherty's obstinacy was holding out. "What about down below?"

"You can't get down there."

"Just satisfy me curiosity for a moment. Is there any security down there?"

"No." The saucier was patient. "There's no need for it. There's nobody down there. There are only a few old dodderers up at the top anyway."

"It's just me curiosity, if you please. There must be diamonds lyin' all over the place down in them shafts?"

"No, that's wrong." The saucier and Pacelli shook their heads emphatically. "People think that, but it's not so. The diamonds are in hard blue rock, a pipe of volcanic rock that comes up from the bowels of the earth. It takes massive machinery to break it down and get to the diamonds."

"Can you never see a diamond in those rocks?" pleaded O'Flaherty.

"I suppose it's just possible once in a while, but you wouldn't recognize it. It's just a dull thing."

O'Flaherty had a cunning gleam in his eye. "Now what about them natives always stealin' the diamonds? How do you explain that?"

"Yes, when there are rock falls there's a lot of grit and blue dust, and if you know what you're lookin for, it's possible to find an occasional stone."

"What was I tellin' yer?" O'Flaherty gave Pacelli a knowing look.

"But you'll never get down there." The saucier was smiling.

"And what about takin' a few small rocks and smashing them up later?"

"That's not how it's done."

"But there could be a diamond or two in them rocks."

"I suppose so." The saucier could only laugh.

O'Flaherty's eyes narrowed as he threw his trump card. "And what about the first diamonds that were ever discovered here? Were they just findin' them on the ground?"

"No, that's different. Those are alluvial diamonds, mostly found around riverbeds."

"Surely they've got a few of those in the mine?"

"No, I don't think so." The saucier could hardly talk for laughing and Pacelli sent him off still chuckling to himself.

"So, you see, Paddi?"

"Sure." O'Flaherty was not arguing. "It's much the way I saw it."

"And Meester Bannock, what he'sa say? He'sa not interested in diamonds?"

"I'm afraid not, Mario. But he's had a bad time, you know. I told you he's lost all his horses, bar one. And when he lost Marcus, well, it changed the man. A real bad blow it was. If it wasn't for them ladies chasin' after him, I don't know what he might have done."

"Ho, ho." Pacelli showed his teeth in a great grin and held up a clenched fist in admiration. "That's Bannock, big *amore*, hey?"

O'Flaherty was also grinning. "For the life of me I don't know how he does it. Every time it happens. You only have to have a woman appear and he's off. It's nothing the man does, never a wink. One moment he's saying, 'How do you do, my dear,' and the next moment he's doin' her."

"Doing her?" Pacelli was not sure.

"On the bed, man, and by the sound of it, bangin' away like a stallion who hasn't seen it for two seasons."

"*Bravissimo,*" Pacelli applauded. He finished his wine and looked around. "You are'a hungry, Paddi?" he asked.

O'Flaherty brightened up. "I wasn't goin' to be the first to mention it." He jerked round at a new sound. "Hey, what's that?"

Every man in the kitchen reacted to the loud report in the distance, quite different and more ominous than the usual sounds of firing and exploding shells. Their attention was riveted on the humming sound that followed, an uneven noise alternating between humming and buzzing, growing in volume, rising in pitch to become a reverberating howl that had everyone in the kitchen exchanging looks of nervous anticipation. In a matter of seconds the howl became earsplitting. Then an explosion shook the foundations and walls of the building, brought glass flying in from every window.

They all went down on the floor instinctively, amidst a pandemonium of falling pots gonging together and crockery crashing from the racks and shattering on the floor. The room was filled with dust that seemed to be sucking in from the broken windows, bringing with it a choking, sulfurous atmosphere. Waves of sound from the explosion echoed away into absolute silence.

Voices began out of the silence, curses and excited shouting. The kitchen staff abandoned their stations and fled out into the open. People from inside the hotel came picking their way through the kitchen out into the yard.

O'Flaherty and Pacelli sat on the floor against the counter, coughing dust and boggling at one another.

"Bejases," breathed O'Flaherty. "What in the name of the saints was that?"

Pacelli took hold of the edge of the counter and slowly pulled himself up, his great fat body quivering with anger.

"I'ma sick of all this bang, bang, bang," he bellowed.

"They smash'a my kitchen, damn, shit. They smash'a everything."

O'Flaherty was concerned with the upturned pigeon pie on the floor beside him. He tenderly turned it over and sampled a piece of the crust.

"Look at'a my kitchen." Pacelli held out a dramatic hand to the empty room like the clown in *I Pagliacci* alone on the stage.

O'Flaherty scooped up a piece of the pie and munched appreciatively.

Cellini came running back into the kitchen from outside, pale and jittery.

"Mario," he shouted. "Ee'sa big gun. The Boers have'a got this'a big gun." He stretched out his arms as he babbled. "It'sa big'a than this'a building."

The broken pigeon pie appeared on the counter, and O'Flaherty's head came up after it.

"Mr. Carloleeni," he said, "this pie is amazing."

The main hall of the Sanatorium was already crowded when they arrived. Emma felt remote from the others as she followed in beside Sarah and Pendleton, with Mark and Major Masefield leading the way through the crush. They soon joined up with a group that included Colonel Thrumpton and other acquaintances.

Emma found herself in the middle of three different conversations, with little inclination to join in any of them. They were all variations on the same topics: food, the shortages in general, the dreaded Long Tom, and its disastrous effect on the day-to-day shelling.

Somebody's wife was saying to Colonel Thrumpton, "I saw Mr. Rhodes but not Colonel Kekewich. I wonder what his excuse will be this time. He is always up in that observation tower, is he not?"

Thrumpton replied, "In this case, it may not be a question of the CO's excuse but whether he was invited in the first place. He and Mr. Rhodes are not the best of friends."

It was a strange atmosphere, Emma decided. An unreal setting for a town under siege—the men in dress uniform, the women in their party best, neither the occasion nor their mood suggesting that some of them might well be dead on the following day. All she could see over the heads around her were people on the gallery above where the buffet was situated and others ranged down on the wide staircase in the center of the hall.

There were native waiters in starched white jackets bearing trays of drinks and snacks. The smell of cooked food that drifted down the hall promised to make nonsense of the desperate shortages. It seemed the rumor was about to be confirmed, that Cecil Rhodes and his luxurious hotel were short of nothing. She saw trays of champagne coming down the stairs, and Emma thought of the notice that had gone around at their hotel, informing everyone that they had virtually run out of all stocks of liquor. Her mother only had sherry by virtue of a secret source of Colonel Thrumpton's, and without much doubt this was the source.

Major Masefield was blocked off from her by some people she didn't know. She wanted to speak to him alone, to find out whether Bart had gotten her note. There were other reasons why she wanted to speak to him. Sarah had virtually snubbed him when he had arrived at the hotel and ignored him all the way here. Emma wondered what the explanation for that could be.

She wondered about something else that had happened earlier. Her mother had gone into one of her nervous declines and decided to go to bed just as they were about to set off. Emma had assumed she would have to stay with her, but surprisingly, her mother had insisted on her going, for some reason wanted her to go. There was only one possible explanation, vague as it may seem. It was her mother who had insisted Major Masefield accompany them. Was he to be the harmless diversion intended to take her mind off

Bart? If it were so, it was almost a clever plan. If she had been seen to smile for anyone, it was Major Masefield. And the reason was simply that he was the most intelligent and amusing subject around. She wished he would come over and talk to her. It was peculiar that he was standing on his own, as unconnected with anyone as she was.

Masefield was being Napoleon again, hands behind back, stomach out, chin up with an expression of disdain for everything that was being said around him. His manner suggested he intended to take no part in the activities other than to acquire a drink from a tray that was conveniently passing near him. He watched the tray idly, as if willing it toward him, and eventually took a glass of wine without having to move a step.

On the heels of one tray came another, containing delicate but delectable-looking snacks, fingers of bread with asparagus, anchovies, and other delicacies from tins. Masefield took one and popped it into his mouth, his hand going straight out like a striking snake to restrain the tray from moving on. To the horror of the lady nearest him, he stacked up three of the fingers, one upon the other, and devoured them as the tray made its escape. He remained in the same position, sipping his drink.

He might have been waiting for what was about to happen behind him. Pendleton excused himself to Sarah in order to speak to a group of officers standing nearby, and before she could join Mark and the others, Masefield turned around, neatly confronting her, stopping her from going past. Sarah's anger showed, but she hesitated, for a moment intimidated by the shrewd-faced major.

He spoke before she could. "There is something which needs to be cleared up between us."

She was on her guard. "I thought I understood you very well."

"Apropos of our last conversation, I think you may have been left with a wrong impression."

"My impression of you is that of a man who cannot be

trusted. I think you are crafty and evasive and, in my case, vindictive."

"You left me with food for thought. Had you not attacked me, we might have reached a better understanding. Had you not been so quick, you might have discovered that we had something in common."

"What could we possibly have in common?"

Masefield's haughty expression had never changed. 'Your sister," he said.

Sarah was puzzled and proceeded cautiously. "But surely that's what we were talking about, Emma's welfare."

"May I give you a word of advice? For all that your intentions might have been very good, your way of achieving your ends was not very effective."

She was immediately suspicious. "You'll have to explain what you mean."

Masefield leaned forward and spoke quietly, confidentially. "Once you have chosen an adversary, you must not waste your emotional energy, you must outwit."

Sarah remained suspicious. "I thought you were talking about Emma."

"Yes," he continued quietly. "You see, I think your sister is extremely attractive." He looked at her meaningfully, and the light slowly dawned.

"Ah," she whispered. "I should have thought of that. Why didn't you say something?"

Masefield allowed himself a thin smile. "You said I was evasive."

Sarah put her hand to her mouth and laughed. "You and Emma." She giggled. "I should have thought of that. What a good idea." Her eyes were far away, evaluating it.

Masefield said nothing, maintaining the smile. He waited for her to catch up.

She laughed again. "That explains quite a few things," she said very quietly. "I suspect Mother has had you in mind. Has she said anything to you?"

He shrugged noncommittally.

Sarah was transformed into whispering enthusiasm. "Am I to understand you were using tactics about Bannock?"

"You are very quick."

"Then you were using tactics on me as well? You are an absolute rogue, sir," she said, but she was pleased.

He smiled slyly, and let her go on.

"Do you know how angry I was at the thought of you being on Bannock's side? It threw me right out. I must confess to you that Mother had no idea I had visited you the other day. You see, she hasn't been at all well, and no matter how angry I was, I thought it best not to report the matter to her. I didn't want to upset her further, you understand."

"How very fortunate."

"Yes, it was, under the circumstances." Sarah was glowing with repressed excitement. "I think we should leave you to do all the outwitting from now on. None of us are very good at it, you know. I suddenly realize why I have always been a little nervous of you. You are an expert at outwitting people, are you not? How do you do it, Major?"

"I don't do it every time," he said modestly. "You see, there is a criterion. When you set out to outwit your adversary, you must first establish that he or she, as the case may be, is not capable of outwitting you."

Sarah smiled uncertainly, then brightened up. "You and Emma, imagine that."

Masefield frowned. "Do you mind if we keep this to ourselves for the moment?"

Sarah giggled and nodded her agreement.

Masefield noticed Pendleton, who had been looking over his shoulder for some time, turn and come to join them. He wasted no time.

"Will you excuse me," he said to Sarah. "I must see whether your sister needs anything."

Emma saw him coming. She had heard Sarah's laughter and wondered at her extraordinary change of heart. Masefield came up beaming, with none of his usual style of arrogance. Was he the person to look to for help? Should she assume that he would be sympathetic, or even that he was a friend of a sort? Do shrewd, astute people of his type use charm to exploit every situation to their own ends? Her judgment told her she could trust him; her instincts wavered on the subject. She prepared her question, but somehow he anticipated her.

"I delivered your message," he said, and added, "Personally. I'm sorry to have left you alone so long, but there was a small matter I had to attend to."

Emma had one thing on her mind. "How is he?" she asked.

"You mean Bannock? He is not in very good shape. Before, he was difficult; now he's impossible. I don't believe he'll ever be normal again."

"Nor will I." Emma was past caring what she said.

"So I gather. I think what you both need more than anything else at this moment is to see one another."

Judgment took over from instinct, and a smile was exchanged. "You are right," said Emma, "and it will have to be soon, very soon."

She studied him for a moment. "You seem to know all about me. I think you are not a man who opens up, yet you know everything that goes on. Should I be saying this to you?"

"I'm delighted." Masefield was amused. "I am forever being accused of being cunning and devious."

But Emma was serious. "What do you think about me?"

"I think you are in a trap, one partly of your own making. A difficult one to spring."

A gong announced supper from the buffet in the gallery. Emma surprised Masefield by taking his arm, saying,

"A friend of mine taught me a technique. It's called walking and talking. It is a way of having a private conversation in a room full of people."

"Excellent plan," said Masefield, and they both set off walking against a slow but definite surge toward the stairs and the buffet.

Emma spoke first. "If I were to ask you something and tell you something, can we deal on a simple basis of truth?"

Masefield's brows came down and he pondered. "The truth I cannot offer you, but I can help."

"Do I need help?"

"Not exactly. You need an ally in a war of nerves."

"I am not good at riddles, Major. Maybe that's my problem. You must be too clever for me. Why can't you offer me the truth?"

"My dear, you should never insist on the truth. It is such a difficult thing to believe in."

Emma made an exasperated face. "That's a contradiction," she said, but she was enjoying it.

"Is it?" Masefield looked too serious to be enjoying it. The lecture went on. "Truth is something you can only evaluate by evidence. What you need is trust. Trust is a much more dependable condition, and you can stake your life on it just as easily as you can on truth. Trust is something you would give carefully or dearly try to earn. At least with trust you reserve the right to let yourself down, but truth is the flag waved by liars. There is no defense against it. It is what everybody demands, and what do they get? They put it into agreements which are broken and proclamations that talk of meat, implying beef but meaning horse."

Emma laughed at another clever Masefield theory as much as at the joke.

"You are talking to an old-fashioned believer," she said.

"All I'm suggesting is that you organize your beliefs. If I can give you a guiding slogan it would go like this: Li to the liars and reserve the truth for people you trust."

Emma refused to be serious. "Then cunning is a virtue," she parried.

They stopped, and Masefield looked at her, impressed. "I knew you were clever," he said admiringly.

They were at the high, open doors at the entrance to the room.

"Shall we step outside and take the air for a moment?" he suggested.

Emma went first and Masefield followed after, immediately looking around for any sign of Bannock. They stood at the edge of the narrow verandah facing out while Masefield rocked impatiently on his heels, peering about at the dim shadows of carriages and sparse trees but seeing nothing. He leaned on a pillar and watched the beautiful girl in black looking out into the night, calmer than he had ever seen her, quite unsuspecting.

There was a buzzing of cicadas and the steady note of crickets. The carriage horses stamped in the dust, and somewhere beyond those sounds were the hoofbeats of an approaching horse.

Emma turned and asked, "Will you explain something to me? This evening, when you arrived, Sarah refused to greet you. She appeared to have some private argument with you."

"That is correct."

"Yet a short while ago she suddenly became your greatest friend. What was the reason for that?"

"I lied to her."

"Lie to the liars," she reflected.

"Yes, siege fever is running high. She told a few lies and caused a fair measure of mischief, and I made the mistake of challenging her. But once I realized the mistake, I threw her off the scent, so to speak. Do you need the details?"

"No, I can imagine what happened. I'm not even curious. I've long since given up regretting that there was no way of making friends with Sarah. I've never been able to understand her. She is a contradictor. Why does she always contradict?"

Masefield took it up. "If you contradict everything, then you are not listening. The problem is with people who will not listen. They become the victims of their own one-sided assumptions." Masefield heard the hoofbeats stop somewhere among the trees. He heard the boots crunching on the ground. He watched over Emma's shoulder, waiting until he saw the white breeches and black top boots emerging into the light.

"I'm keeping us from supper," said Emma. "You must be hungry." She had already turned to go in when Masefield put a hand on her arm.

"You said you wanted to see Bartholomew Bannock," he said simply.

Emma was unprepared for the statement.

"Turn around," he said gently, taking her arm and making her turn.

"Bart," she whispered as she saw him.

Masefield said, "The sooner you come back, the sooner I shall be able to eat." He leaned down to see her face, lips faintly open, staring out as if in a dream. "Did you hear me, Emma?" he asked.

She beamed at the sound of her name from her new friend. "I heard you," she said, and then she was running down the steps and across the gravel toward Bannock.

When Emma reached Bannock, she stopped for a moment, looking up, straining to see his expression. He was frowning and anxious, his tanned face shaved and gleaming, the untidy hair framing his dark eyes, accentuating the two points of reflected light. He remained still, awkward, as if undecided, only moving when she did, meeting the embrace the moment her arms came forward. He held her off the ground, turning easily on his heels, turning her slowly around him.

He whispered into her hair, "I thought I would never see you again."

Her whisper came back: "We are forever."

She clung tightly. They said nothing. He walked slowly, carrying her into the dark, and there among the carriages he lifted her weightlessly onto a driver's seat. It seemed unimportant that he could not see her features. She was there, close again and real again. Their hands clung together the way they had done that night in the veld. The two occasions became one.

He said, "Whenever I really wanted something, when I desperately wanted something, I made myself imagine it was impossible to have. You know that feeling?"

"I know," she whispered.

"You break it down and hope it is building itself up. I wanted you so badly that I convinced myself you could not possibly want me. I even criticized you in my mind, called you naive and vulnerable. I decided you had done something you were regretting. I saw you as Sarah's sister; as impetuous, maybe, but never as foolish as Sarah. I saw you as utterly confused, and that was the worst of all. I tried to imagine you had no resolve, that your family would talk you round and put you down. It was the worst because it was the most logical. It was almost enough to make a man stop fighting. I tried to hide behind pessimism like that, but it failed. Unless you reject me, I will fight for you to the death."

Emma leaned down closer. "I feel I ought to laugh at you saying that, but it's too serious. I only want you."

"Then why—" Bannock realized he was raising his voice and started again in a heavy whisper. "Then why are you here while I am there?" He pointed in the direction of the racecourse.

"Oh Bart, I feel the same way, but I think I have an advantage. I have only just discovered optimism. It makes it so much easier to cope with everything. With my mother's sadness and my mother's anger and, saddest of all, her scheming. I must explain about my mother; may I explain?"

He could not see her face, but he knew she had become upset. "Of course," he said softly.

"She is keeping us apart, yes. But she has been worn down by the siege and what has happened. When the Long Tom started firing and the ground began to shake, she began to crumble with the town, and for a short while, I must let it be. I am part exploited and part needed. It is my own decision, Bart."

"Yes, yes." He tried to calm her.

"But as they are laying plans for me, I am planning for us. You must allow me to do that. Three days, Bart, that is all I will give them now. Have you heard about Lord Roberts? They say everything is different since he has taken over. A few more days, Bart. I only need a few more days."

He knew she couldn't see his smile. "Every day since the beginning of this siege it's been a few more days." The irony was unavoidable for him.

"I know." She was upset again. "But can you wait?"

He let go of her hands and ran his own up under her petticoat onto her thighs. "Do you imagine I could ever give up waiting for you?"

She laid her hands on her skirt, caressing his through the material, gripping them tightly. "Relief or no relief, I will give them three days."

"They will never condone that, Emma."

"I know. They will attack us."

He gripped her thighs, she gripped his hands more tightly. "There is so much to attack," he said. "That is the part you don't know about me. I am so open to attack."

"You could have done anything and I would defend you. We shall defend ourselves. I know how they will see us, and I don't care. I must seem to them as though I am riding on dreams when I am simply grasping at reality. Do you understand why I need time?"

He felt the emotion shivering in her thighs. "Of course, of course," he soothed.

"In a few days, I must put aside a lifetime. I must come out of inactivity. It's the only word I can think of. Inactivity is a confused state to be in. It is an impotent waste of life." She waited for him.

"Emma, if you could hear yourself as I do, then you would understand my fears. I have never known a woman as intelligent as you. And you have never known anyone who groped and battled his way through life the way I did."

A small hand came down to his mouth. "How is it that I know you?" she whispered. "Because I know you so intimately. Bart, this is how love works. We could be speaking different languages and we would still know we were meant for one another. Love is the translator, not the storybook kind, but the embracing, sexual kind that begins in the mind and puts every other good instinct to work. The smallest touch takes on a meaning; being alive becomes a luxury."

"But you still have to stay alive. Every time I hear that massive gun go off, I think of you and where the shell will land."

Emma slid off the seat down into his arms again.

"You have no need to worry, my love. I am cooped up in a cellar with the rest of the guests. It is a ghastly place, but quite safe, I am told."

They hugged each other, and she laughed at the thought that he could not possibly know his own strength. She choked and laughed as the breath was squeezed out of her, but she clung with all her strength.

"Please be a coucal," she whispered.

"Be a what?"

"The coucal knows when to fly and when to stay under cover."

"It's a bird?"

"Yes." Emma pretended to be serious. "A rare bird that defies the balance of nature, somehow contrives to bite without being bitten. It's the bird world's master of survival. And if you'll forgive me, I think you can learn from it."

Bannock clung to her and laughed into her ear. "If you want me to be a coucal, I'll be a coucal."

They turned when they heard voices from the direction of the verandah. The light from the door silhouetted Masefield's large frame as he straightened up from leaning on the pillar. Someone else was there talking to him. It was Emma's brother.

Mark had taken Masefield entirely by surprise, and he had not directly answered the firm query regarding Emma's whereabouts.

Mark was saying, "But I don't understand. Where is she?"

Masefield made a dignified effort to take control of the situation. "She is over there talking to someone." Nothing was going to sound convincing. "You wait here, my dear chap, and I'll fetch her." He went purposefully down the steps and into the dark.

His behavior left Mark standing dumbfounded for a moment staring after him. But only for a moment. Then he set off, to follow just as purposefully.

Masefield walked faster as he heard the footsteps behind. He called out, "Emma," and it sounded ridiculously matter-of-fact. But they were already coming up to him, and they all three turned to deal with Mark.

Mark was visibly flabbergasted at the sight of Bannock. "Emma, you, you disappeared," he stuttered.

Emma ignored him and addressed herself to Masefield. "I'm sorry to have been so long, Major. Shouldn't we go back inside now?"

"Excellent idea," said Masefield, eyes going upward in mock innocence.

Emma turned impulsively and hugged Bannock and they laughed softly. She whispered in his ear. "Do you realize, if I hadn't embarked on my mad escape, we would still be . . ."

"What?" he whispered.

"Searching for one another," she finished.

Mark cleared his throat uncomfortably. "I say, Emma, the supper is almost over."

Emma turned to him and grinned, pointing back at Bannock. "Do you see this incredible-looking man here?"

"Emma, really." Mark blustered to cover his embarrassment and looked helplessly at Masefield.

Emma was still involved in a staring farewell with Bannock when Masefield took over. He gripped Mark's arm firmly and led him up the steps.

Mark lowered his voice. "What on earth are you getting yourself mixed up in?" he complained.

"Heaven only knows," answered Masefield.

"Don't you realize those two have nothing in common?"

"Well, almost nothing."

"I can't understand Emma," said Mark, looking back. "I really cannot understand her."

Masefield sniffed. "I think your sister's behavior is reprehensible and inexcusable."

Mark looked faintly perplexed. "Her behavior?" He was ready to defend her. "What precisely do you mean, Masefield."

"She is keeping me away from my supper." He called out loudly, "Emma," then returned his attention to Mark. "You wish to know what I am getting myself mixed up in? It is one of those inevitable games, which if you fight you will lose and if you play along with you may win. There is a small matter of infatuation here. Let them get together, because nothing will stop them from so doing. But Emma, as I have told her, is an intelligent girl, and infatuation when it is as spontaneous as this can be a short-lived furnace that soon burns itself out. She will soon be able to judge what she has chosen."

Mark watched him in surprise. Masefield had been caught off guard. His expression had turned sour.

12 · A PLACE FOR EMMA

The turns and jerks of the gold propelling pencil made no sense. Once again, it was obviously not writing, but doodling.

Major O'Meara seemed to have become aware of it. He paused in his lecture to look in Masefield's direction, causing other of the officers present to do the same for the moment.

The gold pencil also paused, as if discovered, but as O'Meara resumed, returned to doodling.

His deceptively cheerful voice chattered on in the face of a gloomy audience. He fought their despondency, constantly looking around and demanding their attention to his map on the blackboard, firmly tapping the chalked-in details of each enemy gun position with his baton as it was mentioned. The lack of nourishing food was beginning to tell. So was the boredom of waiting for an attack that never came, let alone the relief that never came.

O'Meara tapped in a wide circle at the Boer gun positions of Carter's Ridge and Johnstone's Kopje in the southeast, Wimbledon Ridge, Alexandersfontein, and Olifantsfontein in the south, and Dronfield Ridge and Kamfersdam in the north.

"At least the Boer gunners can be relied upon to maintain their reputation for missing whatever it is they are aiming at, at all times. If it were only the nine- and fifteen-pounders we were concerned with, we could manage quite nicely. I do believe that the only time they succeed in hitting anything worth hitting is when they are aiming at something else." Chamier paused for a moment, with a faint grimace at the failure of his attempted humor.

The baton came down hard on the heavily chalked-in letters *LT* at the Kamfersdam position.

"The Long Tom, of course, is a nag of another color. There seems to be little we can do about this monster. It has sent us to ground, and there is no effective answer to it. Long Cecil is neither long enough nor strong enough. I think we must accept that, from now until relief, the town will be pounded and smashed by this devil of a gun. But that does not mean we are doing nothing. We are worrying them, if we are not stopping them. So let's consider what we are doing about Long Tom, alias Schneider, alias Creusot." He smacked his baton loudly on the trestle and waited to get the wandering attention of some of the men. His eye became fixed on the reflecting movements of Masefield's gold pencil.

"Major Masefield, I'm sure this subject hardly warrants the taking of copious notes."

Masefield looked up. "I am not taking notes, I am merely scribbling, sir."

"To pass the time?" O'Meara's sarcasm brought roars of laughter. At last someone had plucked up the nerve to show dislike of Masefield, who shrugged.

"Thank you." O'Meara went on. "The gun, as you know, is operated by a French crew, whose aim would be better were it not for the erratic behavior of the projectiles. You are all now accustomed to the weird noises these shells make. They actually veer around in the air before landing, and because of the closeness of the site at Kamfersdam, there is a tendency for the shells to bounce and ricochet without detonating, only to explode or not, as the case may be, at some farther point. I'm sure some of you have witnessed this alarming occurrence."

Masefield settled back in his chair, half closing his eyes. Boredom was becoming sleepiness. Under the hoods, the eyes followed O'Meara with menace.

"For the elucidation of those of you who are not aware of the nature of this shell, it weighs as near as dammit a hundred pounds. It is designed to scatter shrapnel, which it does very effectively over a radius of some two hundred yards. It is also extremely effective in starting fires, and whenever a fire has started, the French gunners concentrate on that same target, making life quite impossible for the fire brigade."

Masefield's eyes kept closing. The mop of hair came forward, the face settled down onto the double chin, the double chin onto the collar, the small, hard line of mouth became more relaxed.

O'Meara turned from the blackboard.

"Why is there so little we can do about it? The answer is that the Long Tom is virtually hidden in the Kamfersdam mine heap. They have dug out a deep channel, wide enough for the crew and long enough for the run-up. The gun fires from a narrow port that is heavily reinforced with stone and cement, so that all Long Cecil has succeeded in doing so far is to hit the heap and shower the gunners with sand. Why don't we charge straight out and launch an attack on Kamfersdam? Because the position is covered by the batteries at Dronfield and Carter's Ridge, as well as by a fifteen-pounder close by at Diebel's Vlei. They are watching over their Long Tom, I can assure you."

Once again O'Meara became conscious of Masefield, slumped down comfortably in his chair.

"Major Masefield." O'Meara waited for the officers to become aware of Masefield with his eyes closed. He raised his voice. "Major Masefield." But in that moment Masefield jerked away, anticipating the efforts of his neighbor to tap him on the shoulder.

O'Meara smiled icily. "Major Masefield, I wonder if you could assist us with some information. Can you tell us the weight of a Long Tom shell?"

Masefield sat up straight. "We don't have that information."

"Indeed?" There were the beginnings of laughter.

"No, sir." Masefield kept it going.

"Strange, I was under the impression that we did." The laughter increased.

Masefield had to raise his voice. "We only know approximately. About a hundred pounds, if your information is to be trusted."

The laughter stopped abruptly.

Bannock waited outside the northern barricade until it began to get dark. He could see through the opening of the guard post to the pall of smoke that still hung over the town from the day's bombing.

The Town Guards leaned on their guns and regarded him suspiciously where he lounged against a dry, blackened tree holding Lady Potter's reins. The sergeant obviously didn't believe his story about meeting Masefield, but fortunately for him, two of the others had been present on previous occasions when he had returned from riding dispatch.

Eventually the hooves were heard, and Masefield emerged out of the gloom, a thinner Masefield on a still thinner cob. Bannock was not particularly pleased to see him, since he had come without Emma.

The guards saluted, and Bannock was mounted by the time Masefield came through and rode up to meet him.

"What happened to Emma?"

Masefield shrugged. "I did my best, old boy. The hotel was struck by a shell today." He stopped Bannock from interrupting. "No, no, they are quite safe. But the mother is in a fever, and Emma is busy nursing her."

"Did you tell her about the house?"

"I could tell her nothing. Sarah was there giving me knowing looks over her shoulder. She thinks I am enamored of her sister."

The old suspicion came back. "What makes her think that?"

"I told her."

Bannock was definitely not satisfied. "Well, are you?" he demanded.

"Don't be silly, my dear fellow. I was simply leading her astray. But worry not, I am seeing Emma again tomorrow. It's arranged. There was much innuendo. She knew I had something to tell her."

"Damn." Bannock jerked the mare around impatiently. "Let's get moving. Paddy is at the house with the chef. He's cooking some food and you might as well eat it."

They set off north toward Kenilworth, following the unused tram lines that led under the long, low wall of the dried-out northern reservoir.

"Slowly, please," Masefield complained as Bannock bounced ahead on Lady Potter. "My animal is in a weak state, not full of grass like yours."

Bannock pulled back alongside him.

"What is the story of this house?" asked Masefield. "I trust you have not just taken over someone else's dwelling."

"Not at all. The house belongs to MacGrath. Ever since Kenilworth was abandoned there has been a bit of looting, so when MacGrath heard I was looking for a house, he asked me to look after his place. It has all the necessities except water. We'll have to cart that."

"Do you seriously expect Emma to live in a ghost village that was vacated for the sake of the safety of the occupants?"

"They don't fire on Kenilworth, you should know that. The Boers know it's empty so they don't waste their ammu-

nition on it. It's the safest place in Kimberley, with the main
perimeter behind and the outer barricade and fort in front.
It's the perfect place, admit it."

Masefield looked ahead at the stark outline of the village—no sign of life, no lights showing anywhere. "I think
you're being a little hysterical. Why don't you wait? By the
time you can arrange to bring Emma out here, the relief
column will have arrived."

Bannock laughed scornfully. "Are you really serious?"
he taunted. "Is that a promise, Masefield?"

"It's a guarantee," Masefield replied moodily. "You
may depend upon it. We'll be relieved in a few days."

Bannock was still scornful. "Nobody in Kimberley
would believe you, not for the hundredth time. Although I
must admit, MacGrath seems to think the same way."

"He would, because he knows."

They rode for a while in silence. Eventually Masefield
voiced his thoughts.

"Was MacGrath asking you to ride to the column?"

"No," said Bannock, preparing his answer. "No, we
only discussed the house."

"Come on, Bannock, you can tell me. MacGrath has
no problem with me. Unlike some of my colleagues, I have
the healthiest respect for De Beers. Really, they have no
problem with me."

"You think not? You may like them, but I'm not sure
they like you. Once they picked up that I was riding for the
army, they stopped using my services. They know everything that's going on. They even know about the fiasco of
the two guns."

"That hardly surprises me, but I would be surprised to
discover that they had any finer feelings about who you
worked for."

"Now you're being a little too innocent for belief. They
don't want their messages read, do they?"

"In other words, if you were riding for them, you
couldn't admit it to me?"

"Come on, Masefield, you're not a lawyer trying to trip me up in court, and if you were, you'd trip yourself up with that kind of question. Can't you understand that I either say what I mean or I say nothing?"

Bannock kept Lady Potter back to the slow pace of Masefield's mount as they approached the darkened main street into Kenilworth.

"All right, I'll tell you what he asked," Bannock conceded. "Like you, he thinks the relief column will be here in a few days. There are a bunch of newspaper correspondents with the column, and he wants them here when the relief arrives, if not sooner."

"You mean he wants them to arrive at the Sanatorium first, rather than army headquarters. When are you to go on this ride?"

"He didn't say and I haven't agreed."

"It would seem you have no choice. A house for a ride."

"It's not quite like that. MacGrath is not a blackmailer like you. It's up to me. And in any case, they have other people who could do this kind of thing."

Bannock led the way down a side road between the hedges. They could hear noises from one of the houses ahead and the faint glow of a lamp showed through a flyscreen.

"You've always had me blackmailed, haven't you Masefield? And you had to use trickery. I never needed you before, but now I need you." He thought about it. "Why should I have to need you?"

"Make up your mind, old chap."

"All right, I know why I need you. You can get to Emma easily. If there are any problems, if anyone tries to attack her, you can help. I frankly don't think much of you as an ally, because you always have some trick up your sleeve. That's why you were asking me about MacGrath wasn't it? Now that you know about the reporters, you're going to get me or someone else to nobble them for you."

"The thought never crossed my mind." Masefield sounded innocent enough.

Bannock rode ahead through a gate into a small front driveway, where the Watson gelding was tethered beside the mule and an outspanned Cape cart. They dismounted and tied their horses in front of the gloomy facade of a typical colonial bungalow, with a sloping tin roof and wide screened-in verandah that extended around three sides.

O'Flaherty was waiting for them as they went in.

"And where's the little lady?" he asked.

"She's not coming," snapped Bannock. "Major Masefield is hungry and so am I, so let's get on with it."

O'Flaherty made a great show of snapping to attention and marching in front of them as they trooped through to the dining room, where candles lit the white tablecloth.

"It's all ready," O'Flaherty announced, "and you'll naturally be wantin' a small drink to start off with."

"I can see you've already started," remarked Bannock, who could recognize every subtle stage of intoxication in O'Flaherty.

O'Flaherty struck a sober and dignified pose. "Mario had to have somethin' to keep him goin'. It's a fine meal he's preparin'." He brandished a bottle of brandy over some glasses at a side table.

Masefield inhaled a smell of cooking the quality of which he had not experienced since his arrival in Kimberley. He saw the box the brandy had come out of, with other bottle tops showing, and was immediately suspicious.

"Where did you get all this stuff?"

Bannock reacted aggressively. "Now listen, Masefield, we did all this for Emma and we also did it for you because of the way you've helped. I took it for granted you would appreciate a good meal, no matter where it came from. We've got the best chef in Kimberley."

"One of the finest in the world," O'Flaherty interrupted.

Bannock went right on. "So before you ask where thi stuff comes from, you'd better decide whether you're goin; to ask before you partake or after."

"What an interesting proposition," said Masefield "You mean that if I am to sin, it must be an honest-to goodness sin. Very well, but before I decide, I must know the extent of it. How much of this largesse have you sto len?"

O'Flaherty stopped in the act of pouring the drinks. He was outraged. "Sure, it's not stealin' at all," he exploded "Mario is the head chef, is he not? And the Sanatorium ha: all these things lyin' in great stores. Mario was quit shocked when he discovered it. They've got boxes of foo and drink there you could never count. And now they'r goin' to take it all down the mine, can you believe that? can see you're not believin' me. They've got more than the know what to do with."

They were interrupted by Mabala, who appeared from the kitchen self-conscious in a white coat a few sizes to small for him, a napkin over his arm, and bearing a tray with a large flat pastry concoction on it.

"What on earth is that?" Masefield asked enthusiasti- cally.

"Pâté en croute." The deep, resonant voice of Pacell rang out as his huge bulk loomed in the doorway and hi doleful eyes fixed on Masefield.

Mabala took a bowl of salad from the chef and placed it on the table beside the tray.

"This is Mario Pacelli." Bannock made the introduc- tion. "Head chef of the Sanatorium. He's on sick leave tonight."

"Delighted to meet you," said Masefield, still eyeing the pastry roll. "Pâté en croute, you said?"

Bannock struggled to look serious. "The major is try- ing to decide whether or not this meal is going to take place."

Masefield went to the table and leaned down to inspect

the salad and smell the pâté. He absently took the glass of brandy handed him by O'Flaherty and put it to his nose, sniffing appreciatively.

"You realize," he said, "that corruption is one of the realities of life. It is a condition only normally allowable to politicians and others in positions of high responsibility and trust. In other words, what other people don't know is not going to lose them any sleep."

Bannock broke in. "There you are, you've justified the whole thing."

Masefield continued, oblivious. "Just as the criteria for whether I sleep well tonight will be judged by the quality of the food and whether the Sanatorium discovers that these goods are missing."

"Never for a minute," reassured O'Flaherty.

Pacelli went over and began to carve and pass the pâté, while Masefield settled himself at the head of the table. He sipped the brandy and looked at the glass.

"Did you steal any wine?" he asked.

"Who'sa steal?" demanded Pacelli.

"He doesn't mean that, Mario." O'Flaherty smiled ingratiatingly at Pacelli and glared at Masefield. "He's just jokin'."

Bannock and O'Flaherty sat down while Pacelli fussed back to the kitchen, grabbing the napkin from Mabala's hand and firmly replacing it on his arm on the way out. Mabala shrugged good-naturedly and followed him.

Masefield cut a piece of pâté and held it up for inspection. He popped it in his mouth and chewed thoughtfully. "This is exquisite," he pronounced. "What's in it, do you know?"

"Eat your food and give thanks," said Bannock.

Masefield had no argument with that. He tucked into the pâté, relishing each mouthful, cutting the pastry in careful strips, laying them just as carefully on an equal part of pâté, and chewing with a quality of enjoyment that bordered on reverence.

"Well, bless the saints, me glass appears to be empty." O'Flaherty was up to fetch the bottle.

"Now that you mention that, my plate appears to be empty," said Masefield, with an expression of hopeful anticipation.

Bannock pushed the tray over to him. "Help yourself. But take it slowly, there's more to come."

Masefield cut a slice and put it on his plate. He took a sip of brandy and watched first Bannock and then O'Flaherty empty their glasses at a gulp. He waited for the brandy to be poured again and allowed his own glass to be topped up.

"May I propose a toast," he said. "Here's to the luckiest man I've ever met. Yes, my dear chap." He nodded at Bannock. "For a racing man, you have incredible luck."

"I know what you're going to say," said Bannock. "I keep surviving, and that's no thanks to you."

"Oh, no, it's not just that." Masefield paused, chewing at his pâté. "It's the way everything happens for you. Look at this food. It's a feast in a famine. And look at Emma." A look of anticipation gleamed in his eyes from the sound of sizzling and the smell of good cooking that permeated in from the kitchen.

Pacelli's rich baritone echoed through, demanding O'Flaherty's presence, and the Irishman, who was watching Bannock, waiting for him to strike back, went reluctantly, taking his glass of brandy with him.

Bannock brooded over his drink, expecting Masefield to go on about Emma. But the other merely sipped his brandy and smiled, leaving the subject in the air.

Bannock broke the silence. "I wonder what's going on in your cunning mind. You're after Emma, aren't you? Do you think I haven't noticed how you're organizing things? You've seen her today, you've arranged to see her tomorrow. All you have to do is arrange for me to go out through the lines again and get me killed."

"Perish the thought, my dear chap."

"You've tried a few times already, haven't you? You work it all out at your desk, how to use people like me. And in that sense, if I did not exist, you would not exist."

"You are alluding to my fat arse again."

"No, I am alluding to your fat mind and the way you are able to rely on your own lousy judgment."

"We've had all this before." Masefield sighed and chewed.

"You can only do it by virtue of your position. You have the advantage, haven't you?"

Masefield held up his glass in a mock toast. "All right, Gunga Din, you're a better man than I am, and I'll say that even though you're still alive."

"As I said, in spite of you. And I know you; you're going to end up by being a fat general, but you'll never get Emma."

Masefield raised his fork for attention. "Permit me to explain. Let me give you an analogy your racing mentality might comprehend. You understand about winners and losers. What you don't understand is that by suppressing the usual illusions of success and glory and romance, one can contrive to be a winner."

"That's you," Bannock agreed. "You are a game player."

"Oh, what a silly idea. I am above that. Unless you mean I am careful and calculating; then I will agree. No, Bannock, I am a winner. If I ever lose it will be by an act of God and in spite of much careful calculation. That is why I am not angling to be a general. I might lose that bet. I just don't bet. And about Emma, who I think is an extraordinary lady: once I established that she was looking for a stallion, I knew I was out of the running."

Bannock gulped at his brandy. "You fat bastard, you were never in the running."

"Be that as it may, I decided that Emma would always be my friend, and since you don't have to tame a stallion to be friendly with it, I could be a friend to both of you.

Come on, let's drink to that." He poised his glass and waited for cooperation.

Bannock brought up his glass with his own toast. "Here's to the man who makes men hop and skip and roll over and die. Here's to the man who is cleverest of them all, a man who fires questions and orders but never guns. Do you know what you are, Masefield?"

"Go on. I'm fascinated."

"You are a mere observer of things."

"I could hope for nothing more. It's only by observation that we learn. You should try it yourself. You would learn all sorts of useful lessons . . ."

"What fucking cheek," Bannock retorted.

"Like the virtue of restraint. But then, I must concede you might have taught me something—to be a little more impulsive, perhaps."

"When were you ever impulsive?"

"Right now," said Masefield. "This food is forbidden, this drink is illicit."

"I'll drink to that," said Bannock, and they tapped their glasses together.

Masefield sniffed the air again and listened to the splattering sound from the kitchen. "There is no point in guessing about that smell. That is beef. This time there is no denying it. I can only pray it is not being overdone."

Bannock was thinking of something else. "What's going to happen to you once the siege is over?"

"That depends on God and Lord Roberts and whether Lieutenant-Colonel Kekewich gets a pat on the arm or a kick up the derriere."

"Kekewich? I've seen him riding around. What's his problem?"

"In a word, Rhodes. It's a case of one man trying to be in charge of a town that belongs to another man. I'm sorry for Kekewich. He is truly the right man in the wrong place. A sound commander, boring but reliable. He lacks both the humor and the cunning to deal with a man like

Rhodes, who is just as boring but far more powerful. I fear he will pay with his career."

"I don't understand. If he's done a good job—"

Masefield interrupted. "Politics outweighs rank, old boy. And when the self-interest of the politician comes up against the duties of a British officer, you have an impossible situation. Just as the former may be vindictive to the point of destruction, the latter must resist interference to the death. You see, principles of profit are as intractable as those of honor."

"No, I don't see that at all. Why should Rhodes make difficulties for the very people who are defending him?"

"Because his empire has stopped building. Because his diamond mines are lying idle. Come now, Bannock, why do you imagine Rhodes needs his own runners and riders, which the garrison ostensibly knows nothing about? Why do you think you are asked to bring the journalists to the Sanatorium first?"

Bannock was taking it all in. He was intrigued and he was thinking. "What about Charlie Watson? He was riding for Rhodes and he was also dealing with the Boers."

Masefield raised his eyebrows at his glass. "I shall not comment on that, but you are quick. I should not even be commenting on my commanding officer. But if I am all the names you call me, I am still some kind of soldier. Understand, I would follow Kekewich to hell before I took a penny profit from a civilian. You needn't smile at me."

"I'm not smiling. I'm sorry for your CO."

"So am I. He has so much against him, when you consider that the civilians and most of the volunteers are in Rhodes' employ. Even the newspaper works for that man. As you say, poor Kekewich. He is an honest man who will never be believed. He is even a great man who will never be great."

Masefield finished his drink and got to his feet. "He must be ruining that beef," he complained. "Will you excuse me." He disappeared through the dark doorway following the scent of cooking and found the kitchen, full of smoke and noise.

Pacelli was shouting, "Not'a brandy, I said'a oil, oil, oil."

"Here's the right bottle, Mario." O'Flaherty handed over the bottle and took a swig from the other. "Ah, there you are, Major. The dinner's almost ready."

But Masefield's attention was riveted over Pacelli's shoulder. He blinked in the acrid smoke and watched a whole fillet of beef blackened and glistening, being carefully turned on the almost red-hot coal stove with flames forcing their way through around the edge of the plates. Pacelli poured a little oil over the beef, which promptly ignited in a tall sheet of flame. He skillfully turned the beef, extinguishing the flame.

"It ee'sa ready," he shouted. "It must'a be eat *immediatamente. Servizio, servizio, presto, presto,* Paddi, the beans, the beans. Mabala, the potatoes, the potatoes." Pacelli neatly rolled the fillet off the top of the stove onto a dish. "Cognac, cognac," he shouted.

O'Flaherty handed over the brandy bottle, and they watched as Pacelli poured a little with a flourish over the meat and reached down to light a taper.

"*E pronto,*" he shouted, lighting up the meat and rushing through to the dining room holding the dish up high.

"Flambé," whispered Masefield. Then, "Haricot verts à la Lyonnaise," as O'Flaherty went through. Then "Pommes de terre à l'Anglaise," as Mabala passed by. He followed after them into the dining room, where Bannoch was opening another bottle of brandy while Pacelli sharpened his knife on a steel.

"I don't know what all them fancy names mean, but it sure smells good," remarked O'Flaherty.

"It means," said Masefield, his attention glued to the spread, "good old mashed potatoes and green beans from a tin mixed with onions."

They all remained standing, their eyes transfixed by the unique and gleaming joint. Pacelli carved a slice, to reveal the perfect reddened texture of the meat.

"Bravo," breathed Masefield, and the big chef paused to confer a smile on him before getting down to carving the slices quickly and expertly.

"Sit down please, gentlemen," invited Bannock. "Mr. O'Flaherty will pour the wine. It's not red and it's not white, but a robust vintage, I think. Come, sit down, Mabala." Bannock saw the slight hint of surprise on Masefield's face. "Mabala is our guest of honor," Bannock explained. "If it wasn't for him you wouldn't be eating meat tonight. And apart from that, he is my friend." He held his glass up to Mabala. "Here's to you, chief."

Mabala made his own toast. "*Bayete, nkosi,*" he gave the Zulu salute.

Pacelli sat down and the room fell into silence save for the noise of knives and forks busy at plates. They ate the meal slowly, savoring each mouthful until the meat on every plate was finished. The candles flickered, turning a few circling mosquitoes into shadowy monsters on the ceiling. They sipped the brandy while Pacelli carved what was left and passed the dish around.

Masefield emerged from his gastronomic trance. "I would like to give a toast to Signor Pacelli, who has demonstrated once and for all what culinary genius can create in adversity."

Pacelli gave a modest laugh and went on eating while Masefield rambled on.

"I stood there in the kitchen and watched this meat being cooked and, gentlemen, such sensitivity, such panache. Words fail me to describe the flavor that has been captured here. Just look at this meat, the dark surround, the magical red of the center. Enough said, I think." And he returned his attention to his plate.

Another mouthful, another sip of brandy, and he became vocal again. "Do you realize it took a siege to bring

us together? We are a bunch of unrelated strangers, trapped
in one vast fort and brought together by need and by threat.
The threat from without combines with the need within to
create a new smaller world, where friends and enemies are
made, loves and hates are formed. It's an excellent way of
meeting people, don't you think?"

"Sure, I'll drink to that," O'Flaherty called out, beginning to sound more than a little drunk. He picked up the
brandy bottle and leaned forward to focus on the glasses,
then smiled apologetically at Masefield, who was waiting to
go on.

"Our resources are shrinking by the day, but somehow
we will come through. That's what forts are built for. Excuse me one moment." Masefield went back to his food
without realizing that the others, with the exception of
Mabala, who was head down asleep, had finished and were
watching him, hanging on his words.

"Have you ever heard a speech go so slowly?" complained O'Flaherty.

Masefield stopped chewing. "Are you suggesting that
I am slightly inebriated, Mr. O'Flaherty?"

"Not at all, at all. You're lookin' fine." O'Flaherty
struggled to his feet to fetch another bottle. "We've only
just started on this stuff, haven't we?"

Masefield tapped his plate with a knife to keep their
attention. "Of course I'm a little intoxicated; we all are.
And for once, I'm not in the least worried about it. Do you
know, I just can't stop marveling at the way we have come
together." He was looking at Bannock. "When I first met
you, do you remember the time I caught you trying to sneak
out of Kimberley? I didn't like you, Bannock."

"I didn't like you either," said Bannock.

"I thought you were a trouble-making rat."

"I called you a fat shit."

Masefield took another mouthful and chewed thoughtfully. "It's good to get these things off your chest."

O'Flaherty stood up and banged the brandy bottle on

the table until they were all looking at him. "Now it's meself will be givin' a toast to the son of George Bannock, God rest his soul."

Bannock interrupted. "You got it wrong, Paddy. I'm still alive."

"I said George Bannock, God rest his soul."

"You said the son of George Bannock, God rest his soul."

"Well, bugger what it is I said. The great man is dead and you're his son. Have I got that right now?"

"Get on with it, Paddy."

O'Flaherty poured himself some more brandy and held up his glass, swaying slightly and squinting at it.

"Now you've all heard of George Bannock, the greatest non-Catholic trainer of this century. Everybody thought he was a gamblin' man. They only saw the races he won and lost, but it was few who realized that he had the heart of a great sire. Sure, it was the blood that counted with him. It was the horses he loved. He would give anythin' for them horses. Now I'm comin' to the toast, so have the glasses ready. This Bar'tolomew, this boy is his father. He's his father t'ru' and t'ru'."

"Thank you, Paddy," Bannock tried not to laugh. He watched O'Flaherty sway forward until he had to lean on the table to steady himself. "You can sit down now. That was a fine speech, Paddy."

O'Flaherty screwed up his eyes and tried to see him across the table. "It's meself who's makin' this speech, and the speech is not over yet. Havin' dealt with the great man himself, I'll be sayin' a few words about me other friends. Mabala there, who is sleepin' nicely on the table. You must excuse him. He had a late night last night, bringin' in the very beef we've been enjoyin' here. Here's to you Mabala, me boy." He drank the toast and leaned back on the table. "And now I'll be askin' you to raise your glasses once again, o me dear friend Mario Paddykelly."

"Yeh, yeh," said Bannock.

"Absolutely," added Masefield.

Mabala lifted his head from his arms, blinked, and went to sleep again.

O'Flaherty staggered back and held out his glass toward Pacelli. "It's not just a great chef that he is, he is a jewel of a man." He leaned across and nudged Pacelli's big arm. "Hey, did you get it, Mario? Jewel, glitterin' jewel."

"Ha, ha." Pacelli caught on. "You mean'a diamond?"

"Shhh." O'Flaherty almost fell over when he had to use the hand he was leaning on to put a finger to his lips.

Masefield was puzzled. "What's that about diamonds?"

"Nothin' at all. Sure, it's just an expression." O'Flaherty tried to look innocent.

"What's a diamonds? What he talk'a diamonds?" Pacelli also tried. "Come on, Paddi, we must make'a dessert." Pacelli heaved himself to his feet and grabbed the swaying Irishman, dragging him toward the kitchen.

O'Flaherty weaved over to the left, pulling free from Pacelli's grip. He was still holding his glass and, for a drunk man, took an agile downward swing at the box sweeping up another bottle of brandy before he followed his friend out. The last thing they heard, as they both stumbled into the dark passage, was Masefield asking again, "What was that about diamonds?" and Bannock's accompanying laughter.

Pacelli went straight into the kitchen and set to work on the next course, kicking open a damper on the stove and pulling a pan and a bowl of previously prepared mixture onto the top.

O'Flaherty leaned against the door with a benign but glassy-eyed expression. "Did you hear Bart laughin', the bastard?" he slurred. "You know what he thinks, don' you? It's a couple of fools he sees us as. Thinks we only talk about the diamonds."

"Si, si." Pacelli was busy. The ladle moved swiftly, expertly throwing batter into the splattering pan.

O'Flaherty took a swig out of the bottle. His eyes became animated for a moment as a pancake flipped and landed on target in the pan.

"He'd be gettin' quite a surprise if he knew about the mine being used as a shelter for the women and children."

The batter was poured, the mixture hissed, and the next pancake flipped. "I think it ee'sa too much risk, Paddi. If you come down'a the mine with me, they catch you."

"Never in your life, Mario. You just get me one of them chef's hats and I'll walk along with you and your fellers and they'll never be tellin' the difference. We'll all go down the mine together, and while you're lookin' after the food, sure, I'll be chippin' away at them rocks."

Pacelli poured the next ladle of batter, shaking his head doubtfully. "Paddi, I'ma not sure. I think'a they catch you. The manager he says we must'a take all the food down, then all the people are coming down to hide away from'a the bombs." He flipped the pancake.

"Well, there you have it, Mario. The people go down, and sure as heaven is above, they'll be comin' up again, and when they do the son of O'Flaherty will be right there among them, this time without the white hat and, God willin', with a few small diamonds to share out."

"I'ma not sure, Paddi." Pacelli flipped the next pancake, still looking doubtful.

"Think of it, Mario." O'Flaherty's slurring voice took on a dreamy note. "Remember what you were tellin' me? That little restaurant in Rome with the great food. If we found some diamonds, you could be havin' that. And I could be havin' a few fine horses of me own workin' in the string."

"Paddi, everybody is'a tell you it'sa no good. What'sa the matter with you?"

"Now you listen to me, Mario. Where there's a diamond mine, there are diamonds. You say they're not, but if they are there, it's a good gamble." This was O'Flaherty the dreamer speaking, O'Flaherty the obstinate. "It may not be the odds-on favorite, but a good long shot, to be sure."

Pacelli was too busy to argue, kicking open the oven door and depositing the last pancake onto a dish containing the others. "Hold'a this pan," he ordered, and O'Flaherty lurched forward to help.

From a small bowl, the chef poured a new mixture into the pan. He took the brandy bottle from O'Flaherty and poured some of it into the mixture.

"This stuff smells good enough for the angels." O'Flaherty sniffed at the pan while Pacelli brought up the dish of pancakes onto the stove. Taking the pan, he poured the thick mixture on each layer, then doused brandy over the top of them.

"*E pronto, presto.*" He lit a taper and the dish sprang into blue, flickering light.

O'Flaherty watched, mesmerized, as the flaming dish passed by and out of the kitchen. He turned to follow but instinct sent his arm back for the brandy bottle. Then he lurched into the passage and swayed about in the dark, one hand out to feel the way and the other clasping the bottle protectively to his chest.

Sounds of enthusiasm came from the dining room, the voices of Bannock and Masefield praising the flaming dessert. Pacelli's voice announced, "Crêpes Marianna."

O'Flaherty aimed for the light from the doorway at the end of the passage, but he walked sideways rather than forward and ended up chuckling to himself and leaning against the wall. In his happy delirium, he heard another noise, a whining sound that grew steadily in volume. It was a familiar sound, but it had no right happening at night and in this quiet spot.

The whine grew still louder, fluctuating between waves of whining and buzzing, and soon the screaming reality dawned and O'Flaherty's presence of mind returned in an instant and he threw himself to the floor. The explosion shook the house from the foundations to the roof. Pots and crockery clattered in the kitchen. There was an anguished bellow from Pacelli in the dining room.

O'Flaherty got up, dusted himself off, and went through, to find Bannock and Masefield helping themselves to the pancakes while Mabala helped the quivering chef out from under the table.

Pacelli waved his arms around and shouted, "What you say, bleddy shit? You say not'a bomb. You say no bomb here. What'sa this, hey? Can'a you tell me?"

"Easy, Mario," soothed O'Flaherty. "You can ask these gentlemen—"

"What they say? Bleddy hell, I get'a killed."

"Calm down, chef." Masefield chewed and swallowed. "They never bomb this area. It must have been a mistake." He held a piece of pancake on his fork. "These crêpes are quite incredible."

But there was no mistaking the whining sound that started up again and grew quickly in volume.

Pacelli groaned and went to earth again under the table, and O'Flaherty might have joined him but for the challenge of Bannock and Masefield calmly eating their dessert. As it was, the explosion was farther away, causing comparatively less of a shock. The plates on the table hardly moved, and Bannock took another pancake from the dish.

Outside, the animals were giving voice to their fear, neighing and blowing noisily.

Pacelli gave voice to his as he climbed out from under the table. "*Mama mia,* I'ma leaving, I'ma leaving. This bomb ee'sa going to kill me." He grabbed O'Flaherty's arm. "It'sa going to kill me, Paddi, I know it."

"Now you're not to worry, Mario," O'Flaherty comforted. "I'll be gettin' you out of here in no time."

Bannock gave orders without taking his attention from his food. "Get the cart ready, Mabala, and drive Mr. Pacelli to the Sanatorium."

"*Yebo, nkosi.*" Mabala was already on his way out as he answered.

"You lead the way for them, Paddy, and I'll see yo
back at the stables. Thank you, Mr. Pacelli," he called
O'Flaherty led his unhappy friend out by the arm.

"*Si,*" answered Pacelli without a backward glanc
looking up nervously at the soft, sinister beginning of th
next whine.

Bannock turned his attention to Masefield, who wa
cutting his second pancake and chewing rather too sel
consciously to be calm. "Aren't you going to make a bo
for it?" His tone was mocking, and the question became
challenge.

Masefield looked at him haughtily, still chewing as th
buzzing rose to a screaming pitch. There was a glisten
perspiration on his forehead, yet his eyes were steady ar
unblinking. The challenge was met. "These crêpes are to
delicious to leave, wouldn't you say?" His teeth locked f
only a moment, when the shell exploded nearby and th
table shook visibly in front of them.

They heard the cart rumble out into the road, ar
Bannock passed the dish, offering the last of the pancake

"Quite delicious," repeated Masefield, helping himse
"I think you should go easy on that brandy, old boy.
gather you won't be spending the night here and you'll ha
to find your way back in the dark."

Bannock didn't have to be told, he knew he was drun
They were both drunk. He also knew that Masefield wou
never tire of tilting at his slightest weakness.

"I'm impressed with you, old boy," he mimicke
Masefield. "I didn't know you could be brave."

"There comes a time." Masefield poured himself a
other brandy, looked dubiously at Bannock's almost emp
glass, and started again. "I could only be brave if I w
forced to be. It is not a condition I believe in, and unli
you, I think that all situations that evoke the instinct shou
be avoided."

"You're talking your usual clever shit." Banno

reached for the brandy. "There is an essential difference between you and me. I'm the one who does it because I have to; you do it for reasons of honor."

"Oh, I don't know." Masefield was off on one of his lectures. "Honor is only something we would like. It is a position you get yourself into. It is a shining medal. It's not for the asking, and it's nothing much if it's not recognized."

Bannock was listening for a whine in the distance that never came. "There seems to be a blockage in the Long Tom."

Masefield stayed with his thoughts, staring at the candle, which was almost burnt out. "I may not have gone into battle, but I've seen them go."

"And not come back," prompted Bannock.

"Yes, that is where I shall never be a true soldier. You see, I cannot abide waste of any sort, much less a waste of life. And honor requires that the best men lead the way. It is so awful to think that it is the intelligent ones who die first. Has it occurred to you that they are too intelligent to simply wish to die?"

"You mean that's the price of honor?"

"No, it is the price of pride. I mean the real motivation is fear."

"Your mind is wandering." Bannock tried to shake himself out of his drunken stupor. "What utter nonsense you're talking."

But Masefield was far away, introspective, dejected. "I have come to believe that in the final moments of confrontation, bravery is an aberration. It is a quality of fright, a nervous reaction to fear that makes one lunge out for survival when invariably it is too late."

"What shit." Bannock stared into his glass. "The trouble with you is you never tried it."

"Colonel Scott-Turner did. Major Stevenson did."

"Wait a minute." Bannock swung round suspiciously. "What is this? Why are you bringing up Stevenson?"

"He was brave."

"That's right." Bannock came wide awake. "I neve doubted he was brave—damned brave."

"I think you know he had his problems."

Bannock's temper was showing. "That has nothin to do with me," he warned. "Just what are you sugges ing?"

"You should know. You were faced with it head on.

"We had an argument, that's all."

"You saw the twitch."

"The man is dead."

"The wife is alive, so the man is not altogether dead.

Bannock was astounded. "Damn you," he said slowl and ignored the distant beginnings of another whine. "Yo are degrading Emma."

The whine grew louder, echoing and changing to reverberating buzz.

"What nonsense," said Masefield, who was sweatir freely, this time struggling to control his nervousness.

Bannock shouted over the screaming of the missi "You are degrading both of us."

The shell exploded somewhere farther south, ar Masefield breathed out with relief. But Bannock was st staring at him, demanding an answer.

"You are degraded by your circumstances, my de chap. By your problems and your weaknesses."

"My weaknesses?" Bannock got control of his feeling "I'm beginning to sort you out in my mind, Masefield.'

"Your worst problem is the one, or should I say tw of divided loyalties. A lady called Emma and a horse call Marcus. A lady you won't give up for anything, and a hor you won't give up for anything. And if retrieving the latt is a matter of principle, it's one you may well have to gi your life for. You're going to chase after that horse, are y not?"

"You're drunk, Masefield."

"And you'll never find your stallion again."

"He's at Carter's Ridge, waiting for me."

Masefield grinned triumphantly. "There you are. Didn't I say you'd be going after him?"

"You're drunk and you're scared. Why don't you go home to your bomb shelter?"

Masefield was staring as if he had difficulty in focusing. "You're weaker than you think, Bannock."

"I'm beginning to understand you at last. I think fat shit was the right name for you."

"You're in the middle. You're caught by the balls, my friend."

"Now you listen to me." Bannock waved a hand in the air. Masefield, misunderstanding the gesture, ducked his head, causing his elbow to slip off the table. Realizing his mistake, he pulled himself up straight and sulkily replaced the elbow.

Bannock kept a finger poised to shut him up. "I've been listening to you and all your clever talk, but when you listen to it, when you really listen to it, it's not as plausible and as clever as it sounds. Do you know what you've been saying?"

"For heaven's sake." Masefield looked away long-sufferingly.

"I'll tell you what you've been saying. Firstly, that you're not brave."

"Yes, yes, very well."

"That you despise honor."

"That is not quite what I said."

"It's near enough. You sneer at pride. You never take bets, which means you never take a risk, which means you're wrong about being a winner. You've got to take risks to win the best prizes. You're a fake, Masefield. You're just a big, fat cynic."

"I prefer realist."

"That's right, a big, fat, cowardly realist. Your only vital organ is your mouth."

"You're being extremely insulting."

"And so are you. You are suggesting I would trade one principle for another. If you think I would value a horse above Emma, you are mad. You know nothing about me and you know nothing about Emma." He suddenly stood up, almost knocking over his chair, staggering around and leaning on the back of it. "I must be mad letting them keep me away from Emma. I'm going to see her now, do you hear?" he shouted. "Now."

Masefield shook his head contemptuously. "That won't do, my dear chap. It will be midnight by the time you get there. You're very drunk, and you would regret it. Don't be foolhardy."

Bannock flung the chair against the wall and stood up straight, swaying unsteadily on his feet. "You've got to be brave to be foolhardy. You just taught me that, and I'm feeling bloody brave and bloody foolhardy. I'm going to see Emma now, and bugger the lot of them."

Emma was fumbling with the door of the living room, trying to keep the candle straight in her free hand, when Mark appeared in the passage. He was as surprised to come upon her wandering around in her dressing gown as she was to see him in his uniform.

"I thought it was your night for sleeping?" she asked as he helped her with the door.

"It is obviously not yours," he countered, and they went in.

Inside, he took the candle from her and set it down on the table.

"Come and sit down, Emma. I want to have a word with you. It's been impossible to get you alone these last few days."

"Why are you dressed for action?" She allowed herself to be led to the window seat.

"It's the rules, my dear sister. When the Boers fire a

night our nights off are cancelled." He sat down on the window seat beside her.

"But the shelling stopped ages ago."

"I know, but from the sound of it, they were shelling the defenses for a change, and I just feel I ought to appear in case I'm needed."

They looked out at the ominous sky. The moon showed ghostly patches of smoke rising in the distance toward the north.

"They seemed to be aiming at the inner perimeter, near Kenilworth. It's rather hard to tell," he said, staring out into the dark.

"What was it you wanted to talk about?" asked Emma.

He turned to face the open, trusting eyes. "Shall I give you a guess?"

"Why not? How about the bad sister who is about to disgrace the family?"

Mark sighed. "I think you know I could swallow almost anything that made you happy, and you also know that I would speak out if I disagreed with your behavior. But for once, I am at a loss to understand you, or at least understand you to the point where I would give judgment. I know you, Emma, and I know you have never ever rushed into anything."

"You think I am rushing now?" She watched his serious profile, silhouetted in the candlelight.

"No. I think you have made a decision you believe in, and nothing is going to stop you, is it?"

"No, Mark." She shook her head, but he was staring at the candle.

"You understand, it is Mother I am worried about. We all assume she is the real strength of the family, but the castle starts crumbling when a wall is breached."

"I am not so indispensable."

"You are the only person who can handle her. She will not take it from me, and she will not listen to Sarah."

"It's not quite that, Mark." She knew what she had to say, but how to say it? To explain her position was to attack her mother, and to do that might alienate Mark. She had to say it.

"I am simply the focus of Mamma's attention at present. She is intent on squashing my rebellion and, sadly, she thinks she'll succeed. That is the problem as it stands, and I'm afraid the time has almost come to resolve it. Is it true this time that relief is imminent?"

"It seems to be. The news has come direct from Rhodes. He informed the town yesterday that Roberts is making his final push on the thirteenth." He turned an incriminating look on her. "But you are digressing. We are talking about Mother."

It was Emma's turn to sigh. "What can I possibly say? If to defy Mamma implies disaster, then there is to be disaster. You think me heartless? You must see my point of view. I feel exploited, because the prejudices at work here are hardly surprising ones. Mamma's definition of how to behave in terms of Geoffrey's dead image is as known as her definition of what kind of man would be appropriate for me to marry."

"I never thought you would be the one to rebel," said Mark gently. "You were always so sensible. But I wonder whether you can be emotionally involved and sensible at the same time."

"I am not pretending to be surprised by these things or even tortured about them, but they force a decision on me."

"Emma, you make me wonder." He paused. "I have always seen myself as logical and independent of mind, but you have only made me realize how subject I am to the very values you are having to break from."

"Do you think I enjoy that? Do you think I relish being seen as a destroyer of convention? If it was possible to conform to all the indoctrination of my youth, I would rather conform." She felt grateful that there was still no real argument between them. She took his hand and patted and held it. "Let me explain something to you that is so clear to me. It is no longer a matter of diverging loyalties. It is now one loyalty, not to my mind or my body or my instincts, but to someone else's. That is what my instincts say. Love works in reverse. It reflects back to you from what you give, and once it is love, you give everything."

Mark let go of her hand, got up, and walked restlessly in a circle around the table until he was facing her again. There was a hint of amusement.

"You must not assume that I'm ignorant of the ways of love or of the strange ways of lovers. They are such helpless victims, not so much of their partners in love as of something in themselves. It's a hopeless condition, is it not? You see, we are all able to recognize that."

"Are we, Mark? I've only just discovered it."

"You are going to go off with him, I take it?"

"Yes."

He was serious again. "Can I ask you to wait until the relief is confirmed? If you walk out now, you will leave me with a problem I cannot cope with. It's not just that I can't deal with Mother; I'm in the Town Guard, and my time is not my own. If you leave, she will go to pieces."

Emma recognized the predictable line of persuasion, the family duty. "She will appear to have gone to pieces," she argued. "And if I wait, Mark, how is relief going to solve the problem?"

"By geography, my dear girl. We can all go our own way."

"What will you do?"

"I've given that a lot of thought. Everything seems to be against my plans here. It's not just that Geoffrey was killed, it's the war. I mean, it isn't what they thought it would be. This is going to be a long, sad war, a stupid, mindless slugging match that won't easily be resolved, and even when it's finished, it won't be resolved."

"Why do you say that?" Emma watched him pacing round slowly on his circular course.

"Oh, it's quite ironic. I was always a misfit in the family, was I not? The first non-military Freestone-Grant in three generations, and here I am in a uniform, be it ever so humble. A private volunteer by day and hobnobbing with the senior staff at the Club in the evenings. I don't know which is the greater education. But I'll tell you this Emma: I've learned a lot." He stopped his pacing. "Am I boring you?"

"Please don't stop." Emma was listening, fascinated. The reticent brother was emerging with a passion she had never seen in him before.

He began to pace again. "I learned something about war. It may be naive to talk of the futility of war, but war is not for me. Do you know what I've learned from the volunteers, from sitting out there on the defenses doing nothing? Well, nothing describes the whole situation. We are trapped in here doing nothing, the Boers are waiting in a great circle of ennui, and the might of the British army is camped on their backsides at the Modder. We are all waiting for the next battle and the next lugubrious, trundling juxtaposition of armies. It's like a painfully slow game of chess, but chess was never as boring as this. And what is it all for? I mean, on our side, what is it all for? Is it for the gold and the diamonds? Does it come down to mere business? Because if that is the reason, I would rather trade in the market I know, in the familiar fog of London, where there is no cause for which one's partner need die. Forgive me, Emma. I'm sorry to mention Geoffrey."

"You don't need to apologize. You were his friend. I was his wife in every sense but passion. There is no ghost for me, no haunting."

"And no recriminations, I trust?"

"None at all." Emma felt enormous relief. In just a few words she had explained to Mark something she'd wondered whether he was sensitive enough to have guessed while Geoffrey was still alive.

"So you'll go back home?" she asked.

"I'll take Mother back to Birchleigh and myself off to London to pick up the threads. As for Sarah . . ."

"She will marry Pendleton."

"No doubt." He stopped on his rounds and tried to see her expression. "Do you think me cowardly?"

Emma was more aware than she had ever been of the great affection she felt for her brother. She had not expected such tolerance. She wondered whether she had ever really understood him, whether perhaps behind that gentle manner there was a source of strength that could transcend all of them.

"You are the best man this family has ever produced. You are the first to have questioned all our simple values."

He was standing near the candle, and she could see that he was smiling. He teased, "You only want to see me as a rebel like yourself."

Emma laughed. There was rapport with at least one member of the family, and she was grateful.

He came to the window seat and sat down beside her. He was on the point of speaking when a noise came up from the courtyard below. Someone was shouting, bellowing out one word again and again.

Emma and Mark looked at one another in a moment of astonished recognition.

"Emma!" The shout rang out and echoed around the courtyard.

Mark snapped open the window and they both knelt on the window seat, leaning out and looking down. There was the shadowy form of a tall man down there. Emma recognized the leather jacket, top boots, and long legs, braced apart in that arrogant stance typical of Bannock.

"It's Bart," she said. "I must go and change."

But Mark stopped her. "Was this arranged?" he asked suspiciously.

"No," said Emma in a fuss. "I'm sorry, Mark, I must go down and see him."

Her brother looked down again with a puzzled expression. "I do believe the fellow is drunk."

The shout came again: "Emma."

"My God," said Mark. "I must put a stop to this."

They rushed from the room, Emma to change, Mark to deal with the emergency below.

He hurried down the stairs, feeling his way in the dark, almost tripping more than once. In the dimly lit hallway, the night porter looked relieved to see him, following him nervously to the door that led out to the courtyard.

Bannock saw him coming and stood his ground, swaying slightly on his heels. He may have been drunk, but his appearance was formidable as he glared down at Mark, a head shorter than him.

"Where is Emma?" he demanded.

Mark bravely went right up to him.

"I say, Bannock, do you realize what time it is?"

"I don't care about the time. I came to speak to Emma."

"By now I am quite aware of that." He tried to reason. "Shall we go over there into the street?"

"No you don't." Bannock shook his head and waved a hand around furiously. "I'm going to see Emma if I have to break this whole bloody building apart."

"Heaven preserve us," whispered Mark. "Look here, Bannock." He kept his voice low. "My mother is not at all well. If she wakes up, it's going to be devilish awkward. You don't know my mother."

Bannock swayed toward him and whispered back. "I didn't come here to see your mother. Are you going to call Emma, or do I start shouting again?"

But at that moment he saw her, the blond hair dancing as she ran, the small hands clasping a cape around her. Bannock could take only one step before she was there in his arms and he lifted her up to his height, swinging her around in a clumsy dance.

"That blasted porter wouldn't tell me where to find you."

"It's all right, Bart, it's all right," she soothed as he let her down.

"I found you a house. I thought it was safe, but the bombs started falling so I got drunk, and I couldn't spend another night without seeing you."

Mark cleared his throat self-consciously. "I have to be off to the perimeter," he said.

They watched him as he walked away. Then he hesitated, turning back. "I say, you two, I trust you will behave sensibly," he blustered. "I mean, try to keep out of trouble." He began walking away backward. "Oh, hell, where is all of this leading?" he muttered as he disappeared into the dark.

Bannock whispered down into Emma's ear, "I know where it's leading."

"So do I. I told you we are more together than you think."

"Come with me," he urged. "I can't spend another night without you."

"I feel the same way." Emma feared her dilemma, dreaded to speak of it. "Will you let me explain?" She shivered and clung to him.

"Your mother?" Bannock prompted.

"My mother and my brother. He knows I won't give you up, but he wants me to wait until relief arrives. He maintains he cannot cope on his own."

"You had to give him your word?"

"No, I promised nothing. I can see his point of view, but I feel I am being coerced, if not used. I am even sorry for my mother. It's a duty I have no heart for." She made her decision. "Tell me to come with you, Bart. Demand it, and I'll simply come."

"I can't do that. I can't afford to take one wrong step with you. We have waited this long."

"One or two more days. If relief takes longer than that, I'll come whether you ask or not."

Bannock swayed and stumbled. "I'm not quite sober," he said shamefacedly.

Emma tried not to laugh as she reached up to her unsteady lover, pulling him gently toward the garden seat in the middle of the courtyard.

They sat down, and he groped clumsily for her.

"What have you got on under this blanket?" He reached inside her cloak. "What are you hiding from me?" He felt through the material to her body, her breasts, her thighs.

She jumped. "You're tickling me," she whispered hoarsely. "And we have an audience."

They looked up at the building, where a head disappeared at one window and a curtain fell closed at another. Emma was glad that both Sarah and her mother's rooms faced in the opposite direction.

"Forget about that." Bannock stared down into the eyes that had started up a passion in him he was incapable of understanding. "I can't tell you what I felt about that house. It was going to be a proper place for you. And when the bombs arrived, it was like the worst failure of all."

"I would live with you in a tent."

But Bannock was still harping on his disappointment. "It drove me a little insane. I kept on drinking, without thinking of what I was doing. I kept thinking of how much I wanted to be with you. Can I really deserve someone like you, Emma?"

Emma leaned into his chest to hide her amusement. "Bart?" she interrupted.

"Yes?"

"It really is about time you made me a proposal."

"I thought I'd been doing that all along."

"Not in so many words."

"I'd give my soul and my life for you," he said softly. "I haven't got much else. Is that a proposal?"

"It's not the classical one," she said into his chest, then lifted her head. "Bart, do you wish to marry me?"

"Ask me to marry you. Come on, ask me."

"Very well. Will you marry me?"

"Do you take this man who has nothing to offer but love and good intentions?"

"I do," she said seriously.

He took her shoulders and held her slightly away, to give weight to what he had to say.

"I know what I'm getting, but do you know what you're getting?"

"Yes, I do."

"You're getting a horse trainer who has almost run out of horses."

"That can be made right."

"And with precious little money."

"I have enough for both of us."

Bannock took a slow, inward breath. He shook Emma's shoulders very gently.

"Emma, it's not as simple as that. When I was on my own, it was simple, but now everything is changed. You and I must go back to England, do you agree?"

"Of course, Bart, but I would go anywhere."

"There is a problem. If I go back, I must take Marcus with me." He held up his arms in a gesture of exasperation. "Why do I assume you know about these things? You know nothing about me."

"I'll take you as you are."

"Marcus." He came back to it. "I must tell you about Marcus. You see, I took him illegally when I left. I traded my inheritance for a horse. You're going to learn what an idiot I am."

"I'll take you as you are," she repeated softly.

"I must try to get Marcus back—buy him from the Boers, if necessary."

"How could that possibly be done?"

"If and when the Boers retreat, I could ride out after

them, try to talk to them. I can see what you're thinking and you're right. There is not much chance of success. It's the story of me and the siege, such a sad story until I found you."

She caught hold of his hands and held them, waiting for him to speak again.

"I saw myself as waiting for fate to sort me out, to decide how many of my horses would be killed, lost, or taken away from me, and whether I would survive each of those times through the Boer lines. I've ridden scared over the Magersfontein hills with sacking tied to my horse's hooves. I've been pushed down the Kimberley Mine, shot at in the dark, crawled on my face in the mud, but somewhere along the way I became aware of you and I stopped crawling. I knew before I ever touched you that fate was not going to hold me back where you were concerned. You brought me alive, and tonight I realize how alive I need to be."

Again she waited for him to speak. He swung his head about restlessly, coming back to settle on her steady gaze.

"You must understand about that stallion."

"I am committed to understand."

"Masefield put his usual twisted meaning on it. He says I am obsessed with a horse, but he would call love an obsession, and in a way, I do love Marcus. He was all I had before you. It was not just his breeding or that he represented my livelihood; he was the horse my father loved above all others. He was my strength, and when I lost him I felt I'd lost everything." Only the words were emotional. Bannock had suddenly become less drunk, more articulate. "How can I explain to you the beliefs I was brought up on? How could I explain them to Masefield, who sneers at racing and racing men?"

"I would treasure your beliefs."

"If racing is an obsession, it's not just with the game of racing, it's with the breed that created the game, and the game only served to perpetuate the breed."

"I understand, I understand." Emma tried to calm the emotion that was starting up again.

"You only see this so-called sport, that has to exist on bets that are lost."

"I only see you."

"Even my family. If you were to understand them, you would have to understand their involvement in breeding. Do you see, Emma, that's what makes racing worthwhile. Somewhere in history, there was one horse that ran faster than another, then one was fastest of all. Then there was an Arab that could run so fast, it upset the applecart. And the Arab was mated to the fastest, and the progeny became a new kind of animal."

"Like Marcus?"

"Like Marcus." He smiled when he became aware of the anxious eyes looking at him. "I am involved with Marcus. I am obsessed with you," he said.

"I understand all of it, Bart. You should not upset yourself over Major Masefield. He is an expert at trite meanings. Plausible, but somehow too clever."

Bannock nodded. "You are very perceptive."

"But he did help us to see one another."

He folded her up in his arms. "That's the only good thing that fat manipulator ever did."

They were being watched from yet another quarter. Masefield leaned on a pepper tree in the darkened street, his hands in his pockets, the normally emotionless eyes piercingly intent on their every movement. He watched when they stood up; the eyes blinked as their laughter came back to him. He watched them, the tall figure of Bannock with the blonde head leaning against his chest as they walked as one toward the hotel entrance.

O'Flaherty looked around and decided it was going to be easier than he had thought. He had imagined there would be just the small detachment of kitchen staff going

down the mine to accompany the food supplies, but instead
the place was alive with people moving about like gray ant
in the gray light of early dawn. Pacelli was the nervous one
standing apart at the head of his band of assistants as if h
were trying to pretend his friend was not there. In front o
them a gang of workers were busy loading provisions, uten
sils, and furniture into a procession of ore trucks lined u
on tracks that led to the minehead.

O'Flaherty looked up uneasily at the high winding gea
with its thin cables extending down to the cage at groun
level. Not a sight to bring confidence to the heart of anyon
but a miner.

The winding wheels were turning, the cables vibratin
down to where the cage had gone out of sight.

It was going to be easier than he'd thought, but ther
were still problems. The chef's jacket was a good disguise
except for the way the miner's pick underneath stuck ou
at its two extremities. As long as the group stayed togethe
and he could get himself into that cage at the back, it woul
be plain sailing after that.

A man O'Flaherty remembered as one of the organiz
ers of the soup kitchen approached Pacelli.

"Righto, chef, you can bring your chaps along." H
went on talking as they all followed, O'Flaherty bringing u
the rear. "We've got lots of trestle tables down there, an
all the equipment you'll need. Did I tell you, we've decide
to handle all the preparation at the top? It's just the tea urn
down below, and the service, of course. But I think you'
agree that we must have everything down in relays befor
the bombing starts."

"What'a time?" asked Pacelli.

"Well, when do they normally start popping off
About seven, wouldn't you say? Let's aim for six-thirty.

They congregated around the minehead, with O'Fla
herty at the back bending his knees to come into line wit
the average height, leaving Pacelli as the only conspicuousl
tall member of the group.

The winding wheels turned above, creaking on their mounts. The cables vibrated in front of them and the cage came up, appearing empty behind the mesh iron gates.

Pacelli was not happy. He looked like a man going to his doom as the gates clanged open and he was pressed forward, gingerly trying a foot on the floor of the cage before stumbling in, forced by the pressure from behind.

O'Flaherty, with knees still bent, got himself into the middle of the crush of kitchen hands, carefully wriggling his way to the back of the cage, as far as possible from the man who accompanied Pacelli. At first, they all stiffened up nervously for the descent, but nothing happened, and they waited.

After a while, a group of what looked like senior officials gathered at the open gate. O'Flaherty began to worry. They all seemed to be concerned with a gray-suited man who stood in the middle, conversing with him in hushed tones. Finally, one of the men stepped forward to the open gate.

"Will you take your place, sir?"

The gray-suited man entered the cage, looking suspiciously at the occupants.

"Make room there, please," the man at the gate ordered, and the kitchen staff pressed back for the important newcomer.

"Braithwaite, my typewriter?" asked the gray-suited man.

"It's all down there, sir. You'll find everything you require, I assure you."

"Very well," came the resigned reply.

The man outside stepped back to allow an official to close the gate.

O'Flaherty was unnerved. Was this a security man? No, he was altogether too elegant. A big official of some sort?

A bell rang. The cage bobbed slightly. The collective tension was high. Pacelli was white-faced. The man in the gray suit looked apprehensive. For O'Flaherty, it was a time for prayer.

"Hail, Mary, full of grace . . ." he began in a whisper.

The cage rumbled and squeaked against its metal guide rails and disappeared into the depths.

It was not until Bannock reached the outskirts of New ton that he realized the extent of the onslaught, and felt his first misgivings. He hesitated, holding up Lady Potter, letting her turn in restless circles while he tried to see some pattern in the falling bombs. It seemed that every gun on the Boer defenses was pouring in its spite on the town setting up a deafening din in chorus with the feeble effort of the defense batteries firing out. Before there could be relief, there was to be revenge. Kimberley was being punished for holding out.

The sky was a suitable backdrop for the destruction, gray and steel-blue, with rolling clouds that banked up into threatening thunderheads. If the storm would only break, the enemy gunners might take to their shelters for a while. But this kind of storm could break in a moment or hang on for another day, as Bannock well knew. The sulfurous smell that filled the air whenever the Long Tom was firing was more acrid and choking than ever.

Bannock looked for a clear way through, but the fire and swirling smoke from the explosions rose everywhere and shells kept whining in at the buildings.

Emma was somewhere in the middle of it.

He had wasted two days listening to the guns at work, the bass boom of the Long Tom deeper than the incessant thumping from the southern ridges that sometimes took on a primitive drumming rhythm. If Emma was in there, he was going to be in there. If she could only agree to come back with him, he would be able to relax for the first time since he had last seen her.

The waiting had tired him out. It was Masefield who

ad stopped him from going after her the day before. His
ews that Emma was safe and his advice that it was not
imely to go there created only faint suspicion for Bannock.
But the suggestion, once again and true to form, that he ride
ut with dispatches was too close to the deep suspicion that
ept coming back stronger each time. After the usual argu-
ent with Masefield—"It wouldn't be advisable, old boy.
he mother, you know—" he had shrunk from going. But
ven the fear of yesterday, his one fear, of compromising
mma in front of her family, was gone. If her family were
threat, they were a threat to both of them. He could wait
o longer. The bombing was intensifying, there was no sign
f relief, and Emma was in the wrong place.

Bannock's hesitation was over. There was no point in
ooking at it any longer. There was no safe way through.
ust go, fast and furious, and let the odds hang in the air
ke the rising smoke.

He sent the mare off at a gallop, brave and trusting
ady Potter heading straight in among the explosions she
ad come to know, but disliked no less. He knew that once
e entered the street ahead, there would be no point in
irning back. From here on, the gauntlet ran both ways.

Smoke billowed around the mare's head, catching Ban-
ock's nose and throat. The waft of heat passed by from a
urning building on his left as he approached the first turn-
g. Three more streets, three more turns, and he would be
ere. The mare quivered under him at the sound of a blast
om behind, then shied away to the right as the ground
xploded out from the turn-off just ahead. There was the
apping and crackling sound of shrapnel striking up at the
alls and shattering window panes. Bannock gathered up
ady Potter and held her back, giving thanks that he had
ot been crossing that street where the smoke still circled
d a giant dust devil now rose, beginning to dissipate itself
gainst the buildings.

They were moving again through the second turning,
ining over to avoid the shallow crater, picking up to a

gallop again. Lady Potter was worked into a frenzy, the froth flicking off from her neck where the reins pulled taut, and Bannock was pulled through the next turn with little control. She would have carried him past the next turning again but for a burning building where the fire belched out from every window. The hooves went down, skidding and scraping on the hard ground, and the mare swung in a circle of following dust. Debris showered off the top of a building, scattering across the street behind him. There were explosions all around, deafening reports, followed by the ripping spray of shrapnel. Then a deep burst of rumbling from directly above; the sky had opened up with its own crackling artillery in sinister harmony with the exploding shells. Bannock felt the first drop of rain on his face as he struggled with the mare, forcing her past the burning edifice in a wild canter that sometimes carried her sideways and sometimes into a mad, chopping reverse.

He guided her into the final street, restraining her to an excited walk, keeping close in under the buildings that gave shelter from the guns to the south. The storm broke noisily overhead, bringing a flurry of rain that flattened the dust in a sweeping path up the street.

Bannock was relieved to see the hotel intact, except for the wing that had been previously damaged. The rain was coming down heavily by the time he rode into the courtyard, making for the shelter of the big central tree. It had become difficult to tell the thunder from above from that of the guns. The heavy downpour splattered the dry ground into mud and dribbled noisily off the thin foliage.

He dismounted quickly, tethered the mare, and made a dash for the side entrance to the hallway. Inside, he began to shake off his wet head. It occurred to him that he had seen no sign of life from the time he began the ride into town, not even the usual fire-fighters. Everyone had gone to shelter. Even here the hallway was deserted.

On the wall facing him he caught sight of a large notice

nat read: SUNDAY: I RECOMMEND WOMEN AND CHIL-
REN WHO DESIRE COMPLETE SHELTER TO PROCEED TO
IMBERLEY AND DE BEERS SHAFTS. THEY WILL BE LOW-
RED AT ONCE IN THE MINES FROM 8 O'CLOCK THROUGH-
UT THE NIGHT. LAMPS AND GUIDES WILL BE PROVIDED.
. J. RHODES.

Had he wasted his time coming here? Had Emma gone
o take shelter down the mine with her family? He felt
eaten and disappointed. It was logical that most of the
own would have taken advantage of such an opportunity,
nd at least Emma would be safe.

But he had to make sure. He looked around for an
ntrance to a cellar and saw the small, narrow stairway
oing down beside the main staircase that came from above.

The noise of the thunder and rain receded as he went
own, and the soft mutter of voices rose up. There were
male voices, and Bannock allowed himself to hope that
mma's was among them. He descended into a passage of
ndbags that extended up to a ceiling reinforced with
eavy beams. More steps went down in the passage and
ore again went off to the left, where the sandbags spread
vay in a structure that became the walls of a long, narrow
oom. Along the sides of the room, seated or lying asleep
n benches, were members of the hotel staff, and at the far
nd, others, more likely residents, were settled in comforta-
e chairs. Faces turned toward him, then turned away
gain listlessly.

Bannock went into the room stepping over out-
retched legs. He made his way toward the far end where
.e light was dim and individual features difficult to distin-
uish. Then he saw Emma's golden hair. In the same mo-
ent she saw him. She was on her feet immediately and
ey came together calmly, hands out to one another.

"Bart." She touched his soaked leather jacket. "You
e wet through."

He studied her anxiously. "Am I doing wrong?"

Emma was smiling. "I wished you here. I wished f‹ it, do you understand?"

His anxiety became worse. "I came here so dete‹ mined. I wanted you to come away with me."

The smile remained. "You don't have to ask, I'm cor ing with you. We can't be apart any longer."

They were speaking too softly to be heard by the grou at the end of the room, but Sarah had recognized Bannoc She was staring in slack-mouthed disbelief and it was son time before she found her voice.

"How dare you," she yelled. "How dare you con here." But she was confused and uncertain and looked fir to her mother, who sat silent and expressionless beside he then at Colonel Thrumpton, who blinked himself out sleep, contracting his spiky gray eyebrows as he reacted her voice and, at the same time, caught sight of Banno‹ with Emma.

Emma moved forward toward them, defiantly holdi‹ on tightly to Bannock's hand. Her mother ignored her a‹ looked down at her folded hands with no expression, ‹ emotion, no sign of recognition of what was happening.

Before Emma could speak, Sarah attacked again.

"How could you invite him here?" she complaine‹ "What kind of mischief are you up to?"

Emma was not going to be intimidated. "Oh, dry u‹ Sarah," she retorted.

"You are upsetting Mamma." Sarah's high-pitched i‹ troduction to temper began.

Then her mother spoke up. "Be quiet, Sarah," s‹ ordered firmly, and slowly raised her eyes from her han‹ to demand Emma's attention. "Come here, Emma." It w‹ said gently; only her children would have recognized t‹ threat.

Emma let go of Bannock's hand and whispered to hi‹ "You will have to bear with this for a moment." She we‹ forward and knelt down in front of her mother.

Bannock put his hands in his pockets and waited.

The confrontation began. The others remained silent.
"Mamma, I told you about this."

The hawk eyes restrained her. The habit of respect made her wait to be spoken to.

"Kindly ask that man to leave. You are not to make a spectacle of yourself. It is time I spoke to you very seriously."

Emma was not going to be intimidated. She met the relentless bullying eyes calmly.

"You must listen to me, Mamma, because if you don't, there will be no further opportunity."

Her mother only stared and said nothing.

Emma kept going. "I have become absolutely clear, just as you were that evening we spoke. There was no disrespect for Geoffrey's memory then, just as there is none intended now. It's quite certain you didn't understand why I did what I did. I was beyond caring, Mamma. I was going to kill myself. And if I could sacrifice myself for some empty concept of despair, and the option was to live and love, then I must be prepared to face anything for that. Can you understand?"

"You are in a vulnerable state." Lady Freestone-Grant looked over her daughter's head, refusing to meet her eyes.

"Will you listen to me, Mamma?"

"You are confused."

"Will you kindly listen?" Emma's irritation was evident, but her mother ignored her. She continued to look away, and, for the first time, raised her voice.

"You must give yourself time. You are utterly confused. You are affected by all this destruction."

Emma slumped back on her heels, pressing her lips together in an expression of hopelessness.

"Tell that man to leave," her mother demanded. "Simon," she commanded without looking around, "kindly ask that man to leave."

The colonel sat up, appearing thinner and frailer in his civilian suit, but he simply looked hesitantly at Emma.

Sarah burst out, "You heard my mother. Why don't you just leave?"

Bannock came closer, leaned down toward Emma, and said, "Stop pleading." He looked at Lady Freestone-Grant, at Sarah, at Thrumpton, and said, "Come, Emma."

Emma nodded without turning around. Her attention remained on her mother.

"You're right, Bart. Why am I kneeling here?" she said wearily, and began to get up.

The hawk eyes followed her. "If you leave here now, you will be disgraced."

"You are threatening me."

The voice rose. "You will be disgraced."

Emma was backing up toward Bannock. "I could always be ordered by you, Mother, but if you think I can be threatened, you are wrong."

The hawk eyes became animated. Lady Freestone-Grant leaned sideways in her chair, looking specifically at Bannock.

"Mr., er . . ." She hesitated.

"Bannock," Emma prompted firmly, recognizing the change of tactics and preparing for them.

"Mr. Bannock," The name seemed to embarrass her mother. "I don't know you, but if you are a gentleman, you will leave now on your own."

Thrumpton cleared his throat as if he might have to say something.

Bannock had taken hold of Emma's shoulders as she backed up to him.

"Madam," he replied, "I don't know you either, but I suspect from what I've seen that I could never share your daughter's concern for you."

Sarah gasped audibly.

Thrumpton struggled to his feet to face Bannock. "You have no respect, sir."

"You should see me when I have no respect." Bannock's voice was hoarse with anger.

Emma took hold of the hand on her shoulder.

She said, "I'll come back to see you," but her mother was looking away.

She went ahead of Bannock toward the far end of the room, between the listless staff members who had become a half-interested audience. It was only when they reached the stairs that she noticed Colonel Thrumpton had come after them. He seemed a little embarrassed, and sniffed and coughed. Emma waited for a rebuke but the old eyes showed only concern.

"You are not to worry, my dear," he said. "These things are said in the heat of the moment. I will try to persuade your mother to go down the mine. I shall offer to accompany her, of course."

"You are so good to us." Emma held out her hand and gripped his.

The old man turned to Bannock as if he was going to say something, but changed his mind and remained watching as the two of them went off up the stairs.

Thrumpton groped his way back through the cellar, frowning, preparing himself for the aftermath. He could see Lady Freestone-Grant uncharacteristically slumped in her seat, staring blindly through the hooded eyes.

Sarah had a stab at breaking the silence. "Emma is bent on upsetting you." She would have bumbled on, but her mother was shaking her head, preparing to speak.

"No." It was barely a whisper. "Emma is thinking of Emma. Sarah is thinking of Sarah."

"Oh, no, no." Sarah managed to gulp back her protest in order to hear the rest.

"And I? I am no different. I am also thinking of myself. I have become quite preoccupied with Birchleigh. Imagine. I thought I wanted to get away from Birchleigh, away from the uniforms." The eyes were closed; the words were thoughts that might as well have been private. "After the general died, the soldiers came marching in, his uniformed relatives and mine, and all the uniformed friends, all those

colors, the red jackets and the green, all those insignia, th
shining boots, the spurs chinking through the hall. If the
had all come together, it would have looked like an inv:
sion."

She looked for a moment as if she would doze off, b
there was more, and they leaned toward her to hear th
almost whispered thoughts.

"Birchleigh was a wood-paneled parade ground of
sort. You could blame the old cousins. I called them the o
soldiers who would never die, but they did, the old dodde
ers.

"It was the same for them as the others. Birchleigh w:
a magnet to them, a good place to plumb the latest intrigu
and keep count of the decimation of the cream of the arm

"They all wanted to go to India. What fun it seeme
Do you know how many friends we lost in India alone? '
when my children wanted to go away . . ." The dark ey
shone and directed themselves at Colonel Thrumpton as
they had come awake and were aware of someone bei
there.

"You see, Birchleigh became a memorial for me,
mass military grave of the imagination.

"I just had to flee from that. It was such a bad drea
at the time. Now I'm awake again, not only back with th
cavalry and the gunners, but the swords are out and t
guns are firing. What that has done for me is that the re
bugles, the real bangs are meaningless. And all that's left
that beautiful place.

"I want to go back."

"We should wait for the storm to let up," he sai
watching her packing the leather valise on the bed.

"No, Bart, we must go now. We must never w:
again." She said it without hesitating, rummaging throug
a drawer to find things she needed. "I'm taking only wh
is essential for the moment."

Bannock felt strange in that room. Apart from the fact that he had been intimidated downstairs, he was uneasy about his own handling of the situation. He saw the rack of beautiful clothes in the open door of the cupboard, the small silver-framed pictures on the dressing table, the perfume bottles and other expensive paraphernalia. The room was part of her family, the comfort she was accustomed to, the lifetime of security she was leaving. It should not have worried him. It was a vague doubt that had no part in his real instincts, nor in Emma's, to see her packing busily. But it had to be admitted.

"I feel I have forced your hand."

Emma stopped in the middle of strapping up the bag, and faced him.

"Bart, I have come to terms with myself about my mother. She is trapped in her own pride. She cannot escape, so I must."

There was more to admit.

"This place," he said. "I feel we will never be truly together until we are out of it and away on our own."

Emma tied the last strap and looked up cheerfully. "Do you mind taking my bag, sir?"

She was ready. It seemed too quick, too easy, and she grinned at him as if it were a perfectly normal thing to do, to throw over everything that was before and go.

And they went, Bannock, almost bewildered, following on with the valise down the stairs, watching the slim figure going quickly ahead, the graceful arms pulling on the cloak. He was transfixed by her every movement. She radiated confidence, holding the cloak wide and wrapping it firmly around her, shaking out her shining hair over the cowl.

The hallway was still deserted. Outside, the rain drummed down on the awnings. They ran to the mare under the tree and Bannock lifted Emma onto the saddle, helping her to arrange her dress and putting up the stirrups. Up went the bag, and Bannock roared with laughter when she hoisted up the front of her skirt to cover it

He gripped her small thigh and looked up at her in wonder. He had the feeling he knew he would have onc they were out of that hotel—just wonder at the idea of suc a perfect woman belonging to him. She stared back, sharin, the moment. The rain was dripping on her hair and over he face, and suddenly she was aware of it. She laughed an pulled up the hood, adjusting it.

They watched the flashes of lightning from under th tree, not so bright and intense as before, and listened to th rolls of thunder, not so loud. By then it became clear tha the bangs and rumblings were only thunder and not artil lery. Bannock was relieved. It seemed that both the Boe and Kimberly gunners had sensibly taken to their shelter for the duration of the storm. When he led the mare int the street, she behaved as if affected by their mood, prancin, on the loose rein, bobbing her head against the downpour As for her owner, he appeared as jubilant as he felt; he fel as if nothing could deter him ever again.

Emma could almost read his thoughts, watching hin ahead. When he turned around, she saw the changed Ban nock, water streaming down through his thick hair, th normally set lips turned up at the corners in a fixed expres sion of good nature; the new, benign Bannock, hardly rec ognizable as the angry man at odds with the siege and th world.

She began a conversation with the horse. "Do yo realize," she addressed the swinging mane, "it was you wh made your master follow us out into the night? It was yo who brought us together."

The long thoroughbred neck arched and straightened and Bannock kept walking, smiling, his eyes fixed ahead

She spoke solemnly to the long neck. "We both rod on one horse that night and I'm sure you could do th same. Why is he walking in front as if he hardly know us?"

Bannock laughed as he splashed through the puddle

Emma kept her attention on the neck. "If he refuses to come up here with me, I'll get off and walk."

He took a step back, throwing the reins over Lady Potter's head, and Emma leaned forward in the saddle, knowing what he intended. He jumped up and fumbled himself onto the mare's back behind her. Lady Potter remained surprisingly calm, waiting while they arranged themselves up above, Bannock sitting loose-legged behind and Emma clutching the valise in front of her.

They rode like that through the outskirts of the town, where each turning told its story of destruction and shattered buildings spread their remains across the streets. Groups of people had emerged from their makeshift shelters carrying bundles of belongings, no doubt heading for the security of the mines. They passed a platoon of bedraggled Town Guardsmen and Bannock called out to them cheerfully, "Good afternoon," and "Rotten weather," and Emma's muffled laughter came back to him from under the hood.

They were soon out of town and on the long, barren track that led to the racecourse. The rain began to thin and they could see the barricade ahead.

"Will they let me through without a pass?"

The thought had just occurred to Bannock when Emma mentioned it. If the guards decided to be difficult, it would mean a return journey to town to arrange the pass.

"We may have to shoot our way through."

They laughed in the way that they were prepared to laugh at almost anything.

Something was happening at the guard post. Voices rose in altercation, and Bannock recognized the tall, fat center of the row. It was Pacelli the chef.

Pacelli was pleading, demanding, and gesticulating all at once. He paused, as the guards did, to examine the approaching horse with its tandem riders before returning to the argument. But in a moment, the chef's attention re-

turned to the horse. He frowned, then waved his arm
wildly as he recognized Bannock.

"Hey, Mario, what are you doing here?" Bannock
slipped off the horse and held the reins while Pacelli ran
puffing up to meet him.

"I'ma come all the way to find'a you. It'sa Paddi, he'sa
lost. He'sa no come back."

Bannock matched the waving gestures with a few
calming ones of his own. "Hold on now, Mario. What do
you mean, he hasn't come back? I've known Paddy to be
drunk and unconscious and lost, but he always comes back.
What do you mean by lost?"

Pacelli struggled with his problems of communication,
beginning with his hands even before he spoke. "He'sa lost
down'a mine. Yesterday he'sa go down'a mine. Today he'sa
not down'a mine. He'sa not up'a mine, he'sa not down'a
mine.

Bannock held up a placating hand in the face of
Pacelli's waving ones. "Steady on, Mario." He waited for
the hands to subside. "You say Paddy is down the mine. He
told me he was spending a few days with you, so what's he
doing down the mine?"

Pacelli looked all around him. He looked behind toward the guards and up at Emma, who gave him a sweet
smile, and still he seemed reluctant to answer.

Bannock was beginning to understand. "Well, come
on, Mario, what was the big idiot doing down the mine?"

Pacelli was on his guard. He seemed offended. "What
do you mean'a idiot?"

"I mean Paddy O'Flaherty, the mug of all mugs, the
biggest bloody fool who ever lived. What would he be doing
down a mine? Come on, Mr. Pacelli, tell me. Would he be
hiding away from the bombs? Not Paddy, as I know him.
So tell me, what was he doing?"

Pacelli drew himself up to his full height to face Bannock. "He'sa my friend, he'sa your friend, why you speak'a
like this?"

"He's down there looking for diamonds, is that right?"

Pacelli struck a dignified pose and refused to answer.

Bannock took it as said. "Do you realize, Mario, what the punishment is for diamond stealing in this town? They send you up for life."

Pacelli was at boiling point. He forced himself to speak.

"It'sa not'a punishment," he exploded. "It'sa not'a stealing. It'sa lost. Paddi, he'sa lost. He'sa no come back. He'sa go down'a mine. Today I go down'a mine, he'sa gone. I ask'a you, what'a must we do?"

Bannock looked solemnly up at Emma and just as solemnly at Pacelli.

"Mario," he said, "it's too late to do anything today. But let me tell you something about Paddy, because I know him well. No matter where he goes or what he does, he always comes back. He'll come back tomorrow. And if he doesn't, we'll go and find him."

Pacelli shook his head and drops of water flew off his thin hair and his thick mustache.

"He'sa bleddy damn fool," he said with feeling.

Bannock pretended to ignore the muffled laughter from above.

· 13 · | EXPLOSIONS AND ECHOES

The large gilt mirror betrayed the presence of Braithwait[e] even before he could complete his inquiries.

Masefield sat back in his favorite chair in the gloom[y] bar lounge of the Kimberley Club, from where he onl[y] needed to raise his head to see, reflected in the bottom [of] the mirror, the reporter questioning one of the stewards.

The unwelcome sight was accompanied by the unwe[l]come sound of his own name being mentioned, and h[e] waited for that pair of myopic lenses to approach in th[e] mirror, peering around the empty chairs until they we[re] virtually squinting at the top of his head.

"What are you doing out at this time of the night?" Masefield didn't bother to look up.

Braithwaite spoke to the top of his head, "It is mo[st] urgent that I speak to you."

"I recognize a remarkably reasonable tone in yo[ur] voice. Let me guess: you are about to ask a favor?"

"Indeed I am." Braithwaite sounded abject, commi[t]ted to suppressing his dislike.

Masefield left him standing. "I'm afraid the banning [of] your newspaper is an irreversible decision."

"It's not just that." Braithwaite came around an[d]

aned on the mantelpiece that supported the mirror, forc-
g a smile, appearing far less sure of himself than on the
evious occasions. "We want the editor freed," he started.
f you will pardon the pun, we want our editor back in
rculation." The humor was as forced as the smile.

"Now listen to me, Braithwaite, listen and don't speak.
our newspaper was closed down because it persisted in
efying the emergency regulations, which, whether you like
or not, exist because they are necessary. You and your
litor caused a lot of panic and confusion, and because you
ntinued in defiance, a warrant was issued for the arrest
your editor. If you wish to make any more of this, we can
sue one for your arrest as well."

Braithwaite seemed more sure of himself. "I think it
ly fair to tell you, Major, that I have it from the most
fluential source in this town that my editor will be vin-
cated and instantly reinstated, once relief arrives."

"There is only one influential source you could mean
d that's Cecil Rhodes."

"I would not take that name too lightly."

"Are you speaking, then, on Mr. Rhodes' behalf?"

"You are twisting my words." Braithwaite remained
niling and defensive.

"I thought only journalists did that."

Braithwaite still refused to be incited. He tried reason-
g again. "Contrary to your suggestion that the newspaper
as causing, how did you say it, panic and confusion? What
more likely to cause consternation, and I think consterna-
on is a strong enough word in any event, is the lack of
formation of any sort. We are, I mean our editorial board
sadly in need of our chief organizer and journalist."

Masefield sniffed.

The thick glasses mirrored the lamp light, jutting for-
ard insistently. "Have you thought, Major, that suddenly
is town is completely cut off not only from the outside
orld but from everything that is happening? They know
thing of the dramatic events taking place. Some are even

unaware that Labram has been killed by a shell from Lor
Tom, and no one—do you hear, no one—has any details
the relief column.

"Major Masefield." Braithwaite was becoming brave
"Let me emphasize to you that, apart from the prejudi
shown by your commander-in-chief to our editor, he is hel
in the highest esteem. I would make so bold as to say th.
that puts him in a position of better influence than yo
commander-in-chief."

Masefield seemed faintly amused. "In whose highe
esteem?" he asked.

"I beg your pardon?"

"You mean Rhodes?"

Braithwaite reverted to being nervous. "I was on
suggesting that my editor will undoubtedly end up on t
right side, and it would do you no harm, let's say it cou
be to your advantage to support him now."

Masefield sank deeper into the chair as if he wished
withdraw from the conversation. "Look here, Mr. Brait
waite," he drawled, "you don't have a newspaper anymor
and I don't care about your precious editor. He can stay
hiding, as far as I'm concerned."

"In hiding?"

"Oh, come now, Braithwaite, you're not going to te
me he's been spirited out of Kimberley in the night. If l
wasn't hidden, he would have been placed under arrest
ordered. My advice to you is to keep him hidden until t
relief column arrives, and then you can carry out all yo
threats to the army, the commanding officer, and myself

"You are determined to twist my words."

"Leave him down the mine."

"Mine?" Braithwaite was startled. "What mine?"

"You have him hidden down the Kimberley mine,
you not?"

"I cannot imagine what you're talking about."

* * *

O'Flaherty was unaware that he was missing.

He struck at the rock in a fever of determination, the pick producing spark after spark in a rhythm that had become a habit for the huge, muscular arm. As long as he kept going, the sweat poured and all thought was blanked out. Each time he stopped to rest, the cold air came up and his spirits sagged.

When he had first explored the main shaft, with its string of weak electric lamps, he had discovered a maze of unlighted passages leading off, some going away at right angles, others veering off obliquely and curving away into blackness, all of them streaked with the magic diamond-bearing rock he was to look for. From the start, he realized there was no point in searching beyond the main shaft; blue stone was blue stone. He settled down to hammer and chip at the sides of that long, ghostly blue cavern.

The impact of the pick rang through the tunnel. When it stopped, there was deathly silence.

He was a long way from the main entry shaft, far enough to be out of earshot of the gallery where thousands of women and children taking shelter from the bombing ate, slept, and waited. For as long as he could still hear the hivelike drone of their voices, he had gone farther up the tunnel. They had faded to silence, and then he had gone farther still. In two days he had discovered no diamonds, but he knew just enough of the crushing and sorting process from Mabala to know that every inch of blue rock held its own promise, so he was collecting pieces of the rock for breaking down at a later stage.

O'Flaherty was not at all in good spirits. Somehow he had imagined that the blue stone would be brittle and crumbling, but he had discovered it was brittle and incredibly hard, of an even consistency that offered few cracks or faults. Each small piece that came away was an hour's work, even for his mighty physique. He was also hungry and thirsty, not having eaten since the previous night, when he'd crept into the main gallery after everyone was asleep and found nothing better than scraps of leftovers and cold coffee. The few women who woke up ignored him, seeing only the chef's jacket, and he was able to exchange his almost spent lamp for a fresh one.

The pick kept flying in at the rock face, each swing producing a strident ring that gave no promise of break-through. Maybe the rock would not be so hard farther along. O'Flaherty gathered up the canvas bag, lamp, and chef's jacket and stumbled away between the rails, deeper into the mine.

After walking for some time, he held up the lamp and searched the wall for a part that showed weaknesses, eventually settling on a jagged seam in the face. The hammering began again, at first producing nothing but sparks and small flying chips. The blows grew harder, louder, the sparks became more profuse, and he heaved a sigh of relief when the rock gave with a loud crack.

He held the lamp high and examined the clean surface, but there were no telltale glints or foreign bodies. The same went for the fist-sized piece that had broken off.

"Clean as a whistle," he muttered, putting down the lamp and throwing the stone into the canvas bag before addressing himself to the rock face once again.

The pick clanged. O'Flaherty kept hammering until he ran out of breath. Had he heard something? He tried to control his breathing and listen, then, at the sound of foot-steps, ducked down against the rock face and covered the lamp. The footsteps stopped, and O'Flaherty kept very still. It was unbelievable that the noise had come, not from the direction of the gallery, but from farther up the tunnel.

There was a movement, and he became aware of the shadowy outline of a man peering at him from the corner of a cutting in the rock.

"What are you doing there?" The deep authoritative voice echoed around the tunnel.

O'Flaherty stood up slowly.

The man came out holding up his own lamp and took

few steps toward him. "What precisely are you doing?" he demanded.

"Who are you?" O'Flaherty asked weakly.

"Never mind who I am, what are you doing there?"

"Well." O'Flaherty held the pick behind his back and gave the question some thought. "It's diggin' I am. Takin' rock samples."

"Are you with the mines?" The voice was suspicious.

"The mines?" O'Flaherty hesitated. "Ah yes, of course. I'm with the mines. Sure, what would I be doin' here if I were not with the mines?"

The man took a few steps backward through the shadows before turning and disappearing into the cutting.

O'Flaherty stayed where he was, trying to decide what to do in a situation that offered little choice but the devil or the deep blue sea: the devil in the form of the gallery and the officials who might see him, or the deep blue yonder of the tunnel. Then he heard a whirring noise like the winding of a telephone set. And he knew he was in trouble. The man had gone to a telephone. O'Flaherty set off in pursuit to find out whether he was right.

He found the cutting and groped his way along, with the lamp held up high. Farther on, he could see a dull light emerging from another cutting that led off to the left, and he could faintly hear the man's voice.

"Will you send someone immediately. . . . Yes, I said digging. . . . No, I am quite sure, but in the meantime I'm here on my own. . . . Yes, yes. . . . Well, get on with it, man."

O'Flaherty turned into the new cutting in time to see the man slam down the receiver of a cable telephone on the wall. He had come into a room hewn out of the rock and lined with heavy timber props. Incredibly, the place was furnished like a comfortable study. There were rugs on the floor, there was a desk with a typewriter and newspapers strewn on top, there was a bed and a bookcase, and two shaded lamps hung from above. He stared at it all in amazement and recognized the man as the gray-suited gentleman

who had joined them in the elevator cage, to whom every
one was paying so much respect.

The man seemed quite amiable. "Would you like to si
down and take a rest?" he suggested.

O'Flaherty knew what was happening. "Not righ
now," he answered. "If you don't mind, I'll be on me way.

He backed up, and the man did nothing to stop him
He made his way back along the cutting and was alread
in the tunnel when he heard the running feet. He looke
around frantically for an escape route, but the next sid
tunnel was a long way off and the cutting behind him wa
a dead end. The footfalls grew louder. There was no poir
in running. He stepped quietly over the rails to the side c
the tunnel farthest from the lights and, extinguishing hi
own lamp, flattened himself up against the wall beside
heavy wooden prop.

Two men ran alongside. O'Flaherty made ready t
dash in the direction from which they had come, when on
of them saw the canvas bag and looked around. In a
instant, O'Flaherty stood exposed. In the next, he took th
same action as the man in front of him and lunged out. Bι
the other man's lunge was a feeble effort by comparisor
and he was sent flying across the rails to the far wall of th
tunnel. The second man came in bravely, and went spraw
ing in the same manner as his companion.

O'Flaherty hesitated for just a moment. He could hea
more feet approaching from the direction of the gallery. H
was not leaving his bag behind. He snatched it up and wer
running down the tunnel in the opposite direction. The tw
men could be heard scrambling to their feet and shoutin
as he reached the first side tunnel leading off to the righ
But once he had made the turn, he realized he was beater
He was without a lamp, and the light soon faded away t
pitch darkness. An alarm bell was ringing from far off, an
he knew that it was only a matter of time before he woul
be discovered.

There was nothing to do but wait or go out and give himself up, and he had no heart for that—at least not until he was forced to. The situation seemed hopeless. They were going to find him sooner or later. If he ran now, they would hear him. He looked sadly at his bag of blue rocks. He was still reluctant to part with it.

Voices echoed up the tunnel in gasps and mutters, and the feet were on the move again. They were running up the tunnel in his direction. Soon a crowd of men ran past, their shadows flickering in where the light faded on the floor.

O'Flaherty gave them a few moments before stepping quietly back into the main tunnel, clutching his canvas bag and checking both ways for any sign of life. If he could get back to the gallery, there was still a chance he could hide himself among the vast throng of people.

He began walking between the rails, but once he was sure there was no one up ahead, he broke into a run. His footsteps sounded very loud to him, particularly as he knew there was nowhere else to hide between there and the gallery itself. The only other turn-off was the one to the room of the gray-suited man, and he slowed down warily as he approached it.

He might have guessed some of them would be waiting for him, and they were. Three men stepped out from the cutting into the middle of the tunnel and squared up for action. One of them shouted through his hands, "He's here, we've found him."

"Oh have you?" O'Flaherty made the quiet words sound like a war cry. He stopped and weighed the heavy canvas bag in his hand, ready to swing it.

The men came forward and the powerful arms swung the bag as easily as if it were a down pillow. The men ducked and swung away, hands up to protect themselves. O'Flaherty darted forward, grabbing one of them by the collar, almost choking him as he prepared to launch him at the other two, but he stopped in his tracks at the familiar click of a gun being cocked. He stared into the barrel of a heavy revolver, ignoring the gasping noises of the man whose collar he held clenched in his hand.

"Let him go," said the man with the revolver, and the other, who was released, went down on his knees coughing violently.

Footsteps sounded again. His pursuers were on their way back.

"Keep still," warned the man with the gun when O'Flaherty turned to watch.

The gray-suited man had come out of the cutting. He looked on without saying anything. The others, six of them, came up out of breath, and one, a tall character with a walrus mustache who appeared to be the leader, went past to speak to the man in the gray suit.

"You can leave this to me, sir. I think the less said the better."

The gray-suited man nodded, but remained where he was.

The walrus mustache loomed beside the man with the gun, and a pair of somber eyes settled on O'Flaherty.

"Who sent you?"

O'Flaherty shrugged. "Nobody sent me."

"You've been spying on the editor."

O'Flaherty looked blank. "What editor?" He peered around at the circle of inquisitorial eyes.

"Answer me." The walrus mustache quivered with the shout.

"You're talkin' fairies. Who's the editor?"

The walrus mustache twitched, the somber eyes blinked, and the voice became more reasonable.

"Are you going to tell me that in the whole of the De Beers mine, with miles of tunnel to choose from, you picked this one spot to sneak up on by accident? Now let's have it. Tell me, who are you working for? It's the army, isn't it? Army intelligence? Give us the whole story and you might get off lightly."

O'Flaherty puffed out his chest proudly at the thought of being a spy, let alone an army intelligence one. He looked upward as if he were considering his answer, then he said, "I'm sayin' nothin'."

The walrus mustache turned to the man with the gun. "If we hand him over, the army is likely to leave him to rot in jail. They're not going to admit anything. They'll call him a liar and we'll call him a liar."

The man with the gun nodded. "But he'll be out of the way."

The walrus mustache nodded. "What do we charge him with?"

"Illicit diamond digging," said the man with the gun. "There's a bag of stone and a pick as evidence."

The somber eyes turned back to O'Flaherty. "Do you know the charge for diamond nicking? That'll keep you out of mischief for years." He raised his voice. "We want to know who sent you, all right?" The walrus mustache posed itself belligerently and the eyes demanded an answer.

O'Flaherty played for time. "I'm thinkin'."

"Give us a statement and we'll see you right."

O'Flaherty looked very solemn. He kept them waiting for a long time before speaking.

"I've thought about what you've said, and it's decided I am. I'll not be givin' a statement at this time."

The somber eyes went hard.

"Right. Take him up and hand him over to the police."

"Blast and bugger O'Flaherty." Bannock stopped himself from saying something worse as he stood up on the buckboard of the Cape cart and steered the mule around a deep bomb crater in the road.

Emma sat beside him hiding her amusement. The heavy wheels of the cart squeaked and grated to the mule's shunting movements. It brought back a memory of riding on the back of a heavy dray as a child, her only other

experience of such a springless form of transport. But she
was enjoying this experience as much as the first, enjoying
everything about her new life in spite of bombs and threat
and anything that might come. The old adage that love
overcomes all was right. Suddenly, there is nothing to over
come. Living in a tent would be a luxury. The bar of the
racecourse was a palace, where the prince of racing cast his
spell without any conscious effort.

There are no degrees of love, she thought, not for the
kind that banishes all doubt at the smallest look, the slight
est touch. For once, there was a future. Everything was
changed. Twenty-five years of halfhearted existence had
changed into a life of meaning, and the meaning came from
a deep need that shouted inside her. Suddenly, I need des
perately. I need to touch him, to passionately come to grip
with him. At last, longing has a satisfaction to it. It come
in cycles, and the cycles only grow more urgent. All suspi
cion of romance and the trance of ecstasy love creates are
gone. The trance has merged into reality, and I can hear
myself babbling those easily despised phrases about happi
ness and still believe in them.

She turned and saw the pall of smoke or dust or both
burgeoning up like a vast earth-bound cloud to the south
always moving, billowing and expanding slowly at the top
It was a compelling sight that no soul in Kimberley could
ignore for long. For three days they had watched the cloud
grow as it came closer, and with it the rising sound of two
armies giving battle, their batteries pounding one another
a deeper sound relative to the explosions and echoes that
filled their days.

Strange to think of relief. The very word had lost its
meaning, to become the weekly wonder that went from
promise to lie as surely as Long Tom opened fire every day
Hard to believe that under that cloud to the south was the
might of the British army, pushing through at last to the
outskirts of the town. Somehow, for her the prospect had
no meaning. If anything, it brought apprehension in the

form of her one intangible fear. This tortured town had become a happy place, and in that way a place of security. It had meant a separate lifetime, where everything changed and the changes came fast and furious. My thoughts are rambling, but not my meanings. The changes are both awful and wonderful. I can think about Geoffrey without much pain. I can love Bart with a ferocity that is beyond understanding.

She had dreamed about Geoffrey as one of those horizontal cathedral knights, the granite ghosts who hung onto their swords in cold stone death. It was a good dream; it put the ghost of guilt to rest, helped to put Geoffrey's memory into perspective beyond judgment and recrimination. She had poured out her ramblings to Bart and he had easily made sense of them. The empathy of her dreams had become real. She had forgotten what fear of loneliness was like, as if nothing could destroy happiness and no threatening influence get through. Even when Bart discovered that Paddy O'Flaherty was in jail and went searching for Major Masefield, she had waited, believing he would come back through the shelling unhurt. It was a state of euphoria that transcended logic and turned doubt and guilt into lesser instincts. It was a mad kind of love, but that was the way Emma wanted it—a love so mad as to have momentum.

For Emma, time revolved around Bart. The waiting, the anxiety, the threat at every possible turn of events were swept aside by love. The five days of separation from her family seemed like months, and in that time she had seen only Mark, who had come on two occasions. Once again, he had surprised her with his understanding and an affection she had always underestimated. He had shown Bart respect, if not friendship, and out of it had come a grateful alliance that formed the first seal on their decision and their future. She knew her mother was safe with Sarah and Colonel Thrumpton down one of the mines, that she was grimly ignoring her existence, which Emma felt was a blessing in disguise for as long as it lasted.

There was only one real flaw in the whole pattern, one fault, one fear that kept creeping back to threaten her otherwise blind belief. A horse, a ghost horse that might become real and vengeful for her. Marcus, the specter on the horizon that beckoned to Bart. Major Masefield had said Bart would die for it, and for a moment she resented Masefield as violently as she did the horse. Was that because she believed it might be true? Was this the pale horse that brought death? She had to stop thinking that way. Maybe he would realize that no animal could be worth the risk.

She watched a plume of smoke spiralling up from one of Long Tom's shells in the direction of the De Beers mine. It was only that big gun that seemed to have remained in action, and she was relieved to see that it was concentrating on the northern quarter, away from the town, sparing them the choking sulfurous smell as much as the ear-splitting explosions. All around them was the evidence of its earlier poundings: houses ripped apart, fire-blackened walls, trees smashed to the roots, fences lying across open gutters.

Bannock balanced himself on the buckboard, leaning one way and the other to see past the mule's head. He flicked the reins and shouted encouragement to force the big animal through another shallow crater in the road. His attention, his own thoughts were elsewhere. Emma made it all so easy, even to laugh at everything. But the problems that had been blinded by frustration had become problems that must be solved. The thought of Marcus fought with the thought of Emma. The image that had ruled his life and his feelings had faded into the background in the face of Emma's safety, Emma's feelings, Emma's very presence. But the vision of Marcus remained and kept coming back with the longing he had always felt. And more than longing, with the realization that all he had to face life with was a woman who was there beside him and a horse that was somewhere else. He thought of how it would be if they escaped Kimberley while he was left with a haunting picture of a horse, destined for greatness, abandoned to waste and work like some farm animal in this wilderness.

He also watched the cloud to the south, which should have been an advancing wall of hope, and saw only an ominous forcing of his own decision. To ride out in search of Marcus was to invite destruction. And if by some miracle he retrieved the stallion, what hope would there be of keeping him in the face of a horse-hungry army whose mounts were dead or spent?

Mabala was the only one of them who still knew the conditions out there beyond the perimeter, and he had shaken his head at any prospect of retrieving the horse. Emma had shaken hers at the thought of the risk. Masefield had made a promise that it was doubtful he could keep, or would want to, at this stage of the game. It was a vague hope, but the only one he could cling to—that the troops riding out might capture the horses with the commandos. For three days, since the cloud of the relief force had appeared, he had searched for Masefield, dodging his way past the worst areas of bombing to army headquarters, north to the number one redoubt, and south to the reservoir. Wherever he went, he was sent somewhere else, until he came to the conclusion that Masefield was leaving a deliberate trail of confusion.

But Masefield had a better reason for avoiding him than the promise he might well have forgotten. He had almost certainly heard about Paddy being in jail and would have anticipated representations being made on his behalf. Bannock's irritation rose at the thought of Paddy. The big fool deserved to go on sitting there.

As they approached Lennox Street, they ran into one-way traffic of mounted troops moving off toward the square, and the cart was forced to rumble its way along the verge of the road to make space for the wide column. More troops were drawn up in front of headquarters. The soldiers looked different, more animated, caught up in an atmosphere of excitement and anticipation not yet shared by the towns people.

Bannock hitched the mule outside of the building and left Emma there to wait. He fiddled with the reins until the sentry was well away on his march along the verandah, then ran up the steps and crossed into the hallway before he could be challenged. Once inside, he marched down the long passage with an air of businesslike involvement, and was through the outer intelligence offices and into Mase field's room before he could be stopped.

Masefield was there, rummaging through papers at his desk. He looked up, reddening with anger at the sight of Bannock.

"How in hell's name did you get in here?" he exploded. "Now get out, damn you, get out before I have you ar rested."

Bannock closed the door behind him. "There are two matters," he said.

Masefield stood up, almost knocking his chair over. "Only two," he shouted. "You must realize the relief force is on its way in and I have a thousand things to deal with."

Bannock came forward calmly. "They've locked up Paddy O'Flaherty."

The pompous poise returned. "What of it? He was digging for diamonds, and I think you know the penalty for that. You can forget about him. By next week he will come up before the civilian court and he'll be put away for years and a good job too." Masefield caught his breath, but obvi ously had more to say. "Oh yes, about Mr. O'Flaherty. Do you know what he did? He had the damned nerve to say that he was a spy in the pay of military intelligence."

Bannock began to laugh.

"You find that funny?" Masefield was far from amused. "Do you know that they actually believed him? And I was put to an awful lot of trouble to convince them that the bloody fool was wasting our time."

Bannock made an effort to look serious. "Come on, Masefield, no one is arguing about Paddy being a bloody fool at times. He gets obsessed. It used to be herbal potions that were supposed to make the horses run faster. It was fairly innocent stuff, but that didn't stop us from being investigated. Or stop him from cooking up new and better brews."

"This is hardly innocent. He broke into a mine."

"He went down to help the kitchen hands from the Sanatorium."

"With proper digging equipment?"

"That's the real joke. Everybody told him it's easier to draw blood out of a stone than diamonds."

"You are wasting your breath and my time."

"Masefield." Bannock was prepared to plead. "I need him to help get my stallion back."

"Indeed? And once again you would like to see the law waived on your account. A pox on your stallion, Bannock. What is it you intended to do? Mount a two-man attack on the Boer forces?"

"You said you would help. You used it as a bargain."

Masefield's eyes flickered. "I remember what I said."

"My side of the bargain was my life."

The eyes darted around. Masefield sighed impatiently. "I said I might be able to help when it came to this point, but I cannot. No one is bothering about the Boers from Carter's and Wimbledon. Kekewich is not interested in them, and if he were, he would have no choice. No wait, let me explain. Besides the force at Alexandersfontein, there is only one active battalion available, and that is setting out north after the Long Tom. So you see, Bannock, there is nothing I can do. I'm afraid you are on your own."

"Very well. If you can't help, I'll ride out and negotiate with the Boers to get my horse."

Masefield's expression made its subtle adjustments to anger. "You are going too far, Bannock. You can't do what you damn well like. If you try to contact the enemy, if you go out after them, I'll have you arrested for treason—and anyone who goes with you."

Bannock was indifferent to Masefield's anger. The roles were reversed, Masefield's voice raised while his remained calm.

"You don't impress me. I have a right to protect what is mine."

Masefield fumed. "You have no rights at all."

"Your threats mean about as much as your promises. You're a big fake, Masefield."

"And you still have no rights. You seem to forget that you are one of the only able-bodied men in this town who is out of uniform, and you have used the freedom that implies to cause more mischief than you're worth."

"We've been through all this before."

"You have caused an inordinate amount of trouble by your hysteria over your horses, while not only horses were being lost but the lives of men."

"You're just repeating yourself."

"You have flittered around with females and not satisfied yourself until you created confusion for the widow of a hero and her family besides." There was open exasperation on the face that normally gave nothing away.

"Then why did you help me with Emma?"

"I hoped that I was helping her to see what you were about."

"That's nonsense. She knows what I'm about."

"You would have met with her anyway in your usual covert manner, lurking in the shadows."

"And that would have worried you?"

"Not at all."

"Yes it would." Bannock pressed the point. "Because you wouldn't have been there, you couldn't have had any influence on the proceedings, you couldn't have manipulated your subjects. You think we're all subject to you."

"What rubbish."

"You let us think you were being positive for a change, when you were being your usual sinister self. What's your problem, Masefield? Are you some kind of voyeur?"

The reddening face belied the soft voice. "Get out of here, Bannock."

Bannock opened the door and left, aware that Masefield was still standing in the middle of the room staring after him. He walked quickly up the passage and out into the hot sun. He was blind to what was happening in the street and saw only Emma on the cart, the straw-colored hair glistening in the sun, her eyes waiting for him, following him down until he stood looking up at her.

"That was a waste of time, Emma."

"You saw Major Masefield?"

Bannock nodded. "He won't help. He will do nothing about Paddy and nothing about Marcus."

Emma frowned down at the worried profile below. She had tried to forget about the stallion. She saw again the passion that showed in his eyes every time he mentioned Marcus, and the fear came back.

"You are going to ride out after him?" She heard the weak challenge in her voice and prayed for a denial.

"I don't know." Bannock was far away. "I don't know whether it's worth it."

"Don't, Bart." She heard herself plead and couldn't stop. "Don't go after that horse. If I am being selfish, I can't help myself. Can I ask you that, Bart?"

He came out of his thoughts and looked up at her without speaking.

She leaned down and reached for his hands. "Don't commit yourself to death." The tears were beginning. "I don't want you to be brave. Brave men die."

"Emma, Emma." He gripped her hands and tried to calm her.

"I know what your stallion means, and I am so afraid. I can't share that feeling with you. I can only see my own need. This is the first time I have ever loved and been loved

the way I should be. Am I walking into the worst nightmar
of all?"

Bannock felt his own hands trembling with hers.

"It's all right, Emma. I won't go against you."

The sky showed through piled-up pieces of broke
masonry, small jagged frames of blue of night streaked wit
the last faint pink of sunset. There was no longer any soun
of shelling, no voices, no sound at all.

O'Flaherty was on his back, pressed against the wa
by the long bench he remembered sitting on earlier. Ther
was just enough room for him to raise an arm and feel fo
his head. He felt the grazes at his forehead and looked a
the blood and loose hair that came away on his fingers. Bu
the eyebrows worked up and down, and so did the jaw. H
shifted his legs and arched his back. It all felt fairly intac
God be praised; he was alive, all right. This was not wha
heaven would be like. This was still the jail—or what wa
left of it.

He struggled to move the bench, and the debris ba
anced above began to shift, plaster grinding against ston
It all moved down on him, cascading off the arms he hel
up to protect his head, the dust and grit showering dow
and rising up again, choking him. He pushed away th
broken rafters and tumbling masonry, forcing himself firs
into a squatting position, then sliding his back upwar
against the wall until he was standing waist-deep in rubbl
coughing to get his breath. The dust cleared, and the eve
ning sky spread itself out above him as an unexpected inv
tation to freedom.

He leaned against the wall, held onto his throbbin
head, and tried to remember. He had heard the shell ap
proaching, just like the others that had come at staggere
intervals throughout the day. Some had landed close by
close enough to bring plaster down from the ceiling an
crack the walls of the cell. But that one shell had sounde

different. The whine had become too loud. And yet he could not recall an explosion, just a sensation like a sharp crack and that was all.

There was no sign of life, no one to call out to. He began to lift away the stones that hemmed him in, finally using a loose rafter propped against the wall to pull himself out and crawl across the wreckage to a place where he could stand again.

Only then did he realize the extent of the destruction. The entire jail was flattened. The only wall partly intact was the one he had been leaning against. In what was left of the charge office he could see an arm, the elbow bent over a section of broken wall, the hand hanging limp. That was MacDonald, the warder, and on closer inspection the arm was all that was left to be recognized. MacDonald of the jokes. O'Flaherty tried to feel sorry for him, but he hardly knew him. The man must have a family. He tried to think of his family and feel sorry that way.

It was a fine evening, with battlements of storm clouds in the distance. Fine but eerie, the hot wind adding to the sinister atmosphere of this new ruin. O'Flaherty stood on the street, feeling somehow guilty and undecided about what to do next. He walked up and down slowly, waiting for something to happen, for a police detachment to arrive or the Town Guard or the army. But there was no one in sight, and it was growing steadily darker.

It would be ridiculous to wait there, but where could he go? The moment he walked away from the jail he would be a fugitive. But why not? Why not make a bolt for it now, with all the confusion and the relief force on its way in? After all, he would not be missed. They would think he had been killed in the blast.

What he needed right now above all things and before any further decision was a drink, any kind of drink as long as it was alcoholic. And the only place to find such a drink was not far off. He must get to Mario and, if nothing else, say farewell to his dear friend. Suddenly, O'Flaherty was walking fast, keeping in the deeper shadows, drawn like a magnet to his greatest need.

It struck him on the way that there were lamps lit in some of the buildings, their light streaming out unashamedly, something he had never seen in the center of Kimberley for four months. There were also more people than usual in the streets for that time of evening, yet no military activity, never a soldier in sight. And that was even more peculiar. But strangest of all was the Sanatorium. As he approached from a block away, it was a blaze of light, electric light. The siege must be over.

O'Flaherty ran the last few hundred yards, beginning to hear a hubbub of voices from the building and see the silhouettes of dozens of horses outside the front. Then he remembered that he was a fugitive and decided to give the front a wide berth on his way to the kitchens. But the sight of the horses stopped him. Where the light shone on those nearest the entrance, he saw the typical thoroughbreds of senior officers, and remounts beside them in full campaign tack. That they had once been fit and sound animals had to be imagined. They appeared gray and powdery from dried mud. They were emaciated, worked to death, and incapable of lifting their heads. A number of troopers who looked just as spent were carrying feedbags and buckets to the listless mounts.

O'Flaherty stared at the scene in a dumb realization of what the war was really about. He had imagined a relief force on shining chargers with pennants flying. He hated to see the horses like that, betrayed by men who could never explain to them why they must fight and die or waste away.

For a moment the alcohol was forgotten, but only for a moment. The sound of loud cheering and merriment from inside the building urged him on. At a time like this, who was even going to think about the charges brought against him? And for that matter, who knew about it, apart from a few mine officials and the army people? He would spend short while with Mario and his men, then go back to the racecourse to see what the plans were.

The sounds of revelry ended at the kitchen, with the usual noise of pots and plates and shouted orders taking over. O'Flaherty was through the scullery and in among the cooking ranges before anyone became aware of his presence. There were looks of surprise and greetings from all round, but they all went on working furiously; there was no time for idle chatter. O'Flaherty almost forgot his need of a drink as he inspected the mountains of food about him. Whole baked hams, caviar, pâtés and terrines, roasted joints, molded desserts, food of a kind he hardly knew or had forgotten existed.

Cellini could be seen listening sullenly to Mr. Henderson from the bar.

"Now listen to me, chef. We've got to pull out all the stops for General French. Don't you realize, man, this is it? Relief, old chap, do you hear; no more siege. Lord Roberts is not coming tonight. He doesn't have to come. General French is doing the whole thing."

Cellini appeared unsatisfied. "When ee'sa coming Lord Roberts?"

Henderson shook his head, exasperated.

"It doesn't matter about Lord Roberts. I told you, this is the official thing. As soon as service is over, there'll be drinks in the kitchen and we can all celebrate."

Henderson swept out through the swing doors. Cellini made a rude sign after him and was taking a swig out of a bottle of cooking wine when he saw O'Flaherty.

"Paddi," he called out, then stood still, looking dumb.

O'Flaherty made his way round the ranges and went up to him. "Ah, Carlolini, are you goin' to be after handin' me that bottle? There was never a time when I needed a drink more."

O'Flaherty took the bottle that was offered him, upended it, and glugged with serious preoccupation. Even when he put the bottle down, he remained unaware that the

entire staff of the kitchen had stopped what they were doin
and were staring at him.

"Where is Mario?" O'Flaherty asked jovially.

Cellini stood with his arms slack beside him, avoidin
O'Flaherty, looking past him into infinity.

O'Flaherty turned to see what he was looking at, the
turned right around when he became aware that every ma
in the kitchen was watching them. They all looked dow
and they looked away and continued to do nothing. Apa
from a few bubbling pots, there was absolute silence in t
kitchen, the sounds of celebration coming through muffl
from beyond the swing doors. O'Flaherty returned his a
tention to Cellini.

"Well, come on, man. Where is Mario? Why are yo
lookin' like that?"

Cellini shook his head slowly. "Mario ee'sa gone,"
said softly.

"Gone? What do you mean he's gone? He said nothi
about goin' anywhere."

"He'sa dead." The words came out hoarsely. "H
was'a walking in the road . . . there was'a bomb." Celli
hung his head, unable to meet O'Flaherty's gaze.

The big Irishman stood still for a long time. Event
ally, he picked up the bottle, raised it to drink, but chang
his mind. He looked at the bottle for a moment befo
flinging it at the wall. It smashed into a thousand fragmen
leaving a splattered patch of red. He turned without sayi
anything further and walked away as if he might be leavir
But as he reached the first of the stoves, he brought his ar
around in a mighty swing at the pots on top of the rang
sweeping them away onto the floor, where they crash
down, spilling their contents.

The kitchen hands scrambled for safety as O'Flahe
swung again at the next range. His eyes blazed, his f
dripped with blood, but he was not finished. The fist ca
up at a rack of plates that were smashed before they hit t
ground.

O'Flaherty was shouting, "You won't be needin' all these fuckin' plates now." He tore down the rack that had held the plates and smashed it to matchwood on the nearest counter.

"You won't be needin' all of this rotten fuckin' stuff," he shouted through the ranges to Cellini, who had not moved. "He didn't belong in this rotten fuckin' siege." O'Flaherty had reached the side wall, where the fists swung again and smashed the panel of a cupboard. He grabbed the cupboard and flung it sideways, buckling it out of shape on the edge of a counter, the contents sliding out onto the floor.

O'Flaherty stepped over the cupboard and looked at Cellini, who had still not moved.

"Do any of you realize what kind of man Mario was?" he yelled. "He was a great man. He could have done anythin'. Did you ever hear the man sing?"

Cellini nodded. He couldn't speak; there were tears running down his cheeks. O'Flaherty kicked one of the pots out of his way and came forward. He had more to say.

In that instant, the swinging doors burst open and Henderson, with two other men, came in and looked around the inactive kitchen. For a moment, Henderson was speechless.

He exploded. "What on earth is going on in here?"

Cellini came to life. "Get'a out!" he shouted.

Henderson looked startled. "I beg your pardon," he protested.

"Get'a out'a my kitchen!" Cellini shouted again.

O'Flaherty seemed not to have noticed the interruption. His voice sounded almost normal. "I've had friends who borrowed money from me and never repaid it. Sure, 've had friends who needed me, wanted one thin' or another from me."

"What is this man doing here?" demanded Henderson, looking a little nervously at the big Irishman, whose dangerous mood was apparent.

"He is Mario's friend." Cellini kept his attention on O'Flaherty, who went on as if nothing had been said.

"In my whole life, it was only one friend I had who needed nothin' from me. All he wanted was a small restaurant in Rome."

O'Flaherty had gone inert. He was weeping.

"I rode this horse once." Emma reached up to run her hand along the long, mobile muscle of Lady Potter's neck. She said it more to herself than to Mark, who was standing beside her.

He sounded hurt. "You were not listening to what I was saying."

She was still not listening, running her hand back across the loosely hanging reins, the rifle holster, and the saddle. "It was an extraordinary ride. One of those mad exhilarating moments you can never forget. I was flying into blackness, with no control, no need for control. I can close my eyes and relive that moment whenever I wish. It was on a night just like this." She looked up from the saddled mare at the moon, floating clear from the mountain of storm clouds spreading out to the west. Its pale light threw a block of shadow from the grandstand toward the stables where they stood.

Mark bent his head closer, studying her to see if he had her attention. "Now may I say what I was trying to say?"

She nodded, but still only half listened. She was watching past his profile, only seeing the two figures of Bannock and Mabala, in earnest conversation in the shadows beyond.

Mark was saying, "It's none of my business, I know, but I would have thought he would be uninvolved in any army matters by this time."

"Who?" Emma guiltily became conscious of the question put to her.

"You're still not listening to me. I was talking about

—he hesitated at the name—"Bart. I'm not trying to interfere, Emma. I know that would be a waste of time. But this
is all very mysterious."

"I'll tell you about it later."

Mark persisted. "It's not that I'm interested in why he
should be riding out armed to the teeth for whatever reason,
at a time when all the fighting seems to be over and the
Boers on the retreat. That doesn't worry me at all. What
worries me is you. I've never seen you in such a state
before."

"I'm fine," she murmured, and her anxious expression
remained directed at Bannock in the shadows.

He kept at her. "Would you like me to speak to Bart?"

"No, please." She shook her head vehemently without
looking at him.

"Isn't this fight over? Shouldn't we all be thinking of
getting away out of here? The siege is over, Emma. It's
absolutely official. I understand that the railway to the
south will be in operation within a few days. I want Mother
out of here as soon as it can possibly be arranged. I can only
assume that Bart has some bee in his bonnet and is not
really thinking of you."

"I'll tell you about it later, Mark."

They looked up at the sound of a horse approaching.
The monotonous rhythm of a trot grew louder until they
saw the outline of the rider, an easily recognizable large,
round figure.

Bannock was on his way over to them. His voice came,
sharp and irritable. "You won't believe it, but that's Masefield. That man is going to drive me too bloody far. Every
time I move, his fat shadow crosses my path. I seem to have
some ugly attraction for him."

He waited for the horse to approach.

"What are you sneaking around here for, Masefield?
Have you thought of some new reason to arrest me?"

Masefield heaved himself from the saddle and breathed
out heavily before he spoke.

"I'm not sure why I should be taking this trouble, bu I've come to give you some information which could decid you against taking whatever ill-advised action you may b considering."

Bannock shook his head in mock wonder. "Do yo really wish me to believe that you have my interests a heart?"

"Don't be ridiculous. I don't care whether you live c die. If I have any concern, it is for the unfortunate peopl you affect." He looked momentarily at Emma, then exam ined the saddled-up mare, nodding thoughtfully. "Befor you set out on your foolhardy mission, there are a fe things you ought to know."

"You said all that earlier. I'm not interested in you threats."

Masefield put a hand on the stock of the rifle in from of the saddle. "What have we here?" His surprise was exa; gerated as he pulled the weapon slightly from the holste and dropped it back into position again. "A German Mann licher, no less; a veritable Boer rifle."

"It was Watson's rifle," Bannock snapped.

Masefield beamed. "A Boer rifle. How very suitabl You look for all the world like a Boer." He eyed the bulle packed bandolier strapped across Bannock's chest. "Has occurred to you that if you ride out now, you will be sh by the first British soldier who sees you?"

Emma looked anxiously at Bannock.

"What is going on here?" Mark was puzzled.

Emma took Bannock's arm, but he was becomin more impatient with Masefield by the moment.

"What is it you want? I haven't got time for this."

Masefield made a pretense of not hearing and smile at Emma and Mark. "You'll be glad to hear," he a nounced, "that relief is official. General French has arriv in the town and there is a huge reception at the Sanatoriu The food and drink are flowing. The poor man and his sta are in a state of complete exhaustion and so are their horses. You should see those animals. They are spent, finished. They have come over a hundred miles in the last four days on a long roundabout route from the Modder. You really should be there, not here."

Bannock broke in. "So should you. I'm not interested in this. If you have something to say, say it and get back to your celebration. I have other things to do."

"Ah, yes." Masefield turned his attention to him. "You don't seem to understand that that is precisely what I am talking about. If you are going out after your stallion, so much the better. The army is going to be delighted with you, and if I am any judge, it will be General French himself who nabs your horse."

Bannock ignored him and turned to Emma. "Come over here. I want to speak to you."

But Masefield was not finished. "There is an option open to you. Instead of chasing after the horse, which is a futile waste of time, you can chase after a cannon and be rewarded for your trouble. Rhodes has offered a thousand pounds for the capture of the Long Tom, which is presently being hauled away to safety by the Boers. Since you have the only fast horse left in existence, you have more hope than anyone else of tracking down the position of the gun. It's a better alternative, don't you think? And the army would be grateful, too."

Bannock led Emma away into the dark without replying or reacting in any way. When they were far enough off not to be heard, he took her by the shoulders and felt her small hands gripping at his sleeves.

"Emma, my mind says go and your eyes still say stay."

"Ignore my eyes."

"You begged me not to go, then you changed your mind. You only have to ask me again and that will be the end of it."

Emma pulled at the sleeves. "I know what Marcus

means to you. I remember the way you spoke about it, tha
your greatest dream was a horse. I won't be the destroye
of your dream."

"You took over from that dream. That is not why
want the horse back. I need Marcus if we are to pick up th
pieces. It's become part of justifying my life with you."

"You must justify nothing. You are my life, you your
self. Just you. You are everything, so there is nothing yo
need to prove. I must not confuse your decisions. If we ar
to live together, I must live with myself and you must liv
with your decisions. Just go, Bart. Don't let my feeling
confuse you."

Bannock pulled her into his arms. "If only the decisio
was a simple one."

Her head was flat against his chest, and in a blu
through the tears that were forming she could see Mabal
lighting extra paraffin lamps.

"What did Mabala say?" she asked.

"He said the Boers are moving off and they have t
move slowly because they're pulling wagons. They ar
going due west, away from the action. The army is doin
nothing. They are camped outside the town in a state
exhaustion."

"I have ears, you know. I know why you paced up an
down all day. I heard you asking Mabala to go out to th
ridge. I heard you asking Mabala for that gun."

"He had it hidden away in one of the stables."

"You said you needed an accurate rifle. Is that a
accurate rifle?"

"Yes, very accurate."

"If you shoot, you will get shot at." She gripped hi
tightly, holding back the emotion. She could hear Mas
field's voice raised for a moment somewhere behind her

"Good heavens, man, it's only starting." Masefield ha
gone to his horse, hitched farther along the rail, and Mar
was forced to follow along and listen.

"Oh, no." Masefield leaned on the saddle. "This wa

not over. And if it were not for Rhodes, this siege would
not be over."

Mark's attention was divided. He could see the vague
figures of Emma and Bannock clinging together like one,
but his eyes became distracted by the lamps carried by
Mabala, who placed one beside the mare and brought the
other to where they stood beside Masefield's cob. The lamps
lit Masefield's eyes, and Mark was forced to look back at
him and listen.

"Rhodes has had his way in everything. Quite predictably, of course. It took a bit of time, but he has had his way.
Even locked away here, he has been the shadowy threat
behind the General Staff. His own war is over. His railway
to Cape Town will be open again and the mines back to full
production. It has really been a marvelous example of influence. He has swept away the enemy outside; he will sweep
away his enemies inside."

Mark's surprise was noted and enjoyed. Masefield
waited for a reaction.

"I don't understand. What enemies inside?"

"Ah, you could say the whole garrison, but that would
be too general. It begins at the top, with Kekewich."

"You amaze me."

"It remains to be seen how far down the scale the
recriminations will work. I would not be honest if I did not
admit to a faint tremor of concern."

"For yourself?"

Masefield seemed amused. "You never know, you
never know." He noticed that Mark had become distracted
by something. Emma and Bannock had come into the light
beside the mare. The reins were thrown over the horse's
neck, and the tall, lean figure was in the saddle.

Emma took hold of the bit with both hands and looked
up into Lady Potter's face.

"You are to look after him," she said quite seriously
to the mare. "At the first sign of indecision on his part, you
are to gallop back, do you hear?"

Bannock leaned down and took hold of her hand but she could not look up at him.

"Stay close to Mabala," he said. "He has strict instructions to look after you. I should be back by dawn."

She felt pain from the tight grip. She looked up and tried desperately to maintain the smile as he turned the mare and rode away. She held back even as the mare disappeared into the dark. And then her fury burst out with angry tears coming. "Damn, damn, damn," she cried out.

Masefield heard and sighed. He kept his voice down to Mark. "Your family problem is about to be solved. Bannock is a dead man. Your sister is waiting for a dead man. If the Boers don't get him, the army will. They can't be expected to know he's not enemy. And even if he were to live and get the horse, the army would commandeer it. You had better take your sister back with you."

But Mark had stopped listening. He began running. He ran past Emma into the dark shouting, "Bannock, Bannock, come back here." But the sound of the cantering hoofbeats was lost in the silence. He came slowly back until he stood beside his sister.

He tried to see her face. There was a reflection of tears but no sound of crying.

"Where is this damned horse?"

She replied, almost inaudibly, "With the Boers."

"You are a couple of fools," he whispered. "How much do you mean to him that he would risk his life for a damned horse? How much does he mean to you that you would agree to such nonsense?"

"It's not simply a matter of the horse," she said quietly. "It's also a matter of pride."

"What a price he may have to pay for his pride."

"Our pride."

Mark was more gentle. "You're not making sense, my sister."

They stopped talking as Masefield's boots crunched

oward them. His tone was charming. "If there is anything can do . . ."

Mark cut him short. "If you knew all this, I mean what ou have just told me, why didn't you make some attempt o stop him?"

"I clearly warned him."

"But you made no reasonable attempt to stop him."

"Surely your sister is the one to have stopped him?"

Emma turned around to face Masefield, and in that noment she saw O'Flaherty come around the end of the able block. She resisted the impulse to call out to him hen he stopped short on seeing them, ducking back out of ght.

Masefield addressed himself to her. "Am I being so nreasonable?"

"You are being what you always are. Utterly reason-ble. Tactically reasonable. I am tired of your tactics gainst Bart."

"What tactics?" Masefield even made the question und reasonable.

"Your manipulations of events, Major. Your threats, our style of innuendo."

"You are upset," Masefield countered carefully. "I ave never meant you any harm."

"Will you do what I most want?" She sounded decep-vely calm.

"Anything."

"Please leave."

Masefield took a step back, unable to hide his discom-rt, but needing to have the last word.

"I believe that in your case I have been misunderstood. you have any problem, I hope you will call on me." He azened it out a little longer in the face of silent rejection om both of them, then nodded sternly and went away ward his horse.

It was not until the hoofbeats had all but died away at O'Flaherty emerged into the light and stood in front

of them. He looked tired and dishevelled, his hair matte
with dust. Mabala gathered up the light that had stoo
beside the cob and came to join them. The eyes of th
African watchers showed in the shadow of the grandstan

Emma held a hand out to O'Flaherty. "I'm glad to se
you're out of . . ." she hesitated. "You're free, Mr. O'Fl:
herty."

"Yes, ma'am, in a manner of speakin'. It's by the grac
of God it is and not the authorities." O'Flaherty looke
around. "Where is Bart? Is he here?"

"Bart has gone out after the stallion."

O'Flaherty nodded as if he expected it. "Now that's
fool thin' to do."

Emma went closer to him. "Will you go and try to hel
him?"

O'Flaherty avoided her gaze. "I'm tired, ma'am," h
said. "I'm very tired."

"I believe he would help you. He tried to get you ou
of jail."

O'Flaherty looked up and down and away. "Do yo
realize how much hope there is of findin' him out there
the veld and the kopjes? And if you'll pardon me sayin' s
he hasn't a hope of gettin' back Marcus from them Boer
Nobody's even goin' to think of partin' with an animal
that quality."

"I will go, *nkosazana.*"

They all looked round at Mabala, including O'Fl
herty, who began to laugh.

"Oh, you will, will you?" O'Flaherty jeered. "We
there's only one horse, and as it happens it's me who'll
goin' after him on the horse. Did you get that, Mabala?

Mabala drew himself up proudly. "I go on my feet,
he announced. "My feet know the way. I tell *nkosi* Ba
where the big horse goes. I can show you the way."

Mabala went toward the grandstand and shouted, ar
feet came running. He chose his men, and they turned
go without another word. As they went from the lamp

hey looked impressive, the light reflecting on their backs
nly for an instant before they became part of the blackness
f the night.

Emma and Mark remained where they were, holding
ands, while O'Flaherty went to saddle the gelding.

Mark said, "I feel a bit helpless."

Emma squeezed his hand. "You have other respon-
bilities."

She looked up at the sky, where the storm clouds
oved still closer to the moon, threatening to swallow it up.
here were dull rumbles and orbs of flashing lightning com-
g from deep inside the clouds. Emma let her thoughts
ander up there, but there was no joy in it. Bart was doing
mething hopeless. Maybe he would have realized that by
ow. Maybe he would look up the way she was doing and
e the approaching storm, see it as an omen and just decide
come back.

Please, please do that, she begged.

·14· | RELIEF AND RETRIBUTION

Another of the countless champagne corks popped, and Captain Pendleton weaved toward Sarah, bumping against the buffet table, waving the bottle's neck toward the glass in her hand.

"Why has the band stopped playing?" Sarah tottered in a dancing circle, checking on the enormous main reception room of the Sanatorium, the gallery leading to the carved wooden staircase still crowded from top to bottom with people resting from the feast, the two long tables aglitter with silver, damask, gold-figured bone china, and the almost burnt out remains of hundreds of candles.

"What happened to the band?" she whined again, refusing to hold out her glass.

"It collapsed." Pendleton took a swig from the bottle. "Someone was sneaking them drinks, and they collapsed and went away."

"They couldn't go away if they collapsed, silly." Sarah began to giggle. She had become aware of Masefield on the other side of the buffet table, stacking up a silver tray with a selection of sandwiches and other items of food, together with a large goblet full of champagne.

"I say, Pendle." Sarah prodded her inebriated partner

"Did you know there is a major offensive taking place on the other side of this table?"

Pendleton leaned to see around the tall centerpiece. He blinked over the glare of the candles, and immediately looked a little nervous when he recognized the subject of Sarah's jibe.

Sarah laughed at her own joke, pointing across at Masefield with her empty champagne glass. "He has hardly stopped all evening." She punched the reluctant Pendleton to keep his attention. "Look, Pendle, look, have you ever seen a major subject taking a major mouthful?"

Masefield used Pendleton's reticence to get her attention without even having to look at her. "Captains, my dear girl, are not at liberty to make light of major anythings." And in the moment of confusion he created, he disappeared in the direction of the staircase.

But Sarah was ready to finish what she had started. She brushed aside Pendleton and the proffered bottle and went off in pursuit, searching from one tightly packed group of revelers to another, becoming visibly irritated by a forest of low-reacting arms and shoulders. Finally, she saw him when she happened to look up. He was partway up the staircase, slowly lowering his bulk into a sitting position from where he could eat, drink, and survey the room.

By the time she had picked her way between the people sitting on the stairs, Masefield had almost finished his champagne and half the contents of the tray. He made no sign of recognition when she spread her wide taffeta skirt and sat down beside him.

"You seem to have lost all interest in Emma," she started.

Masefield chewed and watched the high jinks below.

Sarah was watching him. "Well, what are you going to do about it? Are you going to leave her in that filthy stable?"

Masefield chewed and shrugged.

"I can't believe it. Have you nothing to say? If you had cooperated with me, this would never have happened."

Masefield chewed and waved to an acquaintanc
below.

Sarah leaned back on the banister without taking he
eyes off him. "You don't like me, do you?"

He chewed. No reaction.

"I don't like you, either."

Still no reaction.

"If battles were fought over plates of food, you woul‹
beat all."

At last he spoke. "If wars were fought in the dead o
night, you would come out on top."

"Oh, really," she bridled.

"Without ever getting off your back."

"You're drunk," she screeched, and glared around a
the attention she had caused. In the next moment she wa
on her feet, fuming quietly down at him. "Listen, you.
think it is time you were put in your place, and all tha
would require is a colonel. You are not at liberty to mak‹
light of a colonel, I believe." She straightened up and sur
veyed the room. "Now where is our commanding officer?

While she looked around, Masefield went on chewing
"Colonel Kekewich has retired," he observed, "dismisse‹
by General French. Lieutenant-Colonel Chamier ha
retired, defeated by whiskey and champagne. Colonel Peak
man has retired, with the order of the hangover and tw‹
bars. And Rhodes has gone the way of all the colonel‹
They've all given up, and so should you. Sit down, Sarah.

He had something to say and she sat down, respondin‹
to an impulse of curiosity rather than obedience.

"You think I am in league with Bannock," he begar

"You said he was your friend."

To look at Masefield, a slight smile on the thin lips, th‹
eyes vaguely taking in the crowd below, it would hav‹
seemed he was enjoying himself.

"I loathe him," he said mildly. "I despise him."

Sarah was looking surprised.

Masefield waved absently to someone else below. "Yo‹

may reassure your mother, Emma will be back quite soon."

She was becoming really puzzled. "What about him?" she asked.

"He is dead." Masefield was smiling broadly. "I must fetch some more champagne." He picked up the empty goblet but remained sitting there.

"How do you know?" she whispered to him.

"He is dead, you have my word on it. Mr. Bartholomew Bannock is a dead man."

Sarah came closer, barely whispering. "Have you heard something?"

"No, in fact, I may be just a trifle premature, but if he is not dead yet, he will be . . . presently."

Sarah almost warmed to him, even smiled, "Why do you say he should be dead?" she persisted.

But Masefield was somewhere else. "The laughable part is that everybody's going to want that mare he's riding."

"You hate him, don't you?" She was watching him carefully.

He remained oblivious of her. "A horse like that would stand out in the veld."

Her smile had narrowed. "You said 'if' he is not dead yet, so you're just assuming it anyway."

"The average Boer would kill for a horse like that."

Sarah was hating him again. "You just can't take your mind off him, can you?"

That got him back listening to her.

"What I don't understand is, if you hate him so much, why were you so set on throwing them together?"

"I did it to frustrate you."

"You what?" Sarah went on guard.

"I did it to annoy you."

"You beast." The tremolo note was rising. "What precisely is your problem? What have I done to you?" Curiosity kept the tremolo in check. "Why do you dislike me so?"

Masefield was peering downward through the banisters. "I wonder if there are any more of those excellen tinned salmon sandwiches."

"I'll tell you why you dislike me, and everyone else, fo that matter."

He turned back so abruptly that she let him speak.

"I do wish you'd make up your mind whether you're asking me something or telling me something."

The tremolo tone went shrill. "I'm asking you, yo great sarcastic . . . sarcastic . . ." She struggled for the word chose another route. "You're a great obstruction. Great fa enigma. Enigmatic hippo. Yes," she trilled triumphantly "Hippo—that's the word I was looking for."

"There is a word for you, too," Masefield said mildly

"Hippo," she taunted loudly.

"If we are to look for animal analogies, the word fo you is hyena."

"Oh, this is sour grapes."

"And you are surely the sourest grape of all." Mas field swayed toward her.

"How dare you." Sarah shrunk away from him.

"You're so inept." He gave a loud burp.

"What do you mean?" Sarah rasped out.

"It means your mind slips before your tongue does. means your fatuous frills are a good match for your witle laughter. It means you keep your tactics up your skirt." F smiled.

She stood up and shrieked, getting the attention of a the late carousers. Everyone in the room and on the stai case froze and looked up. The only immediate point action was Pendleton, spilling his drink, hurriedly findin a place to put it down, and charging up the staircase come to Sarah's aid. But having negotiated his way between the others sitting it out on the stairs, he was su prised to find Sarah seated again, very tight-lipped, b relatively calm.

"Sarah, is something amiss?" he asked anxiously.

Masefield turned a vengeful eye on him. "Sarah is amiss," he said, leaning his bulk back onto the upper step, waiting smugly for a reaction from Sarah. But she spoke instead to Pendleton.

"Leave it, Pendle." Sarah seemed to have had enough. "He's like a vicious dog. If you make one move, say one thing, he starts snapping."

Pendleton nevertheless decided to make his gesture of disapproval. "Now look here, sir," he addressed Masefield, but was cut short.

"Captain?" Masefield was smiling unpleasantly again. "Yes?"

"What do you say, Captain?" Masefield enunciated as if to a child.

"Yes, sir." Pendleton grudgingly added the rank.

"Kindly fetch me another glass of champagne." He held out the large goblet.

Pendleton sighed with exasperation, looked to Sarah for guidance, but was left standing on the lower step.

Sarah had undergone one of her abrupt changes of mood. She prepared herself for a final stubborn attempt to satisfy her curiosity; not even humiliation was going to stop her.

"We're all still a bit on edge. I realize that." The soft tone of reconciliation was almost pathetic. "I shouldn't have called you what I called you. I'm only a woman, you know."

"I do understand that." Masefield sympathized.

She was going to resist the sarcasm, no matter what.

"Come on, you old devil, tell me," she cajoled, turning on all the charm she could muster. "Why did you help them? Why did you help that rotten fellow if you despise him so much?"

"Sarah?"

"Yes," she urged. It seemed she was about to know.

"You're quite sure in your mind that I helped them?"

"Yes. Well, didn't you?"

"It's no good. You're never going to know, are you?"
He proceeded to ignore her.

She prepared to explode again.

The ground was still dry and dusty, waiting to b
turned to mud. The thunder grew steadily louder from th
direction of the town. Even at this early hour, the hea
building up with the imminent storm weighed on Bannoc
and the mare. He felt the sweat pouring down inside hi
leather coat. Sweat from the mare's neck dripped from hi
hands where he held the reins.

He could see the Boer party about a mile ahead: tw
covered wagons, seven riders, exactly as Mabala had de
scribed them. And one of those small bobbing forms wa
Marcus.

Seven hours; it had taken seven long hours to fin
them. From the time the moon had been swallowed up b
the storm clouds, he had groped on through the dark, wor
dering if there was any hope of finding the Boer colum
When the first faint light came, there was nothing, just th
flat barren veld with a kopje here and there. It was almo
a relief to have to admit defeat and return to Emma. Th
farther he went, the more Emma called, and the more futi
this exercise seemed to him.

As a last resort, he had sent Lady Potter scramblin
to the top of one of the low hills and scanned carefully wit
the binoculars. Only at the point of finally giving up an
turning back had he seen a faint movement in the distanc

The decision remained, drawing him in inevitably li
the coming storm. The darkness began to give way to daw
the light emerging slowly through the dense cloud.

It was too late to argue with the decision. It was mad
and remade, and the steady trotting action of the ma
shortened the distance to the time of confrontation wit
every minute.

But the arguments raged in his head, and there would be no stopping them. The whispers of others with other motives: "If we are to live together, I must live with myself and you must live with your decisions." She said, "Just go, Bart." She said, "Don't let my feelings confuse you." But poor Emma, you had no idea of what this decision really entailed. If you had known, you could never have agreed. You were duped, Emma. This great love of ours has begun with a flaw. I have been dishonest with you. Because you are too gentle to understand what I'm doing. Who could understand? Not Paddy. "You're mad in your head," he had said. Not Masefield. "I'll have you arrested for treason —and anyone who goes with you." Even he had no idea. There is only one treason that means anything, and that you commit against yourself. But this was one of those times when the cause was not quite clear, nor was the possible sin against it, nor even the future guilt. There is just something that has to be done, something confused. Yet confusion or not, the action had begun, the decision must be carried out.

When Masefield had said he would look like a Boer, he had wanted to laugh at the irony of it. The man could never have realized the extent to which he wanted to achieve that very illusion. He wore the soft felt hat he had kept in the saddlebag, and the rifle was slung across his back commando style. And the illusion was already working as he rode to one side and clear of the small column, close enough to see that heads had turned. The riders wee watching him with only normal curiosity. They must have assumed he was a Boer making his own way to safety. If there was anything about him that really raised their interest it would be the mare, a thoroughbred almost as rare as the big chestnut stallion one of them rode.

He kept the mare at a steady trot, looking straight ahead, consciously avoiding the compulsion to turn and stare at the stallion. But Marcus was there, in front of the wagons. He could see him out of the corner of his eye, and the awareness was overpowering.

He turned for a moment, and it only took that long to tell the whole story: a stallion that could win a classic. Or a ghost version of him. Marcus Aurelius, thinner, wasted to the very muscle; dry-coated, all the shine of condition gone. But the class, the breeding showed through. The muscle once covered by rounded flesh, rippling stark at the shoulder, at the quarter. The eyes still blazed, and the action was still there. Long, fine legs reached out and pumped down in a stylish walk that made the mounts of the other riders look like mules by comparison. Those great equine eyes had reason to blaze with anger, and the reason was a bit. A crude curb bit, of a type he had never known, worrying his mouth, sending his neck jerking down and jerking up at the humiliation of the harsh hands that controlled it, the unyielding weight of the long-stirruped giant on his back.

He was past the leading wagon and the men who rode in front. They were moving at a listless walk, with the exception of Marcus, who was being restrained, while Lady Potter gained ground at more than double the pace. One of them shouted to Bannock, and he pretended not to hear. His objective was close at hand, a low kopje covered in boulders.

This was where it could all go wrong. If they rode him off and confronted him, he would be as good as dead once they discovered he was English. Even considering the lack of condition, he could never outrun Marcus. He resisted the temptation to gallop to the kopje. It was just conceivable that they might decide he had not heard the shout or had gotten it confused with the loud groan of thunder that came straight after.

There was another shout, but he was well ahead and alongside the kopje. When he dared to look back, they were out of sight, obscured by the mound of boulders that separated their course from his on either side of the kopje. He continued on past the kopje to the far side, then rode the mare up among the rocks at the lower end of the slope.

There was no time to find an ideal position. He dismounted and unshouldered the rifle, laying it out in front of him on a platform of rock.

The bullets, bandolier. Get the damn thing open. Bolt out. Loading.

The bolt of the Mannlicher clicked in like the perfect piece of machinery it was.

The thunder sounded, but still no rain. He waited.

The hoofbeats began, faintly at first. They were still at a walk, seemingly unconcerned. The decision was final, it was about to be done, and he felt lonely and stupid and, for the first time, not just confused, but unsure. It was too late to be unsure.

Bannock wound the reins around his arm. He changed his mind and brought them over his shoulder. There must be no chance of the mare breaking away. He leaned on the rock and brought up the rifle, aiming at the first possible point where the riders could appear.

The hoofbeats sounded very loud, and then the first rider came into view, quite unaware of the threat from above. The next rider moved through the sights, and then the next. And then it was Marcus.

The rifle was poised, the bead precisely in the sights, wavering slightly but ready for the steadying moment, the critical moment.

The sights moved over the bounding target as Marcus pranced. The sights ranged from the horse to the big rider and back to the horse. The hand gripped at the stock, the fingers slowly squeezing in on the trigger, and in the instant before firing the target was found: down from the wither, back from the shoulder.

The Mannlicher fired. The bullet found the heart of Marcus, who was dead as he fell.

Bannock's feelings exploded into an uncontrolled shout of anguish. He waited just a moment to see the great stallion bowl over and lie still, the rider falling aside and scrambling to his feet. He saw the other riders turning in confused circles as he shouldered the rifle and fought with

the frightened mare, struggling to mount her. She was dow
at the quarters, rear legs almost touching the ground, pul
ing back, stepping backward over the rocks.

Somehow, Bannock got the reins over her neck, gral
bing at the leathers to pull himself alongside, literally craw
ing into the heaving saddle. He hit at the mare's neck
force her down the slope and out of sight of the riders whe
the first shots rang out, some ricocheting off the rocks, som
finding their target. He felt the shock of pain as he was h
in the leg. Lady Potter was also hit. She reared and whi
nied pathetically, while the firing continued fast and accu
rate. Bannock gasped at a new pain in his shoulder. H
hands fell helplessly from the reins, and as the mare scran
bled around in confusion, he heard bullets ripping into he
side. She staggered and collapsed down under him, and h
felt himself sprawling among the rocks.

He tried to get up, but the pain overwhelmed hir
knives of pain at his shoulder and leg. He looked stupidl
at the prone animal with her blood pouring over the rei
at her neck. The riders were approaching, hoofbeats thum
ing on the ground, clattering on stone. Bannock lay bac
still helpless, and waited, listening to the sounds of th
riders dismounting and the boots climbing the rocks.

A tall figure loomed over him, then another and ai
other. They came over the top and surrounded him in
silent circle, silhouetted against the glare of the stor
clouds above. They stood very still, the hats, the ragge
clothes, bandoliers, and rifles colored red with the dus
Thunder rumbled down between them like an angry chor
of their voices, but only one spoke.

"*Ek het jou mos gesê hy's 'n Engelsman.*"

Another said, "*Hy's definitief 'n Engelsman.*"

The first man spoke again. "Why are you shooting a
us? You are only one man."

Bannock hardly heard the question. He was only real
conscious of the pain, and when he tried to move, his shou
der burnt and throbbed. He groped out with a hand an

ecoiled as it touched on the still warm fetlock of the mare.

The guttural Dutch accent came again, insisting, Why are you shooting at us?"

Bannock's voice was almost inaudible. "I was shooting t the horse."

The man bent down on his haunches and leaned closer. What was you saying?" he demanded.

"I only wanted to kill the horse," Bannock got out. He nade the effort and forced out the words again. "I was hooting at the horse, not at you."

The man hesitated. Bannock could see the dust-cov- red beard, hear the heavy breathing.

"You are mad." He said it slowly, then the beard urned to address the others. "*Hy's mal. Hy sê hy wou die erd skiet.*"

"*Hy's van sy kop af,*" one of the others said belliger- ntly. "*Hoe kan hy 'n perd skiet?*"

The beard was close again. "Why do you want to shoot good horse?"

Bannock lay shivering with emotion as much as pain. That is not a good horse," he choked out, "that is a great orse. That is my horse, do you understand?"

The beard turned. "*Hy sê dis sy eie perd.*"

One of the others shouted impatiently, "*Hy's mal, kom ns ry.*"

But the beard leaned down again. "You say this is your orse? Why do you shoot your own horse?"

Bannock leaned up on his arms, anger mounting above e pain. He looked defiantly into the bearded face and aited for enough breath to speak.

"You can't have that stallion. That is Marcus urelius. That is the progeny of a century of great breeding. ave you ever heard of Eclipse?"

The shadows hung over. A voice said, "*Wat sê hy?*"

"That's the greatest breeding line of all. Have you ever eard of Saint Simon? That's the greatest racehorse of all me, and Marcus is his grandson."

"Wat sê hy? Wat is die Simon?"

The bearded face remained still and attentive.

Bannock swayed on his trembling elbows as he stared into the face. "You can't have Marcus Aurelius." His voice vibrated with emotion. "He doesn't belong here. You can't put a great stallion with farm horses. You can't put him to a common mare." He shouted, "Dammit, you will never understand." His elbows gave way and he slumped, his face against the cold stone. His eyes stared into the ground, but he knew they were still there, watching. They said nothing. And then the boots shifted and moved over the rocks, and they were gone.

He vaguely heard the sound of hooves and voices coming from over the rise, but they soon faded away to nothing. He was left with the thunder and a momentary glowing reflection on the sand from the lightning.

He slowly sat up, holding his shoulder and watching the blood ooze between his fingers. All he could see beyond the rocks was flat barren veld with stubbles of low bush. There was a dust trail out there to the north, but it went too high and the color was wrong. That's not dust going up, that's rain coming down. Maybe the rain won't come that far, but if it does, it will hide the tracks and anyone who comes looking is going to have a hard time.

Emma, can you understand this? If there had been only one rider . . . if there had been only two riders, I might have got him back. I almost shot that rider. But that would have been like shooting myself. No matter which way Marcus had bolted, I would have had to follow out into the open. I would have been a sitting duck.

Bannock sighed, and decided that if he tried to walk he wouldn't get very far. He felt very tired, but resisted the idea of lying down again. If he lay down, he might just stay like that and never be found.

The gun. He could fire the rifle and someone might hear. Slowly, he pulled the strap over his head with the arm that worked, and let the rifle fall beside him. It was luck

hey had not taken it away from him. It was going to be
useful. A distress signal and a crutch. He held up the rifle,
planting the butt firmly on the ground so as to pull himself
up, letting the hurt leg hang. The horizon hovered and
danced and the pain ran up from his leg and down from his
shoulder, sending his entire body into convulsions.

How do you walk on a crutch? The barrel was too thin
to hold on to. But a rifle is the right shape and the right
length. The butt fits under the arm like the armrest of a
crutch. Turn it over the other way and it's made for the
purpose.

You're sticking the barrel of a fine rifle into the grit,
and chances are it will blow up the next time you fire it. But
it works as a crutch, as long as you don't let the sore leg
bang against it. You won't get far this way, but you'll get
farther than sitting down. Emma is waiting, and there is
nothing else to do but get back there. She will understand
what I almost don't understand myself. Marcus was never
going to exist again. She knew that before I even set out.
Even I didn't know that. If I had known that, I could have
saved myself a lot of trouble and two bullets in the body.
And Marcus could have lived on as the happy sire of a lot
of half-bred farm horses. Fine chestnut farm horse, by Mar-
us Aurelius out of farm mare. Sire by Magnus, by Saint
imon out of Minerva. By Caligula out of Merian.

Marcus Aurelius is dead. There will be no progeny.
The one dream is over, and somehow the other has to begin.
But it would have been good. It would have been very good.
Marcus Aurelius standing at Newmarket. Owned and
trained by Bartholomew Bannock, that man with the beautiful wife, Emma Bannock. Emma Bannock. Emma Ban-
ock.

He repeated the name aloud each time the rifle barrel
drove into the ground, but the effort was too much and he
topped, swaying on the butt, clutching with his one good
hand at the top of the barrel.

I am turning in circles around this rifle. Everything is

turning, but I can think clearly enough. If I could only straighten up, I could go on. What would a coucal do "Please be a coucal," she said. Emma belongs to the coucal who should have stayed in the bush. Emma belongs to the coucal with no wings. She used to belong to a sword. I had that sword in my hand. I wouldn't take it by the hilt. No that would have been wrong. Hold it at the middle. I want to give it to her myself, but what would she think? I'll use this sword to get to her. I'll use it to get her.

I can't rest. I must keep going. I feel so tired, but this is more than tiredness, this is delirium. I can't see properly Everything is going round, yet I can hear every sound perfectly. The thunder. The barrel striking the ground. That was a jackal barking.

But Bannock was totally unaware he had stopped again. He began to fall, and clung instinctively to the rifle the good arm sliding down the barrel, which finally toppled over next to where he had fallen. He blinked as a drop of rain splashed on his face, and then another. It brought back consciousness. He could see out along the barrel of the rifle to the horizon.

I'll rest here for a while. Then I'll try again.

When Mark returned to the racecourse, he found Emma standing in the rain, watched by an audience of Africans spread out on the parapet of the grandstand and squatting inside the stable doors.

He tried to move her. "Come along, Emma, you'll be drenched through."

She resisted and remained facing the open veld, but she was smiling. "I'm not being tragic, if that's what you think."

Mark knew it was useless to insist. He made the best of it, pulling up his collar about his ears and waiting beside her in the rain.

"We all have to leave," he said. "It's been arranged. Simon Thrumpton has managed by some miracle to organize a coach to take us to the Modder station, and from here we have been promised seats on the train to Cape Town. It means we will have to leave later on today. I think you must be sensible and come with us."

Emma shook her head slowly without answering.

Mark tried again. "We can leave messages for Bart to follow on to Cape Town. I'm sure he will understand. There may not be another opportunity like this in a hurry. You see, once the main body of the column proceeds north, there will not be enough troops to guard the line south. At the moment, with reinforcements coming up, it's about as safe as it's ever going to be."

Emma remained silent. The smile looked out of place with the rain dripping down her face, creating at least an illusion of tears.

"We are committed. We've got to go. Mother says she will agree to anything, but you must come. We have to stick together, she said that. Even Sarah wants you with us."

Emma nodded. "I understand that you are committed. I am also committed."

"Whenever I wanted you to do something you didn't want to do, you made me feel sad and helpless."

She reached for his hand, but continued to face out into the distance.

Mark came closer and put an arm around her shoulder. "I knew what you would say, but I had to try," he said gently. "I've spoken to old Simon, who will be staying on, and he says you are to call on him for anything you need."

"He is a dear old man."

He watched her wet profile, the distant smile. "Emma." Mark fumbled. "It is going to feel very strange leaving you behind."

She said, "Mark, do you see anything out there?"

He could only see the vague outline of the ridge through the thinning rain.

"No," he answered. "What is it you're looking at?"

"Can't you see anything? Can't you, Mark?"

"No, Emma."

"Well, I can."